The Gathering Company

The Gathering Company

Part Three of *The Marshes of Mount Liang*

A New Translation of
the *Shuihu Zhuan* or *Water Margin*
of Shi Nai'an and Luo Guanzhong

By

John and Alex Dent-Young

The Chinese University Press

The Gathering Company: Part Three of **The Marshes of Mount Liang** *by Shi Nai'an and Luo Guanzhong*
translated by John and Alex Dent-Young

ISBN: 978-962-201-847-1

First edition 2001
Second printing 2016

Published by The Chinese University Press
The Chinese University of Hong Kong
Sha Tin, N.T., Hong Kong
Fax: +852 2603 7355
E-mail: cup@cuhk.edu.hk
Website: www.chineseupress.com

Printed in Hong Kong

Contents

Acknowledgements

As for the previous volumes, we are indebted to many people's help and encouragement. In particular we would like to thank our editors at The Chinese University Press for their patience and support. Our biggest debt of all is to Esther, our wife/mother, whose assistance on so many fronts has always been taken for granted, and without whom the project would never have begun or continued.

The illustrations are from two series of old engravings from the Ming dynasty. One is known as the *Rongyutang* 容與堂本, and the other as *Yang Dingjian* 楊定見序本. These illustrations have been published in two different volumes respectively entitled *Rongyutang ben Shuihu Zhuan* 容與堂本水滸傳 (China: Shanghai Chinese Classics Publishing House, 1988), and *Shuihu quanzhuan* 水滸全傳 (China: Zhong Hua Book Co., 1961). We are grateful to Shanghai Chinese Classics Publishing House for granting us free use of these illustrations.

Introduction

As we said in the introduction to Volume 2, this translation is aimed at the general reader. Comments from such readers have further convinced us of what we already knew — that for the English reader, Chinese names are a major obstacle. We have therefore done our best to anglicize names, using English nicknames for the heroes and somewhat fanciful inventions for place names that play an important part in the story. We have to hope that the result is not too confusing a mix of English and Chinese associations. In some cases where we feel a name has no importance to the action we omit it completely.

Since the action of the novel becomes increasingly involved with battles and political background, we have tried imperceptibly to reduce the amount of stylization in favour of a more modern, direct and idiomatic English, again hoping that the anachronism does not jar. The challenge for the translator in the later parts of the *Shuihu* is to keep the narrative going as smoothly and swiftly as possible. In some cases this will involve cutting out name lists, though we do not want to remove them completely because they are so much a part of the original text. The same goes for repetition. Some degree of repetition seems essential to the rhythm of the text, but in cases where it sounds too un-English we may cut or vary a phrase.

We repeat here our note on *pinyin* pronunciation for those who are completely unfamiliar with it. Those who do know it may wonder, incidentally, why we use Ho for the name which is properly spelt He in *pinyin*: the reason is that since names and pronouns can occur in the same position, it is awkward to have a name that looks like the English pronoun he.

A Note on *Pinyin* Pronunciation

Chinese names, except for a few like Tao already well-known in English, are given here in *pinyin*. *Pinyin* is the standard modern system of transliteration, but it presents a few major problems for the uninitiated, mainly with the use of consonants:

c = ts
z = dz
q = ch as in *cheap*
x = sh as in *sheep*
zh = j as in *judge*

If the reader should wonder about the reason for these outlandish spellings, it is basically because there are two different sets of consonants representing sounds that resemble the English *ch*, *sh* and *j*, so extra symbols are needed to distinguish them.

Vowels mostly resemble those in a European language like French or Spanish. Two vowels together represent a diphthong. But again the double set of consonants produces a problem:

Shi, Zhi, Chi	=	sh etc. followed by a sound like English r — approximately the first syllable in *Shirley*, spoken with an American or West of England accent
Zi, Ci	=	a similar vowel sound to the above

Xi, Ji, Qi	=	the sounds in *she*, *gee* and *chee(se)*
o (in Poxi)	=	the o in *for*, so that Poxi rhymes with *for she*
ü	=	the French sound in *tu*

Chapter 44

Panther and Magic Messenger on a byway meet;
Morbid encounters Madcap in the street!

Let me remind you now how Iron Ox levelled his halberd and charged Green-Eyes and there beside the highroad the two of them fought several bouts and neither had the advantage. Then Zhu Fu, known as Smiler, interposed his weapon to separate them, saying: "Cease fighting and listen to me!"

The two put up their weapons and Smiler said to Green-Eyes: "Hear me out, master. I know I have received from you more honour and love than I deserve, not to mention instruction in the use of spear and staff. How could I ever forget it? But you see, my elder brother, the Crocodile, has become one of the leaders in the Marshes of Mount Liang, and he was entrusted by Song Jiang, the Opportune Rain, with the task of looking after our friend Iron Ox here. Supposing our friend were arrested by you, how would my brother be able to go back and face Song Jiang? That's why we had to drug you and rescue him. Iron Ox even suggested using this opportunity to finish you off but I wouldn't let him, so he confined himself to killing some of the troops. We were about to make a clean getaway, when it occurred to me that you wouldn't go back without giving chase. So remembering how kind you've always been to me, I waited for you here. Master, you're smart, you know the score. A lot of your men have been killed and you've let Iron Ox, the notorious Black Whirlwind, escape. How could you go back and face the governor now? You'd be in deep trouble, and there wouldn't be anyone to come to the rescue. Wouldn't it be better to come with us to the mountain and join Song Jiang's band? What do you say?"

Green-Eyes pondered this at some length, before saying: "Suppose he doesn't want me?"

Smiler dismissed the objection with a laugh. "Surely you know about Song Jiang of Shandong, with his reputation for welcoming all kinds of good men and seeking the friendship of heroes?"

Green-Eyes gave a sigh and said: "I certainly seem to be in the position of having a home I can't call my own and a country I can't return to. The one consolation is that I have no wife and children, so I don't have to worry about reprisals. I'd better go with you."

Iron Ox was delighted. "Why didn't you say so in the first place?" he exclaimed, honouring Green-Eyes with a bow.

Green-Eyes in fact had never married and had no family responsibilities or possessions, so right away the three of them set off together to join up with the cart. When he saw them coming the Crocodile was greatly relieved. All four now went on their way with the cart and nothing worthy of narrating occurred. When they were approaching the Marshes of Mount Liang, they met the Magic Flautist and Whitey, who said: "The two chiefs sent us down the mountain to seek news of you. Now we've found you we'll rush back and report." They did so, and the next day the four travellers together with Smiler's family found themselves in the Assembly Hall of the stronghold on Mount Liang.

The Crocodile stepped forward and introduced Green-Eyes to the two chiefs and all the other leaders, saying: "This is Li Yun, otherwise known as the Green-Eyed Tiger, sergeant of the Yishui constabulary." Then he introduced his brother, saying: "This is my own dear brother, Zhu Fu, otherwise known as the Smiling Tiger, or Smiler." Iron Ox paid his respects to Song Jiang and his two axes were restored to him. He told the story of how he had taken his mother to Yiling Heights and how she was eaten by the tigers and he killed all four of them. He also told how the false Li Kui had tried to rob him and got himself killed, a tale which made everyone laugh. The two chiefs said: "You killed four fierce tigers, and now our stronghold has gained two living tigers. That certainly calls for celebration." Amid general rejoicing, goats and horses were slaughtered and a great banquet was held in honour of the two new leaders. Chao Gai then gave them seats on the left immediately above the Daytime Rat.

The Professor now spoke. "Recently," he said, "our enterprise has prospered exceedingly. Our fame, it seems, is drawing good men to us here from all quarters. We must put it down to the quality of our two beloved leaders and to the good fortune of you all. Anyway, I would now like the Crocodile to take up the reins again at the inn, replacing Shi Yong the Guv and the Ape. A house should be prepared for Smiler and his family.

"Our activities have now expanded considerably. It is not as it was in the old days. I think we should set up three more inns to serve as listening posts and to direct good men who wish to join us. If the court sends troops out against us we will have news of their coming and will be able to prepare. Over to the west there is a broad plain. The two Tong brothers, the River Rider and the Cave Dragon, will take a dozen companions and open an inn there, whilst the Executioner will take a dozen to the south side of the mountain and open another, and the Guv will open one on the north. They are to set up the old system of the water pavilion and the signal arrow, backed up by boats, that word may be brought immediately if a military threat arises.

"On the approaches to the mountain we will build three new gates with Skyscraper in overall command of defence. That will be his sole responsibility and he will not be assigned any further duties, but he is to be on call day and night and not absent himself without cause.

"The Nine-Tailed Turtle will be responsible for digging canals and channels and maintaining the waterways, keeping open the access by water, and ensuring that the Place of Many Meanderings is in a proper state of repair. He will also be in charge of the main route up the mountain. Having been a farmer, he must be familiar with this kind of work.

"The Magic Calculator will be responsible for stores and provisioning, for keeping tabs on all our income and expenditure and maintaining proper accounts. Magic Hand will devise security passes for all who need to move within the camp or without, either on the mountain or in the world below, or to pass through the three gates. He will also register all the leaders, greater and lesser. The Craftsman will be so good as to engrave all the necessary identifications, seals, plaques and so on. The Ape will see to the making of clothing and armour and the various banners and pennants. Green-Eyes will supervise the provision of housing and halls for the fortress and the Magic Flautist will be in charge of the building of boats of every kind. The Door-God in the Clouds and the Daytime Rat will move down to the lower camp at Golden Sands Landing. Short-Arse and Whitey will move to the camp at Duck's-Bill Landing. The younger Mu brother and Smiler will receive all incoming cash and provisions. The Little Duke and the Halberdier will supervise the rest chambers on either side of the Assembly Hall. Iron Fan will be in charge of banquets."

When all the duties had been allotted, there was feasting for three days, but of this no more. Hereafter things were quiet on Mount Liang. Every day there was drill for the troops, together with martial arts instruction and demonstrations. In the waterside camps the leaders gave instruction in boatmanship, swimming and naval combat. We say no more of this.

Then one day Song Jiang happened to say to Chao Gai, the Professor, and the assembled company: "Here we are, all gathered here today, and there is just one person missing: Taoist Gongsun, of whom there is still no sign. I remember that when he left for Jizhou to visit his old mother and his teacher, he promised he would be back in a hundred days. It's been a long time now and we've had no news of him; I hope he isn't going to fail us and not return. I would like to ask the Magic Messenger to go and make inquiries for me, to find out if anything has happened to him and why he hasn't come."

Song Jiang was pleased when the Magic Messenger cheerfully agreed. "No one could go as quickly as you," he said, "we'll expect to hear news in ten days or so." The Magic Messenger bade them all farewell that same day and left early next morning, disguised as an imperial staff officer. Then it was like this:

Though he goes as a soldier he commands no company of men. But to be a traveller is nothing new to him. His legs eat up the

> *miles. As overseer of income and expenditure he carries a certificate hanging from a rattan cane; as commander of troops he carries a yellow scroll inscribed with orders. Three hundred miles from home, he needs but a day to return; in a military emergency, he's there in a moment. In the morning he could still be in the far north eating gruel, by evening he's in the south eating yellow pears.*

So the Magic Messenger left Mount Liang and took the road to Jizhou. He fastened the four magic amulets to his legs and initiated his magic walking mode. On the way he paused only for an occasional cup of plain tea and some simple vegetarian fare. After three days he reached Yishui district. When he questioned the people there he was told: "That there Black Whirlwind were in action here t'other day, and he injured a mighty number of people and that Sergeant Li Yun, him as they call Green-Eyes, got mixed up in it. We don't know where he went to, but to this day he's not been caught." This caused the Magic Messenger some amusement. The same day, as he was proceeding on his way, a man appeared in the distance carrying a hollow-shafted steel spear. This character, when he saw the speed at which the Magic Messenger was travelling, stopped and cried out: "Ho there, Magic Messenger!"

The Magic Messenger glanced behind him and saw it was a big fellow, standing on a little path that ran across the hillside. He had a round head and big ears, straight nose and square-cut chin, finely arched eyebrows with the eyes set well apart, narrow waist and broad shoulders. The Magic Messenger turned right round now and said: "I've never met you before, how pray d'you know my name?"

The other answered immediately: "Then you really are the Magic Messenger!" He lowered his spear and prostrated himself. The Magic Messenger hurriedly raised him up and returned the compliment, then said: "May I know your name?"

"I am Yang Lin," the other replied. "I am from Zhangde. I have long frequented the greenwood, and the rivers and lakes fraternity call me 'Elegant Panther.' A few months ago at an inn I met

錦豹子小徑逢戴宗

Taoist Gongsun. We spent some time together, eating and drinking, and he told me all about Mount Liang, where the leaders Chao Gai and Song Jiang welcome good men. He wrote a letter for me and told me to go to the stronghold and join the company, only I didn't feel I could go just like that. However, he also said: 'On the road to Leeside there's an inn, it's been there for years, run by one Zhu Gui, the Dry Land Crocodile. All who want to join the stronghold are first received there.' And he told me there was a special messenger in the stronghold, Superintendent Dai, known as the Magic Messenger, who can do three hundred miles a day. When I saw you scorching along just now I gave you a shout, just to see. I didn't know it was really you. What an unexpected piece of luck!"

"It's precisely to look for Taoist Gongsun that I'm on my way to Jizhou right now," said the Magic Messenger. "We've had no news of him and the two chiefs have sent me to Jizhou to make inquiries and to find him and bring him back, so it's quite a coincidence, meeting you like this."

"Although I'm from Zhangde," said Panther, "I've covered every inch of this district of Jizhou. If you've no objection I'll come with you and show you around."

"I'll be delighted to have your services. When we've found Taoist Gongsun we can go straight back to Mount Liang together."

This was most satisfactory to Panther, and he asked the Magic Messenger to treat him as younger brother. The Magic Messenger put away his magic amulets and the two of them went on their way at a leisurely pace. At evening they found a village inn to rest in. Panther ordered wine and wanted to invite the Magic Messenger. The latter said: "I have to abstain when I'm in my magic walking mode." So they both ordered vegetarian food.

They were up early next morning, and having breakfasted and packed up they set off again. Panther asked: "If you're going to use your magic walking, how will I be able to keep up? I'm afraid it's not convenient for us to travel together."

"The magic walking will do for a companion too. I'll tie two of the amulets on your legs, and when I start the walking you'll go as fast as I do. When I go, you'll go and when I stop, you'll stop. Otherwise you certainly couldn't keep up with me."

"But I'm just made of ordinary flesh and blood, I haven't got your spiritual powers."

"It doesn't matter," said the Magic Messenger. "In the magic walking mode I can take anyone with me. With the aid of the magic you'll go just like me. So long as I fast and abstain, there'll be absolutely no problem." So saying, he took the two amulets and bound them round Panther's legs. The other two he tied on himself. Then he performed the magic, blew lightly upon the amulets, and the two of them soared off, speeding up or slowing down all according to the pace set by the Magic Messenger. As they went they chatted about matters of the rivers and lakes, and although they proceeded so easily they covered a considerable distance without knowing it. Around midday they arrived at a place that was ringed with high mountains, a stage road running through the middle of it. Panther realized where they were and said: "Brother, this is the spot people call Waterworld. A formidable band of robbers used to frequent that mountain up ahead, though I don't know what it's like nowadays. They call it Waterworld because these slopes are full of winding streams and picturesque scenery."

Just as the two men were approaching the hillside, there was a sudden peal of gongs, drums and flutes and a hundred or more bandits rushed out and blocked their way, a couple of stalwarts at their head wielding halberds. "Halt!" they shouted. "Who the hell are you, and where do you think you're going? You'll pay the toll, if you know what's what, and make it snappy if you want us to spare your lives!"

"Just watch this, brother!" said Panther gleefully. "Just watch me flatten the stupid bastards!" He levelled his spear and charged.

Impressed by the ferocity of this onslaught, and with the benefit of a closer look, the more senior of the two shouted: "Hold your hand! Isn't it my friend Yang Lin?"

Panther recognized him. Putting aside his weapon, the first man stepped forward and paid his respects, and then bade his tall companion do likewise.

Panther said to the Magic Messenger: "Please come and let me introduce you to two friends."

"Who is this and how does he come to know you?" the latter asked.

"This is Deng Fei, from Xiangyang in Gaitianjun. Among the rivers and lakes he is known as the Red-Eyed Lion, because of his bloodshot eyes. The way he handles an iron chain, no one can get near him! We used to be associates, but we parted five years back and I hadn't seen him since. What a surprise to meet him here today!"

Redeye asked: "Tell me please, who is this? He looks to be someone quite out of the ordinary."

"This is my friend Dai Zong, the Magic Messenger, from the company on Mount Liang."

"Would that be Superintendent Dai of Jiangzhou, who can do three hundred miles a day?"

"That's correct," said the Magic Messenger.

Both newcomers hastened to show their respect, saying: "We have often heard your name. We never expected to have the honour of making your acquaintance here today."

Here is a poem to describe this Redeye:

In his hometown the days he just idly wasted,
Till the joys of the vagabond life he had tasted.
Eyes bloodshot from many a cannibal feast,
Deng Fei is the name of this red-eyed beast.

"And may I know his name too?" the Magic Messenger said, indicating the second man.

Redeye said: "This is my friend Meng Kang of Zhending. He's an expert boat builder. One day he was supposed to construct a large boat for transporting marble but the official in charge gave him so much stick that he upped and killed him, so then he had to leave home and take refuge in the rivers and lakes and become an outlaw. That was a long time back. They call him 'Jade Flagpole,' because he's tall and pale, and held to be good-looking."

There's a poem to describe him:

Grasping the bow he'll lead the charge,
Or build you a trim fighting barge.
This shipwright's name they Meng Kang call,
Or Flagpole, because he's white and tall.

This meeting was most pleasing to the Magic Messenger. As the four of them conversed, Panther happened to ask: "When did you two meet up?"

"I'll tell you," said Redeye. "It was over a year ago. Six months ago we met someone else in these parts called Pei Xuan, from Jingzhao. He was an officer of the district court and he's wonderfully skilled in drawing up legal documents. Being honest and clever and absolutely incorruptible, he's known round here as Sterling. He's also expert with spear and staff, a great exponent of fancy sword play and as brave as they come. But the court sent us a corrupt governor, who picked a quarrel with him and had him exiled to the island of Shamen. When they were passing here we killed his guards and set him free, so he agreed to join us. We've got a band of several hundred. Sterling is a great hand at fighting with two swords and since he's the senior of us we've made him our chief. I'd like you both to come to our stronghold now so you can meet him." With this he ordered his men to bring horses and invited the Magic Messenger and Panther to mount. Together they rode off towards the mountain stronghold.

They soon arrived. As they were dismounting, Sterling, who had been forewarned, hurried out to meet them at the bottom of the steps.

He was an imposing figure. He was pale and somewhat portly, and had a calm and steady manner. There's a poem for him:

In questions of law he knows what is right;
When his brush starts to move, the devils take fright.
To be just and unselfish he'll always aspire;
This sterling official is Pei Xuan the lawyer.

Sterling invited the two heroes into their assembly hall where courtesies were exchanged. The Magic Messenger was honoured with the first place, then Sterling, Panther, Redeye, and Flagpole in that order. They were entertained with a banquet and there was great feasting that day. You must understand, friends, that these were all members of the company of stars, destined to come together when the time was ripe. As the poem says:

For these heroes to meet there's a very good reason,
Each link of the chain its neighbour must seize on.
The founders of Han performed menial tasks,
So why think Mount Liang hasn't got what it asks?

Later, while they were all feasting, the Magic Messenger told them about the leaders Chao Gai and Song Jiang, how they welcomed good men, seeking the acquaintance of heroes from every corner of the empire; he told of their kindness, bravery and generosity and their many other good qualities. He told of the spirit of cooperation among all the leaders and of how secure was the territory of Mount Liang, a hundred leagues in circumference, with the Place of Many Meanderings and Duckweed Marsh in the centre surrounded by vast expanses of misty waters, and he told of the hundreds of troops and the system for raising the alarm if government troops should approach. The three from Waterworld were fascinated by all this. Sterling said: "We've a few troops of our own here too, three hundred or so, and something like a dozen cartloads of booty, as well as ample provisions and fodder. If you don't think it presumptuous, would you consider taking us to join the band on Mount Liang? We would like to offer our humble services. What do you say?"

The Magic Messenger replied with great satisfaction: "The two chiefs welcome every addition, you can stake your life on it. Obtaining your valuable services would be a real plus for us. If you're serious, why not get your things together and wait while Panther and I go and find Taoist Gongsun in Jizhou? Then when we come back with him we'll all disguise ourselves as government troops and march by night to Mount Liang."

Everyone expressed their satisfaction with this arrangement. There was much drinking, and later they moved to the Golden Pavilion so they could enjoy the Waterworld scenery while they continued their carousal. It was indeed beautiful:

> *A vast expanse of wild water, and all around it the dark blue hills. A number of ancient trees reflect the declining sun, shreds of coloured mist drift among distant peaks. Lonely are the empty fields, there are no children watching cattle here; it is cool at the old ferry, here no one comes to water their horses. There is nothing to be seen but the stockade the robbers have built to protect their camp, and the banners they have hung all about.*

The Magic Messenger kept exclaiming: "What beautiful scenery, it's truly sublime! How did you two come here?"

Redeye said: "A pack of useless bastards used to hang out here, but we kicked them out," and everyone laughed.

The five of them were quite drunk that night. Sterling stood up and performed a sword dance, inspired by the wine. The Magic Messenger couldn't stop applauding. When evening fell they all went back to the stronghold to rest. The Magic Messenger and Panther insisted on leaving next morning and the other three, finding there was nothing they could do to make them stay, accompanied them down the mountain to see them off. After this they went back up and set about packing and preparing for their departure. Of this no more.

Meanwhile the Magic Messenger and Panther left the Waterworld stronghold and travelling from dawn till dusk were soon at the gates of the city, where they found themselves an inn for the night. Panther said: "Listen, Taoist Gongsun is a monk, so I assume he will be staying out in the wilds, at some remote little place; he won't be within the city."

The Magic Messenger said: "I'm sure you're right."

So the two of them first made inquiries outside the city, asking everywhere for news of Taoist Gongsun. But no one had heard of him. On the second day they went even further afield to ask, but still found no one who knew of him. They returned to their inn to rest. On the third day the Magic Messenger said: "Maybe there's someone in the city who knows him." So that day they started inquiring in the city. They asked a number of elderly people, but only got the answer: "Never heard of him. Reckon he's not from here. Perhaps he lives at a big temple out in the country, somewhere in the mountains maybe."

Now as they were walking along a certain main street, they saw in the distance a group of musicians greeting someone who was coming down the road. They stopped at the side of the road to watch. Two prison guards led the way, one of them carrying a number of brightly wrapped gifts, the other a quantity of satin and brocade. Behind them, shaded by a black silk umbrella, marched an executioner. This gentleman was a most impressive figure. He was dressed in an embroidered robe of indigo silk, had thick eyebrows stretching right to the temples, slanting eyes and a yellowish skin, and a few whiskery hairs on his chin. He was in fact from He'nan and his name was Yang Xiong. He had come here with a cousin who had been appointed governor and he had remained ever since. The next governor to be appointed was also his friend and made him warden of the two prisons, with the additional duty of serving as the city executioner. Because he was extremely skilled in martial arts and because of his unhealthy complexion, people called him the Morbid Swordsman. There is a poem which details his qualities:

> *His arms are adorned with carved stones of varying hues, his turban ring elegantly set with gems. Jade hibiscus flowers are stuck in the long hair at his temples. His vest displays his rank of executioner, his robe is dyed scarlet. At an interrogation he officiates with confident skill, his axe bites like the wind. His complexion is a shade yellow, his eyebrows are bushy. This is Yang Xiong, whom men call the Morbid Swordsman.*

Well then, this Morbid was marching along amid his followers, a prison officer behind him bearing a blade with a demon-headed handle. At the time when the Magic Messenger and Panther saw them in the street, Morbid was returning from a public execution in the main square and his friends and admirers had decked him with red streamers and were accompanying him home. A crowd of people who had gathered with winecups in their hands at the crossroads blocked their progress. At this point seven or eight armed men also appeared from a side-street. The leader of this group was one Sheepsbane Zhang Bao. He was a member of the city guard and was friendly with a bunch of ne'er-do-wells who spent their time extorting contributions to their own welfare from people within and without the city. Innumerable brushes with authority had failed to persuade Sheepsbane to mend his ways. Because Morbid was a relative newcomer to the city and because many people feared him, Sheepsbane chose to treat him with insolence. On this occasion, seeing Morbid loaded with so many gifts of good silk, and being seconded by this rabble who had all been drinking heavily, he was particularly eager for a confrontation. When the crowd with winecups had brought Morbid to a standstill, Sheepsbane thrust himself forward and shouted: "Greetings, Mr. Gaoler!"

"Come and have a cup of wine, my friend," said Morbid.

"I don't want your wine," Sheepsbane replied. "I've come to ask you for the loan of a few hundred strings of cash!"

"But we're mere acquaintances, we've never had any financial dealings, why ask me for money?" said Morbid.

"I can see you've been robbing the people of a fair old quantity of goods, why shouldn't you lend me some?" said Sheepsbane.

"What do you mean, 'robbing the people,' these are all gifts!" said Morbid indignantly. "You can't threaten me like this. I don't have to answer to you, we have separate jurisdictions."

Instead of replying, Sheepsbane goaded his gang into action. Pressing forward in a boisterous throng they seized all the embroidered silk.

Exclaiming "These hooligans are intolerable!" Morbid tried to move forward to attack them, but Sheepsbane held him by the collar in front, while two others secured his arms from behind. When the mob went into action, the prison guards had melted away. Morbid was so hemmed in by Sheepsbane and his two companions that he couldn't strike a blow. He was obliged to swallow his rage, as he was quite unable to break loose from their hold.

At the height of the confusion, a big man carrying a load of firewood appeared. He saw how Morbid was being obstructed and could not free his arm, and he decided an injustice was being committed. He set down his load, thrust his way through the crowd and said: "What are you doing to the Warden?"

Sheepsbane glared at him and shouted: "You mangy cur, you lousy starving beggar, who asked you to butt in?"

Thus provoked, his temper flaring, the big man responded with a rapid move that threw Sheepsbane down on his back. When some of Sheepsbane's cronies tried to intervene, the big man dealt out blows which sent them flying in all directions. Freed at last, Morbid was now able to deploy his own skills and began to throw some useful punches, and soon after the whole pack of vagabonds were flat on their faces.

Sheepsbane had seen there was no future for him here and crept away. The enraged Morbid now bounded after him. In pursuit of Sheepsbane and the silk thieves Morbid disappeared up a side alley. The big fellow, however, still did not pause but went on chastising the culprits at the crossroads.

Meanwhile the Magic Messenger and Panther were exclaiming to themselves in admiration: "What a fellow! Just look at him: 'He sees an injustice and whips out his sword to set it right!' He's a real hero!"

Truly it was a case of:

To leap from its scabbard the noble blade longs,
Because in the world it can see there are wrongs.
But aiming to right them, just watch how you go;
Are you sure you can tell who's friend and who's foe?

The Magic Messenger and Panther now approached the man and said: "My friend, we beg you now to rest your arm." They led him aside into an alleyway. Panther relieved him of his load and the Magic Messenger took him by the hand and invited him to enter a wineshop. Panther put down the load and joined them in an alcove. Crossing his hands in sign of respect, the man said: "Thank you most kindly for your help, good sirs."

"We are both strangers here," they said. "But when we saw how valiantly you were fighting, we feared lest you hit somebody too hard and accidentally take his life. So we decided to come

病關索長街遇石秀

forward and invite you to drink a few cups of wine with us. Please let us be friends."

"I already owe you for getting me away from there, how can I drink your wine as well? That's really too much!"

"Within the four seas all men are brothers," said Panther. "What is there to feel bad about? Please take a seat."

The Magic Messenger offered him the place of honour, but there was no way he would accept it. In the end the two of them sat down together and the stranger sat on the opposite side of the table. The waiter was called and Panther took out a tael of silver and handed it over, saying: "No need to ask anything, just make sure we're supplied with food to go with our wine, whatever you've got, we'll reckon it all up afterwards."

The waiter took the silver and disappeared for a moment, returning with dishes of vegetables and nuts and stuff to go with the wine. The three men drank several cups, and then the Magic Messenger asked: "May I ask your name and where you are from?"

"My name is Shi Xiu," the other said, "and I am from Jiankang in Jinling. I learnt a little spear and staff play when I was young, and I've always held to one principle: when I see a wrong being committed I do what I can to help. Because of this people call me Madcap. I came here with an uncle to sell sheep and horses, but unfortunately he died on the road. Since I'd spent all my money I couldn't get home, so I had to stay here and sell firewood for a living. Because you've honoured me with your friendship, I have told you the exact truth."

The Magic Messenger said: "And we came here on an affair of our own, my friend and I, that's how we happened to meet you. This business of selling firewood, now, I don't see how it's ever going to get you very far. Wouldn't you be better off if you opted for the rivers and lakes? — you could have a great time, for all the rest of your days."

"But I only know a few tricks with the staff, I've got no other talent; how can I hope to find success and happiness?"

"In these times truth is not honoured. In the first place the Emperor is not clear-sighted, and in addition he is obstructed by corrupt officials. My example may not count for much, but for my part I went and joined Song Jiang's band in the Marshes of Mount Liang, where everyone has their share of gold and silver and clothes come in whole suits. We all hope that there'll be an amnesty later and we'll be given official posts."

Madcap sighed and said: "I'd like to join them, but I've no way to get in."

"If you'd really like to go, I can give you a reference."

"Might I ask the names of you two gentlemen?"

"I am Dai Zong and my friend is Yang Lin."

"I've heard stories in the rivers and lakes about someone called the Magic Messenger, is that you, by any chance?"

"It is," said the Magic Messenger. He told Panther to look in the pack beside him and take out a ten tael silver ingot and give it to Madcap, who refused three times before they prevailed upon him to accept it. Now finally convinced that he was talking to the genuine Magic Messenger from Mount Liang, he was on the point of expressing what he really felt about joining the band on Mount Liang, when they heard someone outside demanding entry. As they were wondering what was going on, Morbid rushed in with a score of others, all police officers. Seeing so many people, the Magic Messenger and Panther took fright and profited by the general confusion to slip away.

Madcap stood up and said by way of greeting: "Well, Warden, where did you get to?"

Morbid said: "I've been looking for you all over the place, my friend. And here you are drinking wine. That bastard had got me jammed in so I couldn't lift a finger until you came to the rescue and got me out of trouble. At first I was too busy chasing the bugger, to make him pay for it, and I forgot about you. These people all heard I was being attacked and came to help. We got all the silk back, everything was fine except I couldn't find you. Then someone said two strangers had taken you to the inn for a drink. That's how I managed to track you down."

"Yes," said Madcap, "two strangers invited me here to have a few cups and some talk. I didn't know you wanted me."

"Please would you tell me your name? And where you come from and why you are here?" said Morbid, with the utmost cordiality.

"My name is Shi Xiu, I am from Jiankang in Jinling. People call me Madcap because it's my nature to rush in and help when I see an injustice. I came here with an uncle who sold sheep and horses. He died suddenly on the journey. I ran out of money and stayed here selling firewood for a living."

Morbid took a good look at him. He was strongly built and everything about him matched:

The physique of a wild mountain tiger, a temper like oil poured on fire. A brave and noble heart, allied to a cool mind; everywhere he renders assistance. He fights with a staff or relies on his two fists. His mighty reputation has spread throughout the world. This is Shi Xiu whom men call Madcap.

Morbid asked Madcap: "What happened to the two strangers who were drinking with you?"

"I suppose they thought something was up when you came in with such a crowd. That must be why they left."

Morbid said: "I see." Then he said to his companions: "Let the waiter bring in two bottles of wine. You can each have three big bowls, then you can leave. I'll see you again tomorrow." The policemen drank up and left.

"Don't think this impertinent of me, but I assume you've got no family here," Morbid said to Madcap, "so I'd like from now on to call myself your brother, how about it?"

Madcap was flattered. He asked: "May I make so bold as to ask your age?"

"I am twenty-nine."

"And I am twenty-eight. So please, sit down and let me pay my respects to you, as the elder."

Madcap kowtowed four times to Morbid, who expressed his pleasure by ordering the waiter to bring some special delicacies to accompany the wine. "You and I are going to get really drunk," he said. Whilst they were drinking, Morbid's father-in-law, Old Pan, appeared with a small search party. Morbid leapt to his feet and said: "Father-in-law! What are you doing here?"

The old gentleman said: "I heard you had got into a fight with someone, so I came to find you."

"Luckily my friend here came to the rescue and beat that scoundrel Sheepsbane so badly he'll be scared of his own shadow from now on. Now Mr. Shi and I have got to know each other and become brothers."

The old man said: "Good, that's fine, you can treat these people to a bowl of wine and then they can go home."

Morbid ordered more wine. Everyone drank three bowls and then left. Morbid made his father-in-law sit down between them, while he took the head of the table and Madcap the other end. When they were seated, the waiter poured for them. Noting with satisfaction Madcap's strong, heroic build, the father-in-law said: "My son-in-law needs a friend like you, so there won't be problems when he performs his official duties. No one will want to mess him about now." He also asked what sort of trade Madcap was involved in.

"My father used to be a butcher."

"Do you know how to slaughter cattle then?"

Madcap laughed: "I was brought up in a butcher's family, of course I know how to slaughter cattle."

"I used to be a butcher, but now I'm too old for it. I've just got this one son-in-law and he joined the government service, so my old trade has to be abandoned."

They drank till they were quite tipsy, then the bill was reckoned up and Madcap left his load of firewood at the inn in payment. They went back to Morbid's house. As he entered, Morbid shouted out: "I want you to come and meet someone, dear!"

From behind the curtain came an answering shout: "Who is it, my love?"

"Don't ask questions, just come and see!"

The curtain was raised and the wife came forth. What was she like then?

Luxuriant black hair, finely arched eyebrows, lustrous eyes, perfumed breath, a true straight nose, tender pink cheeks, perfect complexion, an airy figure, delicate white hands, a reed-like waist, soft full hips, little pointed toes, slippers crowded with embroidery, bounteous breasts, white, white legs, and something more, something narrow, tight and hard of access, crimson, crammed and close — but who can tell what thing that was?

Or as the poem says:

Eight and twenty summers, a tasty morsel!
Such dangling moons a poor fool's heart can harrow.
No need to have heads roll, for such a force'll
Suck up invisibly the living marrow.

She had been born on the seventh day of the seventh month, and she was called Felicity, because of the festival on this day. She had been married first to an official, a local man, but he had died two years before so then she married Morbid. They had been married for less than a year.

When she came out, Madcap hurriedly stepped forward and bowed. He begged her to be seated and then began to kowtow.

She said: "I am too young to accept this honour."

Morbid said: "This is my new friend, we've just become brothers. As my wife you can accept half the honour."

Accordingly Madcap kowtowed four times, performing the obeisance with a flourish. She returned the compliment gracefully and asked him to come in and sit down. An empty room was prepared for him to rest in. We will not bore you with more of the details.

Next day when Morbid left for the office he told his household: "Prepare Madcap some proper clothing." He also gave instructions for some baggage Madcap had left at an inn to be brought and stored in the house.

As for the Magic Messenger and Panther, when they saw that crowd of officers arrive at the inn in search of Madcap, they had slipped away in the confusion and returned to their inn outside the town. Next day they made further inquiries about Taoist Gongsun and continued for two days, but to no avail. No one knew him or could say where he might have got to. After some discussion, they decided to return. They packed their things and went back to Waterworld, where they were joined by Sterling,

Redeye, Flagpole and their troops, and that same night, disguising themselves as a government force, set out for Mount Liang. The Magic Messenger was glad of the opportunity to show proof of his value to the stronghold. His arrival with so many additional troops was celebrated on the mountain with a feast, of which we need say no more.

Meanwhile Morbid's father-in-law had been having discussions with Madcap. What he wanted to do was set up a butcher's shop. "At the back of the house," the old man explained, "there is a cul-de-sac, with an empty building at the end. It's got water, so it would make a fine workshop. I suggest you set things up there and take charge."

Madcap had a look at the place and agreed that it was ideal. Old Pan found one of his former assistants, an experienced hand, to do most of the work so Madcap would only have to supervise the accounts. Madcap agreed and instructed the assistant to paint the meat counter, tubs and chopping block black and green, sharpen the knives, and set up the counters. The workshop having been fitted out, with a pen for the pigs and a dozen fat pigs to go in it, an auspicious day was selected and the shop opened. Neighbours and friends all flocked to the opening when the shop was festooned with red decorations, a deal of celebratory wine was drunk and all of Morbid's family declared themselves well pleased with the new shop under Madcap's supervision. No more of this.

Madcap and Morbid's father-in-law busied themselves with trade. Time sped by and soon it was more than two months since the opening. Autumn was ended and winter approaching. Madcap looked a different man now; he had a whole set of new clothes. One day he rose early, at dawn, and went out into the country to buy pigs from another district. He was away for three days and when he got back he found the shop closed. Arriving at the house he found the chopping block had been put away and the knives locked up in the store.

Now Madcap was not slow-witted. When he'd thought it over, he believed he understood. He said to himself: "No man's happiness lasts a thousand days, no flower blooms for a hundred. My friend must be away on official business and isn't looking after things at home. No doubt his wife saw me having new clothes made and started to say things behind my back. And because I was away for a couple of days tongues started to wag. They decided something was going on and closed the business down. Well, I won't wait to have it out with them, I'll leave before they tell me to and go back home for a bit. Like they say, it's always a mistake to plan too far ahead."

He drove the pigs into the pen and went into the workshop to change. He collected his stuff and carefully drew up a final account. He entered the house from the back door. The old man had arranged some vegetarian food and wine and invited him to sit and have a drink. "You've had a hard journey," he said, "it's a tiring business collecting the pigs."

"I only did what had to be done, sir. But see this, I've drawn up a clear account, and may heaven strike me dead if there's the least gain for me in it."

"Why ever should you say something like that?" said the old man. "No one supposes there's anything wrong."

"Well anyway," said Madcap, "I've been away from home six or seven years, I want to go and spend a bit of time at home now, that's why I've made out the account for you. I'll say goodbye tonight and leave first thing tomorrow."

The old man began to laugh. "You've got it all wrong," he said. "You don't need to go. Let me explain."

The old man held forth for quite some time, and spoke with emphasis. And as a result of his words,

The avenger draws his deadly blade,
The faithless priest is sent to hell.

If you want to hear what the old man told Madcap, you must read the next chapter.

Chapter 45

Morbid gets drunk and scolds his wife; Madcap ends the lecher's life!

When Madcap returned and saw that the shop was closed he wanted to leave, but Old Pan said: "Wait a minute. I know what you're thinking. You've just got back after two days absence and you see all the butcher's implements have been packed away, so you think we've decided to close the shop and you have to leave. But even if it wasn't such an excellent business, even if we did decide to close the shop, we'd still keep you here and look after you. No, let me tell you how it is. This daughter of mine was previously married to a certain Registrar Wang of this district. Sadly he died and this is the second anniversary of his death. We are going to have some prayers said for him, that is why we've closed the business for a couple of days. Tomorrow I have asked some monks from the Temple of Divine Favours to come and perform the rites and I'd like to ask you to take charge of it all. I'm an old man and I can't manage late nights. That's why I'm telling you this."

"Now that you've told me," said Madcap, "I shall just be patient."

"Then from now on please don't have any more suspicions. I hope you will carry on as before."

They drank a few cups and ate some vegetarian food, and then cleared up the cups and dishes.

Some lay brothers turned up carrying the scriptures on a pole. They set up an altar and arranged the Buddha images and the dishes for offerings, together with drums, cymbals and gongs, incense, lamps and candles, while vegetarian dishes were prepared in the kitchen. In the afternoon Morbid came home and said to Madcap: "Dear brother, this evening I am on duty at the prison, I won't get home till late. I shall have to rely on you to see to everything."

"Don't worry, brother," said Madcap. "I'll take care of it for you."

When Morbid had left, Madcap went to wait in front of the door. In a little while he saw a priest approaching with a chicken. This is what met his eyes:

> *A gleaming pate, fresh from the razor, assiduously perfumed with musk; a warm yellow cassock, newly stitched, exuding a heady odour of sandalwood; curling slippers, stained deep green by the craft of Fujian, a sash of nine tassels, dyed with true purple fetched from the west; bold staring eyes, forever turning after beautiful women, a sensual mouth, full of sweet words, apt for seducing young women at funerals. In the extremity of his lust, he searches out the nuns in their convents; when the lecherous fit is upon him, he ambushes pilgrims in the abbot's quarters.*

This priest entered and greeted Madcap most reverently. Madcap returned the greeting and said: "Please have a seat, father." An assistant bearing two containers followed immediately behind.

Madcap went to call the old man: "A priest has come, sir." When in due course the old man appeared, the priest greeted him with: "Godfather, why do you never come and see me at the temple?"

"Well, you see," the old man answered, "I've got this shop now, and I haven't had time to go anywhere."

The priest said, "Here are a few poor gifts to celebrate the Registrar's anniversary. Just a few noodles and some dates."

"Oh dear," said the old man. "There was no need for that, it's really too generous of you!" He told Madcap to take the gifts. Madcap took them inside and ordered the servants to bring tea, which was served to the priest at the door.

At this point the woman came downstairs. She didn't have to be in deep mourning, but was just plainly dressed with scarcely any make-up. "Who sent these things?" she asked Madcap.

"A priest," he replied. "He calls your father godfather."

She looked pleased. "It must be Brother Hai — Pei Ruhai that is, a very good man. He used to manage the family silk shop, but then he left the world to enter the Temple of Divine Favours. Since his superior is a secular prelate, he was able to name my father as his godfather. He's just two years older than I am, so I call him elder brother. At the temple everyone calls him Father Hai. Just wait till you hear him chanting the prayers this evening, he's got a lovely voice!"

"I see," said Madcap. But in his heart he felt certain misgivings.

When the woman went down to see the priest, Madcap with his hands behind his back followed her some of the way, but then stood and watched from behind the curtain. He saw the priest rise to his feet and with joined hands greet her most effusively.

"You are really too generous, elder brother," she said.

"Just a few trifling gifts, my dear, nothing to make a song and dance about."

"How can you say that? How can we accept things from someone who has renounced the world?"

"Our temple has just built a new oratory for the souls of those who suffered violent death by land or water. I would have asked you to come and view it, only I wasn't sure if your husband would approve or not."

"My husband's not narrow-minded. Actually when my mother was dying I made a vow to have prayers said for the release of her soul. I have been meaning for some time to pay you a visit at the temple and trouble you to arrange it for me."

"But that is absolutely one of my duties, how could it be any trouble? You have only to say the word and all shall be done according to your wishes."

"Well, then, elder brother, let me request you to read some more sutras for my mother."

At this point a servant brought tea and the woman took a cup and wiped the rim with her handkerchief and offered it with both hands to the priest. Receiving it, he stared greedily at the woman, while she simpered back at him. Lust, as they say, engenders boundless audacity. The fact that Madcap was watching behind the curtain was no hindrance. Madcap said to himself: "'Virtue's not always what it seems, morality is oft a sham.' The hussy likes to use flirtatious language to me, I've observed it more than once.

But I always treated her as if she were my true relative. Now it's clear she's no better than she ought to be. Still, if I catch her at it, it's no good her thinking I won't act on behalf of my friend."

Madcap was by now highly suspicious. He drew aside the curtain and made his appearance. The lecherous bonze put down his cup and said: "Please have a seat, sir." The woman said: "This gentleman is a brother my husband has just adopted."

Smiling meekly the priest said: "May I be permitted to ask your name, sir, and where you are from?"

"Shi Xiu from Jinling," he replied shortly. "They call me Madcap because I've a habit of helping people just for the hell of it. I'm a pretty ordinary type, with no airs and graces, I trust you'll forgive me."

"No offence, no offence!" the monk replied. "I'd better go and fetch the other monks for the service," he said and prepared to take his departure.

"Come back soon, brother," the woman said.

"I will, I will," said the priest.

After seeing the priest off, she returned. Madcap was standing by the door with lowered head, lost in thought. No doubt you've heard it said, my friends, that among all the people of this world, it's the priests who are the most lecherous. Why should this be? Seeing that laymen and priests are all men, born of the father's seed and the mother's blood, why should the priests be more lecherous? It's like the story of Pan's donkey in the Three Books. Of all the people in the world it's the priests who have the easiest life. Three meals a day, with good food supplied free by benefactors, a monastery full of spacious rooms and grand halls to live in, no worldly affairs to cause unrest, a comfortable bed with fine covers to sleep on, nothing to tax the brain and all the time in the world to dream. Compare this with the rich man, who even if he lives in plenty, each day has so many tiresome affairs to worry him, and can't sleep at night because his mind is obsessed with money and possessions, not to mention the women who share his bed and trouble him with their demands. Or compare the life of the common man, every day spent in bitter toil, longing when he rises in the morning for evening to come, up at dawn and not in bed till late at night, and when at last it's bedtime unable to go to bed without first feeling around in the rice bin and finding it empty, knowing tomorrow there's no money left. Even if the wife has some charms, he can't work up much enthusiasm. Now, if we bear in mind all these facts about the monks and their easy life, we can understand this kind of affair. People in the old days used to satirize such things, they said the monks were really terrible. Su Dongpo for instance wrote: "A smooth shaven head and poisonous as a snake, the two things simply can't be separated." There's also a little verse about monks:

In one word you can call him bonze
Or bald pate does as well,
Devil's fiddler if you like,
Or sex-crazed fiend from hell.

Madcap stood in front of the door thinking for a long time. Then he went to help welcome the priests. In a little while a cleric appeared and lit candles and joss-sticks. Then came Father Hai, mustering a whole company of bonzes to attend the altar. Madcap and the old man received them together. When they had been served tea, drums and cymbals began to sound and the singing of the praises of the dead man commenced. Father Hai and another young monk of about the same age officiated, wielding the bells and pestles, dispatching written prayers by burning them, making offerings to the defenders of the faith and the guardians of the altar and praying that the spirit of the departed registrar be soon permitted to enter the kingdom of heaven. At this point the woman appeared, got up in her widow's weeds. She approached the altar with a little incense burner in her hands and lit joss-sticks as she worshipped the Buddha. Father Hai waved his bells and chanted with redoubled vigour. And when the other priests caught sight of Morbid's wife, they were all plunged into confusion. Here's how it was:

The deacon reads the litany crazily, he gets it all back to front; the preceptor makes a thorough mess of reciting the scriptures, you can't make head or tail of it. The acolytes lighting the incense

> *knock over the vase; the brother who's supposed to carry the candle picks up the joss-sticks instead. During the antiphons and the homily, the Song Dynasty is read as Tang; in the penitential ritual Registrar Wang is called Bailiff Wang. The person shaking the bells lets them fly from his hand. The one beating the cymbals falls senseless to the ground. The rhythm blurs, the sounds become harsh. The whole place is in turmoil, the ceremony in chaos. The keeper of the scriptures is so confused he absent-mindedly beats the acolyte's hands instead of the drum, the choir-master's vision is so dazzled he beats out a rhythm on an old monk's bald pate. After ten years of asceticism, they let go for an instant, and then a thousand door-gods would not suffice to hold them back.*

Now when those priests saw Morbid's wife at the ceremony, unconsciously their hands began to dance and their feet began to tap and all thoughts of piety and spirituality were scattered to the winds. They were totally unable to control themselves. It's due to this kind of thing that you'll seldom meet a truly virtuous priest!

Madcap was watching from one side. "Talk of piety!" he scoffed. "They say true who say ''tis easier far to put on piety than to avoid sin.'"

In a little while when the ceremony for the dead was finished the priests were all invited inside for a vegetarian meal. Father Hai stationed himself at the back where he could leer at the woman, who laughed back, covering her mouth with her hand. The two of them went on ogling each other, making no attempt to hide their feelings. Madcap observed it all, with considerable distaste. The monks sat down at the table. First a few cups of simple wine were drunk, then the vegetarian food was served and the gift of money distributed. "Please tuck in, fathers," the old man said.

In no time the priests had scoffed their food and stood up to take a post-prandial stroll. After a few turns, they returned to the altar. Madcap was very ill at ease, and complaining of a stomach pain went to rest in the room next door.

Now her lust had been aroused, the woman seemed not to care at all about being observed and went to serve the priests herself. The drums and cymbals sounded again and a little later tea and snacks were served. Father Hai exhorted the monks to pray earnestly, begging the lord of heaven to show his mercy, as they scattered holy water about and worshipped the Three Treasures. The service continued till nearly midnight. The other monks were exhausted, but our friend Father Hai still went on chanting at the top of his voice. As the woman watched behind the curtain in the doorway, her passions blazed up, she was overcome with desire. She told the maid to tell Father Hai she wanted to speak to him. Eagerly the bald lecher approached her. Grasping his sleeve, she said: "Dear brother, tomorrow when you come to receive the fee, please speak to my father about the prayers for my mother. You won't forget, will you?"

"I won't forget. I shall tell him a vow's a vow and ought to be fulfilled," said the priest. Then he added: "That brother-in-law of yours looks pretty fierce."

"You needn't worry about him," she replied. "He's not even a real relation."

"Then I won't. I supposed he was a real brother of the Warden's."

The two of them chattered happily together for a while, until the priest went off to scatter grain for the ghosts. They didn't know that Madcap was in the room next door, pretending to sleep and taking note of everything. That night at three in the morning when the altar had been dismantled and all the paper offerings burnt, the priests gave thanks and departed. The woman went upstairs to sleep. Madcap thought to himself: "My friend has such a noble spirit, it's really bad luck he picked a bitch like that!" But he kept his indignation to himself and took himself off to sleep in the workshop.

No one said anything about all this when Morbid returned next day. After eating he went out again and immediately Father Hai was there knocking on the door, having changed into a smart new robe. When the woman heard he had come, she hurried downstairs to receive him, inviting him to come in and sit down, and ordering tea. She thanked him for the service the day before: "We put you to a lot of trouble yesterday and you still haven't received the fee," she said. "It's nothing," he replied. "I've come to tell you about those prayers for your mother's soul we talked about yesterday, dear sister. When I go back to the temple I shall be chanting the sutras. Just write out the prayer you want said, that's all it needs."

"All right," she said. She told the maid to go and ask her father to join them. When he came in the old man thanked the priest. "I'm an old man and I haven't much staying power nowadays," he said. "I'm afraid I neglected my duties as host last night. It was most unfortunate that Mr. Shi was also indisposed and there was no one to look after you properly. Do please forgive us."

"There's nothing to worry about, godfather," the priest said.

The woman said, "I want to renew the service for mother's soul. Brother Hai says he will be performing a service tomorrow at the temple and will add the prayers for mother. Let him go back to the temple now and recite the sutras and we will go along after breakfast tomorrow and write down her name on the prayers that are to be chanted. It will mean we have fulfilled our duty."

The old man said: "It sounds a good idea, only tomorrow we may have a lot of business and there won't be anyone to look after it."

"We can leave Mr. Shi to look after it. What's the problem?"

"We'll do as you say then. Tomorrow we'll go to the temple."

The girl went and got some money for the offering and gave it to the priest. "I fear this is very little recompense for your pains, Brother Hai. Tomorrow we'll come to the temple and beg a bowl of plain noodles from you."

"I shall await your coming to burn incense." Having received his fee he stood up and thanked them: "It is more than I merit. I shall go back now and share it with the others, and later I shall expect you, sister, for the ceremony."

The woman saw him off. Madcap, after resting a while in the workshop, rose to get on with his work of slaughtering pigs.

When Morbid came back that evening, his wife waited till he had eaten and washed his hands and feet. Then she prompted her father to say to him: "My daughter here promised my old lady on her deathbed to give her a service for the dead at the Temple of Divine Favours. I want you to know that we are going to go and perform the sacrifice there tomorrow. We won't be long."

"Why couldn't you tell me that yourself?" Morbid said to his wife.

"I thought you might be angry if I said it. I didn't dare," she said.

Nothing of importance happened that evening. They all just went to bed.

Next day Morbid rose at dawn and went off to report for duty at the office. As soon as Madcap got up he went to work in the shop. The woman began by painting her face and dressing herself up to the nines. Then she packed some incense, bought paper offerings for burning and candles, and ordered a sedan chair. Madcap was busy with the shop from early morning and he paid no heed to all this. When breakfast was over the maid, Ying, also dolled herself up and a little later the old man, in a new suit of clothes, came to Madcap and said: "I shall have to trouble you Mr. Shi to keep an eye on the place for me while I and my daughter go and fulfil our vow. We won't be long."

"Of course I'll look after everything," Madcap replied. "Take good care of your daughter, burn plenty of incense, and come back soon." But he was full of forebodings.

The sedan set off for the Temple of Divine Favours, with the old man and Ying, the maid, walking beside it. There is an old poem which comments aptly on all this:

You may study your scriptures all morning,
And chant your fine prayers until late
But the finest of prayers and intentions
Can nowise alter your fate.
How can the heart that's not blind
Ask heaven to change its mind?
If it's melons you plant you'll have melons,
And if you plant beans you'll get beans.
So it's what's in the heart from the outset
That determines what everything means.
Is it Hell, is it Heaven, who knows?
Each one of us reaps what he sows.

These words, handed down from olden time, tell us that good and evil get their desserts, as sure as shadow follows substance.

Best stick to the six virtues and the ten thousand reasons, respect the Three Pillars — the Buddha, the Law and the Monkhood — and the Five Precepts — kill not, steal not, lust not, gossip not, drink not. Unfortunately the clergy can turn into dogs and swine, a disgrace to their tradition and a legacy of shame to future generations.

Now it was solely on account of this woman that the bald lecher, Father Hai, had asked Old Pan to be his godfather. He had however been so far prevented by Morbid's watchful eye and could not proceed in the affair. Since he and the woman had first been acquainted, eyes and looks had spoken volumes, but as yet nothing of substance had occurred. Nevertheless, on the night of the ceremony he had seen that she was really interested. The appointment was duly made, and now the bald lecher, having sharpened his spear and polished his sword, that is to say, having girded up his loins, went to wait at the main gate of the temple. When he saw the sedan approaching he could scarcely contain himself. He dashed forward to receive them.

"I'm afraid we are giving you too much trouble," Old Pan said.

Descending from the chair, the woman said: "We are very very grateful to you, dear brother."

"Not at all, not at all," said Father Hai. "I have personally been in the oratory with the other monks chanting the sutras since dawn. I took no rest until just now. I have been waiting for you so we can burn the prayers. This is a most meritorious business." He led the girl and the old man into the oratory, where flowers, fruit, incense, candles and the like had been set out and a dozen or so monks were chanting sutras. The woman greeted them reverentially, wishing them all a thousand happinesses, and then paid homage to the Three Treasures. Father Hai led her before the Buddha of the Underworld to offer prayers for the remission of sins. After the chanting of the prayers paper offerings were burnt and then the priests were invited to a meal, in recompense for their services. Father Hai now proposed that his godfather and dear sister take tea with him in his inner sanctum. He was inviting the woman into his room in the heart of the temple buildings. All had been prepared in advance: the moment he called for tea two novices appeared with it. The tea was brewed from the choicest leaves and served in snow-white cups on a vermilion tray. When everyone had put their cups down, he said: "Please come and sit inside for a while, dear sister." He led her into a small chamber where some paintings by famous artists were displayed on a gleaming black table and sticks of sweet incense were burning on a little altar. The old man and his daughter sat at the table, the priest sat down opposite them and the maid, Ying, stood on one side.

The girl said: "What a wonderful place this is, brother, for a holy person like you. So quiet and secluded, so harmonious!"

"Don't make fun of me," the priest replied. "How can this compare with your great mansion?"

"We've troubled you for a whole day, now," the old man said. "We should be going."

The priest wouldn't hear of it. "You come here so seldom," he said. "Besides, you're like part of my family, and my sister paid for the banquet today, so why don't you stay and have a simple bowl of noodles with me before you go? The brothers will have it ready in no time." He had scarcely finished speaking when two platters were brought in, the kind of stuff that's only brought out on special occasions, rare fruit and exotic dishes as well as every kind of vegetarian fare. This food completely covered the table.

"You've prepared a feast, why have you gone to so much trouble?" she said.

"It's not really worthy of you, it's just a small mark of my esteem," he answered with a smile.

The brothers filled their cups and Father Hai said: "It's such a long time since you've been here, godfather. Please try some of this wine."

The old man drank and said: "Excellent wine, really first-class."

"A benefactor showed us how to make it the other day. We made three or four gallons. Another day I'll send over a few bottles for your son-in-law."

"Oh no, you really shouldn't," the old man said.

"I'm sorry I have nothing better to give you, dear sister," Father Hai said. "But do at least taste a cup of this wine."

The two brothers poured wine in turn, and even Ying was encouraged to have a few cups.

"You're a wonderful host, but really I can't drink any more," the girl said.

"You come so seldom, you've got to have a few more cups!"

The old man asked for the sedan chair carriers to be brought in so they could all drink a cup together.

"No need to be concerned about them, godfather," the priest said. "I've already arranged it. They've got a place to sit and drink with the brothers outside. So don't worry, just relax and have a few more cups."

Of course it was on account of the girl that the bald lecher had arranged to have this exceptionally strong wine. Old Pan needed little persuading. He drank two more cups and became irremediably drunk.

Then the priest said: "We'd better send godfather to bed to sleep it off." He called two brothers to lend a hand, and they helped the old man to a nice quiet room where he could sleep. Then he said to the girl: "Now you can sit back and enjoy a few more cups." Well, in the first place the girl was quite willing, but in addition the wine had enflamed her passions. Is it not said that wine provokes passion and lust ruins mankind? With a few cups of wine under her belt, she felt her head spinning. "Oh, brother," she gabbled, "why do you keep wanting me to drink wine?"

"It's because I hold you in such high esteem," he replied, laughing wildly.

"I can't drink any more," she said.

"Please come up to my room and see my Buddha's tooth," said he.

"Ooh, yes, I want to see your Buddha's tooth," she said.

He led her upstairs, to an upstairs room which was his bedroom, beautifully furnished. She was absolutely delighted with it. "What a beautiful bedroom you have, it's so neat," she said.

"The only thing missing is a mistress for it," he said, smirking.

"Why don't you look for one?" said she, with a giggle.

"Where would I find a benefactor like that?" he said.

"Come on, show me your Buddha's tooth," she said.

"Send Ying away and I'll get it out," he said.

"Ying, why don't you go down and see if the master has woken up?" she said to the maid.

As soon as Ying had gone off to see her master, he locked the door. "Ooh, brother, why are you locking me in?" said she.

The bald lecher's lewd heart was beating wildly. He rushed to the woman and embraced her, saying: "I love you passionately. For two whole years you have filled my thoughts. Now you are here at last, there's this wonderful opportunity, surely you are going to make me happy?"

She said: "My husband's not a good man to get on the wrong side of. You just want to ruin me. If he gets to know he won't forgive you."

He knelt and said: "Take pity on me, I implore you."

She raised her hand and said: "You priests just want to get people into trouble. This hand of mine ought to give you a big slap."

He giggled and said: "Go ahead, do, and please don't spare me."

She was fully aroused now. She hugged him tight and said: "Do you really think I should hit you?"

His reply was to hug her back. Then, after removing all clothing and apparel, they embarked on the delights of the shared pillow. Truly we can say:

> *Where now the teachings of religion, what price moral precept? Crazed with desire, what cares he for the husband's hurt? Consumed by lust, she's out to ensure His Reverence's downfall. In loud pants his breath comes, like an ox snoring under the willows. With coarse meanings her sweet cries blend, like an oriole warbling among flowers. Wanton words and thoughts whispered in the ear by the one, eternal oaths and pillow-vows from the other. The priest's room is transformed into a shrine to pleasure; the Temple of Divine Favours is become a true garden of delights. How shameful to think that the precious seed of enlightenment is all to be spilt in Felicity!*

From ancient times till now, people have handed down a verse which compares these priests to woodworm. There is no timber so sound that they won't bore into it. What defence have ordinary people against them?

As the old poem says:

Like lascivious monkeys these profligate beasts
Reverse the true sense of their calling as priests.
So leave them like beasts in the jungle to roam,
And never admit them into your home!

After they had both come, the lewd bonze hugged her tight and said: "If you love me, even death has no terrors for me. But although I'm glad you've made me so happy today, it is such a brief instant of happiness! If we cannot prolong our pleasures for a whole night, in the end it is going to kill me."

She said: "Don't worry, I have a plan. About twenty nights every month my husband has to be on duty at the prison. I shall bribe Ying and have her stand at the back door every night. When it gets late, if my husband isn't home, she will set out a little altar and burn incense as a signal. Then you will know it is safe to come. If you are afraid of going to sleep at dawn and not waking in time, you can find one of those lay brothers who wake people up and pay him to come to the back door and beat the wooden fish and sing out a prayer, then you'll know you have to leave. If he is in your employ there are two advantages: one, he can keep watch outside for you, and two, he can make sure you don't oversleep."

The monk thought this was a wonderful idea. "Masterly!" he said. "You do just as you said. And for my part, there's a lay brother here called Brother Hu, I can get him to come and keep watch."

"I daren't linger here now, or those oafs will become suspicious," the girl said. "I'd better be going. Do make sure you arrange everything properly." She quickly rearranged her hair and repaired her make-up. Then she unlocked the door and went downstairs. She told Ying to waken her father and they hurriedly left the temple buildings. The sedan chair carriers had drunk and eaten and were waiting at the temple gates. Father Hai escorted her as far as the main gate of the compound and then she said goodbye to him and got into the chair and together with her father and Ying proceeded home. Of this no more.

As for Father Hai, he went off to find the lay brother who did the morning calls. At the temple this happened to be a lay brother called Hu, who lived like a hermit in a little hut at the back of the compound and was known to everyone as Brother Hu. He rose before dawn each day and came to strike the wooden fish, summoning people to morning prayers. As soon as it was light he would go begging for food. Father Hai called him to his room, where he had prepared a few cups of good wine and some silver to give him. Brother Hu stood there and said: "I haven't done anything, how can I take a reward? I've already received so much kindness from you."

Father Hai said: "I know well that you are very conscientious. One day I shall give you the money to help you buy your monk's certificate, so you can shave your head and become my disciple. For the moment take this and go and buy some proper robes." In fact Father Hai had often instructed the other priests to give Brother Hu food for the midday meal, and to take him along when there was a reading of the sutras so he too could receive some alms. Brother Hu was deeply grateful and had as yet been unable to repay the debt. "Now he gives me more silver," he said to himself, "it must be because he wants me to do something for him, maybe I shouldn't wait for him to say it first." So he said: "If you have something that needs doing, Father, or anything in which I can be of service to you, please don't hesitate to tell me."

Father Hai said: "Brother Hu, I know what a good person you are, so I won't beat about the bush. That daughter of Old Pan's wants to have a relationship with me, and we have agreed that when a little altar with incense is set up outside her back door it will be a signal for me to come. It's a bit difficult for me to hang about round there. But if you were to go along first and check for me if the coast is clear, I'd be able to go. It would also be helpful if when you get up at dawn to call the monks to prayers you could go round to the back door again and after making sure there's no one about strike the wooden fish and sing out a prayer so I'll know it's all right to come out."

"No problem at all!" said Brother Hu.

So it was agreed. When Brother Hu went next day to Old Pan's back door to beg for food, Ying came out and said: "You there, you Taoist, why don't you come to the front door to ask for food, what are you doing coming round the back?"

But Brother Hu began chanting his prayers and Felicity heard him. Having taken a look she went to the back door and asked: "Aren't you the disciple who gives the morning call to prayers?"

"That's right," he answered. "I prevent people from oversleeping, and in the evening I light incense and help people to gain merit."

Scarcely able to contain her excitement, she sent Ying upstairs to get a string of copper cash for the brother. When Ying had gone the brother said: "Father Hai has taken me into his confidence. He sent me here to reconnoitre."

"I know about it," she said. "You can come again tonight, and if you see the altar with incense burning, go and tell him."

He nodded. When Ying returned with the money, she gave it to him and he left. She went upstairs again, and there she unburdened herself to Ying. As they say: "A maid should be your slave." But provided there's something in it for her, why shouldn't she be happy to cooperate, even in an important affair? Likewise, the way things are between mistresses and servants, there's mutual exploitation but not trust. All the same, one can't do without them.

Well, it happened that Morbid was on duty at the prison that night. Before evening he came back to fetch his bedding so he could sleep there. Ying, who had already received some small recompense, didn't even wait till evening before starting to prepare the altar and set it up by the back door at dusk. Her mistress concealed herself to one side where she could watch. Some time after seven o'clock, a figure with its head wrapped in a scarf stole through the doorway. "Who is it?" Ying called. She got no reply. But when the handkerchief came off, a shining bald pate appeared. Recognizing Father Hai, the mistress now gently scolded: "You old devil, you know all the tricks!" They went upstairs together with their arms round each other's waists. Ying put away the áltar, locked the back door and went to bed. The other two spent a night of bliss in each other's arms, tight as rubber, close as lacquer, like sugar in honey, like marrow in the bone, like a fish in water. It is said: "Pleasure hates the night to be so short, and only prays the golden rooster will postpone his call." They had only just gone to sleep when the tock-tock of the wooden fish was heard and the loud entoning of a prayer, startling the couple from their dreams. He hastily grabbed his clothes, and said: "I must be going. I'll see you again tonight."

"From now on come any time the altar is at the back door, don't fail me. But if it's not there, you most definitely must not come."

He rose and wrapped his head in the scarf as before and Ying opened the back door and let him out. From now on every time Morbid was on night duty at the prison the priest came to his house. There was no one there but the old man and he went to bed early. As for the maid, Ying, she was already on their side. It was only a question of deceiving Madcap. The woman was so besotted that she took little care. And the priest had tasted woman now — it was as if the two of them were bewitched. Whenever he received word from the brother, the priest was out of the temple like a shot. Felicity had fully involved Ying in the game, instructing her to let him in and let him out. So it was a joyous life for Pan's daughter, secretly entertaining her priest as lover. Soon the affair had been going over a month and the priest had made something like a dozen visits.

Now when Madcap closed the shop each day and bedded down in the workshop, he thought a good deal about this matter. Only he couldn't be sure: he had not actually seen the priest coming and going. Often he would jump out of bed at dawn, hoping to get to the bottom of the affair. All that happened was that he would hear the brother turning into the lane beating the wooden fish and loudly entoning a prayer. Now Madcap was no fool and he already had a pretty good idea what was afoot. This is how he argued to himself. "This lane is a cul-de-sac. Why does this lay brother come here every day, striking the wooden fish and shouting out prayers? There's something fishy about it." Then one day, the tenth of the eleventh month, when Madcap was awake at dawn, he heard the sound of the wooden fish and the brother entering the lane and stopping at the back door to sing out: "O Buddha of all the worlds, rescue all the faithful from hardship and misfortune." His suspicions aroused, he leapt out of bed and went to spy through a crack in the door. He saw someone with a scarf over his head emerge from the shadows and go off with the lay brother. Afterwards Ying came and locked the door. Madcap said to himself: "Brother, you are such a noble soul, this lustful woman is abominable, she's deceiving you, she's carrying on an affair."

As soon as it was light, he hung up his pork in the front of the shop to make some early sales. After breakfast he went to collect some accounts, and then headed for the government offices to find Morbid. He ran into Morbid just as he reached the town bridge. "Where are you going?" Morbid asked him. "I've been out collecting accounts, brother, so I decided to come and see you," he replied.

"I'm always so busy at work," Morbid said, "that I never have time to enjoy a few cups of wine with you. Let's go and sit down somewhere." He took Madcap into a little tavern under the town bridge where they chose a secluded alcove and sat down. Morbid told the waiter to bring a bottle of good wine and some fruit and nuts and seafood to go with it. But even after three cups Madcap remained quiet and thoughtful and Morbid, by nature impetuous, asked: "Is there something troubling you, brother, has something at home upset you or offended you?"

Madcap replied: "I've got no problem with your household. But since you have been so kind as to treat me almost as your own flesh and blood, will you permit me to mention something?"

"Why do you treat me like a stranger today? If you've something to say, then of course there's nothing to stop you."

"Well, when you go out each morning your mind is only on your official duties. You don't notice what is going on behind your back. Your wife is not behaving herself. I've seen things with my own eyes, several times, but I didn't like to say. But what I saw today was so clear I couldn't refrain from coming to find you. Please forgive my bluntness."

"I haven't got eyes behind my back. Who is it?"

"That bloody priest you got to read the service in your house, that Father Hai. He and your wife were making eyes at each other, I saw it all. And three days later when they went to the service in the temple they came back loaded with bottles of wine. Then recently a brother has been coming to our street beating the wooden fish and shouting out prayers. He makes a tremendous din. Well, this morning I got up at dawn to watch. I saw that bloody priest with a scarf round his head coming out of the house. She's a shameless woman, you'd be better off without her!"

Morbid exploded. "The filthy bitch, what's she playing at?"

"Keep calm, brother," Madcap said. "Don't say anything about this tonight. Just behave as usual. Tomorrow morning pretend you're going to be on night duty, then come back after midnight and knock on the door. That blackguard will undoubtedly try to escape by the back door and I'll grab him for you to dispose of."

"Right, that's what we'll do," said Morbid.

"But don't go babbling about it tonight," Madcap warned him again.

"I'll meet you again tomorrow," said Morbid.

They drank a few more cups, then paid the bill, went downstairs together and after leaving the tavern were about to go their separate ways, when suddenly Morbid was hailed by four or five of the Governor's officers. "Warden, we've been looking for you everywhere. The Governor is waiting in his garden; he told us to fetch you for some staff play with us. Hurry up now."

"The boss wants me, I'll have to go," Morbid said to Madcap. "You go on home." So Madcap took himself home, tidied up the shop and went to the workshop to sleep.

But Morbid was summoned by the Governor to the garden of the residence where he fought several bouts with the staff. The Governor enjoyed the spectacle and had wine brought. Ten big cups were drunk off as a prize. After this they left, but Morbid was invited by some of his colleagues to continue drinking with them. It was quite late when they helped him home, by now completely drunk. There's a poem which says:

'Tis said that wine and sex are oft combined;
The drunkard seeks to ease the sexual urge;
But now this hero's something on his mind
To fire a rage which drunkenness won't purge.

When Morbid's wife saw he was drunk, she thanked his friends and then got him upstairs with Ying's help. A lamp was lit and turned up fully. Morbid sat on the bed. Ying went to take off his boots, the wife removed his cap and unwound his turban. Suddenly as Morbid looked at his wife, something arose in his heart. As they say: "In drunkenness the truth will out." He pointed his finger at her and shouted: "You slut, you strumpet, I'm going to do for you, regardless!" She had a great shock and didn't dare answer, but simply helped him into bed. As he drifted off to sleep he continued to mutter: "Slut, filthy whore, that blackguard thinks he can spit in the mouth of the tiger! Don't you imagine I'm ever going to let you off!"

Not daring even to breathe, she waited for him to fall asleep.

Five o'clock. Morbid roused himself from his stupor and asked for a drink of water. His wife ladled out a bowl and gave it to him. On the table the lamp was still burning. Morbid drank and then asked her: "Didn't you come to bed last night?"

"You were dead drunk," she said. "I was afraid you might throw up, I didn't dare undress. I spent the night at the foot of the bed."

"Did I say anything?"

"You can always hold your drink, you just go to sleep, but last night I was worried for some reason."

Then he said: "I haven't had time lately to enjoy a cup of wine with my good friend Madcap. Would you prepare some food so I can invite him here?"

She made no reply, but just sat on the step of the bed with tears welling from her eyes and sighing. Morbid asked: "Listen, I was drunk last night but you say I didn't hurt you, so why are you so upset?"

She pretended to hide her tears and said nothing. So he asked her again and she went on covering her face and pretending to

楊雄醉罵潘巧雲

cry. Finally he pulled her up onto the bed and insisted on knowing what was troubling her. Choking back her sobs she said: "When my parents arranged my marriage to Registrar Wang, I thought I was going to be married once and for all. Who would have thought he'd go and leave me in the lurch? Now I'm married to you, such a great hero, and a gentleman to boot, who would have imagined that you couldn't protect me?"

"Great heavens! Who dares to insult you! When have I failed to protect you?"

"At first I didn't want to say anything. I was afraid you'd only listen to him. Then I thought of telling you but I was afraid you'd just let it pass."

"You'd better explain what all this is about!"

"Don't be too upset, then, if I tell you. It all began when you adopted that Madcap and brought him home. It was all right at first. It wasn't till later he began to make insinuations. When he knew you weren't coming home to sleep, he would look at me and say: 'Brother's away again tonight. Won't you be lonely sleeping on your own?' Of course I paid no attention, even though it didn't happen just once. Anyway, never mind that. Yesterday morning, when I was washing my neck in the kitchen, the blighter came up behind me and because there was no one else about put one arm round and touched my breast and said: 'Are you pregnant?' I slapped his hand away and I would have screamed, only I was afraid the neighbours would laugh at us and make up stories about you. I was waiting till you came home. But you came back drunk as a lord and I didn't dare say anything. I hate him, I can't bear him, and you come and ask me about your dear friend!"

Well it was a case of:

Smart answers the wanton will never lack,
'Tis the husband's role to be misled.
As the front door closes on Morbid's back,
The back door admits the priest to his bed.

Morbid was outraged. He said: "'You can paint a dragon or a tiger but you can't show its bones; you can recognize the outside of a man but you can't know his heart.' The bugger even came and told me to my face a whole lot of stuff about Father Hai, stories without any foundation. Obviously he was scared. He wanted to get in first with this story about you." He kept muttering angrily: "He's not my brother any more. I'll chuck him out, that's what!"

As soon as it was light, Morbid went downstairs and said to his father-in-law: "Kill all the livestock and salt the carcasses. From today the business is closed." In a trice he had broken up the counter and the workbench. When next morning Madcap went to put out the meat he found counter and workbench smashed. Madcap was no fool, he couldn't fail to understand. He laughed grimly: "I see," he said. "So Morbid got drunk and couldn't keep his mouth shut, he let the cat out of the bag. He's listened to that hussy's account of things, she's turned it all upside down and said I misbehaved. She's made her husband close the shop. If I try to have it out with him it'll make him lose face. I'd better back off a bit and find a different way." He went back into the workshop and packed his things. Morbid also kept away, reluctant to embarrass him. Madcap shouldered his pack, stuck a sharp knife into his belt and went to say goodbye to Old Pan. "I've bothered you in your home too long already. My brother has closed the shop now, so I shall take myself off. I've drawn up the accounts perfectly clearly, there's not a cent missing. If there's anything not right, may heaven strike me dead." Following his son-in-law's instructions, the old man made no attempt to detain him. The poem says:

Pillow talk always appeals;
What's behind you can't be seen.
The faithful friend he expels,
And lets the adulterer in.

After saying goodbye, Madcap went and found an inn in a neighbouring side-street and rented a room for himself. He was thinking: "Morbid is my adopted brother. If I don't clear this matter up between us, it'll be putting his life at risk. The trouble is that for the moment he's been convinced by that woman and thinks I'm guilty. I can't prove anything, but I've got to try and make him see how things really are. I'd better go and find out which day he is going to sleep at the prison, then get up before dawn and solve the riddle." After two days at the inn he went to watch at Morbid's door. That evening he saw a servant from the gaol carry out Morbid's bedding, and he said to himself: "That means he's on duty tonight. I must get to work now."

He returned to the inn to sleep but rose during the fourth watch. He took his dagger, quietly opened the door of the shop and stole round to the lane which Morbid's back door opened onto. There he hid in the shadows to watch. Exactly at five o'clock the lay brother appeared clutching the wooden fish. When he reached the mouth of the lane he peered around cautiously. Madcap slipped out from his hiding-place and came up behind him. He laid one hand on him and with the other pressed the knife to his neck, whispering: "Don't move; if you make a noise I shall kill you! Just tell me the truth. Why did Father Hai tell you to come here?"

"I beg you, sir, spare my life and I will tell you," the lay brother stammered.

"Be quick then, or I'll kill you."

"Father Hai is having an affair with Old Pan's daughter. Every night he wants me to look and see if there's an altar outside the back door — that's the sign that says he's going to get it in. He told me to come at dawn to strike the wooden fish and pray to the Buddha — that lets him know it's time to pull it out."

"And where is he now?"

"He's still inside, sleeping. When I strike the wooden fish he'll come out."

"Give me your robes and the wooden fish." As the brother started undressing Madcap grabbed the wooden fish. When the brother got his clothes off, Madcap slit his throat. Then he dressed up in the dead brother's robes and knee-length stockings, put away his dagger, and walked into the lane striking the wooden fish. Father Hai lying in bed heard the tock-tock of the wooden fish and hurriedly rose, threw on his clothes and rushed downstairs. Ying opened the back door and he slipped out. "Why do you keep on beating it?" he hissed to Madcap, who hadn't stopped striking the wooden fish. Madcap made no answer but waited till he got to the mouth of the lane and then threw him to

石秀智殺裴如海

the ground, pinned him down and growled: "Don't make a sound, keep quiet or I'll kill you! Just let me have your clothes."

Father Hai recognized Madcap and was too scared to struggle or open his mouth. Madcap stripped off all his clothes, leaving him stark naked, without a thread. Then silently he pulled the knife out of his stocking and stabbed the priest three or four times, till he was dead. He placed the knife beside the body of the brother, made all their clothes into a bundle and returned to the inn. He opened the door carefully and closed it quietly behind him and went back to bed. Of this no more.

Now in the town there was an old fellow called Wang, who sold rice soup. That morning he had taken up his gruel, and holding a lantern and followed by a young lad set forth to catch the early trade. Just as he came to the place where the corpses lay he happened to stumble and spilt his rice soup on the ground. At the same moment the boy shouted out: "Oh my God! There's a drunken priest lying here." After feeling around with his two hands, the old man discovered them to be smeared with blood. He began to curse loudly. He couldn't think what had happened. Some neighbours who heard all this opened their doors and came out. Torches were shone on the scene, revealing blood and gruel all over the place and two corpses lying on the ground. The neighbours detained the old man and insisted on taking him to the authorities. Truly,

Calamities fall from the skies;
Out of the ground disasters rise.

If you want to know how Old Wang got out of this predicament you must read the next chapter.

Chapter 46

Morbid gets rough on Jade Screen Hill; Madcap burns the Zhu Arms down!

When that group of neighbours detained Old Wang, the seller of gruel, they took him straight off to the government office and reported him. The court was in session. They knelt before the Governor and declared: "This old man was carrying a load of gruel and spilt it on the ground and discovered two corpses there: one was a monk, the other a lay brother. Neither body had a stitch of clothing on. There was a knife beside the body of the lay brother."

The old man gave his statement: "I generally go out in the morning to sell gruel. It's how I earn my living. Most times I get going in the fifth watch. This morning I got up a bit early and I was just walking along with this stupid boy of mine, not looking where I was going, when I suddenly tripped up and went and smashed all my bowls and dishes. That's when I saw these two bodies on the ground — swimming in blood, they were. It gave me a right turn, I can tell you. I started screaming, and those people grabbed me and dragged me here to the court. I hope Your Honour will judge me mercifully."

The Governor had his statement taken and signed an order requiring the local authorities and officials from the coroner's office to go with the neighbours, Old Wang and anyone else involved in the affair to inspect the bodies and draw up a detailed account.

When they had made their inspection, they reported back to the Governor: "The dead priest is a canon from the Temple of Divine Favours, Pei Ruhai; the lay brother lying beside him is Brother Hu, who lives at the back of the temple. The priest was absolutely naked, and he had three or four stab wounds which were obviously the cause of death. Next to Brother Hu there was a sharp knife and his throat was cut. It looks as if Brother Hu picked up the knife and killed the priest with it, then horrified by his crime, took his own life."

The Governor ordered the monks at the temple to be detained and questioned to find out the cause, but none of them knew anything. He was quite unable to deliver a verdict. Then the secretary in charge of the case suggested: "It is evident that this naked priest and the brother were up to something utterly improper and illegal. They killed each other. It's nothing to do with Old Wang. Just release the neighbours on security, to be available if needed, while the bodies are delivered to the abbot of the temple to be placed in coffins, prepared for burial, and then removed, and deliver a verdict of mutual killing."

"Yes, that's what I'll do," the Governor said. Later the witnesses were all released. Of this no more. Some young busybodies of Jizhou made up a poem which says:

This bloody bonze, sad to relate
With a lady made a date,
Gave his evil lust its head,
Coveted the marriage bed.
Forbidden pleasures were his aim,
This monk who besmirches monkhood's name;
Now in the gutter he lies dead,
Naked in a pool of blood.
Mulian died to save his mother
Not so this unworthy brother:
The Buddha's law he set aside.
And for a harlot's body died.

Later some literary gents heard all about it and picked up their brushes and produced an account which goes like this:

Lust among the clergy must end in death, when all's clandestine, nothing in the clear. These two clerics' bodies are quite bizarre, lying on the ground without a stitch, victims of the assassin's knife.

The monk lies dead in a pool of his own blood, the brother has truly reaped the wind. Are they then so keen to die for each other, these monks? Or was it a fight to the death for possession of a single grave? Whichever way you look at it, it's two funerals for the price of one.

This affair had set the whole town talking. Felicity was scared out of her wits. There was no one she could talk to about it, all she could do was secretly lament to herself.

When somebody told Morbid at work that a monk and a lay brother had been killed he half guessed what had happened. "I'll bet this is Madcap's work," he thought. "The other day I wronged him by thinking him guilty for a while. I've got some free time today, I'd better go and see him and get him to tell me the facts."

When he reached the bridge, he heard someone behind him call out: "Brother, where are you off to?" Turning, he saw that it was Madcap. "You're just the person I wanted to see," he said.

"Come to my place," said Madcap, "I've got something to tell you." He took Morbid to a little room in the inn where he was staying, and said: "Do you still think I was lying?"

"Forgive me, brother," said Morbid. "Sometimes I'm a stupid fool and do something silly. I got drunk and couldn't hold my tongue. The woman fooled me. She said bad things about you and I couldn't see the truth. I've come today to apologize humbly and beg your forgiveness."

Madcap said: "Brother, I may not be very clever, but I'm a man of honour, how could I do something like that behind your back? Now, the reason I wanted to see you was that I was afraid later on you might fall into a wicked trap. I have some evidence I want you to see. I've brought the clothes that the monk and the brother were wearing. Look!"

Morbid was furious. "Forgive me, brother," he said. "Tonight I'm going to tear that harlot to pieces, I've got to relieve my feelings."

Madcap said with a grin: "Listen to you! You are a public official, how is it you don't know the law? How can you kill someone if you haven't caught them in the act? I might have just made it all up, then you'd be killing an innocent person."

Morbid said: "But how can I let something like that go unpunished?"

"You just do as I say and I'll show you how to act like a real man."

"What's your advice then?"

"Outside the east gate there is a hill known as Jade Screen Hill. It's a very quiet spot. Tell your wife tomorrow: 'It's a long time since I burnt any incense. I want you to come with me today.' Get her to go with you to the hill and take Ying along as well. I shall be there waiting for you, right at the top, and we'll ascertain the truth of the matter, once and for all. Then you can sign a divorce document and get rid of her, isn't that the best way?"

"Brother, there's no need for all this. I know you're innocent. What she said was all lies."

"All the same, I want you to know exactly what she's really been up to."

"Well, since you've thought it out so carefully, I won't fail you, I'll get the strumpet to come tomorrow, only don't you let me down."

"If I'm not there, everything I've said is false."

Morbid said goodbye and left the inn and went back to work till evening. When he went home he didn't mention it. He kept his mouth shut and just behaved as usual. Next morning he rose at first light and said to his wife: "Last night I dreamed a spirit came and told me I had not yet fulfilled an old vow. I promised to go at sunrise to the Temple of the Sacred Peaks beyond the east gate to burn incense, and I've never done it. I've some free time today so I want to go and do it now, and you have to come with me."

"You can go by yourself, what's the point of my going?"

"I originally vowed to do it when I got married, so you should come too."

"In that case let's have an early meal of vegetarian food and bathe in hot water first."

"I'll go and buy the incense and paper offerings. You order the sedan and bathe yourself, comb your hair, put in your hair pins and wait for me. And tell Ying to come too, for the outing."

Morbid went next to the inn to tell Madcap they'd be going after breakfast and not to be late.

Madcap said: "Listen, when you're nearly there, all of you leave the sedan chair halfway up the hill and continue to the top on foot. I'll be waiting in a quiet spot at the top. Don't let anyone else come up."

Having settled this with Madcap, Morbid went and bought candles and paper offerings. Then he went home and had breakfast. His wife suspected nothing. She took considerable care over her appearance, getting herself up very neatly, and Ying also dressed herself up. The bearers had already brought the sedan chair and were waiting outside.

Morbid said to his father-in-law: "Please look after the house. Felicity and I are going to burn incense. We won't be long."

"Burn plenty of incense, but don't be too long about it," said Old Pan.

Felicity climbed into the sedan, Ying walked alongside and Morbid followed. As they left by the east gate, Morbid whispered to the bearers: "If you go on a bit further to Jade Screen Hill, I'll pay you extra." In less than two hours they reached Jade Screen Hill, which was six or seven miles from the east gate of the city. Here there were a great many tombs scattered about. On top it was nothing but green grass and white poplars, there were no buildings at all, no temple compound. When Morbid had brought his wife halfway up the mountain he told the bearers to put down the chair, take out the poles and draw back the curtain. He told his wife to get out.

"Why have we come to this hill?" she asked.

"You just keep on going till you get to the top," he said. "Bearers, you wait here. Don't come with us. In a little while, I'll give you money to buy wine."

"Fair enough, we'll just wait here," they answered.

Morbid led his wife and Ying up the hill. After the third or fourth ridge, they were able to see Madcap sitting at the top.

"Where's the paper and the incense?" the wife asked.

"I sent someone on ahead with it," Morbid answered. He hurried them onwards until they came to a place where there were some old tombs. Here Madcap, who had placed his bundle, dagger and staff at the foot of a tree, approached and said: "Greetings, sister!"

She promptly replied: "Why are you here too, sir?" But even while she spoke she was trembling inside.

"I've been waiting here quite a while," Madcap said.

Morbid said: "The other day you told me that Uncle made a habit of using suggestive language to you, and also put his hand on your breasts and asked if you were pregnant. Now it's quite private here, let's hear what you both have to say."

"Oh dear," she said. "What's the point of talking about what's over and done with?"

Madcap scowled and said: "What are you talking about? This is no laughing matter. You've got to give my brother an explanation."

"But why should you want to bring it all up again?" she said.

"It's no good trying to brazen it out. I can show you proof." He went to his bundle and took out the clothing of Father Hai and the brother and threw it on the ground. "Do you recognize this?"

She blushed scarlet. She could think of nothing to say.

Madcap whipped out his dagger and said to Morbid: "You've only to ask Ying and you'll know the truth of it."

Morbid forced the maid down onto her knees in front of them and roared: "Now, you little bitch, tell us everything and be quick about it! How was the adultery committed in the priest's room? How were the meetings arranged with the incense altar as a signal? How was the brother told to come and beat the wooden fish? If you tell the truth I'll let you off. But if you tell a single lie I'll make mincemeat of you!"

Ying cried: "Master, it's not my fault, don't kill me, I'll tell you everything. They were drinking wine in the priest's room and they went upstairs to see the Buddha's tooth. They sent me downstairs to look at the Old Master who was sleeping off his wine. They made a secret agreement. Three days later he sent that brother here to beg food. I was told to go upstairs to get money for him, that's when the mistress arranged with him that when Master was on duty at the gaol I would put the altar outside the back door, it was to be the signal. He'd come and look and then go back to tell the father. That night Father Hai came in ordinary clothes with a scarf over his head. In the fifth watch the brother came and beat the wooden fish and prayed loudly to the Buddha — that was the

病關索大鬧翠屏山

signal for me to open the back door and let the father out. You see, when the father came, I couldn't not know about it, I had to be told. The Mistress promised me a bracelet and a set of clothes, but anyway I had to do what she said. That's how the affair was set up, he must have come a dozen times, then he got killed. She also gave me a few pieces of jewellery and told me to tell the Master that Mr. Shi had used suggestive language to her. But that's something I didn't actually see, so I didn't like to say anything. That's the whole truth, I haven't made anything up."

When Ying had finished, Madcap said: "Do you see? It's impossible that I should have told her to say all that. Please ask your wife to explain everything fully."

Morbid seized the woman and shouted: "You filthy whore, the maid's told everything, don't try to deny it. Make a full confession and I'll spare your worthless life."

"I've done wrong," she said. "But for the sake of the love we once had for each other, spare me this time."

Madcap said: "You mustn't be left in any doubt, you'd better ask her for a full account."

Morbid shouted: "Speak, you harlot!"

One by one she told him all the details of her secret affair with the monk, from the evening of the service for the dead up to the time of the regular relationship.

"Why did you say I had harassed you?" Madcap asked.

"The other day when he was drunk he shouted at me and I realized he suspected something. I guessed you had seen my fault. That's why I said it. In the morning he started asking about you, so I just slipped in this story. You are not really like that at all."

"Now you've confessed all this in front of three witnesses. It's up to brother now to decide how you should be dealt with."

Morbid said: "Brother, you can take off the strumpet's hair ornaments and clothes. Then I'll attend to her."

So Madcap stripped her of her hair ornaments and clothes and Morbid cut two of her skirts into strips and with his own hands bound her to a tree. Madcap also removed all Ying's hair ornaments. Then he offered Morbid his dagger and said: "Brother, what's the point of leaving this little bitch alive? Get the roots out all in one go!"

"You're right," said Morbid. "Give me the knife and I'll do it."

Realizing her situation was desperate, Ying started to scream but Morbid, with a flourish of the dagger, severed her neck. Thereupon the wife, tied to the tree, began to implore Madcap: "Do something, please, help me!"

Madcap merely said: "It's his business, not mine."

Morbid advanced on her, dug out her tongue with his knife and cut it off, which put an end to the screams. Then he pointed and shouted: "You worthless whore, for a time I got it all wrong, you nearly fooled me. Quite apart from the fact that my brother's reputation was ruined, it's obvious that sooner or later you would have killed me. Isn't it better I should act firmly now? What sort of heart and liver does a woman like you have, I wonder? Let's take a look!" And with one cut he opened her up from breast to belly and took out the five organs and hung them on a pine tree. Having done this, he tied her hair ornaments and clothes in a bundle, and said to Madcap: "Come, brother, you and I must do some serious thinking. An adulterer and his whore have been killed, the thing is now where can you and I take refuge?"

Madcap said: "I've already thought about that and I know where; get ready to start, we must get going at once."

"But where to?"

"You and I, we've both killed someone, where else should we go but to the Marshes of Mount Liang?"

"Wait a minute! Neither you nor I know any of that lot, why would they ever take us?"

"You're wrong, there. Nowadays Song Jiang of Shandong, the Opportune Rain, famous throughout the rivers and lakes, has declared that he welcomes all honourable men and will receive brave men from anywhere, who doesn't know that? We've both of us got good fighting skills. Why should we be afraid they won't let us stay?"

"One ought to be prepared for the worst, to avoid disappointment. One problem is that I'm a government official. They may well be suspicious and refuse to take us in."

This made Madcap laugh. "Have you forgotten Song Jiang himself was a court registrar? But I'll tell you something to put your heart at rest. Remember the day I met you, and the two men who were drinking with me at the inn before you came in? One of them was Dai Zong, the Magic Messenger from Mount Liang and the other was Yang Lin, the Panther. They gave me ten taels of silver, which I've still got in my bundle. So we can go and invest it there with the outlaws."

"Well, if that route is really open to us, I'll just go and collect some cash for our travelling expenses and then let's go."

"Brother, are you still so muddle-headed? If you go back to the city and get yourself arrested, how are you going to escape? In any case, you've got all those bracelets and jewels you just put in your bundle and I've got some silver. Even if there were twice as many of us it would suffice for our needs. What do you want to go and get more for? If you get into trouble, who's going to rescue you? This business will soon be out, so we've no time to waste. We must leave in the opposite direction."

So Madcap shouldered his bundle and picked up his staff, while Morbid tucked away his dagger and took up his pike, and they were just about to leave the tombs when someone jumped out from behind a pine tree and shouted: "Here you go, in this wide world, in these realms of light, you go and murder someone and now you're off to the Marshes of Mount Liang to join the outlaws, I've heard it all!" He prostrated himself as they stared at him.

Now this man was known to Morbid. He was a certain Shi Qian from Gaotang, and this was one of his haunts. His work was walking on rooftops and scaling walls, vaulting fences and doing dodgy deals. He had been in trouble with the authorities in Jizhou, but Morbid had rescued him. People called him "The Flea on the Drum." There's a poem about him:

His limbs are supple, his body stout,
Beneath thick brows bright eyes peer out.
His appearance is a trifle weird,
He floats as smoothly as a bird.

In the dead of night he'll pass through walls,
In the silent hours he roams the halls.
Men hide their goods when they see him come,
Shi Qian he's called, or Flea on the Drum.

"What are you doing here?" Morbid asked him.

"I'll explain, Brother Warden. Recently I just haven't been able to make ends meet. I've had to come here and dig up tombs, in the hope of finding something to live on. When I saw what you were up to here I didn't dare show myself. But then I heard you were planning to go to Mount Liang to join the company. Well, all I've been able to do round here lately is to nick a few chickens and dogs. There's no future in that. If only I could go with you to join the outlaws! The question is, would you be willing to take me with you?"

Madcap said: "I suppose you can be counted among the bold spirits, and nowadays they welcome all good men, so why not, since there's only one of you? Yes, if it's what you want, you can come with us."

"Then I know a good way to go," said the Flea.

With the Flea leading, they took a small path down the other side of the hill and set off for Mount Liang.

Meanwhile the two sedan chair bearers were still waiting halfway up the hill. They waited till the sun was going down in the west, but there was no sign of their three customers. Since they'd been ordered to wait they had not dared to go on up. But in the end they had to climb slowly up the hill to find out what had happened. What they saw was a great flock of crows that had settled on the tombs, squabbling over something. When they got closer they saw that the crows were tearing at a pile of inner organs and intestines, hence all the commotion. Horror-struck they raced off home to tell Old Pan, who went with them to report the matter to the Jizhou authorities. The Governor immediately ordered a district official and the coroner to go to Jade Screen Hill and examine the bodies and then report back to him. They reported: "We found the body of Pan's daughter, Felicity, mutilated and tied to a tree. The servant, Ying, was lying dead at the foot of a tomb. Near the tomb there was a pile of clothes, women's clothes and the clothes of a monk and a lay brother."

When he heard this the Governor remembered the earlier affair of Father Hai and the lay brother. He interrogated Old Pan. The old man told him how he had got drunk in the monks' quarters and the reasons why Madcap had gone away.

"Obviously the woman committed adultery with the monk," the Governor said. "The servant and the lay brother aided and abetted them. I imagine this Madcap, on account of their wrong-doing, killed the brother and the priest; and now without a doubt Morbid has killed his wife and the servant. I'll wager that's the way it is. Arrest Morbid and Madcap and we shall know all."

He issued notices and a reward for the capture of Morbid and Madcap, while the sedan chair bearers were allowed to go home until the court called them. Old Pan went off to buy coffins and bury the bodies. Of this no more.

As for Morbid, Madcap and the Flea, they had left the territory of Jizhou, travelling in great haste. When they reached the province of Yunzhou and passed Sandalwood Bottom, they saw a high mountain ahead, just as the light was beginning to fade. In front of them there was an inn on the banks of a stream. When they got closer they were able to take a good look:

> *Before it runs the highroad, behind it a broad stream. A thicket of poplars and weeping willows guards the main gate, while one or two white-blossomed plum trees flank the house. A hedge of thorns runs all the way round a pond with reeds and caltrops; in front and behind a reed curtain and barred doorway shield the hearth. On the right an alcove with a line of verse upon the wall: "In the quiet pavilion dawn greets the visitor from the Five Lakes." On the left the matching quotation: "In the rustic abode day welcomes the traveller from the Three Islands." Although this inn is situated out in the wilds, there's many a carriage travels this road.*

Night was falling and the waiter was just about to close the doors, when he saw there were three people wanting to come in. He said: "You must have come from far, to be abroad so late."

"We've done more than thirty miles today," the Flea replied. "That's why we're out late."

When he had let them in, the man asked: "Have you eaten yet?"

"We'll take care of that for ourselves," the Flea replied.

"There's no one staying here at the moment," said the man. "There's two clean pots on the stove, you're welcome to use those."

"Have you any wine and meat we can buy?"

"We had some meat this morning, but we sold it all to the locals. We've only got a pot of wine here now, there's nothing to go with it."

"That's all right. Just let us have five bushels of rice, and we'll manage the rest."

The waiter fetched the rice and gave it to the Flea, who washed it and then cooked it. Madcap arranged the luggage inside their room, while Morbid took out one of the women's hairpins and gave it to the waiter saying that if he would fetch the pot of wine for them they'd settle up in the morning. The man took the hairpin and disappeared inside, coming out with the pot of wine which he opened and placed on the table together with a few dishes of hot vegetables. The Flea brought a bucket of hot water and invited Morbid and Madcap to wash their hands and feet. The wine was prepared and they invited the waiter to sit and drink with them. Four large bowls were poured and drunk.

Madcap had noticed that there were a dozen or so good halberds stored under the eaves and he asked the waiter: "Why do you keep these weapons in your house?"

"The landlord left them here," he replied.

"What sort of a man is your landlord?"

"Come on, you're a gentleman of the rivers and lakes, aren't you? How come you don't know about this place? That mountain up ahead is called Lone Dragon Peak. On this side of the mountain there's a cliff known as Lone Dragon Heights. That's where the landlord has his residence. Zhu Castle, they call it, it covers an area of ten square miles. Baron Zhu, that's the owner, has three sons known as the Brothers Zhu. There's six or seven hundred families living on the estate as tenant farmers and each household has to keep two halberds for the Baron. This place is called Zhu Arms. There's often several dozen people staying here at the inn, that's why the halberds are kept here."

"But what's the point of keeping the weapons here?" Madcap asked.

"The Marshes of Mount Liang are not far off. We're afraid those robbers will come here to get provisions, that's why we've got to be prepared."

"If I gave you some silver for it would you sell me one of those halberds?" Madcap asked.

"Certainly not. There's a number on every one of them. I'm not going to get into trouble with my landlord. His rules are very strict."

"I was only joking," Madcap said with a laugh. "Stop worrying and just drink up."

"I can't take any more," the waiter said. "I'm going to bed. But please feel free to drink more yourselves." He left them to it.

They drank another round, and then the Flea said to them: "Would you like some meat?"

"Our host said he hadn't got any meat," Morbid said. "Where do you propose to find it?"

The Flea sniggered. He went to the stove and pulled out a cockerel.

"Wherever did that come from?" Morbid asked.

"When I went round the back to wash my hands, I saw this chicken in a coop. I said to myself, my friends haven't got anything to eat with their wine, so I crept up close and killed it. I got some hot water and plucked it and boiled it and then I brought it here for you."

Morbid said: "You really are a bloody master thief, aren't you?"

"The leopard doesn't change his spots," said Madcap, laughing.

They all had a good laugh as they pulled the chicken apart and ate it, helping it down with plenty of rice.

Now when the waiter went to bed he felt uneasy, so he got up again and went to make a thorough inspection of the premises. On the kitchen table he noticed some chicken feathers and bones. He went to the stove and saw half a pot of stock. Anxiously he went and looked in the coop at the back of the house. No cockerel! He rushed back inside and shouted: "You're really disgusting, you lot! Why have you eaten the inn's rooster?"

The Flea replied: "You're imagining things! Really! I brought the chicken we ate, I bought it on the way. I haven't seen your rooster!"

"You tell me then, where's it gone?" the waiter demanded.

"Maybe it was taken by a wildcat, or a weasel ate it, or a sparrow hawk carried it off, how should I know?"

"It was in the coop. If you didn't take it, who did?"

Madcap said: "Enough of all this fuss. We'll give you money to pay for the cockerel, and there's an end to it."

"It's the rooster I keep to wake me up, we can't do without it here. Even if you gave me ten taels of silver it wouldn't make up for it. I want my cockerel back."

Madcap started to lose his temper. "Who are you trying to fool? Suppose I decide not to pay you anything, what then?"

The waiter laughed contemptuously. "You're playing with fire you know. This isn't just an ordinary inn. I can take you up to the castle and say you're bandits from Mount Liang and have you handed over to the authorities!"

Madcap was furious. "And supposing we were heroes from Mount Liang, how would you be able to capture us and get the reward?"

Morbid was also angry by now. "We generously offered to pay you. But if we don't, how do you think you're going to detain us?"

The waiter set up a cry of "Thieves!" and immediately four or five bouncers, stark naked, dashed out from the interior of the inn and tried to rush Madcap and Morbid. Madcap raised his fist and knocked them all down, one blow to each. When the waiter tried to cry out, the Flea gave him a slap that caused his whole face to swell and rendered him speechless. The bouncers escaped by the back door.

"Friends, those bastards have obviously gone to fetch help," Morbid said. "We'd better eat up and go."

As soon as they'd had enough, they tied their bundles, put on their shoes, and stowed away their daggers. Each of them also picked a stout halberd from the store of weapons under the eaves.

"All the same, we can't let him get off so lightly," said Madcap. He got some straw from in front of the stove, held it in the flames and set fire to the house on every side. Fanned by the wind, the thatched building began to blaze with a merry crackling sound. In no time the flames were leaping up to the heavens. The three of them now set off, heading for the highroad. As the song says:

All on account of a pilfered fowl,
The Brothers Zhu a-hunting go,
On Mount Liang the storm winds blow,
Zhu Castle is at last laid low.

When they had been going about four hours, they saw an innumerable host of torches, in front and behind. There must have been several hundred people, creating a great hullabaloo, racing towards them.

"Don't worry," said Madcap. "We'll take a smaller path."

"No, let's make a stand," said Morbid. "If there's one, kill one, if there's two kill a pair. We don't want to move on before it's light."

He had scarcely finished speaking when the pursuers closed in on them from all sides. So with Morbid in front, Madcap in the rear and the Flea in the middle, they levelled their halberds and engaged the retainers. The latter at first advanced confidently, whirling their spears and staves. Morbid wielding his halberd quickly downed half a dozen. Those in front fled and those behind did their best to withdraw. Madcap waded in and knocked down half a dozen more. Hearing that a dozen had been killed or wounded, the remainder now, preferring to live than die and judging the situation to be far from favourable, began to retreat, while our three heroes steadily pursued them. At this juncture, there was another burst of shouting and two long hooks reaching out from the undergrowth pinned the Flea and dragged him out of sight. When Madcap turned round to rescue him, two more hooks reached out from behind to catch him. But Morbid spotted them and with a blow of his halberd he cut them off. Then he thrust his halberd into the undergrowth. There was a scream and the hidden

拚命三火
燒祝家庄

enemy fled. The Flea was taken, but the other two decided it was too dangerous to follow and had no heart to continue the fight. Giving the Flea up for lost, they cast about for a way out. They could still see the torches milling about in the distance and there were no bushes or trees around. As soon as they found a path they set off, travelling due east along it. Their assailants lost the trail, so they collected their wounded comrades and with the Flea bound hand and foot withdrew to Zhu Castle.

Morbid and Madcap walked till it grew light and they came to a remote country inn. "Let's go and buy a bowl of wine before we go on, and we can ask the way too," said Madcap. They entered the inn, propped their halberds against the wall and sat down opposite each other. They told the landlord to bring wine and cook something for them. He laid out dishes of vegetables and fruit to go with it, and brought the wine. Just as they were about to start on this, a big fellow rushed in. He was strongly built with a square jaw, piercing eyes, and big ears, an ugly, coarse fellow in appearance. He wore a tea-coloured robe, a cloth decorated with swastikas on his head, a white sash round his waist and a pair of tall boots of oiled leather. "His Honour wants those loads up at the manor right away," he shouted.

The landlord hurriedly replied: "The minute they've loaded up I'll send them along."

The man who had given the order turned to leave, saying "Be quick about it!" On his way out he passed Morbid and Madcap, whereupon Morbid, recognizing him, gave a great shout: "Hey there, young feller-me-lad, what are you doing here? Didn't you see me?"

When he saw who it was, the other shouted: "Benefactor, how did you get here?" Then he prostrated himself in front of Morbid. Now if Morbid had not run into this person, things would have been different. As it was,

The oath of loyalty is to be foresworn;
The roaring of tigers heralds a crisis.

But if you want to know who it was that Morbid and Madcap had met, the next chapter will tell you.

Chapter 47

Skyhawk twice invokes the oath of loyalty; Song Jiang attacks Zhu Castle!

Morbid raised the other man to his feet, and made to introduce him to Madcap. "Who is this fellow?" Madcap asked.

"He's an old friend by the name of Du Xing," Morbid replied. "He's from Zhongshan. Because he was blessed with such a coarse complexion, people call him Uglymug. He was a trader and he came to Jizhou last year on business. But in a fit of rage he killed one of the foreign merchants he was travelling with. He was sentenced and they locked him up. I heard that he was an expert with fists and staff, so I did what I could to help him. It's quite a surprise to meet him here."

Uglymug asked: "What official business brings you here, benefactor?"

Morbid leant forward and said confidentially: "I have killed someone in Jizhou and I'm on my way to the Marshes of Mount Liang to join the outlaws. Last night we stayed at the Zhu Arms and because a travelling companion of ours, known as the Flea, stole the inn's rooster for our supper, we got into a fight with the waiter there. We lost our tempers and burnt the place down. We cleared off immediately, but we had been followed. We did for a number of them, all by ourselves, but some others hidden in the undergrowth stuck out a couple of hooks and collared the Flea. We two ended up here. We were just going to ask the way when we met you."

"Don't you worry, benefactor," said Uglymug. "I'll get them to release the Flea and return him to you."

"Sit down and drink a cup with us, old chap," said Morbid.

They sat down together and as they were drinking Uglymug said: "After I left Jizhou, thanks to your kind assistance, I moved here, and gained the favour of an important man who received me into his household and made me his steward. All his financial affairs are entirely in my hands, he trusts me completely. So I don't plan to go back home."

"What's the name of this man?" Morbid asked.

"Here on the edge of the Lone Dragon mountains," Uglymug began, "there are three bluffs, each with its village. The place in the middle is the Zhu family's estate, to the west are the Hu family and to the east the Li family. Altogether, counting villagers and retainers, there's around twenty thousand fighting men. Chief of the three is the Zhu place: Baron Zhu and his three sons, known as the Brothers Zhu — Dragon Zhu, Tiger Zhu and Wildcat Zhu. They've also got an arms instructor called Luan Tingyu, known as Ironstaff. That man is formidable. In addition the manor has several thousand fearless retainers.

"Over to the west is the manor of Squire Hu. He has one son, Hu Cheng, known as Flying Tiger. He's pretty good, too. But above all he has a daughter, Hu Sanniang, known as Steelbright, because of the two bright swords she wields. She's as bold a horsewoman as you'll ever meet.

"Now the man I serve is the master of the eastern manor, Skyhawk. His name's Li Ying, and his weapon's a solid steel spear. He also carries at his back five throwing knives. With these he can spit a man at a hundred paces, just like that!

"These three villages have sworn an oath of loyalty to each other, to work together, in good times or bad, and to provide mutual assistance. What they fear is that the heroes of Mount Liang may come foraging, so the three villages have made preparations for resisting them.

"I'm going to take you back to my village now to meet Skyhawk and to get him to send a letter requesting the release of the Flea."

Morbid said: "This Skyhawk of yours, would he be the gentleman who's made that name so famous among the rivers and lakes?"

"That's him," replied Uglymug.

"I've heard it many times from the brethren of the rivers and lakes: in the Lone Dragon Mountains there is a certain Skyhawk, who is a bold spirit. So this is where he hangs out! He has the reputation of being a fine fighter and truly a man of parts. Let's go and meet him, then."

So Madcap called the waiter over and asked for the bill. But Uglymug was having none of it, and produced the money himself.

The three left the inn and Uglymug conducted the others to Skyhawk's manor. What Morbid saw was a fine compound, surrounded by a broad piece of water, with a whitewashed wall and hundreds of ancient willows of immense girth. The gate was reached by a drawbridge. Entering the compound, they saw twenty or more arms racks, stacked with gleaming weapons, in front of the main hall.

Uglymug said: "Please wait here a moment while I go in and announce you and ask the master to come and meet you."

He disappeared inside and a few minutes later Skyhawk came out. What met the eyes of Morbid and Madcap was a fine figure of a man, as the poem describes:

> *Eyes like an eagle and head like a lion; a swallow's neck, ape's shoulders and wolf's waist; this is a man who is open-handed and single-minded, truly heroic. He likes to ride a snow-white charger, and is wont to wear a blood red robe. Five throwing knives he carries at his back, and a barbed spear of steel with inlaid hasp. Such a man is not easily gainsaid. This imposing personage is called Li Ying, otherwise known as Skyhawk.*

When Skyhawk came out, Uglymug presented Morbid and Madcap, who prostrated themselves. Skyhawk hurriedly returned the compliment and invited them into the hall. After many modest protestations, all were finally seated and Skyhawk called for wine. Morbid and Madcap again saluted him and said: "Might we ask you to be so kind as to write a letter to Baron Zhu asking him to spare the life of our friend the Flea? We should be eternally grateful to you."

Skyhawk called for the household tutor to perform this business. A letter was composed and duly certificated with Skyhawk's personal seal. It was then handed to the assistant chief steward with instructions to take a fast mount and ride like the wind to Zhu Castle to fetch the gentleman in question.

After the steward had departed on horseback bearing the letter, Morbid and Madcap kowtowed once more. Skyhawk said: "Don't worry, my friends. When they get my letter they're bound to release him." Again they expressed their thanks.

"Come inside and we'll have a few cups together," Skyhawk said. They followed him in, and found a repast awaiting them. After eating they drank tea while Skyhawk quizzed them about shooting and was pleased at finding their answers most sensible.

Halfway through the morning, the assistant steward returned. Skyhawk sent for him and said: "Where's the man I sent you to fetch?"

The steward replied: "I saw the Baron and delivered the letter. I think he was about to release the man when the Brothers Zhu came in and began to kick up a terrific row. They would neither answer your letter nor release the man; they are determined to hand him over to the authorities."

Skyhawk was horrified. "But we've all signed a life or death pact," he said. "They've got to respect my letter. How can they behave like this? You can't have explained properly, that's the problem. Mr. Du," he said, turning to Uglymug, "you'd better go along and see to it yourself, explain carefully what it's all about."

"Of course I'll go, sir," said Uglymug, "only could you write something in your own hand, so when I get there they'll feel obliged to release him?"

"It shall be done," said Skyhawk, quickly taking up a piece of the best paper on which he wrote a letter in his own hand. He stamped it on the front and affixed his personal seal, then handed it to Uglymug. A fast mount was brought round from the stables at the back of the house, saddled and bridled. Uglymug picked up a whip and strode through the gate. Mounting, he applied the whip and shot off towards Baron Zhu's castle.

僕天鵰双修
生死書

"Now you two really can relax," Skyhawk said. "When they receive this letter in my own hand he'll be freed in no time."

They thanked him most sincerely, and the drinking continued in the inner room, as they waited for the result.

It was beginning to grow dark, yet still there was no sign of Uglymug. Skyhawk began to have misgivings. He had just ordered someone to go and look out for Uglymug, when a retainer came in and said: "The chief steward, Mr. Du, is coming."

"Is there anyone with him?" Skyhawk asked.

"No, he's riding back on his own," the man replied.

Skyhawk shook his head. "Stranger and stranger," he said. "He's never let me down before, what's the matter with him today?"

Morbid and Madcap went with him to see. As Uglymug dismounted and came through the gate, they saw his expression: he was purple with rage, his teeth bared in a horrible grimace. It was a while before he could even speak. There's a poem which says:

He was born with a face that's already a curse,
But when he's angry it even gets worse,
Not like a human being at all,
More like the black-faced lord of Hell.

Skyhawk said: "Tell us exactly what happened!"

When Uglymug had managed to catch his breath, he said: "Bearing your letter, I went up as far as the third gate. There I came upon Dragon Zhu, Tiger Zhu and Wildcat Zhu. I saluted and Wildcat Zhu shouted out: 'What are you doing here?'

"I bowed very low and said: 'I have a letter here that my master has written to you.'

"His face changed, the bastard, and he yelled: 'What's he playing at, that master of yours? He sent some lousy beggar here this morning with a letter asking for the Mount Liang bandit, Shi Qian. I'm going to hand him over to the authorities. You're wasting your time!'

"I said: 'This Shi Qian is not one of the Mount Liang bandits, he's a merchant from Jizhou. He was coming to see our master when a misunderstanding occurred and he accidentally burnt down your inn. My master vows that he will restore it completely for you. He humbly begs you to show consideration, exercise restraint and pardon the offense.' But they all shouted in unison: 'We won't, we won't!' So then I said: 'Please read this letter of my master's.' Wildcat Zhu took it and without even breaking the seal tore it into little pieces, saying he'd have me kicked out. Tiger Zhu and Wildcat Zhu said: 'Stop provoking us or we'll have that Skyhawk of yours arrested as well, as an accomplice of the bandits of Mount Liang.' I didn't dare press them further. Truly I was treated disgracefully by those three animals and they slandered you vilely. They ended by ordering their people to seize me but I leapt into the saddle and galloped straight back. I can tell you, though, all the way back I was choking with rage. How dare those bastards flout the life or death pact which has existed between you all these years! They've no loyalty at all!"

This talk of friendship's mere hot air,
When genuine loyalty isn't there,
When things go wrong it's an empty word:
To trust in a pact is just absurd.

When Skyhawk heard what had happened anger rose in him like a column of fire, towering and unquenchable. He called for his horse to be saddled. "Please moderate your anger," Morbid and Madcap pleaded. "You mustn't upset everything on our account."

But Skyhawk wasn't listening. He went back in and provided himself with a suit of gilded chain-mail, wrought with animal heads guarding his breast front and back, donned a red robe, and stuck five throwing knives into the back of his kneeguards. He picked up his steel spear and put on a phoenix-winged helmet. He went outside and picked three hundred stalwart retainers. Uglymug also put on armour, took up his spear and mounted. He collected another twenty or more riders. Morbid and Madcap tagged along, wielding their halberds. Led by Skyhawk on horseback, this entire force set off at speed, heading for the castle of Baron Zhu.

The sun was already sinking towards the mountains when they reached Lone Dragon Heights, where horse and foot deployed.

The castle was of solid construction, set on an eminence at the foot of the Lone Dragon Mountains and surrounded on all sides by a sizeable moat. Besides being built on a bluff, it had three layers of ramparts constructed from large blocks of stone to a height of about six metres. There were two gates, front and back, each approached by a drawbridge. Within the walls, on all sides, there were sheds simply bristling with spears, swords and other weapons, .while the gate tower was full of military drums and gongs.

Skyhawk reined in his horse and shouted up at the castle: "You there, Brothers Zhu, what do you mean by insulting me?" At this moment the gates opened and out charged fifty or more horsemen, led by the Baron's third son, Wildcat Zhu, on a flame-coloured steed.

> *On his head he wears a helmet in the shape of a golden lotus leaf. He's dressed in armour like plum blossom. At his waist swings an embroidered sheaf with bow and arrows. In either hand he grasps a sword and spear of pure steel. Red tassels hang from his horse's brow. He's a sight to fill the heart with dread!*

When Skyhawk saw Wildcat Zhu he pointed a finger at him and said: "Look at you! The mother's milk still wet on your lips and your head still covered in fluff! Your father and I swore eternal loyalty, we agreed to cooperate and made a pact for mutual defence and protection. If there's a problem in your household, if you need extra hands, we send them over at once; if you need supplies we hold nothing back. Today I've twice sent someone to you with a letter asking for something, why did you tear up my letter and insult my honour? What's your game?"

Wildcat Zhu said: "It's perfectly true we have a life or death pact. We vowed to work together, to defend each other against the bandits of Mount Liang and wipe out the mountain stronghold. So why have you gone and joined the rebels, why are you conspiring with them?"

"Who are you calling a bandit from Mount Liang?" Skyhawk said. "Why are you slandering someone, what have you got against him?"

"The bandit Shi Qian has confessed to it himself, so stop talking rubbish," Wildcat Zhu replied. "It's irrefutable. Either you leave now or I'll have you arrested and handed over too as one of them."

Skyhawk was enraged. He settled himself in the saddle, took a firm grip on his spear and charged. Wildcat Zhu likewise gave his horse its head and attacked. Back and forth and to and fro, the pair of them fought hundreds of encounters, there at the foot of Lone Dragon Heights. When Wildcat Zhu saw that he could not prevail, he turned his horse and galloped off. As Skyhawk urged his horse in pursuit, Wildcat Zhu rested his spear on the horse's back, grasped his bow in his left hand and an arrow in his right, fitted the arrow to the string and bent the bow. Twisting in the saddle, he took careful aim and loosed the shaft. Skyhawk tried to dodge but it caught him in the arm and he fell headlong from his mount. Wildcat Zhu then turned his horse and came at him with the spear. When Morbid and Madcap saw this they gave a great shout, twirled their halberds and placed themselves menacingly in the path of horse and rider. This was more than Wildcat Zhu could cope with. He pulled up his horse and galloped off, but not before the horse had taken a blow on the rump from Morbid's weapon. Maddened by pain the animal reared up, almost throwing its rider. The supporting archers however now began to shoot their arrows. Morbid and Madcap had no armour and they were obliged to turn and run for it. Uglymug fled too, once he had rescued Skyhawk and hoisted him onto his horse. Morbid and Madcap escaped with the crowd of retainers. The Zhu forces pursued them for a few miles, but when it began to get dark they went home.

Uglymug reached the manor bearing Skyhawk. He dismounted and took the squire inside and made him sit. All the household came to see. They pulled out the arrow, stripped off his armour and anointed the wound with an appropriate salve. All night there were discussions in the back room. Morbid and Madcap said to Uglymug: "Those villains have insulted your master, they've wounded him with an arrow; the Flea is still being held, and it's all our fault that your master got involved. What we'll have to do is go to Mount Liang, the two of us, and ask for help from the leaders, Chao Gai, Song Jiang and the rest. We'll beg them to come and avenge your honour and rescue the Flea."

Before they left they went to thank Skyhawk.

"I did my best," he said to them. "But it was beyond my power. Please forgive me."

He told Uglymug to get some gold and silver to give them. They didn't want to take it, but Skyhawk said: "Among friends of the rivers and lakes, there's no reason to refuse." So in the end they accepted, thanked Skyhawk and bade him farewell. Uglymug escorted them to the end of the village and then, after pointing out the road, bade them farewell and returned to Skyhawk's. Of this no more.

So Morbid and Madcap set off for Mount Liang. Before long they saw in the distance a newly built inn, with its flag sticking out very straight. They went in and ordered something to eat and drink and asked for directions. This inn was one of the newly established lookouts for Mount Liang and the landlord was none other than Shi Yong, the Guv. As they drank they kept questioning the waiter about the route to Mount Liang, and this drew the Guv's attention: "Where are you two from and why do you keep asking about the way to Mount Liang?" he asked.

"We are from Jizhou," Morbid replied.

The Guv suddenly had a thought: "You're not Madcap by any chance, are you?" he asked.

Morbid replied: "I'm Morbid. My friend here is Madcap. But how do you know about him?"

"I don't know you myself," the Guv said eagerly to Madcap. "But when my friend Dai Zong, the Magic Messenger, returned from Jizhou, he was full of your praises. I've heard so much about you and now you want to go up the mountain. I'm very pleased to hear it."

Having exchanged the usual courtesies, Morbid and Madcap told the Guv about recent events. The Guv ordered his waiter to serve them with the best wine. A window was opened at the back of the inn, a bow was pulled and a whistling arrow fired off. Immediately from the reeds on the other side of the water two soldiers rowed out in a boat. The Guv invited the others to embark and they were rowed across to Duck's-Bill Landing. Messengers had already been sent up the mountain and almost at once the Magic Messenger and Panther appeared to welcome them. When the introductions had been completed they went together up to the fortress where all the leaders, hearing of the arrival of some brave men, had assembled in the great hall. The Magic Messenger and Panther brought the newcomers into the hall to meet the two leaders and all the others. After greeting them, Chao Gai asked them all about their travels. But first they spoke of their experience in martial arts and their wish to enter the company. This pleased everyone and they were invited to sit down. Morbid recounted little by little how a comrade known as the Flea, who also wanted to join, had unfortunately stolen the Zhu inn's cockerel and caused a rumpus as a result of which Madcap had set fire to the inn and the Flea had been taken and Skyhawk had written two letters asking for his release but the Brothers Zhu had refused point-blank to let him go and vowed that they would capture all the heroes of the mountain stronghold, whom they had roundly insulted. "They're a bunch of unmannerly scoundrels," he concluded.

It would have been well if Morbid had held his tongue, but he blurted all this out and Chao Gai flew into a great passion. "Take these two outside and cut off their heads!" he ordered. As the poem says:

Before they recounted the Flea's misdemeanour,
Morbid and Madcap should have thought twice.
Though the heart of a hero may burn like a fire,
The law of the greenwood is rigid as ice.

Song Jiang hurriedly intervened. "Calm yourself, brother," he said. "These gentlemen thought nothing of travelling a long way to join us, why do you want to cut their heads off?"

Chao Gai replied: "Here on Mount Liang, ever since we put paid to Wang Lun, we have been ruled by honour and have always treated the people decently. No one who has gone down the mountain has ever disgraced us. Everyone, whether a new recruit or an oldtimer, has a heroic spirit. These two villains, in the name of the heroes of Mount Liang, have stolen a chicken. Thus they have shamed us all. First we will cut off their heads, then we will take the heads down there with an escort of troops and show them to the villagers to cleanse our name and prove that we are not common thieves. Let them be executed at once!"

"But brother," Song Jiang objected again, "did you not hear what they said? This fellow Shi Qian, the Flea, has always been that way inclined, and it's he who got that bloody Zhu family so worked up. Do you really think these two friends wanted to bring disgrace on our company? Anyway, I've often heard people saying that the Zhu crowd want to fight us. At present, what's more, our numbers are great and money and provisions are getting short. We wouldn't have gone to seek them out deliberately, but since they'll always be looking for a pretext to attack us, we'd better take this opportunity to have a go at the bastards. If we capture their place there's three or four years' supplies there for us. It's not our aim to make trouble for them, but they're really getting too big for their boots! So calm down, please, brother, because whatever my limitations as a commander, I intend to ask for volunteers and assemble a force to go down the mountain and attack the Zhu domain. If we don't make a clean sweep, I vow never to return to the mountain. In this way we'll wipe out any slur on our name, and at the same time avenge all the insults and obtain much-needed provisions for the camp. And we can even ask Skyhawk to join our company."

Professor Wu Yong said: "What Song Jiang says is right. Why should we execute our brothers?"

The Magic Messenger said: "Better you cut off my head than send such a signal to other brave men who might want to join us!"

In the end, after everyone had had a say, Chao Gai relented. Morbid and Madcap kowtowed to express their thanks. Song Jiang tried to reassure them by saying: "Don't be surprised friends. This is the rule of Mount Liang. We all have to submit to it. If I myself commit a fault, I must have my head cut off. There can be no mercy. The lawyer Pei Xuan, known as Sterling, who just joined us, was recently appointed provost marshal and has drawn up the code and established the penalties. So please don't harbour any resentment."

Morbid and Madcap responded by kowtowing and expressing their thanks all over again. Chao Gai then allotted them seats below Panther Yang Lin. All the troops on the mountain were invited to celebrate the arrival of new leaders, cows and sheep were slaughtered and a feast prepared. The two newcomers were allotted quarters so they had somewhere to live, and each was given ten men to serve him. There was more feasting next day, and then a conference to discuss plans.

Having asked Sterling to make a list of those who were going, Song Jiang requested volunteers to accompany him on his raid against Zhu Castle, which he was bent on destroying. It was determined that, apart from Chao Gai who would remain in charge in the mountain stronghold, those who were to stay to defend it were Professor Wu, the Red-Haired Devil, the three Ruan brothers, the Halberdier and the Little Duke. Others were appointed to take charge of the landings, the main gates and the inns. Flagpole, the new arrival, was put in charge of boat-building, replacing the Flautist as supervisor of war vessels. Orders were written out and those who were to go down the mountain and attack Zhu Castle were divided into two contingents: the first consisted of Song Jiang, Colonel Hua, the White-Water Dragon, the elder Mu brother, Iron Ox, Morbid, Madcap, Tamer, Golden Wings and the Panther, with three thousand infantry and three hundred horse. They armed themselves and set off first down the mountain. The second contingent consisted of Leopard's Head, Thunderclap, the Magic Messenger, White Eel, the Pilot, the Flautist, Redeye, Short-Arse and the Daytime Rat. They too would lead three thousand infantry and three hundred horse and would follow on in support of the others. Finally Golden Sands Landing and Duck's-Bill Landing were left in the hands of the Door-God in the Clouds and Whitey, to guard and secure their lines of supply.

Chao Gai saw them all off down the mountain, and then went back to the stronghold.

So Song Jiang and the other leaders pressed on towards Zhu Castle and nothing occurred on the way. Soon they were nearing Lone Dragon Heights. With less than a mile to go, the leading party pitched their camp. Song Jiang sat in his tent in their midst, conferring with Colonel Hua. "I have heard that the roads through the Zhu domain are very confusing and it's difficult for troops to advance there. Before we launch our attack we should send in two scouts to learn the various turnings of the road and find out the best route."

Iron Ox said: "Brother, I've been idle for a long while. I haven't killed anyone recently. Let me go first."

"Absolutely not," Song Jiang said. "When it comes to open fighting, you can go first. But this is a job which calls for attention to detail, you're not suited to it."

Iron Ox laughed contemptuously. "Why all this trouble for the sake of a fucking farmhouse? Just give me a few hundred men and I'll go ahead and kill all those fucking peasants, what need is there to send in scouts?"

Song Jiang shouted angrily: "You're talking rubbish! When we want to storm the place, we'll call for you."

Iron Ox took himself off, muttering: "What a lot of fuss just to swat a bloody fly!"

Next Song Jiang called Madcap and said: "You've been there before, so I'd like you to go with Panther."

Madcap said: "Since we've come here in such force, I can't believe they won't be ready for us. How should we disguise ourselves, in order to get in?"

Panther said: "I shall disguise myself as an exorcist. I'll be carrying a hidden knife and holding a rattle and I'll just amble along quietly till I'm inside. You just listen for my rattle and stay close."

"When I was in Jizhou I used to be a seller of firewood," Madcap said. "I'll take a load of firewood in to sell. I'll carry a concealed weapon too, and in an emergency I can also use the carrying-pole."

"Good," said Panther. "We'll work it all out and make our preparations tonight. We'll start at dawn."

So all because of a row over a chicken, the tigers came out to fight. There's an old poem that says it all:

> *Often it's the weak who have an easy time, the strong are too prone to stir up trouble. Still, though it's good to live without strife, show me the man that's always blameless! A blunt axe serves to smash a brick; with the sharpest knife you can't cut water. The hair turns white, the teeth decay, the tongue's the only part that lasts.*

Madcap went in first, with his load of firewood. He had gone no more than five miles or so when he found he was lost in a maze of pathways that seemed to twist and turn in every direction, obscured by trees and thick undergrowth — impossible to know which way was right. Madcap stopped and set down his load. Behind him he heard the sound of the rattle approaching, and Panther appeared, a battered straw hat on his head. He was wearing an old exorcist's robe and holding the rattle, and he drifted along as if without purpose.

After checking that there was no one around, Madcap called out to him: "It's impossible to find the way among all these turnings, and I can't remember which way we went when I came here the other day with Skyhawk. It was getting dark at the time and the others all knew the way so I didn't pay attention."

Panther said: "Don't worry about all the turnings. Just keep to the main path."

Madcap picked up his load and went on, always following the widest path. Presently he came to a village with several inns and shops. Still shouldering his load he stopped at the door of an inn. The customers had all left their weapons in front of the door and each man wore a yellow singlet bearing the character *Zhu*. Everyone was the same. Seeing an old man, he saluted him and respectfully asked: "Can you tell me something about your customs, sir? What are all those weapons doing in front of the door?"

"Where have you come from?" the old man said. "If you really don't know, you'd better get out of here at once."

"I'm from Shandong and I used to trade in dates," Madcap said. "But I lost my capital and couldn't get home, that's why I've come here to sell firewood. I don't know the local customs and geography."

"You'd better go somewhere else at once and hide," the old man said. "There's going to be a massacre here, before very long."

"It seems to be such a fine place! Why should there be killing?"

"If you really don't know," the old man said, "I'd better tell you. This is called Zhu village, and that place up there at the top is Baron Zhu's seat. Something has stirred up the bandits of Mount Liang recently, and now they've brought a force down to the edge of our territory. They plan to attack us and kill us. The only thing that bothers them is that the roads here are very confusing and they're afraid to advance. That's why they've stopped outside the village. The order's just come down from the castle that every fit man and youth in every household must be prepared, and as soon as the order comes we are to go and help them."

"How many men do you have then, sir, in the village?"

"There's a couple of thousand in this village alone," the old man replied. "And there's two more villages, to the east and the west. The place to the east belongs to Skyhawk Li Ying, as he's called. To the west is Squire Hu's place — he's got a daughter, Miss Hu, known as Steelbright, who's an expert fighter."

"In that case, surely there's nothing to fear from Mount Liang?"

The old man assented: "If we were coming here ourselves for the first time, without knowing the roads, we'd fall into the trap too."

"Why do you say that, sir?" Madcap asked.

"We've got a poem about these roads of ours," the old man said.

A grand old place is Zhu,
Its roads they coil about.
Though 'tis easy to get in,
Once in you can't get out.

After listening to all this, Madcap began to lament. He threw himself down on the ground in front of the old man. "Poor me," he wailed. "I'm just a poor wanderer who's lost all his money and can't get home. Isn't it a bit hard, if I'm just trying to sell a bit of firewood and I meet up with a lot of murderers and can't find any way to escape? Kind sir, have pity on me. I beg you to accept this firewood and tell me how to get out of here."

The old man said: "Why should I take your firewood for nothing? I'll buy it from you. But come inside and let me offer you something to eat and drink."

Madcap thanked the old man and still carrying the firewood followed him into the house. The old man poured two cups of clear wine and filled a bowl with rice gruel. He bade Madcap eat. Madcap thanked him again, saying: "But please tell me how to get out."

The old man said: "As you go towards the village, you'll notice a white willow. That's where you should turn. Don't worry about whether the path is wide or narrow, just look for the turnings where there's a white willow, then there's a way through. If you don't see the tree, it's a dead end. If there's another kind of tree, it also means there's no way through. If you make a mistake you can turn this way or that way, but you'll never get through. What's more, in the dead end paths there's pointed bamboos buried in the ground and barricades of iron spikes, one false step and you'll set off flying arrows, you're sure to get yourself caught."

Madcap thanked him and asked: "Would you please tell me your name, sir?"

"Most people in this place are called Zhu. But I've got a double-barrelled name, Zhongli. This is where I live."

"I've eaten and drunk well. Some day I must repay you."

At this moment a great commotion arose outside. Madcap heard people shouting: "A spy's been caught." Anxiously he followed the old man outside to look. Eighty or so soldiers were carrying a captive towards them. He was soon able to make out that it was Panther, stripped naked and bound hand and foot. Madcap kept his distress to himself and innocently asked the old man: "Who is that they're bringing? Why is he tied up?"

"Can't you hear them saying it's a spy sent by Song Jiang?" said the old man.

"How did they catch him?" Madcap asked.

"They say he was very daring. He came here all on his own to spy on us, slipped into the village disguised as an exorcist. But he didn't know the roads. He always chose the widest paths, turning this way and that till he was caught in a dead end — he didn't know the system of turning at the white willow, you see. People saw he kept making mistakes and behaving strangely, so they reported him to the Baron's people up there, who came to get him. The villain pulled out a knife and proceeded to wound four or five of them. But there were a lot of people around who joined in and so he was taken. There were some who recognized him as a notorious robber, named Yang Lin the Panther."

He had hardly finished speaking when an outcry arose ahead. Voices were heard saying it was the third son from the castle on patrol. Madcap watching through a crack in the wall saw twenty men with tasselled spears and half a dozen horsemen behind them, all equipped with bows and arrows. There was also a group of three or four on grey horses and in their midst a young fellow seated on a pure white horse, fully armed with a bow and a gleaming spear in his hand.

Madcap recognized him, but he deliberately asked the old man: "Who is that young gentleman passing by?"

"That's Baron Zhu's third son. He's known as Wildcat Zhu and he's betrothed to Steelbright, from the Hu village to the west. Of the three brothers he's the bravest."

Madcap bowed and said: "Please now would you point me in the right direction to get out of here?"

"It's getting late," the old man said. "Suppose they're fighting out there, you'd just be throwing your life away for nothing."

"Then please tell me what I can do to save myself," Madcap said.

"You'd better stay the night with me," the old man said. "If we hear it's all quiet tomorrow morning you can leave then."

So Madcap gratefully remained with the old man. In a little while half a dozen mounted messengers came knocking on doors and shouting: "People of the village, tonight you must look for the red signal lanterns. If you all do your best we shall catch those Mount Liang brigands, hand them over and get the reward." When they had gone, Madcap asked: "Who was that?"

"The officer was the chief of our local anti-brigand squad," the old man said. "They plan to capture Song Jiang tonight."

Madcap thought about this for a while. Then he asked for a light, retired to the bedroom, covered himself and slept.

Now as for Song Jiang, encamped with his troops outside the village, he had waited in vain for Madcap and Panther to return from the village and report. So in the end he sent Golden Wings who got as far as the outskirts and then returned and reported: "I heard the people talking there. They're saying a spy has been caught. Seeing that the roads are so devious and confusing I didn't dare go further in."

Song Jiang was extremely disturbed by the news. "How can we wait for a report now before we attack? If they're saying a spy has been caught it must mean our two friends have fallen into a trap. We must attack tonight. We must go in and fight to rescue our companions. What do the rest of you say?"

Iron Ox jumped up and said: "I shall be the first. Now we'll see what's what!"

Song Jiang issued orders, telling them all to arm themselves. Iron Ox and Morbid were to lead the first group, spearheading the attack, the White-Water Dragon and some others were to bring up the rear. The elder Mu brother was given the left flank and the Tamer the right. Song Jiang, Colonel Hua, Golden Wings and others commanded the centre. Thus with waving banners and loud cheers, with thundering drums and piercing gongs, wielding great swords and broad axes, they advanced on Zhu Castle. By the time they had fought their way to the foot of Lone Dragon Heights it was dusk.

Song Jiang ordered the first group to press home the attack on the castle. Iron Ox, in the vanguard, had stripped naked and was brandishing his two axes of tempered steel. His progress was swift as a forest fire. He reached the castle gates and paused to take stock. The drawbridge was raised on high, and no lights showed in the gate tower. Iron Ox was about to dive into the water but Morbid stopped him, saying: "No way! The gate is closed, it must be a trap. Wait till the chief arrives, we'll discuss it with him."

宋公明一打祝家庄

Iron Ox was most reluctant to give up. He stood by the bank, waving his two axes, and shouted: "Come on out, Baron Zhu, you lousy old fox, the Black Whirlwind wants a word with you!" But there was no reply from the castle.

When Song Jiang came up with his troops, Morbid drew near to him and reported that they could see no defenders in the castle, and no sign of movement. Song Jiang reined in his horse to look for himself: no swords, no spears, no men and no horses. Now he began to be afraid. "I've been a fool," he said hoarsely. "The mystic books state categorically that when engaging the enemy one should not act hastily. I had a moment of blindness. I was too anxious to rescue our two companions, that's why I attacked at once, without waiting for scouts to make a reconnaissance. We've reached their castle and there's no sign of the enemy, so they must have something up their sleeves. Order the three columns to retreat immediately!"

Iron Ox shouted: "Brother, now all our troops are here, don't order a retreat. We'll go in and smash them, you and I. Everyone follow me!"

Before he finished speaking the castle seemed to hear him: a rocket went off, soaring into the sky, and on Lone Dragon Heights above them thousands of torches were lit simultaneously, while from the gate tower crossbow bolts began to rain down. Song Jiang hurriedly tried to turn back the way he had come, but an outcry arose from the White-Water Dragon's troops in the rear. "The way we came in is blocked!" they were shouting. "It's an ambush!"

Song Jiang ordered his troops to cast around in all directions for a way out. Iron Ox went on brandishing his axes, searching for someone to kill, but he could not find a single enemy. Then on Lone Dragon Heights there was a second loud report. The sound seemed to reverberate forever, as thunderous shouts rang out on all sides, causing Song Jiang to stand and gape in helpless amazement.

For all your political and military acumen, how will you escape such a comprehensive scheme? For it was a real plan to trap the tiger and catch the dragon that had been devised, to seize the man of whom heaven and earth go in awe.

If you want to know how Song Jiang and his troops escaped from this predicament, you must read the next chapter.

Chapter 48

Steelbright captures Short-Arse Wang; Song Jiang twice attacks Zhu Castle!

So there was Song Jiang seated on his horse and he looked around him and saw that he was in the midst of an ambush. He gave the order to force a way through along the main paths, but at that moment came news that the fifth detachment had been brought to a complete standstill, and despairing cries arose from his men. "Now what's the problem?" Song Jiang asked.

"The roads in front are a complete maze," they replied. "We keep on going and just get back to where we started."

Song Jiang said: "Tell them to look for the way out by following the torches, the places where there are houses and people."

But they had not gone far before the cry arose again from the troops in front: "We took a route which leads towards the torches and lights, and there's sharp pointed bamboos and barbed wire, and they've stuck deer's horns everywhere to block the way."

Song Jiang said: "Is Heaven bent on destroying me?"

At this moment of crisis there was a commotion among the elder Mu brother's troops on the left flank and someone reported: "Madcap is here!" And sure enough Madcap arrived in front of Song Jiang's horse, gripping his blade. "Don't worry," he said. "I know the way. Pass the word quietly to all your forces that they should only take a turning where they see a white willow tree, tell them not to worry about whether the way is wide or narrow."

Song Jiang instructed his men to look for a white willow before turning. They had progressed a little under two miles when it became apparent that the number of enemy troops in their path was continually increasing. Song Jiang was very concerned. He shouted to Madcap: "How is it that the enemy forces ahead keep growing?"

Madcap said: "They're using the lamps as a signal."

Colonel Hua, on horseback beside Song Jiang, pointed and said: "Do you see that lamp in the dark spot under the tree? When we head east the lamp points to the east, if we head west it points west. That must be it! It's obviously a signal."

"Can't we do something about that lamp?" Song Jiang said.

"No problem," said Colonel Hua. He took his bow and fitted an arrow to it. Then urging his horse forward he loosed an arrow into the dark. Just the one shot sufficed, it sped straight to the target and shot the red light out. All around them the troops of the ambush, not seeing the red light any longer, fell into confusion.

Song Jiang ordered Madcap to lead the way and they fought their way through to the edge of the village. At this point a hubbub arose on the hillside and a line of bobbing torches was seen moving confusedly in from one side. Song Jiang ordered the foremost troops to halt and sent Madcap to investigate. He returned soon after and reported: "The second contingent from Mount Liang have arrived to reinforce us and they've routed the enemy." Song Jiang now encouraged his troops to redouble their efforts to break out of the village, as the Zhu troops fled in disarray. After meeting up with Leopard's Head, Thunderclap and the others they bivouacked on the outskirts.

When it was fully light, they built a stockade on top of a high mound and positioned their forces. The Tamer, Huang Xin was not seen among them. Highly disturbed by this, Song Jiang asked why. Some soldiers who had been with the expedition the day before came and said: "In accordance with your orders, General Huang went ahead to reconnoitre. He rashly entered some thick reedbeds where his horse was brought down by two concealed hooks, and half a dozen of them took him alive. There was just nothing we could do!"

Song Jiang was furious. He would have killed the bodyguards for not having reported this before, but Leopard's Head and Colonel Hua restrained him.

The mood was grim. Everyone was saying: "We've failed to take the castle and we've lost two of our comrades into the bargain. What is going to come of all this?"

Morbid said: "We're dealing with three villages that have united. But the one to the east is Mr. Li's, who was shot in the arm the other day by that villain Wildcat Zhu. At present he's at home recovering. Might it not be a good idea to go and consult him?"

"I had forgotten all about him," Song Jiang said. "He must know the local geography and conditions." So he told them to collect a quantity of silk, horses, goats and wine. Then, choosing a good mount, saddled and bridled, he went himself to request an audience with Skyhawk, leaving Leopard's Head and Thunderclap to guard the camp. He took with him Colonel Hua, Morbid and Madcap. They mounted and with three hundred horsemen set off for the Li manor.

When they reached their destination they found the gates bolted and the drawbridge raised, while a good many troops were ranged along the wall. From the gate tower a drum began to beat.

Song Jiang shouted up: "I am Song Jiang of Mount Liang. I have come to consult your master. I have no bad intention, you have nothing to fear from me."

When Uglymug looked down from the gate tower and saw Morbid and Madcap were there, he quickly opened the gates and crossed the moat in a small boat to greet Song Jiang. Song Jiang hurriedly dismounted and returned the courtesy. Morbid and Madcap came forward and said: "This is our friend Du Xing, known as Uglymug, who took us to meet Mr. Li."

Song Jiang said: "So this is Mr. Du! I should be most grateful if you would tell Mr. Li that I, Song Jiang of Mount Liang, am well acquainted with his great reputation, although it has not been my good fortune to meet him yet. Today, because the people of Zhu want to fight with us, I have come here to offer a few little gifts, some silk and a few thoroughbreds, some goats and some wine, and to beg an audience with him, not for any other purpose."

Bearing this message Uglymug rowed back and went to the main hall, where Skyhawk was sitting on a bed, swathed in bandages. When he reported Song Jiang's request for an interview, Skyhawk said: "He is one of the Mount Liang rebels, how can I talk to him? It's out of the question. Go back and tell him that

I'm lying in bed wounded and can't move, so it's impossible for me to see him now. Tell him he can visit me another time. As for the gifts, don't accept them."

Uglymug went back across the water to Song Jiang and said: "My master greets you most respectfully and says he wishes he could receive you, but being gravely wounded he is obliged to keep his bed and is unable to grant you an interview. He hopes it may be possible to meet some other day. As for your most generous gifts, it is quite impossible for him to accept them."

Song Jiang said: "I understand your master's meaning. I have failed to capture Zhu Castle. I wanted to meet him, that's all. But he doesn't want to upset Baron Zhu and his clan, that's why he refuses to see me."

Uglymug said: "That's not how it is at all. He truly is seriously indisposed. But I have lived here a number of years, although I'm a native of Zhongshan, and I know pretty well how things stand. Zhu Castle is situated between our manor here to the east and the Hu domain to the west. These three estates have signed a life or death pact guaranteeing mutual assistance. Now they have injured my master and he will not go to help them. It is likely, though, that the people over to the west, the Hu family, will come to their assistance. Most of that lot aren't up to much, but Miss Hu, the daughter, known as Steelbright for the two bright swords she uses, has true worth. She is betrothed to Baron Zhu's third, Wildcat Zhu, and sooner or later they'll be married. If you want to attack Zhu there's no need to watch out to the east, but you must seal off the roads to the west. There are two ways into Zhu Castle, a front way and a back way. One can be approached from the front of Lone Dragon Heights, the other from the far side. If you only attack from the front it won't be enough. It needs a concerted assault from both sides, that's the way you'll smash them. The front gate is a problem. The approach is complex and difficult, the paths winding and turning all the way, and their width keeps changing. You must only take the turnings where there is a white willow. If there isn't such a tree it's a dead end."

Madcap said: "Suppose they've gone and cut down the trees, how are we going to remember the way?"

"Even if they've cut down the trees, they can't eradicate them completely. There's bound to be a stump left. But you've got to attack by day, it's no good trying to go in there in the dark."

Song Jiang thanked Uglymug for all this information and returned with his troops to the base. When Leopard's Head and his force joined them, they held a meeting in the main camp. Song Jiang told the others about Skyhawk's refusal to see him and the information Uglymug had given them. Iron Ox burst out: "After we'd sent them all those presents, that motherfucker wouldn't even come out and receive you! I'll take three hundred men and smash up his fucking manor. I'll force the bastard to come out and pay his respects."

Song Jiang said: "Don't talk nonsense, brother. He's an honourable gentleman and he doesn't want to get on the wrong side of the law. It's obvious he wouldn't be in a hurry to see us."

Iron Ox muttered: "It's bloody childish. He's just scared." Everyone began to laugh.

"Be that as it may," Song Jiang said, "we've lost two comrades and we don't even know if they're still alive or not. I must ask you all to do your utmost, and renew the attack on Zhu Castle with me." They rose to their feet as one man and said: "You are the leader, no one would dream of disobeying! Who shall go first?"

Iron Ox said: "I shall go first, since all the rest of you are scared of little children!"

"It's no good having you in the vanguard," Song Jiang said. "We can't use you for this."

Iron Ox lowered his head, swallowing his anger. Song Jiang then ordered the Flautist, Redeye, Golden Wings and Short-Arse to march with him in the vanguard. Next he instructed the Magic Messenger, Thunderclap, Morbid, Madcap, the White-Water Dragon, the Pilot, White Eel and the Daytime Rat to muster a band of sailors. Finally he told Leopard's Head, Colonel Hua, Mu the Unstoppable and Iron Ox to form two supporting forces. When all the duties had been allotted, they armed themselves and mounted.

Song Jiang had decided to lead from the front, commanding the vanguard. Preceded by a large banner with characters in red, and followed by the other four leaders, with a hundred and fifty cavalry and a thousand foot, he marched on Zhu Castle. Scouts went in front of them to check the route. Soon they stood before Lone Dragon Heights. Song Jiang reined in his horse to have a good look at the castle. It was indeed a brave sight. There is a poem in praise of it which will tell you what it looked like:

In front of the mountains is Lone Dragon Heights
Where Zhu Castle stands, most wondrous of sights;
On all sides defended by a broad moat,
With clusters of willows scattered about.
Inside the ramparts are weapons in stacks;
In front of the gates there are spears in their racks.
The enemy leaders are strong and aggressive,
Three valiant youngsters whose ardour's excessive:
Dragon is one who'll be hard to defeat;
Tiger's another you won't want to meet;
Wildcat has mastered war's arts most fully,
Shouting insults and curses like a great bully.
Baron Zhu is a man of astuteness and more;
Of gold, silver and silk he has a great store.
A pair of white banners flutter on high,
Proclaiming in words that no clarity lack:
"We shall level the Marshes and capture Chao Gai;
We shall flatten Mount Liang and get Song Jiang the Black!"

Song Jiang was filled with anger when he saw those banners. "If I don't defeat Zhu I shall never return to Mount Liang," he vowed. The other leaders were also outraged. When Song Jiang knew that the rest had all come up behind him, he left the second force to attack the front gate of the castle whilst he led the first force round to the back of Lone Dragon Heights. Seen from this side the castle was a solid mass of ramparts, strongly fortified. As they were surveying it, a column of troops was observed in the west, coming up behind them with a great deal of shouting. Leaving the Flautist and Redeye to seal off the rear approach to Zhu Castle, Song Jiang took Golden Wings and Short-Arse and half the troops to meet the oncoming force. This consisted of around three hundred cavalry, who came streaming down the mountain. In their midst was a woman warrior, exceedingly handsome:

> *A pair of gold pins subdue the curls; phoenix slippers thread the stirrups. Chain mail overlays a robe of red silk; an embroidered belt girds the willow waist. Here is a frosty blade that will strike down the fiercest warrior, a slender force to vanquish the wildest opponent. Radiant as the crab-apple in flower is Steelbright who leads the charge.*

Steelbright it was, Squire Hu's daughter. She rode a horse with a bluish mane, and she twirled a pair of glittering blades. Behind her came three or four hundred retainers. They were on their way to relieve Zhu Castle.

Song Jiang said: "They told me the Hu manor has a woman warrior who's very brave. This must be her. Who wants to fight her?"

Before he'd even finished, Short-Arse, who was a notorious womanizer and reckoned, on hearing talk of a woman warrior, that a single bout would suffice to capture her, cheered and galloped out in front, readying his lance for the charge. There were cheers from both sides as Miss Hu, slapping her horse and brandishing her two swords rode to the encounter.

What you had now was an expert swordswoman pitted against an outstanding lancer. They fought a dozen bouts, until it became evident to Song Jiang that Short-Arse's technique with the spear was failing and he was losing the strength to parry. The fact was that when Short-Arse first saw the girl he just couldn't wait to get his hands on her. He never thought that after a dozen bouts his arm would weaken, his legs grow stiff, his spearsmanship go all awry. He hadn't been looking for a fight to the death, he had just thought to have some fun.

But Steelbright was not to be trifled with. "This fellow's a lout," she thought to herself. Then she went in with her two swords, lunging at once both high and low. Short-Arse had more than met his match. He turned his horse and tried to flee. But Steelbright was on him again at once. Sheathing the sword in her right hand she stretched out a long agile arm, plucked him from

一丈青单捉王矮虎

his embroidered saddle and made him captive. The retainers gathered round and unceremoniously dragged Short-Arse away. There's a poem about this:

The power of lust outweighs discretion.
His life he sets at nought.
The sex destroy his self-possession,
By a woman he'll be caught.

When Golden Wings saw Short-Arse taken, he levelled his lance and charged to the rescue. Steelbright galloped towards him, waving her swords, and the two began to fight.

Now Golden Wings came from a family of famous soldiers and was an expert with the steel lance. Song Jiang watched, silently urging him on. But brilliant as his spearsmanship was, he could not get the slightest advantage over the woman warrior. Redeye, who was watching from afar and had seen Short-Arse taken prisoner and Golden Wings unable to subdue the woman, now urged on his mount and charged to the rescue, whirling a steel chain and letting off a tremendous shout. Meanwhile in Zhu Castle, where they had been watching for some time, they began to fear that Steelbright might lose. They hastily lowered the drawbridge and opened the gates and Dragon Zhu himself, leading out three hundred men, galloped with levelled spear at Song Jiang, hoping to capture him. The Flautist saw this, and waving his two swords galloped to encounter Dragon Zhu. Redeye fearing for Song Jiang's safety stuck by his side, as the fight raged on amid a tumult of shouts. As Song Jiang began to be really concerned that the Flautist could not handle Dragon Zhu and Golden Wings could not get the better of Steelbright, another column of troops came charging in from the side. To Song Jiang's delight it was Thunderclap Qin Ming, who had heard the sound of fighting and was coming to lend a hand. Song Jiang shouted out: "General Qin, look to the Flautist!"

Now Thunderclap was an impetuous man. Moreover, the Zhu forces had captured his friend and disciple the Tamer. He was not in a good mood. He gave his horse a slap and flew at Dragon Zhu, his face set in a terrifying grimace. Dragon Zhu readied his lance to receive the onslaught. The Flautist now led his troops away to try to recapture Short-Arse. Steelbright saw them coming and turned away from Golden Wings in order to receive the Flautist's attack. This encounter, since both were wielding two swords, gave the appearance of wind whirling up powdered jade, of snowflakes scattering among fairy petals. Just to watch it blurred one's vision.

On the other side Thunderclap and Dragon Zhu fought a dozen bouts. Dragon Zhu was no match for Thunderclap, but among his men was Ironstaff, who charged forward with steel chain and lance. Golden Wings rushed to meet him. Before the horses clashed, the instructor put up his lance and rode away to one side. As Golden Wings galloped after him, Ironstaff's flying chain caught him and knocked him headlong from the saddle. Redeye gave a great shout: "To the rescue, lads!" and charged after Ironstaff, whirling his chain.

Song Jiang told his men to save Golden Wings and get him on a horse. Meanwhile Dragon Zhu, unable to withstand Thunderclap, slapped his horse and fled. Ironstaff also broke off combat with Redeye and engaged Thunderclap. The two of them fought some twenty bouts and neither had the advantage. Eventually Ironstaff feinted and then slipped away. Thunderclap gave chase, whirling his mace, as Ironstaff galloped into a thicket. Unsuspectingly Thunderclap followed. Of course the Zhu force had positioned men in ambush in all such places. As soon as they saw Thunderclap they stretched out ropes to trip his horse. Horse and rider crashed to the ground and amid a tumult of shouts Thunderclap was taken.

Redeye saw Thunderclap fall and rushed to his assistance. Too late he saw the trip-wires and tried to turn back, but with much cheering on either side of him a tangle of hooks snaked out and he too was taken.

All that Song Jiang watching from afar could do was curse his luck and see to it that Golden Wings was put on a horse. The Flautist broke off the fight with Steelbright and rushed to support Song Jiang. They rode away southward, with Ironstaff, Dragon Zhu and Steelbright all in pursuit. They could see no way out and they were fully expecting to be captured when they saw away to the south a horseman was galloping towards them with five hundred troops behind him. It was Mu the Unstoppable. Another three hundred or more cavalry with two leaders were racing up from the southeast. One of the leaders was Morbid and the other was Madcap. From the northeast came yet another horseman, who was shouting out: "Get away from them!" It was Colonel Hua, the Archer. These three groups of cavalry converged on Song Jiang, who was immensely relieved to see them.

They now joined forces against Ironstaff and Dragon Zhu. Those watching from the castle feared for the safety of their two champions, so leaving Tiger Zhu to guard the gate the youngest brother, Wildcat Zhu, rode out from the rear of the castle. Mounted on a mettlesome charger and wielding a long lance, he was the leader of over five hundred cavalry, who now flung themselves into the fray.

Meanwhile in front of the castle, the White-Water Dragon, the Pilot and White Eel had crossed the water, but came under a hail of arrows from the castle and were unable to make any progress. The Magic Messenger and the Daytime Rat could only give encouragement from the other bank.

It was beginning to get dark, so Song Jiang hurriedly told the Flautist to get Golden Wings to safety outside the village. He also gave orders for the gongs to be sounded, as a signal to all his commanders to break off the fight and withdraw.

Song Jiang himself slapped his horse and galloped here and there to round up his men. He was afraid some of them might get lost. As he was doing so, he saw Steelbright charging towards him. He was unprepared for this, so he galloped off to the east with Steelbright in hot pursuit.

Eight hooves beat the earth like upturned cups. The chase took them deep into enemy territory. Steelbright was gaining on him and Song Jiang was about to turn and fight when a shout rang out from the mountainside: "What does that bloody woman think she's doing chasing our leader?"

It was Iron Ox, whirling his two axes, racing towards them at the head of a force of seventy or eighty. Steelbright reined in her horse and rode off towards the forest. Song Jiang also halted, and was able to observe another few dozen cavalrymen emerging from the forest. At the head of them rode a fellow who was bravely built and nobly accoutred.

It was Leopard's Head, who shouted as he rode forward: "Where do you think you're going, you bitch?" Steelbright whirling her swords charged him. Leopard's Head levelling his long curved spear rode to meet her. Before they had fought ten bouts he feinted. When Steelbright came in close to slash at him with her two swords, he parried with his spear and reaching out with an easy movement of his agile arm and a bend of his supple waist, plucked her from her horse.

Song Jiang applauded loudly, his delight knew no bounds. Ordering his men to tie her up, Leopard's Head galloped over to Song Jiang and asked: "Are you hurt, brother?"

"No, I'm not hurt," the latter replied.

Iron Ox was now ordered to rush round the village rounding up all the leaders and ordering them to come to the camp outside the village for a conference. He rode off with his troops behind him. Leopard's Head, protecting Song Jiang, with Steelbright in custody, headed back to the camp outside the village.

That night all the leaders gathered anxiously in the camp, worried at not having prevailed in the fight.

The Zhu forces likewise withdrew to the castle. They had suffered countless casualties. Dragon Zhu ordered all the prisoners to be confined in prison carts, to be taken together to the capital, once Song Jiang had been captured, and exchanged for the reward. The people of Hu had already handed over Short-Arse to Zhu Castle.

Having assembled most of his forces on the outskirts of the village, Song Jiang set up camp. He first ordered Steelbright to be brought and instructed twenty experienced soldiers and four leaders on fast mounts to deliver her with all speed, bound hand and foot and also on horseback, to Mount Liang and hand her over to his father, Squire Song, to look after, and then report back. He told them that he would dispose of her when he returned to the mountain. The others all thought Song Jiang wanted the

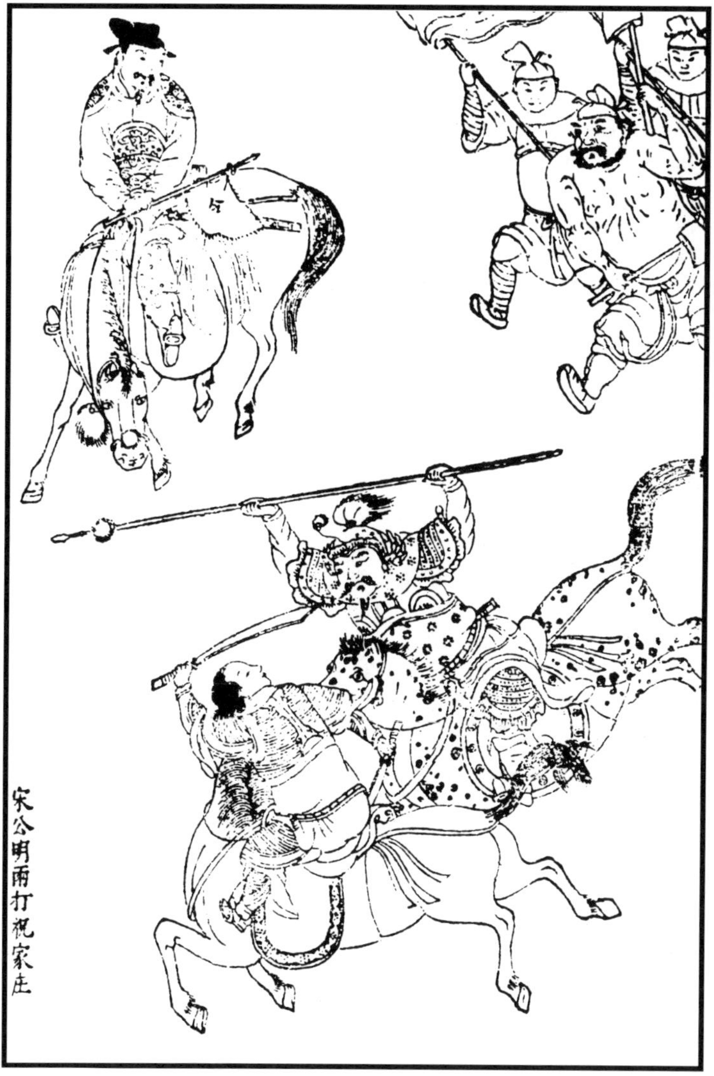

宋公明兩打祝家庄

woman for himself, so the mission was carried out with great care. Golden Wings was also to be sent in a cart back to the mountain to recuperate. Everyone carried out these orders, travelling with all speed. But Song Jiang grieved in his tent all night, unable to sleep. He watched till morning.

Next day scouts came to report that Professor Wu Yong was on the way, with the three Ruan brothers, the Little Duke and the Halberdier, and five hundred cavalry. Song Jiang went out to meet him, and then took him back to the tent. The Professor had brought food and drink with him, and drank a toast to celebrate with Song Jiang and reward the leaders of the expedition.

"Back in the mountain stronghold," he said, "our leader Chao Gai has heard all about your first unsuccessful expedition and has sent me and five others to lend a hand. How did you fare today, well or badly?"

"It's not easy to say in a word. That unspeakable Zhu crowd had erected two white banners over their gate, saying 'We shall level the Marshes and capture Chao Gai, we shall flatten Mount Liang and get Song Jiang the Black!' They are insolent! In our first attack the topography was against us and we lost Panther and the Tamer. We launched an assault in the evening and Short-Arse was captured by Steelbright, while Golden Wings was injured by the instructor's chain. Then Thunderclap and Redeye were unseated and captured by means of trip-wires. With losses like these our morale would have been severely damaged if Leopard's Head had not managed to capture Steelbright. With things as they are, I don't know what we can do next. I'd sooner kill myself right here than fail to destroy Zhu Castle and rescue our comrades. I certainly wouldn't be able to go back and face our friend Chao Gai again."

But the Professor only laughed. "This Zhu Castle," he said, "has really been tempting heaven. And now there's a wonderful opportunity. I should say it will only take us a day and a night to destroy it."

Song Jiang was both astonished and delighted. "How could it take only a day and a night to destroy it?" he asked eagerly. "What is this opportunity?"

Smiling patiently, the Professor laid two fingers together and explained what he meant by an opportunity. Truly this was a case of:

He reaches up into the sky and pulls down the clouds;
He delivers them from the snares of heaven and earth.

But if you want to know what Professor Wu Yong was talking about, you must read the next chapter.

Chapter 49

Colonel Sun and Blackface attack the prison; Snake and Scorpion are sprung from gaol!

What the Professor told Song Jiang was as follows: "We've an excellent opportunity today because someone recommended by the Guv who wants to join our company is a good friend of that Ironstaff's, besides being an intimate of Panther and Redeye. He knows about your not having managed to capture Zhu Castle, and has offered us this scheme in return for our allowing him to join us, as a joining gift so to speak. He'll soon be here. The plan can be carried out within five days. How about that?"

Song Jiang's face broke into a smile of relief. "That's wonderful!" he said.

Now all this, including the plan itself, you shall hear about, friends, all in good time. Just store it up in your memory, because at the same time as Song Jiang started the attack on Zhu Castle something else had happened. It's awkward to describe a little bit of this and then a little bit of that, so for the moment just keep in mind that there are two themes connected with the storming of Zhu Castle and let us concentrate on this someone wanting to join the company and the business of providing an excellent opportunity. Later we will get back to the other story.

On the coast of Shandong there is a provincial capital called Dengzhou. Outside the city there is a mountain. On this mountain there is an abundance of wild animals, wild boar, wolves, tigers and leopards, which often attack people. For this reason the governor had rounded up hunters and charged each of them with catching a tiger on Dengzhou mountain within a certain time-limit. Village headmen on both sides of the mountain were also roped in and told to catch a tiger within the time-limit or suffer the severest penalties.

Now there were on Dengzhou mountain two hunters who were brothers, the elder called Xie Zhen and the younger Xie Bao. These two brothers both liked to use solid steel tridents and their skill in a fight was truly awesome. The local hunters all reckoned they were the best. The elder was nicknamed Two-headed Snake, the younger Two-tailed Scorpion. They were orphans and unmarried. The elder was tall with a red complexion like a crab-apple, a slender waist and broad shoulders. The younger was tremendous: he was equally tall, and his face was round and very dark. Two flying Rakshasas were tattooed on his legs, and when he was angry he seemed about to leap up to the heavens, or to pluck up trees and shake the mountains.

When these two brothers were presented by the authorities with the unwelcome task, they went home and got out their trap with the poisoned arrow, their crossbows and tridents, dressed themselves up in animal skins and set off, steel tridents in hand, for Dengzhou mountain. There they set their trap and waited for a whole day, but to no avail. They picked up the trap and left. Next day they took some provisions with them, climbed the mountain again and waited. When it began to get dark they set the trap and climbed a tree. They waited till just before dawn, but nothing stirred. They picked up the trap and moved it to the western flank of the mountain. There they waited till it was fully light, but again with no success.

They began to be worried. "The time-limit's only three days," they said to themselves. "If we miss it we'll have to pay the penalty. What are we going to do?"

On the night of the third day, in the small hours, despite their cramped and weary limbs, they fell asleep, leaning back to back. But they had scarcely closed their eyes when there was a sudden sound from the trap. They both leapt up, grabbed their tridents and began to look in all directions. What should they see but a tiger wounded by a poisoned arrow and rolling on the ground! They rushed towards it with their tridents at the ready, but at their approach the beast fled, with the arrow still stuck in it. They gave chase. Nearly halfway round the mountain the poison began to take effect and the tiger, maddened by pain, gave a mighty roar and went plunging down a steep slope.

"That's all right," said Scorpion. "I know this mountain. It'll be in Squire Mao's back garden. Let's go down and ask him to let us get it."

They shouldered their tridents and went down to Squire Mao's house and knocked on the door. It was still early in the morning. They were let in and someone went to tell the master. After a long wait, Squire Mao appeared. The brothers put down their tridents, saluted and said: "It's a long time since we've seen you, sir. We come to greet you."

"But why come so early?" Squire Mao asked. "Is there something you want to say to me?"

Snake said: "Of course we wouldn't dream of disturbing you if there wasn't a reason. We've been ordered by the authorities to catch a tiger, and there's a strict time-limit. We've been lying in wait three days, and this morning at dawn we wounded one, but then suddenly it fell down the mountain and landed in your garden. We were hoping you'd allow us to come in and get it."

"Of course you may, if it fell in my garden," said Squire Mao. "Why don't you just sit down for a bit? I expect you're hungry. Have some breakfast before you go and get the tiger."

He told the servants to get breakfast for them. But when he urged them to have more, they stood up, thanked him and said: "We truly appreciate your kindness, sir. But please would you let us go and get our tiger now?"

"If it's in my garden, what are you worried about?" said the Squire. "Do sit down and have some tea. Time enough to get it afterwards."

The brothers could hardly refuse. They sat down and the servants brought tea for them. At last the Squire said: "Now we'll go and get the tiger."

"We are truly grateful," they said.

Squire Mao took them to the back of the house and told a servant to get the key to open the garden door. Try as he would to open it, it wouldn't budge.

"We seldom go into this part of the garden," the Squire said. "I expect the lock is rusty, that's why it won't open. Go and get a hammer to break it open."

The servant brought a hammer and they broke the lock and everyone went into the garden. They searched the whole hillside, but nothing did they find.

"Are you sure you weren't mistaken?" the Squire said to the brothers. "Perhaps you weren't watching carefully. Maybe it didn't fall into my garden."

"How could we be mistaken?" said Snake. "We were born and bred here. We know the district well."

"Well, just go on looking," said the Squire. "If it's here, finish it off and take it away."

"Look at this, brother," cried Scorpion. "There's a patch of grass here that's been rolled completely flat. And look, there's traces of blood. Who says it wasn't here? The Squire's people must have finished it off."

"What are you talking about?" said the Squire. "How would my people even know there was a tiger here, let alone finish it off? You saw for yourselves that we had to break the lock, and we all came in at the same time as you. You're talking absolute nonsense!"

"Just give us back our tiger, sir," said Snake. "So we can take it to the authorities."

"You're both crazy," said the Squire. "Out of the kindness of my heart I offer you breakfast. Then you go and make a false accusation about our stealing your tiger!"

"What false accusation?" said Scorpion. "You are also a headman in your household and the time-limit for catching a tiger applies to you too. Only you haven't the ability to catch one for yourself, so when you see we've got one you decide to take it to get the reward and let us pay the penalty!"

"What's it got to do with me, if you have to pay a penalty?" said the Squire.

Glaring ferociously, Scorpion said: "Do you want us to search the place?"

"This is my house, not yours," said the Squire. "Everyone has a right to privacy. Really! The impudence of these two beggars!"

But Scorpion had already charged into the hall to look. He found nothing. His anger grew inside him and he began to smash everything in sight. Snake likewise pulled out the balustrade and began to hammer things with it.

Squire Mao let out a shout: "Help! They've come to rob me in broad daylight!"

The two brothers smashed up all the furniture in the hall and then as the servants were preparing to attack them, strode out of the front door, pointing accusingly and saying: "You've cheated us of a tiger! We'll denounce you to the court!"

At catching beasts they're most astute;
But the Squire's art is trapping men.
Because a tiger's in dispute,
Mount Liang will take two dragons in.

As they were engaged in this slanging match, some horsemen rode up to the house, followed by a band of men. Snake recognized Squire Mao's son, Mao Zhongyi.

He went over to him and said: "Your people have stolen our tiger, and your father won't give it back. He even wants them to beat us up!"

"They're just an ignorant bunch of peasants," said Mao Zhongyi. "My father must have been deceived by them. Don't be angry. Now I'm home I'll get them to give it back."

The brothers thanked him. He ordered the door to be opened and took them inside. Once they were in, he ordered the doors to be shut and yelled: "Get them!" From the corridors on either side thirty or forty men sprang out, the Squire's retainers plus the group that came with the riders, who turned out to be policemen. The brothers could do nothing. The whole lot fell on them at once and tied them up.

Mao Zhongyi now said: "We shot a tiger yesterday, why did you pretend it was yours? You made it an excuse to come in here looting and destroying our property, what sort of punishment do you suppose that deserves? Well, we're going to hand you over to the court. That'll rid the district of a public menace."

What had happened, of course, was that Mao Zhongyi had already delivered the tiger to the authorities in the early morning, and had returned with a group of policemen to arrest the brothers. The latter, unfortunately for them, had not understood the situation at all and had fallen into his trap. It needs no further explanation. Squire Mao had the steel tridents they had used brought, and a bag of alleged stolen goods; some pieces of broken furniture and other household objects were slung on carrying-poles; the brothers themselves were stripped naked and their hands tied behind their backs. Then the whole lot was sent to the court.

Now in this district there was a clerk of the court called Wang Zheng, who was Squire Mao's son-in-law. Wang had already gone to the magistrate and told him about the case. When the two brothers were brought before the court they were allowed to say nothing in their defence. They were thrown down and beaten, to make them confess that they had cheated over the tiger and that it was all a pretext for them to come armed with tridents to rob the household. Unable to withstand the beating, they were forced to confess to the charges as required. The magistrate ordered them to be fitted with twenty-five catty cangues and thrown into the main prison.

When Squire Mao and his son got back home they considered the affair: "It'll be a problem for us if they release those two fools. Wouldn't it be best to finish them off once and for all, to avoid any further consequences?" So they went back to the government office and made it known to registrar Wang Zheng that they would like him to cut the weeds and pull out the roots so they wouldn't sprout again. They promised they would take care of the magistrate.

The two brothers were assigned to the cells for condemned criminals. They were taken to the central area of the prison, where they met the head warder. This important personage was called Bao Ji. He too had received silver from Squire Mao and had Wang's instructions to finish them off. He was already sitting in the centre of the hall. The junior warder said to them: "Go and kneel down there in front of him, quickly."

"You're supposed to be some kind of two-headed snake and two-tailed scorpion, is that it?" Bao Ji roared at them.

"People have given us some such nicknames," said Snake. "But we've never done any kind of harm to innocent people."

"Well you two animals are in my hands now, and I know how to turn a two-headed snake into a one-headed snake, and a two-tailed scorpion into a one-tailed scorpion! I've got you here in my prison now."

When the junior warder took them to their cell, he looked around to see there was no one and then said: "Do you recognize me? I'm your elder brother's brother-in-law!"

Snake said: "There's only the two of us. We haven't got an elder brother."

The warder said: "Surely you are brothers of Colonel Sun?"

Snake said: "Colonel Sun's younger brother is married to a cousin on my father's side. But I've never met you. Are you by any chance Yue Ho?"

"That's right, I'm Yue Ho. I'm from Maozhou. My family moved here, and my elder sister became Colonel Sun's wife. I got a job here as a warder. I've a good singing voice, so people call me Lungs. My brother-in-law taught me some tricks with the staff, because he saw I had an aptitude for martial arts."

There's a poem to say what Yue Ho is like:

He's smart and he's stylish, his get-up is choice;
He's as lucid a speaker as any on earth.
They call him the Lungs for the power of his voice;
Quick-witted Yue Ho is a hero from birth.

This Lungs was indeed quick and ingenious. He knew every kind of weapon, for whatever he studied he could master. He never did anything by halves. As for the art of staff and spear, he loved it like sugar and honey. He could see that Snake and Scorpion were good fellows and he was determined to help them, only you can't make cloth from a single thread, nor can you clap with one hand. The most he could do on his own was give them some information.

So he said: "There's something I think you ought to know: Chief Warder Bao has been taking money from Squire Mao. It must mean they want to finish you off. Do you have any useful connections?"

Snake said: "Well, now you've mentioned him there's Colonel Sun — if you would approach him, I could give you a letter to take."

Lungs said: "Who should I give the letter to?"

"Like I said, there's this cousin of ours, on our father's side, who's the wife of Colonel Sun's younger brother. She lives outside the east gate, at the third milestone. Although she's really a cousin, we call her Auntie Gu. She runs an inn, but it's also a butcher's and a gambling house. Auntie Gu is a match for twenty or thirty men. Her husband, Sun Xin, is skilled in fighting, but even he can't get the better of her. She's the one person we really get on with. Actually our mother also was the aunt of Colonel Sun and his brother, so they're cousins on our mother's side too. If you would be so good as to secretly carry a letter to her explaining our situation, I'm sure she will come to the rescue."

After hearing all this Lungs said: "No need to worry now friends." He first went and got some provisions — pancakes and meat — and went back to give them to the brothers. Then on the pretext of having some business to see to he locked up, asked another gaoler to keep the door, and set off towards the third milestone outside the east gate. He soon came to an inn. Carcasses of buffalo and sheep were hanging outside the door. Inside, in an inner room, a group of men were gambling. There was a woman sitting at the counter. Here's what she looked like:

> *Thick eyebrows and big eyes, a chubby round face, a whole headful of outlandish hairpins and rings, together with a couple of quite fashionable bracelets. Sometimes when she's angry she pulls up one of the rails from the well and beats her old man about the head with it. When something really sets her off, she grabs a stone awl and raps the servants' legs. This one was not born to handle a needle and thread; she has turned staff and spear play into woman's work.*

Lungs went right in, saluted Auntie Gu and said: "Is this the Sun's?"

Auntie Gu replied cheerfully: "It certainly is. Do you want to drink wine or buy some meat? If you want to gamble, it's in the back."

"I am the younger brother of Colonel Sun's wife. Yue Ho is my name."

Auntie Gu looked pleased. "So it's cousin Yue Ho! I should have known. You're just like sister-in-law. Do please come in and have some tea."

Lungs followed her into the inn and took the guest's seat. Auntie Gu started the conversation: "I've heard that you have a job in the capital. I'm afraid we're worked off our feet here and never have any free time, or we would have tried to see you. What wind blows you here today?"

"I wouldn't have disturbed you either, if I didn't have some important business. We have just received two criminals who happen to have been sentenced by the court. I didn't know them before, but I have heard a lot about them. One is Xie Zhen, the Two-headed Snake, the other is Xie Bao, the Two-tailed Scorpion."

"They are my relatives, " Auntie Gu said. "Whatever have they done to be sent to prison?"

"They shot a tiger and a rich man, Squire Mao, stole it. He turned the truth upside down, making them out to be thieves who had broken into his house, and handed them over to the court. He gave bribes to all and sundry and intends sooner or later to have prison Chief Warder Bao do them in and that'll be that. I saw at once it's a serious business and quite beyond my powers to help them by myself. But for the sake of family ties and even more importantly for the sake of justice, I had to let them know how things stood. They said you were the only one who can save them. But unless you act quickly and decisively, it's going to be impossible to get them out of it."

Auntie Gu responded by expressing her shock, but at the same time she sent some of her people to tell her husband to return home urgently to discuss things. They soon found him and brought him back to meet Lungs.

There's a poem which describes Sun Xin's qualities:

Of fighters the finest,
With bearing most martial,
Penglai now his home,
And Hainan his birthplace.
Endowed with high spirit
And an amazon for mate,
The strength of two dragons,
The strike of a snake,
Still but a young man,
They call him Blackface.

This Sun Xin, or Blackface to give him his popular name, was born in Hainan, to a well-known military family. The father being posted to Dengzhou, the sons grew up there. Blackface was tall and strong. He had learnt all his elder brother's skills, and like him was pretty useful with the spear and whip, which is why people compared him to the black-faced warrior, whose image guards the doors of courtrooms.

Auntie Gu related what she had heard to Blackface.

Blackface said to Lungs: "In that case you'd better go back there at once. Whilst they're in the prison we need you to keep an eye on things. My wife and I will try to work out a long-term solution. We'll come and find you afterwards."

Lungs said: "If I can be of use in any way, I promise to do my utmost."

Auntie Gu brought wine for them and then took out a quantity of small change which she gave to Lungs, saying: "Please would you take this and share it among the people at the gaol so that they will treat my cousins well."

Lungs took the money and thanked her and then went back to the gaol to distribute it. Of this no more.

As for Auntie Gu and Blackface, here is how their discussion went.

"What's your plan to save my cousins?" Auntie Gu asked.

"That Squire Mao has money and influence," said Blackface. "If he's had your cousins thrown into prison it won't end there. He'll definitely want to destroy them; they're certain to die under his orders. It's going to be difficult to save them, unless we can get them out of the prison."

"Let's go then, right away," said Auntie Gu.

"My goodness, you are impetuous! We've got to plan ahead. Once we get them out of gaol, there's got to be some route for them to take. Unless my elder brother helps us, and a couple of others, the thing's not going to work."

"Who are these others?" Auntie Gu asked.

"They're an uncle and nephew, a pair of fanatical gamblers called Zou Yuan and Zou Run. I have just seen them in Dengyun Mountain valley, where they've collected together a band of robbers. They're good friends of mine, and with their help I think we can manage it."

"That's not far," said Auntie Gu. "You'd better go tonight and ask them to come here and discuss it."

"I'll go right away," said Blackface. "You can prepare some food and drink while I go and invite them here."

Auntie Gu told her people to kill a pig, prepare some plates of dried fruit to accompany the wine, and set the tables. Blackface returned at dusk with a pair of stalwarts in tow. The senior was called Zou Yuan and he was from Laizhou. From his youth he had loved gambling and had grown up somewhat idle, but he was loyal and generous and he had, what is more, notable martial skills and a proud spirit: he wouldn't give way to anyone. Among the rivers and lakes he was known as the Forester. The second, who was his nephew, was called Zou Run. He was about the same age as his uncle, and both men were about equal in a fight. He was tall and well built. He had a strange birthmark: a prominent lump on the top of his head. Due to this people called him Rhinoceros. He was very much inclined to pick a fight with people. When angry he would butt people with his head. Once he actually butted a pine tree standing beside a mountain stream and knocked it down, to the amazement of the onlookers.

Auntie Gu asked them to come inside and sit down. She told them what had happened, and they discussed plans for breaking into the gaol.

The Forester said: "Although I've got around ninety men, there are only about twenty I have confidence in. If we do this, it won't be safe to stay around here afterwards. I've got somewhere to go to — I've been intending to go for quite a while. Would you two be prepared to go with me?"

Auntie Gu said: "I'll go anywhere with you, so long as we can rescue my cousins."

"They're doing extremely well at the moment in the Marshes of Mount Liang," the Forester said. "Song Jiang welcomes good people into the company. I know three people there under his command: one is Panther Yang Lin, another is Deng Fei or Redeye and the third is Shi Yong, the Guv. They've all been members for some time. How d'you say if after rescuing your cousins we all go and join the company on Mount Liang?"

"That's fine," said Auntie Gu. "If there's anyone who doesn't want to, I'll take my spear and stick it through him myself."

"There's just one thing," said the Forester. "If we get them out, there are government troops in Dengzhou and I'm afraid they're going to come after us. What are we going to do about that?"

"My brother is commander of the troops in Dengzhou," said Blackface. "He's the only one in the city that really counts for anything right now. Every time bandits have approached, he's always been the one that routed them. He's made a name for himself. Tomorrow I'll go and ask him to join us. If he agrees there'll be no problem."

The Forester said: "But he might object to becoming an outlaw."

"I know how to persuade him," said Blackface.

They went on drinking half the night and slept till it was daylight. Then, having persuaded the two outlaws to stay, Blackface told a servant to get a couple of others and a cart and go to the barracks in town and ask for his brother, Colonel Sun, and his sister-in-law, Mrs. Yue. They were to give them this message: "Our mistress is gravely ill, please come back to see her."

"Say only that I'm gravely ill and have something important to tell them," Auntie Gu admonished them. "Say they must come because it may be their last chance to hear what I have to say."

The servants went off, pushing the cart. Blackface placed himself in front of the door, to await his brother. At supper time the cart was seen approaching, bearing Mrs. Yue. Behind came Colonel Sun on horseback and a dozen or so soldiers, all heading for the third milestone. Blackface went inside to tell Auntie Gu. "My brother and sister-in-law are coming," he said.

"Do exactly as I said," said Auntie Gu.

Blackface went out to receive the visitors. He invited his sister-in-law to leave the cart and step inside to see his sick wife.

Colonel Sun dismounted and strode through the gate. He made an impressive figure: pale yellowish complexion, cheeks adorned with a luxuriant growth of whiskers, immense stature. His true name was Sun Li, but he was also nicknamed the Bilious Marshal, on account of his colour. He was a fine shot with the bow and a masterful horseman; his weapons were the long spear and a long steel whip, which now hung from his wrist, supple as a jointed bamboo and deadly as the gleam in a tiger's eye. Barbarians on distant shores surrendered the moment they saw him.

"What exactly is the matter with my sister-in-law?" he asked as he entered.

"Her illness is very strange, please come inside and talk," Blackface replied. He told some of his people to take the soldiers to the back and give them something to eat and drink, and to look after the Colonel's horse. Then he ushered his brother and sister-in-law into an inner room and asked them to be seated. After a little while he said: "Brother and sister-in-law, please come to see my wife."

They followed him into the sickroom, but there they found no patient. "But where is she?" Colonel Sun asked. As he spoke Auntie Gu entered the room, with the Forester and Rhinoceros at her heels. Colonel Sun asked: "Goodness me, is there really something the matter with you, sister-in-law?"

"Greetings, brother-in-law," she said. "I am infected with a need to rescue my cousins."

"How extraordinary!" said Colonel Sun. "To rescue what cousins?"

"It's no good pretending to be deaf and dumb," she said. "You're there in the city, you don't mean to say you don't know those two are my cousins, and therefore relatives of yours too?"

"I really don't understand," said Colonel Sun. "What two are you talking about?"

"With all due respect," she said, "I have to speak bluntly because it's so urgent. Those two, Xie Zhen and Xie Bao, Snake and Scorpion, have fallen into a trap set by Squire Mao of Dengyun Mountain and the clerk of the court, Wang, who are plotting against their lives. I have just made a plan with these two gentlemen, to go to town and break into the gaol to rescue them. After that we'll all go to Mount Liang and join the outlaws. I'm afraid there's going to be a big to-do, and you may well be implicated. That's why I pretended to be ill, so I could get you here and tell you the whole story. If you don't want to go with us we shall go to Mount Liang on our own. But the way things are nowadays at court, those who clear off escape without consequences, whereas those who remain pay the penalty. As the proverb says: 'Who's closest to the fire is the first to get burnt.' If you get sentenced and sent to prison because of us, there won't be anyone to take you food or look after you. So what do you propose to do?"

Colonel Sun said: "But I am an officer of the Dengzhou army, how can I do something like that!"

"If you won't, then it's got to be either you or me," she said, producing two swords that were by her side. At the same time the Forester and Rhinoceros drew their short swords.

"Wait, sister-in-law!" Colonel Sun cried. "Don't be so hasty. Wait till I've had a chance to consider all the consequences. I must think it over." Mrs. Yue, frightened out of her wits, went on screaming for a long time.

Auntie Gu said: "If you refuse to come with us, send sister-in-law away first, then we can get down to it."

Colonel Sun said: "If that's what we're going to do, let me go home first and pack some things and check up on what you told me, before we set out."

"Brother-in-law, it was one of your Yue relations who told us all this. Whilst we go and break into the gaol, you can go and do your packing, but make it quick."

Colonel Sun took a deep breath and said: "If this is what you've all decided, I don't see how I can refuse. I don't see why I should have to pay the penalty afterwards instead of you. Okay, okay, okay, let's just make our plans and then go."

The Forester was first told to go back to the camp on Dengyun Mountain to collect his valuables and horses, and bring the twenty or so men who were trustworthy to join them at the inn. When he had left, Blackface was sent into town to ask Lungs for the latest news. He would agree a time with Lungs for the raid, and ask him to secretly inform Snake and Scorpion.

Next day when the Forester had collected some money from his camp he returned with his men to lend a hand. There were also seven or eight trusted servants at Blackface's, so that together with the twenty soldiers Colonel Sun had brought they now had a force of more than forty. Blackface slaughtered two pigs and a sheep and everyone feasted. Auntie Gu, having concealed a sharp knife on her person and dressed herself up as a serving woman, left first. Blackface with Colonel Sun and the Forester with his nephew Rhinoceros made up two parties, each accompanied by the men they had brought. Then it was:

Hunting a tiger becomes a tiger hunting;
Wicked officials had better watch their step.
Hard iron cuts through the effects of bribery
An attack on the gaol takes the lid off the pot.

Back in Dengzhou gaol, Chief Warder Bao, bribed with Squire Mao's gifts, was continuing to do all he could to bring about the death of the two brothers. Lungs, meanwhile, was standing staff of office in hand beside the stone lion at the prison gate, when someone rang the bell. "Who is it?" he asked.

"The woman with the food," Auntie Gu replied.

After taking a look, Lungs opened the gate to let Auntie Gu in. He closed it behind her and led her down the corridor. Chief Warder Bao, who was sitting in the central pavilion, saw them and shouted: "Who is that woman? Who told her she could bring food in here? Nothing is supposed to get in here, not even the wind."

"It's a relative of Snake's and Scorpion's. She's bringing food for them."

"Don't let her into the cell," Chief Warder Bao bellowed. "You people take the stuff in yourselves."

Lungs took the food from her. He opened the cell door and gave it to the brothers. "That business you told us about yesterday," they asked, "how did it go?"

"Your cousin has come," he said. "You'll see her soon." He unlocked their fetters for them. At this moment another underling ran in and reported: "Colonel Sun is at the gate, he wants to come in."

"He's the garrison commander," Bao said. "What the devil is he doing in my prison? Don't open."

Auntie Gu now wandered into the central pavilion. Outside someone was shouting: "Colonel Sun is getting impatient. He keeps banging on the door."

Chief Warder Bao angrily started to go out. Shouting "Where are my brothers?" Auntie Gu drew out two gleaming knives. Bao realized trouble was coming and started to run for it. The brothers had lifted off their cangues and slipped out of their cell. They ran straight into the Chief Warder. Bao had no time to react. With one blow of the cangue, Scorpion smashed in his skull. Meanwhile Auntie Gu had got to work and had stuck four or five gaolers through. All shouting together they fought their way out of the gaol. Outside Colonel Sun and Blackface had stopped two of the guards escaping, but four others emerged and went racing off towards the government offices. But the Forester and Rhinoceros were just emerging from the government offices holding up the head of Wang, the clerk of the court. People fled screaming from the streets, as Colonel Sun rode out, grasping his bow with an arrow fitted and ready. The householders had all bolted their doors and didn't dare venture out. None of the policemen, when they saw it was Colonel Sun, had a mind to interfere. The Colonel, with his men around him, charged out of the city gates and headed for the third milestone. Mrs. Yue was helped into a cart,

孫立孫新大劫牢

Auntie Gu mounted a horse, and they were ready to start. But Snake and Scorpion said: "How can we let that villain Squire Mao get away with such an injustice and not pay him back?"

"You're right," said Colonel Sun. He told his brother, Blackface, and Lungs to go on ahead, escorting the cart and said the rest of them would catch them up later. Blackface and Lungs accordingly set off, escorting the cart.

Led by Colonel Sun, Snake and Scorpion, together with the Forester and Rhinoceros and half the troops, rode towards Squire Mao's. It so happened that Mao Zhongyi and his father were having a drink in celebration of the latter's birthday, so they were totally unprepared. With ferocious yells the party charged inside and killed everyone, Squire Mao, his son, and all the household, young and old. Not a soul was left living. In a bedroom they discovered a dozen bags of gold and silver and valuables, and from the stables they took seven or eight good horses, and four pack horses. Snake and Scorpion picked out some good clothes for themselves, and then they set fire to the manor and burnt it down. Then they mounted again. Within ten miles they had caught up with the cart and its escort, and they all rode on together. From landowners along the way they took four or five more horses. They continued on towards Mount Liang by night.

There are some lines which say:

On the one hand loyalty, virtue and independence of spirit; on the other hand debauchery, venality and unpatriotic behaviour. Evil natures, vile fortune and abuse of office heap sorrows upon good men. A shameful plot to steal a tiger gives rise to a scheme to break open the gaol. In a trice the city's bitterness turns to a sea of corpses.

In a few days they reached the Guv's inn. When the Forester saw the Guv he asked about Panther and Redeye. The Guv informed him how Song Jiang had gone to attack Zhu Castle and they had both gone with him. Two attempts to take the castle had failed, and it had been reported that Panther and Redeye had both been taken captive there, but it was not known what had become of them. He also told how the three Brothers Zhu were said to be assisted by an instructor known as Ironstaff, which was why the second attempt had failed. Colonel Sun grinned broadly when he heard this. "We have all come here because we want to join the company, but since we have done nothing to win acceptance, I'd like to offer you a plan for taking Zhu Castle. Do you think this could be our joining present?"

The Guv was delighted. "I can't wait to hear this plan," he said.

"That Ironstaff," Colonel Sun began, "had the same arms instructor as I did. All that I learnt about spearsmanship he knows too; all that he learnt about martial arts, I know through and through. Now, suppose we say we are a company that has been posted from Dengzhou to the garrison at Yunzhou and that I wanted to see him as we pass through. He is bound to come out and receive me. When we get inside I'll get him to collaborate and that will settle the whole thing. How about that?"

Colonel Sun had hardly finished explaining his plan to the Guv when a guard appeared and reported: "The Professor is coming down the mountain on his way to Zhu Castle to reinforce our troops."

As soon as he heard this the Guv told the man to go back quickly and ask the Professor to come and see them. Before he'd even finished speaking, a body of troops halted in front of the inn: they were led by the Halberdier, the Little Duke and the three Ruan brothers. Immediately behind them was the Professor, with five hundred troops, cavalry and foot. The Guv took them into the inn and introduced everyone, explaining that they wanted to join the company and were presenting a plan.

The Professor was delighted. "Since you are all prepared to join us in the mountain stronghold, I suggest that instead of going up the mountain right now, you be so good as to come with us to Zhu Castle so we may bring this meritorious business to a successful conclusion. What do you say?"

Colonel Sun and the rest of his party were happy to agree to this.

The Professor said: "I shall start at once. Let this be our plan: my troops will go first and you will all follow on behind as quickly as possible."

Accordingly the Professor reached Song Jiang's camp first. He found Song Jiang's plunged in gloom, his expression morose. The Professor produced some wine to lighten his comrade's mood and then told him what the Guv, Panther and Redeye all knew, that Colonel Sun, commander of the Dengzhou garrison and the Zhu Castle arms instructor, Ironstaff, both had the same master; and that the eight leaders who would be arriving shortly wanted to join the company of Mount Liang, and were offering to set up this scheme as their joining present. It had been decided to launch a conspiracy within the castle and after the business had been settled this way they would come to meet Song Jiang. When he had heard all this through, Song Jiang's joy knew no bounds, his gloom evaporated. He immediately ordered wine to be prepared to welcome the newcomers.

Colonel Sun ordered his company, with the cart, the troops and the horses, to halt somewhere and wait while he himself took Snake, Scorpion, the Forester, Rhinoceros, Blackface, Auntie Gu and Lungs, a party of eight, to see Song Jiang. After the greeting ceremonies, Song Jiang offered them all wine and a banquet. Of this no more.

The Professor gave everyone secret orders: what to do on the third day, what to do on the fifth day and so on. When they all had their orders, Colonel Sun and the others left as had been agreed, with the cart, troops and horses in a long line, heading for Zhu Castle to set the plan in motion.

Meanwhile the Professor said: "I want the Magic Messenger to go to the mountain stronghold and fetch four of the leaders for me. I have some urgent business for them."

If he had not sent the Magic Messenger post haste to the mountain to fetch these four, things would have been very different:

In the Marshes they'd have had to grow new wings;
Many a post would have fallen vacant on the Mountain.

Which four the Magic Messenger went to the mountain stronghold to fetch and what effect it was to have, you may read in the next chapter.

Chapter 50

The Professor carries out a double plan; Song Jiang attacks Zhu Castle for the third time!

Now the request the Professor made to the Magic Messenger was this: "Dear friend, go back to the mountain and get these four: Sterling, the Hand, the Ape and the Craftsman. Tell them to bring the tools of their trade and to make haste. I have a job for them to do."

The Magic Messenger departed.

At this moment a sentry came to report that young Hu, Steelbright's brother from the Hu manor to the west had arrived, bringing oxen and wine, and was requesting an interview. Song Jiang ordered him to be brought in.

Young Hu marched right into the tent, bowed and declared: "My sister in a moment of madness, due undoubtedly to her youth and ignorance of the ways of the world, foolishly attacked you and has been taken prisoner. I beg you to be merciful. This rash action which brought about her captivity is owing to the fact that she had been promised to the Zhu family. If you will release her, we shall be happy to supply you with anything you may need."

"Please be seated and let us talk," Song Jiang replied. "That unmannerly crowd in Zhu Castle have insulted us without provocation, which is why we have come here to seek redress. We have no quarrel with the Hu family. But your sister led a force to capture one of our leaders, which is why we returned the compliment by taking your sister prisoner. If you will return our leader to us, I will release your sister to you."

"Unfortunately," young Hu replied, "the people from Zhu Castle have already taken him away."

"Then where exactly is he?" the Professor interposed.

"He's locked up in Zhu Castle. It's quite impossible for me to get him."

"If you won't go and get him for us, how can we return your sister?" said Song Jiang.

"Wait a moment, brother," said the Professor. "Let me say something first. Mr. Hu, some time hereafter you're going to hear noises from Zhu Castle. Your people, I trust, will not send reinforcements to help them out. If people from Zhu try to take refuge with you, you had better tie them up. When you have taken some captives your sister will be returned to you. The fact is that at present she is not here in the camp. She has already been sent back to the mountain stronghold and handed over to Squire Song for safekeeping. But you can rest easy. We know what we're doing."

"We will certainly not give them aid now. If anyone from the castle seeks refuge with us we will take them prisoner and hand them over to you," said Hu Cheng.

"If you do that it will be better than a gift of gold and silk to us."

Hu Cheng prostrated himself and left.

Meanwhile, Colonel Sun had changed the emblem on his banner to "Colonel Sun, commander of Dengzhou troops" and was leading his company towards the rear entrance of Zhu Castle. Those watching from the walls saw the Dengzhou banner and went to report. When Ironstaff heard that it was Colonel Sun, he came out to see for himself. He said to the Brothers Zhu: "Colonel Sun is my friend. When we were young we studied martial arts under the same master. I wonder why he's coming here?"

Taking some twenty or more troops, he had the gates opened and the drawbridge lowered and rode out to meet the visitor. Colonel Sun and his men dismounted and after the exchange of courtesies Ironstaff asked: "If you belong to the Dengzhou garrison, brother, what are you doing here?"

Colonel Sun replied: "An order has come from the regional commander-in-chief transferring me to the garrison at Yunzhou, to strengthen their defences against the bandits of the Marshes of Mount Liang. Along the way I heard that you were here at Zhu

吳斈究双掌連環計

Castle, so I came to see you. We approached by the front gate first, but I found the castle was invested by a hostile force encamped outside the village. I thought it unwise to risk an engagement, so I made inquiries in the village and found a way round to the back gate. So here I am, come to greet you."

Ironstaff said: "We've been fighting with the Mount Liang bandits recently. We've got several of their leaders here as prisoners. We now want to capture the leader, Song Jiang, and hand him over to the authorities. Heaven must have sent you at this moment to lend a hand. It's gilt on the gingerbread for us, it's like fresh rain on parched earth."

Colonel Sun laughed. "Don't expect too much of me, but I'll see what I can do to help catch those slaves and complete your good work."

Ironstaff was delighted, and took them all into the castle right away. The drawbridge was raised again and the gates closed. Colonel Sun and all his company were settled in, with their carts, weapons, men and horses. After changing their clothes they all went to the main hall to meet. Courtesies were exchanged and Ironstaff said to Baron Zhu, "This dear friend of mine, Colonel Sun, sometimes called the Bilious Marshal, is a commander of Dengzhou garrison. Now the high command is sending him to reinforce the defences of Yunzhou."

The Baron said: "I too shall place myself under your command."

Colonel Sun replied: "You do me too much honour. I trust you will favour me with your advice and instructions."

The Brothers Zhu now asked everyone to be seated. Colonel Sun began the conversation with: "You have fought many days, you must be weary of battle."

Dragon Zhu said: "But we still haven't won. My brothers and I are indeed weary from long days in the saddle."

Colonel Sun now told Auntie Gu and Mrs. Yue, the two sisters-in-law to go to the back room and pay their respects to the family, and asked Blackface, Snake and Scorpion to come in and be introduced. "These three are my friends," he said. He pointed out Lungs and said: "This is the official who was sent from Yunzhou to fetch me." Pointing to the Forester and Rhinoceros he said: "These two are army officers from Dengzhou."

Now although Baron Zhu and his sons were not stupid, they could see that Colonel Sun had his family and luggage with him as well as the cart, weapons, men and horses, and in addition he was a friend of Ironstaff's, so they suspected nothing. They simply went about killing oxen and horses to welcome the visitors. There was great feasting.

A couple of days later, on the third day, a castle sentry came to report: "Song Jiang has moved his men into position to attack the castle."

Wildcat Zhu said: "I shall ride out and get the villain myself!"

The drawbridge was lowered and he charged out at the head of more than a hundred cavalry. They soon came upon a body of men, around five hundred in all, surrounding a leader, fully equipped with bow and arrows. This leader, who slapped his horse and dashed forward, was Colonel Hua, the Archer.

When he saw him, Wildcat Zhu kicked his horse, levelled his lance and charged. Colonel Hua likewise urged his horse on to the encounter. There at Lone Dragon Heights the two fought a dozen or so bouts and neither had the advantage. Then Colonel Hua gave his adversary the slip, turned his horse and cantered off, tempting his adversary to follow. Wildcat Zhu was just about to give chase when a friend behind him spoke out: "Commander, don't follow him. I'm sure it's a trick. He's an expert archer."

Wildcat Zhu listened to the advice. Reining in his horse, he abandoned the chase and led his men back to the castle. The drawbridge was raised again and they watched Colonel Hua withdrawing also with his troops. Wildcat Zhu dismounted right in front of the main hall and went to an inner room to drink wine. Colonel Sun inquired: "How many brigands did you capture today, Commander?"

"The villains have got a certain Colonel Hua in their ranks. He's pretty handy with a spear. I fought more than fifty bouts with him, but then he ran away. I was going to chase him, but my men told me he's a good archer. So we broke off the engagement and came back."

"I've no skill to boast of," said Colonel Sun. "But another day I'll have a go and see if I can take some of them."

At the banquet that evening Lungs was asked to sing. Everyone enjoyed the performance. After the banquet they all rested. At midday on the fourth day, one of the castle guards reported: "Song Jiang's troops are advancing again!"

The Brothers Zhu armed themselves and hurried to the front gate. Gongs and drums could be heard in the distance, amid shouts and waving banners. Before long the enemy were facing them in battle order. By now Baron Zhu was sitting above the gate. On his left was Ironstaff, on his right Colonel Sun and the three Brothers Zhu. Some of the troops that Colonel Sun had brought were also lined up on either side.

Now from Song Jiang's ranks Leopard's Head emerged and began hurling insults. Dragon Zhu in a frenzy shouted for the drawbridge to be lowered. He grasped his spear and mounted. Followed by several hundred troops he hurled himself with a great shout on Leopard's Head's force. From the castle gate a drum began to beat and from both sides every bow and crossbow opened fire at the opposing lines. Leopard's Head levelled his snake head lance and joined combat with Dragon Zhu. They fought more than thirty bouts, but neither prevailed. Gongs rang out on either side and both men turned their horses. Tiger Zhu was furious. He grasped his sword, mounted and galloped to the front. In ringing tones he challenged Song Jiang to single combat. He had hardly finished when Song Jiang's ranks parted and out rode a horseman: it was Mu Hong the Unstoppable, answering Tiger Zhu's challenge. They fought more than thirty bouts but again neither had the advantage. This enraged Wildcat Zhu. He grasped his spear, leapt onto his horse and with two hundred cavalry launched himself against the front rank. From Song Jiang's ranks Morbid rode forward with his spear and rushed against Wildcat Zhu.

When Colonel Sun saw the two sides engaged in such furious combat, he could wait no longer. Calling to his brother Blackface to bring his spear, armour, helmet and robe, he accoutred himself and went to get his horse, which was a piebald. He fitted the saddle, securing it with three girths, hung the jointed whip from his wrist, grasped his spear and mounted. As a gong sounded in Zhu Castle, Colonel Sun took to the field. On Song Jiang's side, Leopard's Head, Mu Hong, and Morbid all reined in their horses and rejoined the main force. As he galloped forth, Colonel Sun said: "Let's see now if we can capture the bastards." Causing his horse to rear up, he shouted: "You there, you scum, if there is anyone among you who thinks he's good, let him answer me in single combat!"

With a flurry of bridle bells from among Song Jiang's ranks a rider galloped forth. All eyes turned towards him. It was Madcap, taking up Colonel Sun's challenge. The two horses closed, two spears were brandished. They fought fifty bouts before Colonel Sun feinted and allowed Madcap to lunge with his spear, dodging as he did so and lightly lifting the other from his horse and dragging him to the castle gates where he threw him down and shouted: "Come and tie him up!"

After harrying Song Jiang's troops a while, the Brothers Zhu scattered and brought their troops back to the gate tower. There they found Colonel Sun, reclining with a cup of wine among an admiring crowd.

"How many of the bastards have you got?" the Colonel inquired.

Baron Zhu said: "First we got one called Shi Qian, the Flea. Then we got Panther and one they call the Tamer. Steelbright, from Hu manor, took a certain Short-Arse Wang, and our troops took Thunderclap and Redeye. And now you yourself have captured this Madcap, he's the one that burnt my inn down. So we've got seven."

"Don't let any harm come to them," said Colonel Sun. "Have seven prison carts made to put them in, and give them food, to keep them strong and healthy, don't let them wither away, it doesn't look good. Later when we get Song Jiang we'll send the whole lot up to the Eastern Capital and get the Emperor to proclaim it, and make the Brothers Zhu famous."

Baron Zhu said: "We're so lucky to have your help, Colonel. This will be the end of the brigands of Mount Liang, I'd say."

Colonel Sun was invited to a banquet in an inner room, while Madcap was placed in the prison cart.

Now, you must understand, friends, that Madcap's skill in fighting was no less than Colonel Sun's. But they wanted to deceive the people in Zhu Castle. He purposely allowed himself to be taken to make people trust Colonel Sun.

Colonel Sun now secretly sent the Forester and Rhinoceros, uncle and nephew, with Lungs to the back of the castle to examine the gates and see how many ways in and out there were. When Panther and Redeye saw the Forester and Rhinoceros they were very excited. Lungs checked that there was no one around and told them all the news. Meanwhile Auntie Gu and Mrs. Yue were counting all the entrances and exits to the inner rooms.

Until the fifth day Colonel Sun and the others amused themselves strolling in the castle grounds. At dawn on the fifth day, after breakfast, one of the castle guards reported: "Song Jiang is coming to attack the castle and he has divided his forces into four columns."

"Why should he divide them into four columns?" said Colonel Sun. "There's nothing for your troops to worry about. All we need to do is to be prepared. First organize some hooks and ropes. We want to take them alive, dead ones are no use."

Everyone in the castle armed. The Baron himself took a company of men to a vantage point on the gate tower. They saw a body of troops approaching from the east, with a leader at its head. This was Leopard's Head Lin Chong, and behind him came the White-Water Dragon and Ruan the Second, with about five hundred troops. Another five hundred or so were approaching from the west, led by Colonel Hua the Archer with the Pilot and White Eel. And five hundred troops were coming straight towards the observers in the tower over the south gate. These were led by Mu Hong the Unstoppable, Morbid and Iron Ox. There were enemy troops on all sides. Drums and gongs were sounding. The noise was deafening.

Ironstaff said: "It's not going to be an easy fight today. I will go to the back gate and deal with those who are coming from the northwest."

Dragon Zhu said: "I shall go to the front gate and deal with the ones who are coming up from the east."

Tiger Zhu said: "I will go to the back gate too, and deal with the ones from the southwest."

Wildcat Zhu said: "I shall ride out of the front gate and capture Song Jiang. He's the important one."

Baron Zhu was well pleased and offered them all wine. Everyone mounted and with three hundred cavalry they burst out of the castle gates. The remainder guarded the castle precincts and lined up cheering on the battlements. By this time the Forester and Rhinoceros had hidden big axes on the left hand side of the prison door. Snake and Scorpion had concealed weapons somewhere near the back gate. Blackface and Lungs were keeping guard on the left and right of the front gate. Auntie Gu left one of the soldiers to look after Mrs. Yue and with her two swords took up a position next to the hall, listening to the talk, and ready to spring into action.

Now three drums began to beat in the castle, a gun was fired and the gates opened, front and back, the drawbridge was raised, and on four sides the parties went separately into battle. Soon after, Colonel Sun took a dozen troops and stationed them on the drawbridge. Now Blackface by the gate raised the signal flags they had brought with them on the gate tower and Lungs, brandishing his spear, began to sing. When they heard the singing, the Forester and Rhinoceros gave several loud whistles and whirling the big axes cut down the dozen or so prison guards in no time at all and broke open the prison carts. This released seven raging heroes, who each found himself a weapon and began to yell blue murder. Auntie Gu with her two swords charged into the inner chambers and systematically killed every one of the women in the hall. The Baron, seeing the situation had turned so ugly, was on the point of throwing himself down the well, but was stabbed by Madcap first and had his head cut off. A dozen or so heroes went on killing the castle's defenders independently. Snake and Scorpion at the back gate set fire to the piles of hay for the horses and a fiery column of black smoke began to mount to the heavens.

The four columns of troops, seeing the castle on fire, made desperate efforts to push forward. When Tiger Zhu saw the fire he first tried to return. But Colonel Sun guarding the drawbridge, bellowed "Where the hell do you think you're going?" and blocked the way. Tiger Zhu in consternation turned his horse's head and charged Song Jiang's lines again. This time the Halberdier and the Little Duke raised their halberds and brought down both man and horse. The troops then fell on him and turned him into mincemeat. The foremost ranks fled in all directions. Colonel Sun and his brother welcomed Song Jiang into the castle. Meanwhile Dragon Zhu's eastern column had found Leopard's Head too much for them and were streaming back towards the castle. When they reached the drawbridge they saw Snake and Scorpion by the back gate pitching the defenders' bodies one by one into the flames. Dragon Zhu desperately wrenched his horse's head round and fled northwards. Suddenly he ran into Iron Ox, leaping towards him and whirling his two axes. In a trice the horse's legs were cut from under him and before Dragon Zhu could lift a finger he was thrown headlong. One blow from Iron Ox's axe and his head was rolling on the ground.

When troops from the castle reported the situation to Wildcat Zhu, he dared not return so he went straight to Hu manor to seek refuge. There Hu Cheng ordered his people to arrest him and tie him up. Hu Cheng was on his way to hand Wildcat Zhu over to Song Jiang when they had the bad luck to run into Iron Ox who with one blow of the axe cut off Wildcat Zhu's head. The retainers fled in all directions, while Iron Ox, still whirling his axes, turned on Hu Cheng. Things did not look at all good to Hu Cheng, so he galloped off into the wilderness, forsaking all family ties for the sake of preserving his life. He settled in Yan'an district, and later he made good, becoming a famous military commander.

Iron Ox, meanwhile, went on killing as he pleased. He charged into Hu manor and killed Squire Hu and his entire household, every one of them — not a soul was left. He told his men to get all the horses and collect up all the valuables and cash in the manor, which were loaded onto the forty or fifty packhorses they found.

宋公明三打祝家庄

The place was then set alight and Iron Ox returned to hand over his contribution.

Song Jiang was now seated in the main hall of Zhu Castle and the leaders were coming to claim their honours. They had taken four or five hundred prisoners, more than five hundred horses and innumerable livestock. Song Jiang was delighted with the result. "The only pity is that Ironstaff was killed. He was a good man." As he was expressing this regret, someone announced: "Iron Ox has set fire to the Hu manor and is coming to present the heads he has cut off."

"Hu Cheng came and surrendered to us the other day," said Song Jiang. "Who gave Iron Ox permission to kill him? How dare he burn their house down!"

At this moment Iron Ox walked in, covered in blood from head to foot, the two axes swinging at his waist. He went straight up to Song Jiang, saluted and said: "I killed Dragon Zhu and I killed Wildcat Zhu too, cut off their heads. Hu Cheng got away, blast him, but I killed Squire Hu and all his family beautifully. I've come to claim my reward."

Song Jiang roared at him: "We saw you kill Dragon Zhu, but who says it was you that killed the others?"

"I killed whoever I came across, and then when I was pursing them to Hu manor I met Steelbright's brother coming out with Wildcat Zhu so I cut off his head with my axe but unfortunately the other bugger got away. The rest of the family I killed, there's absolutely no one left."

Song Jiang shouted: "You stupid bastard! Who told you to go there? Didn't you know Hu Cheng came the other day to surrender, bringing us gifts of oxen and wine? Why did you contravene my orders and go there to kill them all on your own initiative?"

"You may have forgotten, but I haven't," said Iron Ox. "The other day the bastard told that bloody woman to catch you and kill you. But now you want to be all merciful. You haven't even married his sister yet, but you want to behave like a brother-in-law."

Song Jiang shouted: "You moron, stop talking such bollocks. What do I want with the woman? I've got other things in mind. All right, you black bastard, how many did you take alive?"

Iron Ox replied: "Who the fuck would bother with that? If I saw any alive I cut their heads off."

Song Jiang shouted: "For deliberately flouting a military order, you wretch, you should be executed. But as your reward for killing Dragon Zhu and Wildcat Zhu I will commute the sentence. Next time you disobey orders you will not be pardoned."

Iron Ox merely grinned: "Even if I don't get a reward, I had a great time with all that killing!"

At this point the commander-in-chief, Professor Wu Yong was seen with his troops arriving at the castle to celebrate with Song Jiang. After a discussion, Song Jiang and the Professor decided that Zhu Castle and its environs should be obliterated. But Madcap made a request: "There's an old man here, Zhongli by name, who is truly charitable. He told me the way and I owe my life to him. When there's someone as kind-hearted and good as that around, we surely oughtn't to destroy the place."

When he heard this, Song Jiang told Madcap to go and find the old man. In a little while Madcap returned to the castle with him and brought him in to pay his respects to Song Jiang and the Professor. Song Jiang presented the old man with a bundle of silver and silk, praising him as an example to the people: "But for your kind-heartedness, we would have swept this whole village away. Not one family would have been spared. But because you showed such goodness, we will pardon everyone in the village."

The old man prostrated himself and Song Jiang said: "For many days we have been here turning your lives upside down. But today we have destroyed Zhu Castle and rid you all of a great scourge. Now every household shall receive a hundred catties of rice as a gesture of humanity."

The old man was given the responsibility of distributing the gift, while the bulk of the grain remaining in the castle was loaded onto carts. The valuables and cash were distributed among the men of the three companies as bounty. The oxen, sheep, mules, horses and other animals were sent to the mountain to be disposed of there. The overthrow of Zhu Castle produced five hundred thousand catties of provisions. Song Jiang was delighted.

All the leaders, men and horses now prepared for departure, including all the new arrivals — Colonel Sun, his brother Black-face, Snake and Scorpion, the Forester and Rhinoceros, uncle and nephew, Lungs and Auntie Gu — and the seven who had been freed. Colonel Sun and his party, with horses, possessions and family, including Mrs. Yue and followers headed for the mountain in a big troop. All the villagers, young and old, turned out to see them off, burning incense and lighting lamps to honour them and thank them. As soon as the others had all mounted, Song Jiang divided the troops into three columns. They set off, the leaders knocking their whips on the stirrups, the rearguard all singing a victory song.

Now our story divides in two.

First let us deal with Skyhawk Li Ying, who, now fortunately recovered from his arrow wound, had shut himself up in his manor and would not come out. Secretly however he regularly sent out scouts to gather news of events at Zhu Castle. When he learnt that Song Jiang had destroyed it, his shock and his pleasure were about equal. But then his scouts reported that the provincial governor had arrived with a force of around fifty men to investigate the Zhu Castle affair. Skyhawk hurriedly instructed Uglymug to open the manor gates, lower the drawbridge and let them in. Wrapping a strip of gauze round his injured arm, Skyhawk came out to greet the visitors and invited them into the main hall. The governor dismounted and entered. He took the place of honour, his secretary sat down beside him, after them a police sergeant and several court officers, and below the steps a number of prison guards and attendants.

Skyhawk prostrated himself before the governor and then stood and waited. The governor asked: "What's all this about fighting at Zhu Castle?"

"I had been shot with an arrow by Wildcat Zhu and wounded in the left shoulder. I know nothing about Zhu Castle because I kept my doors closed and didn't go out."

"Rubbish!" said the governor. "Someone in Zhu Castle accused you of being in league with the bandits of Mount Liang and so you invited them down to destroy the castle. The other day you accepted saddles, horses, sheep, wine and patterned silk from those bandits. How can you lie about it?"

"I respect the law," said Skyhawk. "I would never receive anything from them."

The governor said: "Who's going to believe that? You'd better come back to the government offices with me. Confronting you with our witness should settle it." He ordered the bailiffs to arrest Skyhawk and take him to the government offices to find out which of the two was lying — he or the Zhu witness. The two court officers tied Skyhawk up. When the governor, surrounded by his men, had mounted, he asked: "Is that Mr. Du, the manor steward?"

"Yes, sir," said Uglymug.

"Your name is also mentioned in the accusation. We'd better take you along too and lock you up with him."

The party rode out of the manor gates. So Skyhawk and Uglymug both left the manor under arrest and were carried off without delay. But they had barely gone ten miles when from the edge of a wood out rushed Song Jiang, Leopard's Head, Colonel Hua the Archer, Morbid and Madcap, together with a small body of troops, and barred the way. Leopard's Head gave a ringing cry: "The company of the Marshes of Mount Liang are here!"

The governor and his suite dared not put up any resistance. They abandoned Skyhawk and Uglymug and ran for their lives. Song Jiang gave orders for them to be caught. Some of the others went after them, and in a little while returned and said: "We caught some of them and killed that sodding governor, but we don't know where the others went to."

Skyhawk and Uglymug were released from their bonds and let out of the cages. Two horses were brought for them to ride. Then Song Jiang said: "Mr. Li, sir, I would like you to come with us to hide on Mount Liang for a while. What do you say?"

Skyhawk said: "That's quite impossible. Your killing the governor has got nothing to do with me."

Song Jiang smiled and said: "How can you expect the authorities to make that distinction? If we leave you, they will certainly consider you to be implicated. If you don't want to become an outlaw, sir, at least come and rest in the mountain stronghold for a few days. When we hear that it has all blown over, it will be time enough for you to go back."

So, however unwillingly, Skyhawk and Uglymug were obliged to go too, riding with the outlaws. For how could they go back?

They all rode on till they reached Mount Liang. When they got to the camp, the leader Chao Gai came down the mountain with drums and fifes to greet them. Some wine was drunk to welcome them and then they all went up to the Assembly Hall in the main camp, where they sat round in a circle and Skyhawk was invited to meet the other leaders.

After the introductions, Skyhawk had something to ask Song Jiang: "You have brought us here to the camp and introduced us to all the leaders, it wouldn't be difficult to accept your way of life, but what would become of my family? Please let me go back now."

"You are mistaken, sir," said the Professor with a smile. "Your family are all on their way to the camp and your manor is burnt to the ground. What would you go back to?"

Skyhawk couldn't believe his ears, until a moment later he saw carts, arms, men and horses filing up the mountain and recognized the people from his manor, with all his family and household. To his anxious questioning, his wife replied: "After the governor had taken you away, two inspectors and four sergeants came round with three hundred men and registered all our things. They asked us very politely to get in the carts and then fetched everything out of the house, boxes, trunks, cattle and sheep, horses, mules, donkeys and so on. Then they set fire to it and it burnt down."

Skyhawk cursed his fate when he heard this. Chao Gai and Song Jiang got up and came to apologize: "You see, we had heard so much good of you. That's why we thought up this scheme, we do ask you to forgive us."

They spoke so politely Skyhawk felt he had to go along with it.

Song Jiang said: "We would like you and your family to reside in the building at the side of the main hall."

Skyhawk saw that all the members of his own family were now among the leaders in the hall, at the front or at the back, and he said to his wife: "We must do as they say, then."

At the behest of Song Jiang and the others, the time was now devoted to conversation and rejoicing, and Song Jiang now spoke with a big smile on his face. "Sir, I'd like you to meet those two inspectors and the governor." The "governor" was in fact the Hand and the two "inspectors" were the Magic Messenger and Panther. The governor's secretary was Sterling, the court officers were the Craftsman and the Ape. He also introduced the four sergeants, who were the White-Water Dragon, White Eel, the Flautist and the Daytime Rat. Skyhawk looked on open-mouthed and speechless.

Song Jiang quickly called for oxen and horses to be killed and Skyhawk was invited to join them in celebrating the arrival of twelve new leaders, to wit Skyhawk himself, Colonel Sun and his brother Blackface, Snake and Scorpion, the Forester and Rhinoceros (uncle and nephew), Uglymug, Lungs, the Flea, the woman warrior Steelbright and Auntie Gu and also Mrs. Yue. A separate banquet was held for Skyhawk's family in the hall at the back. All the troops who had fought also had their reward. Amid much tootling of flutes and tapping of drums the company of heroes feasted in the main hall and did not break up till the early hours, when the new leaders retired to their allotted accommodation.

Next day another feast was held because there was a matter to be settled by all the leaders. Song Jiang called out Short-Arse and said to him: "Since the early days on Windy Mountain I promised you a wedding. It has been much on my mind that I have not yet fulfilled that promise. But now my father has a daughter whom he will offer you as wife."

Song Jiang asked Squire Song to bring forward Steelbright. He himself proposed to her on behalf of Short-Arse, saying: "This brother of mine, Wang Ying, whose martial skill is great, though not equal to yours, was originally promised a wife by me, but this business has long remained unfinished. Now, dear sister, you are my father's adopted daughter, all the rest of us here are the witnesses, this is a most auspicious day, so then, dear sister, will you accept to become the wife of Wang Ying?"

Seeing that Song Jiang was so honourable and serious, Steelbright could hardly refuse. In reply she kowtowed twice and thanked him. Chao Gai and the others were well pleased. They praised Song Jiang saying he was a true gentleman. The rest of the day was to be entirely devoted to feasting and celebration. During the banquet however a guard came up the mountain to report: "There is someone from Yuncheng district at the Crocodile's inn wanting to speak with you."

When they heard who it was, Chao Gai and Song Jiang were very excited. "If that honourable man is coming to join us, it will satisfy a long-felt wish."

It was truly a case of:

No hero the man who mixes gratitude and revenge;
He who knows black from white is truly a man.

If you want to know who this person from Yuncheng was, you must read the next chapter.

Chapter 51

Sergeant Lei's aroused, a singer's killed; Whiskers loses an innocent child!

Now on the day that Song Jiang arranged the marriage of Steelbright and Short-Arse and everyone praised him for his humanity and a feast was held to celebrate the event, a messenger came up from the Crocodile's inn to report: "Our men have stopped a group of travellers who were passing near the wood on the highway, and apparently one of them is Sergeant Lei from Yuncheng. The Crocodile has invited him to stay. He is being well looked after with wine and food at the inn. They sent me to tell you."

Chao Gai and Song Jiang were very excited by this news, and with the Professor and all the other leaders they went down the mountain to welcome the newcomer, whom the Crocodile had already sent across in the boat to Golden Sands Landing.

Song Jiang hurriedly prostrated himself and said: "It's a long time since I saw you, but you have always been in my thoughts. What brings you here to our place?"

Sergeant Lei immediately returned the courtesy and said: "I was sent by my office on official business to Dongchang district. I was just on my way back when I was stopped at the crossroads by a group of men who demanded I pay a toll. When I happened to mention my name, Mr. Zhu began insisting that I should stay."

"Heaven be thanked for this!" Song Jiang exclaimed. He ushered Sergeant Lei into the main hall and all the leaders were invited to meet him. Wine was served. Sergeant Lei stayed five days and each day conversed with Song Jiang. It occurred to Chao Gai to ask Sergeant Lei for news of his colleague, Sergeant Zhu, and he answered: "Sergeant Zhu is now working in the prison service of our district, the new governor is very pleased with him." Song Jiang brought the conversation round to the subject of Sergeant Lei's joining the company on Mount Liang. He refused, pleading an aged mother as his excuse. He would join them, he said, when she passed away.

Eventually Sergeant Lei prostrated himself and announced his intention of departing. Although Song Jiang and the others repeatedly urged him to stay he would not. All the leaders gave him presents of money and silk; Song Jiang and Chao Gai were no exception of course. With a big bag to carry this booty, Sergeant Lei set off down the mountain, the leaders seeing him off as far as the road. After crossing on the ferry he took the road to Yuncheng. Of this no more.

When Chao Gai and Song Jiang returned to the Assembly Hall in the main camp, they asked the Professor to assign the various duties. The Professor did so, after discussing it with Song Jiang, and all the leaders were invited to assemble to hear the roster read.

"Blackface and Auntie Gu," Song Jiang began, "are innkeepers by trade, so I want them to replace the two Tong brothers, who will be employed elsewhere." He went on to assign the Flea to assist the Guv at his inn, Lungs to assist the Crocodile and Whitey to assist the Executioner, Li Li, so that each of the four inns north, south, east and west, was now provided with two leaders, selling wine and food and recruiting good men from all over the place. "Steelbright and Short-Arse can go to the other side of the mountain and look after the horses. Let the two Tong brothers guard Golden Sands Landing. Let the Forester and Rhinoceros guard Duck's-Bill Landing. The Tamer and the Dandy are to go down to guard the highway on this side of the mountain with their cavalry. Snake and Scorpion must guard the first gate on this side of the mountain. Door-God and Skyscraper will guard the second gate at the Place of Many Meanderings. The Red-Haired Devil, and Mu Hong the Unstoppable will guard the third gate, the entrance to the main camp itself. The Ruan brothers will guard the waterside camp on the south of the mountain. As before, Flagpole shall supervise the boats. Skyhawk Li Ying, Uglymug and the

Calculator will look after the finances and provisioning and treasury in the main camp. The Nine-Tailed Turtle and the Pill Monger can supervise the building of a lookout for the main fortress. The Ape can go back to supervising the manufacture of clothing, armour, banners and war robes. Smiler and my brother Iron Fan will be in charge of banquets. Mu Chun the Irrepressible and Green-Eyes will deal with housing and fences. Hand and the Craftsman will set up an office for correspondence with guests and visitors. Sterling as before will be responsible for military regulations and penalties. The remainder, the Halberdier, the Little Duke, Colonel Sun, Golden Wings, the Flautist, Redeye, Panther, and the Daytime Rat, will each take one of the eight sides of the stronghold to keep watch. Chao Gai, myself and the Professor will reside in the headquarters at the top of the mountain. Colonel Hua and Thunderclap will reside in the camp on the left. Leopard's Head and the Magic Messenger will reside in the camp on the right. The White-Water Dragon, and Iron Ox will be based in front of the mountain in the mountain stronghold. The Pilot and White Eel will be based at the back of the mountain. Morbid and Madcap will guard the Assembly Hall, on either side."

Once all the leaders had been allotted their duties, they took it in turn each day to give a celebratory banquet. The protocol of the camp was now clearly established. As it says in the poem:

At that camp on its lofty mountain crest,
Establishing order is what they do best,
They've all but the trappings of life at the court,
And such fame in the marshes as cannot be bought.

Now when Sergeant Lei left Mount Liang, shouldering his pack and gripping his halberd, he set off for Yuncheng. Arriving there, he first went home to see his mother. Then he changed his clothes and went to the government offices to report to the district magistrate and deliver the reply from his mission. After delivering his verbal report and returning his official warrant to the office, he went home to rest. After that his life continued as before, going in to the office every day, making himself available for the next official mission he might be sent on.

One day as he was waiting outside the office he heard someone calling behind him: "When did you get back, sergeant?"

Turning to look, he saw it was one second brother Li, a well-known local idler.

"Just a few days ago," he replied.

"You've been away, so you probably don't know there's a new singer from the Eastern Capital in town. She's absolutely phenomenal, in every department. Fleur, they call her. The girl called on you but you were away on official business. She's performing at the theatre now, she does all the well-known songs. They put on some kind of variety show every day, with dancing, or music or singing and it draws a huge audience. Why don't you come and take a look? That girl's really something."

Since he had nothing better to do, Sergeant Lei agreed to go with this Li to the playhouse. There were signs written in gold characters over the door and from the flag-pole hung banners as tall as a man. They went in and found seats right in the front row on the left. On stage a comic curtain-raiser was being performed. Li left Sergeant Lei there in the crowd while he went out to get some wine. After the curtain-raiser, an old man came on, with a turban wound about his head and a tea-coloured silk shirt, trailing a long black cloth and carrying a fan. He opened his mouth and declaimed: "I am from the Eastern Capital, Bai Yuqiao's my name. I am old now, but my daughter Fleur supports me with her singing and dancing and her music. She's always at your service, to entertain you."

Next, to the clamour of gongs Fleur Bai stepped out onto the stage and curtsyed in all directions. Taking up the gong stick she beat out a rapid rhythm like the sound of scattering beans, ending with a quick crack of the clappers, and then recited a short poem. After this she said: "My next number is a truly beautiful tale. It's a romantic and refined piece, entitled 'A Yuzhang love story'." She launched into the piece, singing and speaking in turns, to repeated applause from all present. From his position in the front row Sergeant Lei had a good view of her, and indeed she was as accomplished as she was beautiful:

Floating gauzes like the drifting snow, lustrous tresses like massed clouds, a pair of cherry lips, a complexion of peaches and apricots, a willow waist, a seductive manner and a sweet nature. The singing tones soft as the fluting of birds in the branches, the movements in the dance proud as a phoenix stalking through flowers. The melody is classical, nothing forced or unnatural. Between high notes and low, from quick to slow, the voice moves, all in accordance with the rules of harmony; and the variations of emphasis and mood are ruled by superlative taste. The bamboo flute produces ravishing trills, the clappers impart an elegant emphasis to each word.

When the story reached its climax, Fleur's father cried: "Well, we don't grow rich by horse-trading or gambling, but we do provide something to satisfy the thoughtful and discerning. We've had the applause, friends. Now my daughter will take a turn among you for a little number known as drumming up support."

Fleur took up the plate and struck a pose, saying: "At a rich door I begin, on a wealthy spot I stay my steps, I travel to a lucky place, I journey by a happy way, the hand you see before your face, empty send it not away."

Her father said: "Off you go now, girl, our public are eager to show their appreciation."

Holding out her plate Fleur stopped first before Sergeant Lei. But when the latter felt about him for money, he found he hadn't got a cent.

"I'm afraid I haven't got anything on me," he said. "Tomorrow I'll reward you."

Smiling ironically she said: "'If the vinegar on top's got no bite, the rest is going to be too weak.' Really now, sir, you've got a seat in the front row, you ought to give a lead."

Blushing scarlet, Sergeant Lei said: "I really didn't bring anything, it's not that I would withhold it."

"Are you telling me you come to the playhouse and don't think to bring any money?" she asked.

"I'll give you four or five taels of silver, it's no problem," he said. "Only today I really did forget to bring it."

"You haven't a cent, but you talk about four or five taels of silver, that's like telling me to quench my thirst by looking at plums, or fill my stomach with a painted cake!"

Her father said: "Where's your eyes, child? Can't you see this is just a small town person, a bumpkin, why do you go on asking him? You should look for some man of real understanding and culture, and get him to start the ball rolling."

"Are you suggesting I'm uncultured?" Sergeant Lei protested.

"As you don't know what every mother's son ought to know about how to behave, there's as much hope of any culture from you as for a dog to grow horns."

At this point everyone rose to their feet.

Lei Heng gave a roar: "How dare you insult me, you cheeky bugger!"

The old man replied: "And if I say you're a cowherd from the sticks, so what?"

Someone who knew Sergeant Lei shouted out: "That's not right! It's Sergeant Lei, an officer of our district."

"Seems more like an arsehole to me," said the performer.

This was beyond Sergeant Lei's enduring. He leapt up onto the stage and made for the artiste. With one blow of his fist and one kick he split his lip and knocked his teeth out.

When the bystanders saw the man was badly hurt, they intervened to break up the fight, advising Sergeant Lei to leave. The audience dispersed too, amid scenes of pandemonium.

Now Fleur had previously been a close friend of the new magistrate when he resided in the Eastern Capital, which is indeed why she had now chosen to ply her trade in Yuncheng. When Sergeant Lei hit her father and she saw he was seriously hurt, she called a sedan chair and went straight to the magistrate's office to make a complaint against Sergeant Lei for beating her father, breaking up a performance and trying to swindle her. The magistrate was outraged. "Make a written accusation at once," he said. It was a real case of 'pillow power.' The father was invited to write down the accusation, show his wounds and name witnesses.

Now there were plenty of people in the district who knew Sergeant Lei well and they went to the government office to lay out bribes on his behalf. But the girl was already inside the magistrate's, throwing a tantrum, and the magistrate had no alternative but to take action. He gave orders forthwith for Sergeant Lei to be arrested and brought to the magistracy, where he was beaten and forced to confess, placed in irons and paraded through the streets to be publicly shamed. The girl also wanted to show off her power and asked the magistrate to have him exposed at the door of the theatre. So next day, just before the performance, the magistrate ordered Lei Heng to be taken to the theatre door.

Now all the guards were colleagues of Sergeant Lei's. How could they be expected to tie him up? The girl gave it some thought. The news had already got around that she was picking on him and people were going to blame her anyway. So she left the theatre and went to sit in a teashop, where she summoned the guards to her. "I know you're all hand in glove with him," she said. "You don't want to touch him. His Honour told you to tie him up, but you want to be lenient. But when I go to His Honour and tell him, do you really imagine he's not going to take it out on you?"

"Don't be angry, miss," the guards said. "We'll go and tie him up, don't worry."

"If you do I shall reward you financially," she said.

So the guards had to go to Sergeant Lei and say: "We're not trying to pick on you, brother, but we're going to have to sort of tie you up." And then they showed him off in public with his hands and feet bound.

This caused quite a commotion, in the middle of which Sergeant Lei's mother arrived bringing him food. When she saw they had him tied up, she began to weep noisily. "You're all colleagues of my son's," she scolded, "working just like him in the same department. Just look what money can do! Who can ever hope to keep out of trouble?"

"Listen, old lady," they answered. "We'd much rather have let him off. But since the plaintiff has demanded that he be bound we've no excuse for not doing it. If we didn't they'd go and complain to the magistrate and we'd be for it! That's why we've got to do it, see."

The old lady said: "Since when has it been permitted for the plaintiff to set the penalty for the accused?"

"Listen here," the guards whispered. "She's a very particular friend of the magistrate's. One word from her and we'd be done for. So it's as hard on us as it is for you."

The old lady started to undo the bonds, scolding all the while. "That dirty bastard, how he abuses his position! Well I'm going to undo these bonds, and let's see what he says to that!"

When the news reached the teahouse where Fleur was sitting, she came rushing round at once and shouted: "You there, what are you playing at?"

The old lady was in no mood for pleasantries. She pointed a finger and cursed her roundly: "How dare you raise your voice to me, you whore! Thousands have humped you, millions have, you bitch! You're common property!"

When Fleur heard this her willow brows became perpendicular, her starry eyes nearly popped out of her head: "You poisonous insect, you vermin, who gave you the right to shout at me?"

"Why shouldn't I shout at you? You've got no authority here, you're not the governor of this town!"

Enraged, Fleur dashed at the old lady and gave her a slap which made her stagger. When the old lady tried to retaliate, Fleur came in again and started boxing her ears. She showed no sign of stopping.

Now Sergeant Lei was a very filial son, and when he saw his mother being beaten up, anger exploded in his heart. He tore off the cangue and brought it down with a crash on Fleur's head. He hit her with great violence, using the end of the cangue; the blow cracked open her skull and she crashed to the ground. The brains spilled out, the eyeballs burst and she lay without movement. She was obviously dead.

The bystanders who had witnessed the killing of Fleur Bai seized the murderer and went straight away to the magistracy to denounce him and render a detailed account of the events. The magistrate sent men to bring Sergeant Lei to him under arrest. All those involved were collected; the local headman, neighbours,

插翅虎枷打白秀英

friends and such were all summoned to appear, and when the body had been examined, they were escorted to the magistracy. Sergeant Lei confessed everything, quite openly. His mother was released on her own security to wait at home. Sergeant Lei was fitted with a cangue and committed to the cells.

Now the gaoler there happened to be Whiskers Zhu Tong. When Sergeant Lei was brought he did not ill-treat him in any way, rather he laid on wine and food for him, and told the gaolers to sweep and prepare a clean cell to make him comfortable. In a little while Sergeant Lei's mother arrived at the gaol with food. Sobbing she complained to Whiskers: "Here I am, over sixty years old, and this son of mine is my whole life. I beg you sir to be kind to him and take good care of him."

"I assure you, ma'am," said Whiskers, "that you are leaving him in good hands. You don't need to bring him food any more. I shall look after him. If there's the least chance of it I will get him off."

"If you can save my son, I shall worship you like my own parents," she said. "If anything happens to him, I'd sooner die."

Whiskers said: "I shan't forget it. There's nothing for you to worry about."

When the old lady had prostrated herself in thanks and left, Whiskers turned it over in his mind for a whole day, but could think of no means to rescue his friend. He employed people himself to go to the magistracy and buy support and persuade everyone to show leniency. But although the magistrate liked Whiskers, he had it in for Sergeant Lei for killing his mistress and said he could not pardon him. Besides he had the girl's father nagging at him; he was having charges drawn up and urged the magistrate to sentence the culprit and make him pay with the life that he owed.

When Sergeant Lei had been in the gaol sixty days and the interval before sentencing had been completed, it was decided to send him to the provincial capital. The clerk in charge of the case left first, armed with a complete dossier. Whiskers was appointed to escort Sergeant Lei.

Whiskers set off from Yuncheng, with a dozen prison guards and Sergeant Lei in custody. They had barely gone four miles when they saw an inn. "We'll all go in here and have a cup or two of wine," Whiskers announced.

While the others were drinking, Whiskers took Sergeant Lei off to a quiet corner and removed the cangue. Having released Sergeant Lei, he said to him: "Leave now old chap. Go straight home, get your mother, and go as fast as you can to seek refuge somewhere else. I'll take the blame for this."

"I've no problem with going away," said Sergeant Lei, "but how can I leave you to get into trouble?"

"Don't you see?" said Whiskers. "The magistrate blames you for killing his mistress. He has judged it to be a capital offence. He must be sending you to the capital to be executed. I won't get the death penalty for releasing you. Besides, I haven't any parents to worry about, all I'm likely to lose is my possessions. You've simply got to put as much distance as you can between yourself and this place."

Sergeant Lei prostrated himself in thanks, set off by a small back road and raced home. He made all his valuables into a bundle, and with his mother travelled night and day to Mount Liang, to join the outlaws. Of this no more.

Whiskers threw the empty cangue into the undergrowth and then went to tell the guards: "Sergeant Lei has got away, what can we do?"

"We'd better go quickly to his house and pick him up," they said.

Whiskers purposely delayed for as long as possible, which allowed Sergeant Lei to get a good long way away. Then he went back to the office with the guards to own up.

"I'm afraid I've been careless," he said. "I let Sergeant Lei escape while he was in my custody. He fled and we couldn't catch him. I have no excuse and I am ready to pay the penalty."

The magistrate liked Whiskers, and would have liked to let him off, but the girl's father wanted to complain to a higher authority that Whiskers had deliberately let Sergeant Lei escape, so the magistrate was obliged to report Whiskers' crime to the provincial capital. Some of Whiskers' relatives went to the capital to hand out bribes, so when he was sent there and the case was investigated by the court and the facts established, he was only sentenced to twenty strokes and banishment to Cangzhou prison camp. He was fitted with a cangue for travelling and two court officers were appointed to escort him on the road, bearing the dossier of the case. His relatives supplied him with clothes and money for his expenses and gave presents to the two guards. Then they left Yuncheng for the place of banishment. Of the journey we need say nothing.

On arrival they entered the town and went straight to the government office. The Governor had just gone into session, so the two guards took Whiskers to the court and handed over the documents. The Governor read them. He saw that Whiskers was something out of the ordinary, with his ruddy complexion and a fine long beard reaching below the waist. He liked what he saw so much that he ordered the new convict not to be placed in the cells but retained in the government office for special duties. The travelling cangue was removed and the guards were given a receipt with which they returned whence they had come.

Every day then Whiskers waited for orders in front of the courtroom in the government office. All the constables, court officers, door-keepers, messengers, gaolers, prison guards and so on received gifts from him. Seeing that he was so friendly and polite, everyone liked him. Then one day, when the court was in session and Whiskers in attendance, the Governor called him up and said: "Why did you let Sergeant Lei go and allow yourself to be sent here as a convict?"

Whiskers respectfully replied: "I had no intention of letting him go. It's just that I was careless and he escaped."

"Then why did you get such a heavy punishment?" the Governor asked.

"The plaintiff was determined to make me confess I did it on purpose, so my interrogation was severe," said Whiskers.

"How did Sergeant Lei come to kill that singer?"

Whiskers recounted Sergeant Lei's story in detail.

"So you saw what a filial son he was and you let him go out of respect for his virtue?" the Governor suggested.

"How would I have dared to cheat the government and deceive my superiors?" Whiskers protested.

At this juncture a young boy burst out from behind the screen. This was the Governor's own son, a fine looking lad about four years old, the apple of his father's eye. When the child saw Whiskers he went straight up to him and wanted to be picked up. Whiskers had to take him in his arms and give him a hug. The boy grabbed Whiskers' beard in both hands and said: "I want to hug this beard."

"Let go of him, child," the Governor said. "Don't pester him."

The boy said: "I want this beard. I want him to come and play with me."

Whiskers said: "Shall I take him to the area in front of the court and play with him for a while? I'll come straight back."

"Since the child wants you to hold him, you'd better go and play with him for a bit and come back afterwards."

So Whiskers carried the child off to the front of the courtroom and bought some sweets and dried fruit to eat with him. He took him for a little walk and then returned to the courtroom.

"Where have you been?" the Governor asked his son.

"Mr. Whiskers played with me in the street and he gave me some sweets and some fruit and he let me eat them."

"Why did you spend your money to buy things for the child?" the Governor asked.

"It was just some trifles to please the little chap," said Whiskers. "Nothing to make a fuss about."

The Governor ordered wine to be brought for Whiskers. Slave girls appeared with a silver jug and some fruit and nuts. They poured out wine and Whiskers was made to drink three bumpers.

"Any time my son wants to play with you," said the Governor, "just take him out, will you?"

"Your wish is my command," said Whiskers.

From that day on he took the child out for a walk every day. He carried a wallet and in order to please the Governor he would pay out little sums when the child was with him.

A fortnight later it was the fifteenth of July, the festival of Hungry Ghosts, when according to tradition lights are floated on the river and altars are set up everywhere for prayers and offerings. That evening a nursemaid from the residence called out to

Whiskers: "Sergeant Zhu, the young master wants to go and see the lights tonight. The mistress says you can take him."

"I'll take him, then," Whiskers replied.

The child came out, dressed in a green silk shirt, with his hair arranged on top of his head in two little horns braided with pearls. Whiskers hoisted him onto his shoulders and carried him out into the town. They went to watch the lights being floated in the river at the Temple of the Redeeming Buddha. At that time it happened to be the first watch of the evening and they saw something like this:

> *Bells are ringing, clouds of incense rising, pennants fluttering everywhere. Sticks of choicest incense smoulder in the pots, dishes are piled high with every kind of vegetarian fare. Wielding gold pestles, priests intone sacred texts to improve the lot of the dead; people dressed in mourning clothes pile up silver to ease the way to heaven of impeded souls. People gather at the Hall of Benevolence, to view representations of the officials of Hell, the eight obstacles and the three types of torment. Around the temple walls the four ways of birth and the six incarnations are impressively depicted. The branches of the willows are sprinkled with pure water; flaring lanterns float among the water lilies in the pond.*

As Whiskers carried the Governor's son round the temple to see the sights, they came to the pond for releasing fish beside the Water and Land pavilion where people were floating their lights. The child climbed onto the balustrade and laughed gleefully. At that moment someone tugged Whiskers' sleeve from behind and said: "Please give me a moment of your time."

Whiskers got quite a shock when he turned round and saw that it was Sergeant Lei. "Come down from there," he said to the child. "And sit down here while I go and get you some sweets. Whatever you do, don't go away."

"Don't be long," said the child. "I want to go and look at the lights from the bridge."

"I'll be back immediately," said Whiskers, as he turned and went with Sergeant Lei to talk. "Why have you come here?" he asked.

Sergeant Lei led him to a quiet place and prostrated himself. "When you saved my life," he said, "I had nowhere else to go with my old mother, so I had to go to the Marshes of Mount Liang to join Song Jiang's band. When I told them about your generosity, Song Jiang also remembered how you helped him to get away that other time, and Chao Gai and the others were deeply moved. They asked the Professor and myself therefore to pay you a visit."

"Where is the Professor, then?" Whiskers asked.

"The Professor is here," said a voice behind him. The Professor came forward and prostrated himself.

Whiskers hurriedly returned the courtesy, saying: "It's a long time since we met. I trust all is well with you?"

"Many, many leaders in the mountain stronghold send you their regards," said the Professor. "They have commanded me to come here, with our brother Sergeant Lei, to request you to join our loyal band on the mountain. We've been here several days, but we couldn't find a way to speak to you. Today we waited here and managed to catch you. So please agree to come with us to the mountain stronghold and fulfil the wishes of our two leaders."

Whiskers thought about this for a long time before he could find an answer. Eventually he said: "I'm afraid you've misjudged me, sir. Please don't say any more about this. I'm afraid if someone should overhear, it could have serious consequences. My friend Sergeant Lei committed a capital offence. I let him escape for the sake of friendship and loyalty. He can't show his face now, so he went to join the outlaws on the mountain. I got sent here on account of him, but heaven may relent. In a year and a half I may manage to return home, and become a respectable citizen again. How can you imagine I would join you? Please go back now, and don't come here stirring up trouble."

Sergeant Lei said: "My dear friend, you're really nothing better than a servant here. Serving others is in no kind of work for a real man. It's just not manly. It's not only my idea that you should join us on the mountain, our two leaders have long wanted you to come. It's really not very good of you to keep them waiting!"

Whiskers said: "What are you talking about, brother? Have you forgotten that I let you escape because of your old mother and your difficult family circumstances? And now you come here and accuse me of disloyalty!"

The Professor said: "If you don't want to come with us, Sergeant, we had better say goodbye and leave you in peace."

"Please give my humble respects to the leaders," said Whiskers. Together they went to the bridge.

When Whiskers got back, there was no sign of the Governor's son. Cursing his fate, he searched absolutely everywhere, until Sergeant Lei put a hand on his arm and said: "Don't go on looking. I bet it's the two chaps we brought with us. They probably heard you didn't want to come with us and carried the boy off. We'll go with you to find them."

Whiskers said: "It's no joke. His Excellency dotes on that child and he entrusted him to me."

"You'd better come with us then," said Sergeant Lei.

The three of them, Whiskers assisted by the Professor and Sergeant Lei, left the Temple of the Redeeming Buddha and headed out of town. Whiskers was extremely worried. "Wherever have these mates of yours taken the child?" he said.

"Just keep going. When we get to the place where we're staying we'll give you back the child," said Sergeant Lei.

"Time's getting short," said Whiskers. "I'm afraid the Governor will think something's wrong."

The Professor said: "Those two we brought with us aren't very bright, I'm sure they'll have taken the child back to where we're staying."

"These friends of yours, who are they exactly?" Whiskers asked.

"I don't really know," said Sergeant Lei. "But I think I heard the name Li Kui, the Black Whirlwind."

"Not the murderer who killed someone in Jiangzhou?" cried the horrified Whiskers.

"That's the one," said the Professor.

Whiskers staggered a little and then with many a groan hurried on. They were five or six miles from the city when they saw Iron Ox Li Kui up ahead. "I'm here," he called to them. Whiskers raced towards him. "What have you done with the child?" he asked.

Iron Ox saluted and said: "My respects, sergeant. The child is here."

"Then hand him over to me, very, very carefully."

Iron Ox pointed to his own head and said: "This is what he tied his hair with."

Whiskers looked, and again asked where the child was. Iron Ox said: "I had a drug with me and I administered it to him before I carried him off. He's sleeping in that wood now. Go and see for yourself."

The bright moonlight aided Whiskers as he plunged into the wood to look for the child. He found him lying on the ground. But when he put out his hand to touch him, he saw that the head was split in two. The child was dead.

A great rage filled Whiskers' heart. He stumbled out of the wood. The other three had disappeared. He looked in all directions. Then he saw Iron Ox a long way off waving his two axes and shouting: "Come on, come on, I'm going to have a few bouts with you!"

Seething with rage, careless of life and limb, Whiskers hoisted up his robe and bounded in pursuit. Iron Ox turned and ran, with Whiskers hot on his heels. But Iron Ox was a hardened mountaineer and there was no way Whiskers could catch him. Soon he had to stop for breath. "Come on, come on," Iron Ox shouted back at him. "We're going to fight. It'll be you or me."

Whiskers couldn't wait. He would have eaten him alive, only he couldn't get his hands on him. The chase went on and on, till gradually day began to dawn. If Whiskers ran faster, Iron Ox also speeded up; if he went slower, Iron Ox slowed down. But Whiskers could never catch him. Eventually he saw Iron Ox disappear into a large compound. "So the villain's got a bolt-hole, has he? But I won't let him get away with it." he said to himself.

Whiskers went right to the main hall of the house. Here he found stacks of weapons on both sides of the building, and he said to himself: "This must be the house of some official."

He halted and shouted out: "Is there anyone in?"

A man emerged from behind the screen at the back. And do you know who it was?

One of ancient and illustrious lineage, noble scion of a royal line, his portals defended by vermilion inscription and cast-iron guarantee, host to good men from far and wide, provider of faultless hospitality to every guest, dispenser of largesse with a smiling face, skilled exponent of brush and sword, gentleman of Mengchang dubbed Little Whirlwind, the world famous Chai Jin.

He who came out was indeed Chai Jin, the Little Whirlwind. He said: "And who might you be?"

At the sight of such an imposing figure of a man, of such liberal endowments, Whiskers hurriedly bowed and said: "I am Zhu Tong, warden of Yuncheng prison. I was banished here on account of an offence I committed. Last night I took the Governor's little son out to see the lights and he was killed by Iron Ox Li Kui. I saw this Iron Ox enter your compound this morning. I beg you to do all you can to help apprehend him and send him to justice."

Chai Jin said: "You are Whiskers, aren't you? Please sit down."

"Might I ask your name?" Whiskers said.

"My name is Chai Jin and they call me the Little Whirlwind."

"Of course I have heard much about you," said Whiskers, hurriedly prostrating himself. "I never expected to have the chance of meeting you like this."

"I have heard a lot about you too, Whiskers," said Chai Jin. "Please come inside so we can talk."

Whiskers followed Chai Jin inside. Then he said: "How is it that villain Iron Ox dares to enter your house?"

"I had better explain," said Chai Jin. "I have always enjoyed knowing the brethren of the rivers and lakes. Because of the acts of my ancestor and his meritorious abdication, my family enjoy the privilege of a cast-iron guarantee. If anyone guilty of wrongdoing hides in my house no one can come here searching for him. Recently a dear friend of mine, with whom you too have had a connection, and who is now one of the leaders on Mount Liang, namely Song Jiang, the Opportune Rain, wrote to ask me if I would allow Professor Wu Yong, Sergeant Lei and Iron Ox to stay in my place whilst they tried to persuade you to go up the mountain and join the loyal band. He knew that you might refuse to go so he instructed Iron Ox to kill the child, in order to cut off your return route, and leave you no alternative but to take your place among the leaders on the mountain. Professor, Sergeant! Why don't you come out and join our discussion?"

Thereupon Professor Wu and Sergeant Lei emerged from a room at the side. They went straight to Whiskers and prostrated themselves. "Dear brother, please forgive us," they said. "It was on Song Jiang's orders, he told us to do it. If you will come to the mountain stronghold, all will be explained."

"I accept that you had good intentions," said Whiskers. "But that was really too cruel!"

After Chai Jin had done his utmost to calm him, Whiskers said: "I suppose I can go with you, but just let me have a sight of that Black Whirlwind!"

"Mr. Li!" Chai Jin called out. "Come and join our discussion!"

Iron Ox also issued forth from the room at the side and saluted. When Whiskers saw him his heart was filled with an indescribable fury, vast and ungovernable. He leapt to his feet and rushed at Iron Ox, ready for a fight to the death. Chai Jin, Sergeant Lei and the Professor struggled hard to restrain him. Finally he said: "If you want me to join you on the mountain you'll have to promise me one thing, or I won't go."

"Not one but a dozen," said the Professor. "Please tell us what it is."

And if Whiskers had not made this condition, things would have been different.

A tumult in Gaotang district, repercussions on Mount Liang,
Cause a royal friend of the righteous to clash with the law,
Lead to a hospitable royal relative languishing in gaol.

But if you want to hear what condition Whiskers made, you must read the next chapter.

Chapter 52

Iron Ox beats the Chancellor to death; Mr. Chai becomes a prisoner in Gaotang!

Now what Whiskers said to them was: "You want me to go to the mountain with you — well, I'll do it, but only if you can purge this anger of mine by executing Black Whirlwind."

This infuriated Iron Ox. "Well, fuck me! It was the two leaders who ordered it, what's it got to do with me, you arsehole?"

The outraged Whiskers would have thrown himself on Iron Ox, but the other three restrained him. "If he's going to be there," said Whiskers, "you can kill me before you'll get me to the mountain."

"There's no problem, I've got a solution," said Mr. Chai. "Iron Ox can stay here with me. Then you three can go to the mountain, as the leaders have requested."

"But after what's happened," said Whiskers, "the Governor is bound to have made out a warrant, and they'll go straight over to Yuncheng and arrest all my family, what am I to do about that?"

"Don't worry," said the Professor. "By now I imagine Song Jiang has already taken your family to the mountain."

Whiskers felt a bit better after this. Mr. Chai poured wine for them and gave a farewell feast. That very evening they bade him goodbye and prepared to set off. Mr. Chai had his people saddle three horses to carry them to the bounds of his territory. Before they parted, the Professor said to Iron Ox: "You be careful. You're to stay with His Excellency for a while, but don't play the fool and stir things up, or get him into any trouble. In a few months' time, when Whiskers has settled down a bit, we will come to fetch you, and most likely we shall invite Mr. Chai to join our company too." The three men then mounted and left.

We shall not follow Mr. Chai and Iron Ox back to the manor, but tell how Whiskers Zhu, accompanying the Professor and Sergeant Lei, came to the Marshes of Mount Liang and entered the company. When they had travelled one stage and reached the limits of Cangzhou, Mr. Chai's retainers returned home with the horses. The three men headed for Mount Liang, and nothing worthy of note happened on the way. They soon reached the inn of the Crocodile, who sent men up the mountain to report their arrival. Chao Gai and Song Jiang, with all the other leaders, greater and lesser, came down to the accompaniment of drums and fifes and met them at Golden Sands Landing. Everyone was introduced and then they rode up to the main camp where they dismounted and went to the great Assembly Hall, where the events that we already know of were recounted.

Whiskers said: "Now that I have been called here to the mountain, the Governor of Cangzhou is sure to have sent a warrant for the arrest of all my relatives. What can I do about it?"

Song Jiang smiled and said: "My advice is not to worry. Your wife and son were all brought here days ago."

"Where are they then?" Whiskers asked.

"They are resting in my father's house, go and see for yourself." Song Jiang told Whiskers, to the latter's immense relief.

Song Jiang had people take Whiskers to Squire Song's residence, where he found all his family and also all of his valuable possessions. His wife said: "A little while ago someone brought a letter which said you had joined the company on the mountain, so we packed and came here at once."

Whiskers went back and thanked everyone. Song Jiang then invited Whiskers and Sergeant Lei to the lower camp on the mountain where a feast was laid on, and the arrival of these new leaders was celebrated over several days. Of this no more.

Back in Cangzhou the Governor, when it got really late and Whiskers had still not brought his son back, sent people off to search in every direction. They spent most of the night searching. Next day someone found the dead body in the wood, and told the Governor. This gentleman was desolated. He went to the wood to see for himself. His grief was limitless. He had a coffin made and burnt paper offerings. A day later he went into session and ordered notices to be posted everywhere, demanding the apprehension and arrest of the said Sergeant Zhu. The authorities in the Sergeant's home district had already reported that Whiskers' wife and children had fled from their home and their whereabouts was unknown. A reward for the capture was announced in every district and town. Of this no more.

Meanwhile Iron Ox had been living at Mr. Chai's for several months when suddenly one day a man bearing a letter burst through the manor gates. Chai Jin greeted him politely, took the letter and read it. "Then I must go at once," he said in some consternation.

"Is it something serious?" Iron Ox asked.

"I have this uncle called Chai Huangcheng," Mr. Chai began. "He lives in Gaotang. A certain rogue called Yin Tianxi, who is the brother-in-law of the governor there, Gao Lian, has been demanding he give up a garden that he owns. He's had an apoplexy and is lying ill in bed. They think he's close to death and apparently he has some last wishes he wants to make known, so they've come to fetch me. He has no children, so it's essential that I go."

"If you've got to go why don't I go with you?" said Iron Ox.

"Yes, if you like, let us go together," said Chai Jin.

Mr. Chai did his packing and picked a dozen good horses and some retainers to accompany them. At dawn next day Mr. Chai, Iron Ox and their retinue mounted and rode out of the gates, heading for Gaotang.

In less than a day they arrived. They entered the town and dismounted in front of the uncle's residence. Leaving Iron Ox and the rest of the party outside the main hall, Mr. Chai entered the sick room to see his uncle:

This face is like gold leaf, the body a withered branch; the spirit is slow and sad, the breath but a tenuous thread. The teeth are tightly clamped together, neither food nor drink has passed these lips for days. The innards are so swollen no pill can get down. Grievers and mourners are already at hand, the doctors have given up hope.

Chai Jin sat down beside the bed and wept unreservedly. His uncle's second wife came out and tried to comfort him. "You rode here in such haste," she said. "You must try not to upset yourself too much."

When greetings had been completed, Chai Jin asked for a full account. The second wife said: "The new governor, Gao Lian, who is also commander-in-chief of the armed forces, is a cousin of Marshal Gao in the capital. He relies on this connection to do just as he likes here. He brought a brother-in-law of his along with him, Yin Tianxi, whom people call Chancellor Yin. Actually he's only a young man, but he uses his brother-in-law's position to ride roughshod over everyone. A bunch of toadies he goes around with told him that behind our house we have a very attractive garden with a water pavilion. The swine came round here with twenty or thirty scheming rogues and marched straight through to the back to look at it. Now he wants to chase us out and come to live here himself. Huangcheng said to him: 'Our family is of royal descent; we have a charter and a cast-iron guarantee from a previous emperor, which says no one is allowed to annoy us. How dare you try to take our house! Where are my family going to go?'

"The blighter just wouldn't listen. He's determined to throw us out. When Huangcheng tried to stop him, he got beaten up. That's what brought on this seizure. He took to his bed and hasn't moved since. He won't eat or drink, no medicine does any good, it's obvious he's not long for this world. But now with you here to look after things, whatever troubles lie ahead it's not going to get worse."

Chai Jin said: "My dear, don't worry. We'll get a good doctor to treat him. If there's any more trouble, I shall send someone home to get our imperial certificate to convince them. Even if the case goes before the Emperor himself there's nothing to fear!"

"Huangcheng is so hopeless at practical matters. He's not a patch on you, Your Excellency," she said gratefully.

After seeing his uncle, Mr. Chai went out and explained everything to Iron Ox and the rest of his people.

When he heard it, Iron Ox leapt up and said: "What a bloody nerve! I've got my axes here. I'll go and give the bastard a few chops first, and then we can discuss things."

"Calm yourself, Mr. Li," said Mr. Chai. "What's the point in arguing with boors like that? Although he thinks he's powerful enough to bully people, I've got a certificate at home to protect me. It's no good disputing with him here, but in the capital there are people bigger than him, we must prepare our case carefully and appeal to the law."

"The law my arse! If the law means anything, how come the world is in such a mess? Me, I'd strike first and talk later. Then if the bugger still wants to complain, I'd go and cut off the heads of all those fucking officials."

"No wonder Whiskers has got it in for you and you two have got to be kept apart," said Mr. Chai with a laugh. "This is an imperial city. You can't employ your savage methods here."

"So what if it is an imperial city?" said Iron Ox. "Didn't I kill men in Jiangzhou and Wuweijun too?"

"Let me look into the affair first," said Mr. Chai. "If I need your services, I'll let you know. In the meantime there's nothing you need do except sit down in this room and wait."

At this point a maid came out and begged Mr. Chai to go in and see his uncle immediately.

Chai Jin entered the room and approached the bed. Huangcheng's eyes were filled with tears. "My dear and respected nephew," he said to Chai Jin, "I know you will not let our ancestor be shamed. That so-called 'Chancellor' has destroyed my life. On behalf of your own flesh and blood please take this letter to the capital to denounce him and obtain redress. Your kindness will bring relief to me in the underworld. Take care! This is my last and only wish!"

So saying, he gave up the ghost. Chai Jin wept bitterly for a time. Fearing that he was going to faint, the second wife did her best to enliven him. "You've been worried all the day. But now it's time to consider what to do next."

"I have the documents at home," Chai Jin said. "I've sent for them but they haven't come yet. But I'll send someone as fast as possible with all that is needed, to lodge an accusation in the capital. Now we must honour my uncle; we must organize the coffin and the funeral service. When we've completed all the ceremonies we will discuss things again."

Mr. Chai ordered everything to be done properly: the two coffins, inner and outer, obtained, a suitable memorial tablet set up, mourning clothes provided for the whole household. Everyone went into mourning.

Iron Ox had been outside and heard all the weeping in the inner appartments. He rubbed his hands together in eager anticipation of a fight. But when he questioned the servants no one would tell him anything. Meanwhile monks were invited to the house to organize prayers and offerings.

On the third day, the Chancellor turned up in front of the house. He was riding a prancing steed, and had with him a score of hangers-on, with bows and crossbows, some blowing on flutes, or fooling around with balls, staves or musical instruments. They were on an excursion and were all somewhat drunk and pretending to be more drunk than they really were. The Chancellor reined in his horse and shouted that he wanted to speak to whoever was in charge inside.

Mr. Chai responded by hurrying out to receive him, dressed completely in mourning.

"What's your position here?" the Chancellor inquired arrogantly.

"I am a nephew of Chai Huangcheng's. My name is Chai Jin."

"The other day I told them to move out of here. Why have my orders not been obeyed?"

"My uncle was sick and we couldn't move him. He died the other day and we can't move till the seven days period is complete."

"Bugger the seven days period. I'll give you three days to move. If you're not out in three days, I shall order you a cangue and let you have a hundred blows of my staff!"

"You had better not threaten us like this, your Honour! Our family has an imperial lineage, and we have a cast-iron guarantee. That's something you can't ignore!"

"Let me see it then!" said the Chancellor.

"It's at home, but I've sent someone to fetch it."

"This bugger's talking nonsense!" the Chancellor said to his followers in a great rage. "Even if he's got it, this cast-iron guarantee does not impress me. Take him away and beat him for me."

Before his attendants could move, Iron Ox, who had been watching the proceedings from a gap in the door, flung the door open and with a huge bellow threw himself at the Chancellor's horse, dragged him off it and felled him with a single blow of the fist. When Yin's companions rushed to the rescue, five or six of them fell to Iron Ox's fists and the rest fled in confusion. Iron Ox picked the Chancellor up and began to hammer him with fists and feet. There was nothing Mr. Chai could do to stop him. The Chancellor was now indeed in a sorry state, lying sprawled on the ground like a sacrificial victim:

The bully has such a false view of his worth,
He heeds not the justice of heaven and earth.
But Iron Ox is here, so he won't get away,
Till the King of Hell greets him and asks him to pay.

Now that the Chancellor lay there dead by Iron Ox's hand, Mr. Chai could only curse his luck. He ordered Iron Ox into the back room to discuss what to do. "Obviously they'll come here to get you," he said to Iron Ox. "So you're not safe here. Leave me to take care of the authorities. You must go at once to Mount Liang."

"But if I go," said Iron Ox, "you'll get the blame.

"I've got the cast-iron guarantee to protect me," said Mr. Chai. "So you have to go, and without delay."

So Iron Ox picked up his axes, took some money for travel expenses and departed, taking the road to Mount Liang.

It wasn't long before several hundred well-armed men appeared and surrounded the house. Knowing they had come to arrest the culprit, Mr. Chai went out and spoke to them: "I am going to go with you to the magistracy to make a statement."

They tied his hands first and then went into the house to look for the murderer, the big black fellow. Not finding him, they took Mr. Chai still with his hands tied to the courtroom where he was told to kneel. When Governor Gao Lian had heard that his

李逵打死殷天錫

brother-in-law had been killed, he ground his teeth in fury and couldn't wait to get hold of the criminal. Mr. Chai was flung down before the bench while the Governor shouted: "How dare you kill my brother-in-law!"

Mr. Chai declared: "I am of imperial lineage. Our family has a charter and a cast-iron guarantee. It's at my house in Cangzhou. I came here to see my uncle because he was ill. Unfortunately he died. At present we are preparing the funeral. Mr. Yin brought a crowd of people to the house and wanted to drive the family out. He wouldn't listen to what I had to say and ordered his people to beat me. One of my retainers, Big Li, came to rescue me and happened to kill Mr. Yin."

"Where is this Big Li?" the Governor roared.

"He was frightened and he ran away," said Mr. Chai.

"If he is a retainer, how could he kill someone unless you ordered him to? You let him go on purpose, because you want to pull the wool over my eyes! You're a villain! You obviously won't confess till we beat you. Guards! Take him and thrash him within an inch of his life!"

Mr. Chai protested: "Big Li was protecting his master. If he accidentally killed someone, it's not my fault. Since I have the imperial guarantee it's quite illegal to beat me."

"Where is this imperial guarantee?" said the Governor.

"I've sent someone home to fetch it," said Mr. Chai.

This incensed the Governor still further. "The villain is opposing the authorities! Thrash him!" he roared. "Give him all you've got!"

The guards set to work. They beat Mr. Chai till the skin was in shreds and the blood flowed, and got him to confess that he had ordered his retainer Big Li to kill the Chancellor, Yin Tianxi. Then a twenty-five catty cangue, appropriate for a condemned man was fitted and he was consigned to prison. The body of the Chancellor was prepared for burial and the coffin was interred. Of this no more.

The Governor's wife was determined to avenge her brother. She urged her husband to confiscate Chai Huangcheng's property, imprison all his people and seize the house and all the lands. This was a bitter time for Chai Jin, languishing in prison:

柴進失陷高唐州

The words of a woman are like a snake's poison,
The power of the charter an empty illusion.
Just to think that the ancestor gave up a throne,
While his grandson can't even defend what's his own!

Meanwhile Iron Ox had rushed straight back to Mount Liang. Arriving at the stronghold he went to see all the leaders. When Whiskers Zhu saw him, he exploded with anger and reaching for his halberd tried to hurl himself upon him. Iron Ox took out his two axes to retaliate. Chao Gai, Song Jiang and the rest rushed forward to separate them.

Song Jiang tried to placate Whiskers by saying: "The business of the little boy was not Iron Ox's fault. It was a plan of the Professor's, because he could not persuade you to join us on the mountain. Now you are here with us, forget the past and try to work with us in order to strengthen our reputation for loyalty, lest outsiders deride us." He then called upon Iron Ox to apologize to Whiskers.

Scowling ferociously, Iron Ox exclaimed: "But he started it all! I've put in a lot of work for the mountain stronghold, he hasn't deserved half as much as I have, and now I'm the one who's asked to apologize!"

Song Jiang said: "But you're the one who killed the child, even if it was on the Professor's orders. And again, he is your senior. Please, for my sake give him a few courteous words and I'll prostrate myself before you."

Iron Ox had to give way before Song Jiang's insistence. He said: "I'm not afraid of you, and this is only because the boss makes me do it and leaves me no alternative: I apologize to you." And at Song Jiang's insistence he also threw down his axes and bowed to Whiskers twice. Whiskers' anger was at last appeased. Chao Gai ordered a feast in the camp to celebrate their reconciliation.

Iron Ox now explained how Mr. Chai had gone to Gaotang to visit his sick relative and how the Governor's brother-in-law had wanted to seize the garden and threatened to beat Mr. Chai and been killed by himself. Song Jiang was greatly disturbed by this account. "So you ran off and left Mr. Chai to face the music," he said.

"Let us keep calm, friends," said the Professor, "and wait till the Magic Messenger gets back. Then we'll hear what's happened."

"Where has the Magic Messenger gone?" Iron Ox asked.

"I was afraid you might make trouble when you were staying at Mr. Chai's," said the Professor. "So I sent him to call you back. When he got there and found you gone, he must have gone on to Gaotang to look for you."

He had hardly finished speaking when one of the men came in to report that the Magic Messenger was back. Song Jiang went to receive him and then brought him into the hall. When he was seated they asked him about Mr. Chai.

"When I got to Mr. Chai's manor," he replied, "they told me he had gone with Iron Ox to Gaotang. So I went there straight away and made inquiries. I found everyone in the city was talking about how the Chancellor in a dispute over Chai Huangcheng's estate had been killed by a big black fellow and how Mr. Chai was held responsible and had been bound and thrown into prison. All Chai Huangcheng's property has been confiscated and Chai Jin's life is under grave threat."

Chao Gai said: "This big black idiot has done it again! Wherever he goes he stirs up something!"

Iron Ox said: "Chai Huangcheng was beaten up by that bastard and died of chagrin. He came to grab their house and threatened to beat Chai Jin. Not even a living Buddha could put up with all that!"

Chao Gai said: "Mr. Chai has always been a friend of the mountain stronghold. Now he's in trouble. How can we not go to his assistance? I shall go myself."

"You're our commander-in-chief," said Song Jiang. "You can't act like that without a plan. I myself have long been a friend of Mr. Chai, please allow me to go down on your behalf."

The Professor said: "Although Gaotang is only a small administration, it's densely populated and has a big defence force and ample supplies, we mustn't underestimate them. I propose an advance guard of twelve leaders, Leopard's Head, Colonel Hua,

Thunderclap, the White-Water Dragon, the Little Duke, the Halberdier, Colonel Sun, Golden Wings, Panther, Redeye, the Flautist and the Daytime Rat, with five thousand cavalry and foot, and in support a force led by Song Jiang and myself, with Whiskers, Sergeant Lei, the Magic Messenger, Iron Ox, White Eel, Morbid and Madcap, ten leaders in all, with three thousand horse and foot."

After bidding farewell to Chao Gai and the rest, these twenty two leaders left the mountain and set out for Gaotang. Indeed, they marched out in perfect order:

A swirling of embroidered banners and signal flags, a medley of trumpets and gongs. Forks, three-pronged and five-pronged, glitter like autumn frost; spears with steel or wooden points slant thick as winter's snow. Fierce warriors fill the road, archers and crossbowmen in the lead; guns follow on carts, stout halberdiers and lancers pressing after. The commanders on horseback have the ferocity of the tiger of the Southern mountains, every one of them a stern, indomitable warrior. Their mounts are like the green dragon of the northern sea, battle-steeled and unscareable. Here are engines of war as powerful as a flood; here are the troops to sweep all before them like a tempest.

When the advance guard of the Mount Liang forces reached the border of Gaotang, some government soldiers reported it to the Governor. "Aha, you rebellious rabble hiding away in the Marshes of Mount Liang," said the latter, with a cold smile. "I was intending to come and get you anyway, but now you've come to me of your own accord! Heaven must want me to succeed." To his minions he shouted: "You there, quickly pass on the order for the army to advance and engage the enemy and for the people to man the ramparts." For this Governor had two hats: he commanded the army and he governed the people. The moment the order was received all the army officers and government officials of every rank took up their positions to receive the enemy.

Under Gao Lian's immediate command there were three hundred special troops known as the Celestial Guard. These were all picked troops from Shandong, Hebei, Jiangxi, Hunan, or from either bank of the Huai river, or the east and west parts of Zhejiang. These three hundred Celestial guards were indeed a sight to behold:

> *Wild and dishevelled is their hair, their heads framed in an aura of mist. They are dressed in gourd-shaped armour, and a thousand flames leap up behind them. Their foreheads are daubed yellow and painted with the eight diagrams. They are cloaked in protective leopard skins; they wear face masks of copper like burnished gold and carry hard steel scourges like brooms. Front and back they are protected by bright steel. Their banners dazzle the eye, as they spread out on either hand like countless black vapours. One could be witnessing the heavenly powers descending from the Dipper, or some comet falling from on high.*

So the Governor led out his three hundred guards, fully armed and accoutred; he rode forth, with the rest of the army under his command drawn up around him in battle formation. The three hundred guards were in the centre. Waving their banners and cheering, with thundering drum and shrilling fifes, they awaited the enemy.

Leopard's Head, Colonel Hua, and Thunderclap now arrived on the scene with their five thousand troops. The two armies met, flags and drums facing each other, while bows and crossbows on either side set up a deadly fire at the front ranks. Bugles rang out and drums thundered in both armies. Colonel Hua and Thunderclap with ten other leaders galloped to the front and reined in their horses. Leader Leopard's Head slanting his eight-pronged lance galloped out in front and shouted out: "Let the commander of Gaotang show himself!" Giving his horse its head, Gao Lian with some thirty or so of his officers, galloped to the pennants gate, and reined in his horse. He pointed at Leopard's Head and bellowed: "You foolhardy gang of rebels, how dare you flout my authority?"

Leopard's Head shouted back: "You vicious tyrant and plunderer! One day I shall go to the capital and get that Gao the Ball, oppressor of the righteous and despoiler of the people. I shall cut him into ten thousand pieces! Then I'll be satisfied!"

Gao Lian was outraged. He turned and asked: "Who wants to be first to go and get the scoundrel?"

One of the group of officers, a commander named Yu Zhi, rode forward, slapping his horse and whirling his sword.

Leopard's Head charged him at once. Before they had fought five bouts Yu Zhi received a thrust in the chest and was knocked head over heels from his horse.

Greatly shocked by this, Gao Lian asked: "Who will go and avenge him?"

Another captain rode forward, named Wen Wenbao. He wielded a long lance and rode a handsome bay and his harness bells and the jade ornaments on his belt all jingled as he rode out in front. Four hooves hammered the ground as he charged Leopard's Head.

Thunderclap immediately gave a great shout. "Wait, brother! Just watch me cut his head off!"

Leopard's Head reined in his horse and rested his lance, allowing Thunderclap to fight Wen. After about ten bouts, Thunderclap left an opening, allowing his opponent to lunge forward. Thunderclap raised his arm and struck down and sliced off half Wen's head. He died in the saddle. The horse galloped back to the enemy ranks. A great tumult arose in the opposing ranks.

When Gao Lian saw two of his commanders defeated he reached behind him and drew his magic sword. After muttering a spell, he gave a loud cry of "chrr!" Immediately a column of black smoke rose from his lines. As the black smoke filled the heavens, sand and stones began to blow about, heaven and earth shook and a strange wind blew, sweeping towards the opposing army. Leopard's Head, Thunderclap, Colonel Hua and the other commanders could not face it. The terrified pack horses whinnied and bolted. Everyone turned and ran.

With a wave of his sword. Gao Lian signalled the three hundred Celestial guards to charge, with the regular troops following in support. They routed Lin Chong's troops, who scattered like falling stars and driven clouds, in total panic. It was like some natural disaster when brother loses brother and children are separated from parents. Of the five thousand troops more than a thousand were annihilated. The remainder fled back more than fifteen miles before daring to stop and make camp. After observing the rout, Gao Lian recalled his own troops and retired to the city to rest.

When Song Jiang arrived with the support force, he was greeted by Leopard's Head and the others, who told him what had happened. Song Jiang and the Professor had a shock. "What kind of trick is that, to have such a terrible effect!" Song Jiang said.

"It's some kind of magic," said the Professor. "You'd need to be able to stop the wind and turn back fire to defeat such an enemy!"

Hearing this Song Jiang opened his mystic books, and in the third volume found a method for stopping the wind and turning back fire. Delighted with what he'd found, he diligently committed the spells and magic formulae to memory. Then he made dispositions for his forces. They breakfasted at dawn and with waving banners and beating drums marched on the city.

Their approach was reported in the city. Gao Lian called up his victorious army again, including the three hundred Celestial guards. The gates were opened, the drawbridge lowered, and they marched out of the city and deployed in battle formation.

Waving his sword Song Jiang galloped to the front. A cluster of black pennants could be seen in Gao Lian's lines. "Those black pennants among their forces indicate masters of wizardry," said the Professor. "I'm afraid with a weapon like that we won't be able to stand up to them."

"Fear not, Professor!" said Song Jiang. "I have my own secret mode of offence. Let every man go forward without fear or hesitation in his heart."

Gao Lian now ordered all his commanders not to try and challenge the enemy to single combat but to observe the signals and together use all their strength to seize Song Jiang. He himself offered a big reward.

Shouts arose now on both sides as Gao Lian rode out in front of his troops. He had hung on the pommel of his saddle the bronze shield which gave him the power to summon beasts, decorated with dragon and phoenix insignia, and he was brandishing his magic sword.

Song Jiang pointed a finger at Gao and upbraided him: "Yesterday before I arrived my commanders carelessly suffered some casualties. Today I shall most certainly punish you."

"You bunch of rebels!" Gao riposted. "Get down off your horses double-quick and let us tie you up, to save me the trouble of soiling my hands and muddying my feet!"

And with this he waved his sword, muttered a spell and cried: "Chrr!" Immediately the column of black smoke arose and the strange wind began to blow. Song Jiang did not wait till the wind reached him. He also uttered a spell, formed a secret sign with his left hand while raising the sword in his right, and also pronounced "Chrr!" Immediately the wind stopped blowing towards Song Jiang's forces and turned back against Gao's ranks.

Song Jiang was about to give the order to charge, but Gao had seen how the wind had changed. He hurriedly took his bronze shield, rapped it with his sword and then rolled a ball of sand towards the company of celestial guards. From among the troops a pack of fearsome beasts rushed forth:

> *There are wildcats with darting claws, lions with shuddering heads. Flashing chimeras reveal their savage ferocity, rearing monsters parade their awesome power. Wolves and jackals become rows of snarling teeth, vomiting fearsome warriors; tigers and leopards turn into bevies of gaping mouths, spitting out wild horses. Bristling wild boar burst through the ranks, curly-haired mastiffs savage the men. Python like dragons rear into the sky, vicious serpents that could swallow an elephant infest the earth.*

When Gao's bronze shield rang out, this pack of weird beasts and venomous reptiles poured forth, while Song Jiang's troops gazed on in horror.

Song Jiang was the first to throw away his sword, clap heels to his horse and lead the retreat. The other leaders fled for their lives all in a bunch. The lesser commanders also took flight, so tightly packed together you could not tell one from the other. Gao was after them, waving his sword and urging on his troops, the celestial guard in the lead and the regulars behind them. Song Jiang's army suffered a huge reverse. Gao harried them for half a dozen miles before giving the signal for his men to regroup and return to the city.

Arriving at the foot of a hill, Song Jiang halted his troops and made camp. Although they had suffered losses among the troops, the leaders were fortunately all unscathed. Having settled his troops, Song Jiang held a discussion with the Professor. "This time in the attack on Gaotang we have lost a second battle. We've no means of overcoming the celestial guard, what shall we do?"

"If this blighter can employ wizardry," said the latter, "he will surely come tonight to raid our camp. We must have a plan to pre-empt him. Let's leave just a small force here, while the rest of us go back to the old camp."

Song Jiang gave the orders. Only Panther and the Daytime Rat were left in charge of the camp while the others went back to the old camp to rest.

Now Panther and the Daytime Rat disposed their troops in an ambush several hundred yards outside the camp. About the first watch this is what they saw:

> *In every quarter the murk deepens; from every side the mist spreads. A violent gale arises, shaking heaven and earth. Driving rain causes the seas to boil and the rivers to burst their banks. The Lord of Thunder rages, riding backwards on the Firebreather to vaunt his might; the Lightning Goddess spits, goading the Golden Snake into a venomous display. Great trees are torn up by the roots, deep waters emptied to the dregs.*

During the big storm that night as Panther and the Daytime Rat with their three hundred men lay hidden in the undergrowth, they watched Gao stealthily approach with his three hundred Celestial guards. After certain secret signals, they charged into the camp. They found it empty and were turning round to leave when Panther and the Daytime Rat raised a great shout. Gao and his men suspected they were caught in a trap. They scattered and fled, each of the Celestial guards taking his own path to escape. Panther and the Daytime Rat began loosing crossbow bolts at random, firing for all they were worth, and one of the bolts struck Gao in the left shoulder. Braving the elements they spread out and attacked the fleeing enemy forces. But when Gao and his Celestial guards had put some distance between themselves and the camp Panther and the Daytime Rat, not having many troops at their disposal, dared not continue the pursuit.

A little later the rain had ceased and the sky cleared. The stars were visible again and in the moonlight they found that more than twenty of the Celestial guards had been shot or wounded at the foot of a grassy knoll. They took the wounded to Song Jiang's camp and also told him about the storm. Song Jiang and the Professor were alarmed by what they heard. "We are only a mile or two away, but we had no rain or wind!" they exclaimed.

"It must be the magic," everyone concluded. "It was only in that place and from a height of a few hundred metres. The moisture must have been drawn up from nearby ponds."

Panther said: "Gao Lian charged into our camp, with his hair flying and waving his sword. One of my crossbow bolts hit him and he retreated to the city. We didn't have enough men so I didn't dare pursue him further."

Song Jiang rewarded Panther and the Daytime Rat, the wounded Celestial guards were executed, and the rest of the leaders were ordered to set up seven or eight small camps around the main camp, to protect them from further attacks, while someone was sent to the mountain stronghold to fetch reinforcements.

Meanwhile the wounded Gao was convalescing in the city. He ordered the army to man the defences and to be on the alert night and day. He ruled out any further offensive until he was recovered from his wound, when he vowed he would capture Song Jiang.

When Song Jiang saw his troops defeated his heart was filled with gloom. He discussed matters with the Professor. "Once again we haven't managed to break the power of Gao Lian. Suppose they raise more troops and mount a stronger attack, what then?"

The Professor said: "We'll only break Gao Lian's magic if we do this and this. Unless I can get a certain person to come, it will be difficult to save Chai Jin and we'll never take Gaotang."

Indeed, in order to overcome the power to raise fog and clouds it was necessary to invite a master of the most transcendental and profound knowledge. If you want to know who this person was that the Professor spoke of you must read the next chapter.

Chapter 53

Magic Messenger wins the argument by using his wits; Iron Ox believes he's chopped the Sage to bits!

Now what the Professor told Song Jiang was that they would never break the magic power unless they quickly sent someone to fetch Gongsun Sheng, the Taoist.

Song Jiang said: "But last time the Magic Messenger spent a long time looking for him and drew a complete blank. Where are we going to look now?"

The Professor said: "Just think how many towns, villages and hamlets there are under the jurisdiction of Jizhou. He can't have searched them all. The way I see it, Taoist Gongsun is a very spiritual person, he must be staying in some famous hermit's cave or some blissful abode beside a rushing stream. This time tell the Magic Messenger to go and have a good look outside the city, wherever there is a famous mountain or sacred spot. I am confident that he'll find him."

Accordingly Song Jiang summoned the Magic Messenger and said: "You are to go to Jizhou and fetch Taoist Gongsun."

The Magic Messenger said: "I will gladly go. But it would be good if I could have a travelling companion."

"But how can anyone keep up with you when you start your magic walking mode?" said the Professor.

"If I have a companion, I tie the magic amulets on his legs too," said the Magic Messenger. "That enables him to travel fast as well."

Iron Ox said: "I'd like to accompany Superintendent Dai."

"If you want to go with me, you'll have to eat vegetarian food for the whole journey and obey my orders," said the Magic Messenger.

"No problem," said Iron Ox. "I'll do whatever you say."

Song Jiang and the Professor said: "You'd better watch out on the journey. Don't stir up any trouble. If you find him come back as fast as possible."

Iron Ox said: "It was me who killed the Chancellor and got Mr. Chai into trouble, so naturally I want to save him. I'm certainly not going to cause any more trouble."

The two men concealed weapons on their persons, tied their bundles, bade farewell to Song Jiang and the others and left Gaotang by the Jizhou road.

When they had gone about six miles, Iron Ox stopped and said: "I'd travel more easily if we could stop and have a bowl of wine for the journey."

"If you want to do the magic walking with me you can only have a non-alcoholic drink," said the Magic Messenger. "And we must go straight on afterwards."

"We could eat a little bit of meat, what's wrong with that?" said Iron Ox.

"There you go again," said the Magic Messenger. "But anyway, it's late. Let's look for somewhere to stay. We'll have an early start tomorrow."

After another couple of miles, as dusk was falling, they found an inn where they stopped and lit the fire to cook their rice and procured some wine. Iron Ox brought in a bowl of vegetarian food and a bowl of vegetable broth and gave it to the Magic Messenger.

"Why aren't you eating?" the latter asked.

"I'm not hungry," Iron Ox replied.

The Magic Messenger thought to himself: "He's cheating me, the rogue. He must be eating meat behind my back."

The Magic Messenger finished his vegetarian meal and stole to the back to investigate. There was Iron Ox with two measures of wine and a plate of beef, eating away. "What did I say!" the Magic Messenger exclaimed to himself. "I won't expose him now. I'm going to have some fun with him tomorrow."

The Magic Messenger returned to the room and went to sleep. After eating for a while, Iron Ox began to worry about what the

Magic Messenger had said, and crept back into the room and went to sleep.

The Magic Messenger woke at dawn and told Iron Ox to light the fire and cook some vegetarian food for breakfast. Then they shouldered their bags, paid their bill and left the inn. Before they had gone a mile, the Magic Messenger said: "We didn't do any magic walking yesterday. We need to get on a bit faster today. So make sure your pack is tied on securely, because I'm going to say the spell over you and then we'll do three hundred miles without stopping."

He took out four amulets and tied them on both of Iron Ox's legs. He said: "Wait for me when you get to the next inn." Then he pronounced the formula and blew on Iron Ox's legs.

Iron Ox shot off. It felt just as if he was riding on a cloud, he seemed to be flying.

The Magic Messenger laughed to himself: "He's about to suffer a day of hunger." He fastened on his own amulets and followed.

Iron Ox had no understanding of this mode of travel. He tried to walk just as usual. But the sound of wind and rain was in his ears, houses and woods appeared to fall away as if in long lines on either side, the clouds and mist beneath him seemed to speed his feet on their way. He started to feel afraid. He made several attempts to stop but his two legs would not respond. It was as if there was someone underneath pushing him, his feet simply would not touch the ground, they just kept on going. When he came to an inn and couldn't just pop in and buy something to eat, he cried out: "Please, old chap, let's take a break!"

When they had been travelling till the sun was going down red in the west, Iron Ox was hungry and thirsty. But still he couldn't control his legs. Fear brought him out in a stinking sweat, his breath came in short pants. The Magic Messenger drew closer and called out: "Iron Ox, my friend, why don't you go and buy some snacks to eat?"

"Brother, help me please," Iron Ox replied. "I'm starving!"

The Magic Messenger took some cakes out of his pocket and started eating them.

"I can't buy anything because I don't know how to stop," Iron Ox cried. "Give me a couple, please, to ease my hunger."

"Come a bit closer and I'll give you some," said the Magic Messenger.

Iron Ox stretched out his hand, but he couldn't get closer than three metres and he couldn't reach the cakes. "Please, please brother," he implored. "Wait for me a minute!"

"There's something funny about it today," said the Magic Messenger. "I can't stop either."

"Aiya!" Iron Ox moaned. "These fucking feet of mine won't obey me at all, they just keep going on their own like this, I'd like to get an axe and chop of my bottom half!"

The Magic Messenger said: "Perhaps that's the only solution. Otherwise we shall just keep on going till next New Year's Day and we still won't be able to stop!"

"Please, don't laugh at me!" said Iron Ox. "If I were to chop off my legs I know you'd laugh at me!"

"Maybe you didn't do everything I said yesterday?" said the Magic Messenger. "Today even I can't stop. You'll just have to keep on going!"

Iron Ox cried: "Please, old chap, please let me stop."

"When you're using this magic of mine you mustn't eat meat. Beef above all things is forbidden. If you eat a single piece of beef, you'll have to go ten thousand miles without stopping."

"Then it's a disaster! I deceived you last night, I was a fool. I did secretly buy a few little pieces of beef to eat. It was so good!"

"No wonder then that today even I can't stop going. We'll just have to go on till we reach the end of the sky, it'll take us about three or four years to get back!"

Iron Ox began to shout his complaints to heaven. The Magic Messenger was laughing his head off. "If from now on you'll do everything I say, I'll make the magic stop," he said.

"I will, old chap, I will!"

"Are you going to cheat again and eat meat?"

"If I eat meat again after today, may a boil the size of a rice bowl grow on my tongue! When I saw you were going to eat vegetarian food I simply couldn't stomach it, that's all. But I won't do it again!"

"All right then, I'll let you off!" He took a step back and flapping his sleeve against Iron Ox's legs cried "Halt!", just once. Iron Ox's legs stopped going immediately and remained as if nailed to the ground. They couldn't move.

"I'll go on ahead," said the Magic Messenger. "You follow on slowly."

Now when Iron Ox tried to move his feet, they wouldn't stir from the spot; he tugged at his legs but they wouldn't budge. It was as if they had been cast in iron.

"Oh no! Not again!" Iron Ox exclaimed. "How am I going to get anywhere now?" Then he yelled: "Brother! Help! Help!"

The Magic Messenger turned round, laughing. "Are you going to listen to me now?" he asked.

"I shall respect you like my father, I will never dare to disobey you in anything!"

"This time you'd really better do as I say!" said the Magic Messenger. Touching Iron Ox with his hand, he said "Go!" and they both began to walk easily on.

"Brother, please take pity on me and let's soon have a break!" Iron Ox said after a while. And before long they came to an inn where they stopped for the night. When they went to their room the Magic Messenger took off the amulets, burnt some paper money as an offering, and asked Iron Ox: "Well, how do you feel now?"

Iron Ox said: "These two legs belong to me again."

"Who told you to go and secretly buy wine and meat last night?"

"It's only because you wouldn't let me eat meat I ate some secretly, so now you've had a good laugh at my expense."

The Magic Messenger got Iron Ox to prepare some vegetarian food and non-alcoholic wine for their supper and warm the water to wash their feet. Then they lay down to rest. They slept till dawn. When they had completed their toilet, breakfasted and paid the bill they set off. Before they had gone a mile the Magic Messenger took out the amulets and said: "I'm only going to give you two today, so you'll go a bit slower."

"I'd rather not have any at all, old man," said Iron Ox.

"If you do as I say, we're going to achieve something very important, you and I. Why should I try to make fun of you? But if you don't do as I say, I shall nail you down again like I did yesterday, and you'll have to wait till I've been to Jizhou and found Taoist Gongsun before I can come back and release you."

Iron Ox hurriedly said: "I will, I will."

This time the Magic Messenger and Iron Ox both put on two amulets and when they started the magic walking the Magic Messenger held Iron Ox's elbow. This magic, you see, enabled him to move or stop just by willing it. Iron Ox from now on didn't dream of disobeying him. For the rest of the journey they just bought vegetarian fare, ate and then went on. To cut a long story short, by using the magic walking they were soon outside the walls of Jizhou, where they found an inn to stay.

Next day they went into the city, the Magic Messenger dressed as the master and Iron Ox got himself up as his servant. They searched all day, but no one had heard of Taoist Gongsun, so they retired to their inn to rest. They spent the whole of the next day searching all the little side-streets and alleys, but heard no news. Iron Ox was getting restive. "That bloody monk, where the fucking hell is he hiding?" he complained. "When I find him I'm going to take him by the scruff of the neck and drag him to our leader!"

"There you go again! If you don't listen to me, I'm going to make you regret it!"

"I was only joking," said Iron Ox with a sheepish grin.

But the Magic Messenger went on grumbling for a while and Iron Ox did not dare to answer back. They reached the inn and rested.

They were up early next morning and searched every neighbourhood outside the city walls. Every time he saw an older person, the Magic Messenger bowed and respectfully asked where Taoist Gongsun's house was, but not a single one knew him. He asked in a dozen different places. In the late afternoon when they were really hungry from so much walking they came upon a vegetarian restaurant beside the road and went in to have a snack. But all the tables were taken, not one was free, so they had to go out and stand in the road. The waiter said: "If you want some noodles, sirs, you'd better sit here with this old gentleman."

The Magic Messenger saw an old man all by himself occupying a big table, so he greeted him respectfully and they both sat down opposite. Iron Ox, who was sitting a little behind the Magic Messenger, told the waiter to bring them four bowls of noodles. The Magic Messenger said: "One bowl for me and three bowls for you, are you sure that will be enough?"

"No point in economizing," said Iron Ox. "Make that six, I'll take care of them."

This made the waiter laugh. But they waited hours, and still the noodles didn't come. Watching all the noodles being taken in for other people, Iron Ox became pretty impatient. Then the waiter brought a bowl of steaming noodles and placed it in front of the old man. Without a word of apology, the latter began to eat. Since the noodles were very hot, he lowered his head and leaned forward over the table. Iron Ox lost his temper. Because the noodles hadn't come, he gave a great shout of "Waiter! We've been waiting here half the day!" and banged the table, splashing hot soup all over the old man's face and spilling his noodles. Highly incensed, the old man got up and grabbed Iron Ox. "Where's your manners? Why did you spill my noodles?" he said indignantly.

Iron Ox clenched his fist and was about to strike the old man, but the Magic Messenger hurriedly intervened. He apologized to the old man. "Don't waste your time with him, sir. I will buy you another bowl," he said.

"That's not the point," said the old man. "I've got a long journey ahead of me, and I want to eat quickly so I can go back to hear the talk. If I take too long it will ruin my journey."

"Where are you from, sir?" the Magic Messenger asked. "Whose talk is it you want to hear, and what is he talking about?"

"I am from Nine Halls Village by the Two Immortals Peak in this province. I came here to get some good quality incense and I'm going to hear the Blessed Sage on the mountain speaking on 'The Secret of Longevity.'"

It occurred to the Magic Messenger that this might be where Taoist Gongsun was, so he asked: "Do you by any chance have a Taoist called Gongsun Sheng in your village?"

"Anyone else wouldn't be able to answer your question," said the old man. "Not many people know him. We are neighbours. He's got an old mother. He spends his time wandering about begging, this monk, and nowadays he's called Gongsun the Pure because recently he changed his name to Brother Purity and is no longer Gongsun Sheng. No one knows his old worldly name now."

"It's just like they say," said the Magic Messenger. "You can wear out a pair of iron shoes in the search and still not find what you're looking for; but then you get it without lifting a finger!" He respectfully asked the old man: "How far is this Two Immortals Peak from here?"

"It's just fifteen miles," the latter replied. "Brother Purity is the chief follower of the Blessed Sage. The master won't let him out of his sight."

The Magic Messenger was delighted. He got them to bring the noodles quickly and ate in the old man's company. When they'd paid the bill, they left together. After asking the way, he said to the old man: "You go on ahead, sir. We'll buy some incense and paper to burn and then follow you." The old man said goodbye and left.

The Magic Messenger and Iron Ox went back to the inn to collect their luggage. Then they tied on the amulets again and set off for Two Immortals Peak in Nine Halls Village. With the magic walking they did the fifteen miles in no time. When they asked in the village for Two Imortals Peak, a resident gave them directions: "Out of the village go east and in a mile and a half you're there."

They followed these directions, and just as they had been told, they were soon looking at that mountain, which was indeed outstandingly beautiful:

The mountain is green as if carved from jade; the emerald peaks are swathed in clouds. On opposing cliffs tigers crouch and dragons coil; on every side the howling of apes, the call of the crane. In the morning the summit is lost in cloud, at nightfall the sun hangs in the branches of the trees. Everywhere the tinkle of running water, as if each stream stirred a string of jade pendants. Waterfalls seem to hang in the air and in the mountain cave the zither softly sounds. Perhaps it's a Taoist busy with his rites, or maybe some saintly elder preparing potions.

When they reached the mountain, the Magic Messenger and Iron Ox met a woodcutter. The Magic Messenger greeted him politely and said: "Can I ask you where Brother Purity lives?"

The woodcutter replied: "Just past yon eastern spur of the mountain, 'tis the place with a little stone bridge in front of the gate."

Beyond the spur they found a collection of thatched huts surrounded by a low wall, outside which was a tiny stone bridge. As they reached it a peasant woman came out carrying a tray of fresh fruit.

The Magic Messenger said: "You've just come from the house of Brother Purity, is that right? Is he at home?"

"He's at the back, making up pills," she answered.

Inwardly rejoicing, he told Iron Ox: "Go and hide behind a tree while I go inside. If I find him, I'll come and fetch you."

He entered what was apparently a typical three-room house with a reed curtain hanging over the doorway. At his shout, a white-haired old lady emerged from the inner room. Here's what he saw:

A grey-haired old crone, but still with a rubicund complexion; eyes misty as the smoke of an Autumn Festival lantern, eyebrows white as sunlight glittering on frost. She wears a plain black skirt, like a female immortal in the heavens. Her outer robe is sackcloth, like the old Dame's on Mount Li. In her figure you seem to see a crane soaring among the clouds, in her face the look of a mountain pine proudly standing against the snow.

The Magic Messenger greeted her most respectfully and said: "My greetings, madam. I would like to request an interview with Brother Purity."

"What is your name, please?" the old lady asked.

"My name is Dai Zong, and I have come here from Shandong.

"My son has gone out begging. He isn't back yet."

"I am an old friend, and I want to speak to him about a most urgent matter. Please let me see him."

"He's not at home. If you've got something to say to him you can certainly wait here. When he gets back he'll come and see you."

"I'll come back."

He took leave of the old lady and went out to find Iron Ox. "Now I need to make use of you. Since his mother insists he's not home, you go in now and ask for him. If she says he's not in, threaten her, but remember she's his mother, don't hurt her. When I come in and tell you to stop, do so at once."

Iron Ox first took his two axes out of his pack and tucked them behind his back. Then he went into the house and shouted: "Come out!"

The old lady hurriedly received him and said: "Who is it?"

When she saw Iron Ox scowling at her she was very scared. "What do you want, sir?" she asked.

"I am the Black Whirlwind from the Marshes of Mount Liang," said Iron Ox. "Under orders from my leader I have come to ask for Taoist Gongsun Sheng. Ask him to come out and I'll behave nicely. If he doesn't, I shall start a fucking fire and burn your house to the ground. No arguing now. Just make it snappy!"

"Please be patient, sir," she said. "This is not Gongsun Sheng's house. It belongs to Brother Purity."

"Just ask him to come out, that's all," said Iron Ox. "I'll know him by his fucking face."

"He's gone out begging and he hasn't come back yet."

Iron Ox took out an axe and began to hack at a wall. When the old woman rushed forward to stop him, he said: "If you don't ask your son to come out, I'm going to kill you." He raised his axe as if to strike and the old lady collapsed in a heap. At this moment Taoist Gongsun rushed out, crying: "Stop this disgraceful behaviour!" As the poem says:

This mountain hideout's the perfect place
Pharmacy's secret arts to trace.
Only a rude and rough onslaught
Will persuade the Taoist to come out.

The Magic Messenger also rushed in shouting: "Iron Ox, why are you frightening the old lady?" He hurriedly helped her to her feet.

Iron Ox threw down his axe and respectfully saluted Taoist Gongsun. "Don't be angry with me," he said. "If I hadn't done it you weren't going to come out."

Taoist Gongsun first helped his mother into the inner room. Then he came back and greeted the other two and invited them into a clean room to sit. "What caused you to look for me here?" he asked.

The Magic Messenger said: "Since you left the mountain I have already been once to Jizhou in search of you and couldn't find any trace. I did however get together a band of brothers to join the company on the mountain. Now Song Jiang has gone to Gaotang to rescue Mr. Chai and he has lost several battles to the governor, who has been using magic. He doesn't know what else to try, so he sent me with Iron Ox to find you and ask you to come. We looked all over Jizhou but couldn't find you. We chanced upon an old man from this district in a vegetarian restaurant, and he led us here. We met a peasant woman who told us you were at home preparing pills and potions. But your mother kept denying it, so I got Iron Ox to provoke you into coming out. It was a bit of a nasty trick but please forgive us. For our leader in Gaotang every day that passes increases the danger. Please agree to come with us, for the sake of loyalty to our great enterprise."

Taoist Gongsun said: "It is true that in my youth I used to frequent the rivers and lakes and enjoy the companionship of brave men. But since the time I left Mount Liang and returned home I have had no taste for that life: in the first place I have an aged mother with no one else to look after her; secondly my present master, the Blessed Sage, wants me to stay. I was afraid someone might come looking for me, that is why I changed my name to Brother Purity and hid myself away here."

戴宗智取公孫勝

The Magic Messenger said: "But right now Song Jiang is in extreme peril. Please, out of compassion, Father, come with us, if only for a little while."

Taoist Gongsun said: "The problem is there will be no one to look after my mother. And I doubt if my master would allow it. No, really I can't."

The Magic Messenger threw himself down in supplication. Taoist Gongsun raised him up and said: "Let's think about it later." He left them sitting there in the room while he went to arrange some vegetarian food for them.

When the three had been eating for a while, the Magic Messenger said with many a sigh: "If you won't come with us, Song Jiang will be captured by Gao Lian and from now on the loyal company of the mountain stronghold is no more!"

Taoist Gongsun said: "Let me go and ask my master. If he gives his consent I will go with you."

"Then go and ask him right away."

"Just be patient for this one night. I will go first thing tomorrow morning."

"But for our leader every day that passes is like a year, please let's go now."

So Taoist Gongsun stood up and together with the other two set off on the path to Two Immortals Peak. It was that season when autumn is turning into winter, when the days are short and the nights long and it is easy for the traveller to be benighted. When they were halfway up the mountain a red sun was already sinking in the west. Through the shadow of the pine trees a little path led directly to the hermitage of the Blessed Sage. Before it was a red sign with three gold characters saying "Temple of the Purple Void." The scene that met their eyes when they arrived there was indeed impressive:

The dark green pines stand thickly, the paler green cypresses are luxuriant. A bunch of greybeards listen to the scriptures, while a group of black-robed priests mix medicines. The green wutong trees, the green bamboos, are like a jade screen at the mouth of the cave shutting out the cold; white snow and yellow shoots seem to

> *seal in the heat of the furnace in the pill manufactory. Wild deer wander down the paths, trampling the flowers; mountain apes leap across the gorges picking fruit. The sound of Taoists reciting the scriptures is wafted to the ears, hermits can be seen discussing the law. From the altar to the Heavenly Void the sound of priests chanting the litanies carries on the breeze, from the phoenixes atop the Hall of the Dipper comes the tinkling of jade. Veritably one thinks oneself in heaven, for where else could one go to seek paradise?*

In the vestibule the three of them arranged their dress and then entered from the corridor passing the main hall to the Pines and Cranes Pavilion at the back. Two acolytes, seeing that Taoist Gongsun was bringing two strangers, went and reported it to the master. They returned with an invitation to enter.

When the three men entered, the master had just been praying and was seated on the monk's throne. Taoist Gongsun stepped forward and greeted him reverently, then waited with bowed head. The holy man whom the Magic Messenger and Iron Ox now observed had a truly other-worldly air:

> *His monk's circlet is bedecked with jade leaves, his crane robe is embroidered with gold thread. He has long whiskers and broad cheekbones, and is a steadfast practitioner of the rule to suppress passion; he has green eyes with large pupils, and is replete with longevity pills. He is always nibbling Anqi dates or gobbling Fangshuo peaches. His solar plexus is filled with* qi: *he is brimming with health and vitality. His name is inscribed in the mystic register: he is a pure and unblemished immortal. This is indeed one who loves to stroll at night under the moon and barken to the distant cry of the peacock, or travel a thousand leagues soaring among the clouds on the crane's back.*

The Magic Messenger hurriedly bowed, but Iron Ox simply stared. "Why are these two here?" the holy man asked Taoist Gongsun.

"They are the two young friends I told you about," said Taoist Gongsun. "They are loyal friends from Shandong. It's because the governor of Gaotang has been using magic powers that our friend Song Jiang has sent them here to summon me. Of course I wouldn't go without your permission, so I have come to ask you for it."

"My son, if you wish to escape the burning pit and prepare yourself for longevity, how can you have any desire to return to those realms?"

The Magic Messenger bowed again and said: "I beseech you to give Taoist Gongsun leave. As soon as Gaotang is defeated we will send him back."

"You know nothing about it," said the Blessed Sage. "It is not for the laity to involve themselves in our affairs. Go, take yourselves off."

Taoist Gongsun had no alternative but to take them away. They left the hermitage and went down the mountain that same night.

Iron Ox asked: "What did that old monk say?"

The Magic Messenger said: "Didn't you hear what he said?"

"I know, but I can never work that kind of crap out."

"Well, the upshot of what the master said was that he couldn't go."

Iron Ox began to rave. "The two of us have come all this way, and had a world of trouble finding him, and now he comes out with that shit? That really makes me sick! I'm going to get that bloody monk, I'll twist his crown off with one hand, grab him round the waist with the other and pitch him down the mountain!"

The Magic Messenger gave him a look and said: "You want to have your feet nailed down again?"

Iron Ox said hastily: "I don't mean it, I don't mean it. I was just joking!"

They went back to Taoist Gongsun's house, where a supper was prepared for them. Taoist Gongsun said: "Please stay here tonight, and tomorrow I'll go and plead with my master again. If he gives his permission I'll go with you."

So the Magic Messenger bade him goodnight and the two of them collected their things and went to the clean room. They both went to sleep, but around midnight Iron Ox stealthily got up.

Judging by his companion's heavy breathing that he was soundly asleep, he said to himself: "Isn't it fucking stupid? You're a member of the company of Mount Liang, yet you have to come and ask permission from some fucking priest! If the bugger refuses again tomorrow morning, all our leader's great enterprise goes to pot. I can't stand for that. It's only a question of killing that bloody Taoist, and then he's got no one to ask and he'll have to come with us."

He groped around for his axes and then quietly opened the door and set off up the mountain, moving forward steadily by the light of stars and moon. When he reached the Temple of the Purple Void, the main gates were shut. But the fence was not particularly high. With a spring he was over it. He opened the main gate and entered stealthily. When he got to the Pines and Cranes Pavilion he heard someone behind the partition reciting the Jade Pivot sutra. He crept up close and made a hole in the paper window with a wettened finger: the Blessed Sage was there alone, seated on his throne. On a table before him burnt a little pot of choice incense, and two painted lamps were lit, throwing a bright light on the text.

"This bloody Taoist deserves to die!" Iron Ox said to himself. He crept up to the door and then gave a single push, so that both halves sprang open with a shuddering groan. He rushed inside, raised the head of his axe and brought it crashing down on the Sage's head. It cut right through into the chair. The blood that flowed out was white. Iron Ox chuckled at this. "The bloody Taoist's a virgin, obviously," he said. "He hoards all his spunk and won't let a drop of it go. There's not a trace of red blood."

Looking carefully, he saw that even the priest's crown had been cut in two and the skull was split down to the spinal column. "Well, that's the end of that problem," he said. "He won't be making any more fuss about Taoist Gongsun's going." He turned and ran from the Pines and Cranes Pavilion, leaving the temple by the main corridor. On the way he came upon a black-robed acolyte who barred the way and shouted: "You have killed our master, where do you think you are going?"

"You can have a taste of my axe too, you young bugger!" Iron Ox yelled. He raised his arm, the axe fell, and the head went

李逵斧劈羅真人

bounding along the temple floor. That made two he had killed. "I'd best be off now!" he said with a laugh. He made his way to the main gate and positively flew down the mountain. Arriving at Taoist Gongsun's house he slipped inside and bolted the door. Back in the room he could hear that the Magic Messenger was still fast asleep. He went back to sleep again too.

In the morning Taoist Gongsun got up and prepared breakfast and told the others to eat.

"Please will you go with us again to the mountain and plead with the Sage," the Magic Messenger said to Taoist Gongsun. This caused Iron Ox to smile ironically to himself.

Taking the same road as before, they returned to the mountain. They went again to the Pines and Cranes Pavilion in the Temple of the Purple Void. Two acolytes met them. "Where is the Sage?" Taoist Gongsun asked.

"The Sage is on his throne nurturing his spirit," the acolytes replied.

Iron Ox had a huge shock. His mouth fell open and it was quite a while before he closed it. When they drew aside the curtain and entered they saw the Blessed Sage seated on his throne in the middle of the room. Iron Ox thought to himself: "Can I possibly have killed the wrong person last night?"

"Why have you three come again?" the Blessed Sage asked.

"I have come to implore my master's compassion," said the Magic Messenger, "to help rescue our company from their present straits."

"Who is this big dark fellow?" the Blessed Sage asked.

"He is my comrade, his name is Li Kui," said the Magic Messenger.

"I had not intended to allow Taoist Gongsun to go," said the Blessed Sage with a slight smile. "But for the sake of his honour I shall allow him to absent himself for a little while."

The Magic Messenger prostrated himself in gratitude. Iron Ox thought to himself: "The bastard knows I wanted to kill him, that's why he fucking says it."

At this point the Blessed Sage said: "Shall I have all three of you transported to Gaotang in an instant of time?" They thanked him and the Magic Messenger thought: "It seems as if this Blessed Sage knows some trick like my magic walking."

The Master told his acolytes to bring three handkerchiefs.

The Magic Messenger said: "May I ask, Master, how you propose to transport us to Gaotang?"

The Blessed Sage rose and said: "Come with me." They all followed him out to the cliff. First he took a red handkerchief. He spread it out on the rock and said: "Let my disciple climb onto it." Taoist Gongsun placed both feet on the handkerchief and with a flap of his sleeve the Blessed Sage shouted "Rise!" and the handkerchief turned into a red cloud and Taoist Gongsun went soaring into the sky till he was two hundred feet or more above the mountain. The Blessed Sage shouted "Stop!" and the red cloud became stationary. Then he spread out a blue handkerchief and made the Magic Messenger step onto it. He shouted "Rise!" and the handkerchief changed into a blue cloud and rose up into the sky with the Magic Messenger on it. The two clouds, red and blue, about the size of two rush mats, floated there in the sky above them, while Iron Ox watched open-mouthed. The Blessed Sage now spread a white handkerchief on the rock and bade Iron Ox step onto it. Iron Ox grinned nervously and said: "No tricks now. If I should fall off, I'd look a proper idiot."

"Don't you see the other two?" said the Blessed Sage.

Iron Ox stood on the handkerchief and the Blessed Sage pronounced "Rise" and the handkerchief changed into a white cloud and flew up into the sky. Iron Ox shouted: "Aiya, mine is unstable, bring me down again!"

The Blessed Sage motioned with his right hand and the red cloud and the blue one gradually sank back to earth. The Magic Messenger prostrated himself and stood with bowed head in front of the Sage, while Taoist Gongsun stood on his left. Above them Iron Ox was shouting down: "I've got to relieve myself, I'm going to pee and shit, if you don't bring me down I'm going to do it on your head!"

The Blessed Sage said: "I am a contemplative, I never did anything to upset you, why did you come by night and break in and try to chop me with an axe? If I had not been protected by my virtue, I would be dead. And you killed one of my acolytes too."

"Not me," said Iron Ox. "Perhaps it's a case of mistaken identity!"

The Blessed Sage laughed. "Although you actually only split two of my gourds, your intention was evil, and for that reason I am going to make you suffer for a time." And he signalled with his hand and shouted "Go!", and an ill wind arose and blew Iron Ox off into the midst of the clouds. At this point two yellow-turbanned strong men took charge of Iron Ox. With the sound of wind and rain roaring in his ears he was gradually swept into the territory of Jizhou. He was frightened out of his wits and his hands and feet trembled violently. Then there was a sudden swishing sound, and he fell slap bang into the middle of the Jizhou court of justice.

Governor Ma was actually sitting in his court, with quite a number of officials present in the courtroom, when suddenly, to everyone's utter amazement, this big swarthy character fell from the sky.

"Bring him here!" Governor Ma shouted. Immediately a dozen guards and gaolers dragged Iron Ox before the bench.

"Where the devil have you come from?" the Governor roared. "How do you manage to fall out of the sky like that?"

Iron Ox's pate was cracked and his forehead cut by the fall and at first he was simply unable to speak.

The Governor said: "He must be some kind of magician. This calls for the instruments of justice to be employed." The guards and gaolers tied Iron Ox up and dragged him to an open space in front of the court-house. One of the officers fetched a bowl of dog's blood and plunged his head into it, while another brought a bucket of shit and poured it over Iron Ox, drenching him from head to foot. Iron Ox's mouth and ears were filled with piss and shit.

"I'm not a magician," Iron Ox protested. "I'm a follower of the Blessed Sage."

Now of course everyone knew that the Blessed Sage was a living saint and for this reason they were reluctant to do him any injury. They dragged him before the bench again and one of the officials said: "This Blessed Sage of Jizhou is renowned throughout the world as a living saint. If this is one of his followers we cannot punish him."

Governor Ma merely laughed. "I have read thousands of books and have heard of many wonders ancient and modern, but I never heard of a holy man having a disciple like this one. He's a magician, I tell you. Give the bastard a good hiding!"

The guards were obliged to throw Iron Ox down and beat him to within an inch of his life.

"Confess you're a magician and the beating will stop!" the Governor shouted.

So Iron Ox had to confess that he was "Second Brother Li, the Magician." A heavy cangue was produced and fitted, and he was escorted to the main gaol. When he arrived at the cells for the condemned, he said: "I'm one of the top brass of the spirit world, how dare you put a cangue on me? You people of Jizhou are all going to come to a sticky end."

Now every officer in the gaol knew that the virtue of the Blessed Sage was immense, all held him in the greatest respect, so they said to Iron Ox: "Tell us honestly who you are."

"I am the Blessed Sage's favourite disciple and chief bodyguard. But I committed a small fault and the Sage was angry with me and has cast me in here, allowing me to suffer like this. In two or three days' time he will come to get me out. If you don't provide some food and wine for my comfort I shall see to it all of you and your families die."

This put the wind up all the officers of the gaol and they bought wine and meat which they pressed upon Iron Ox. Seeing how scared they were, Iron Ox invented even more stories. More and more frightened, they brought him hot water to wash in and clean clothes to put on.

"If you don't bring me enough wine and food," Iron Ox told them, "I shall fly off, and you will really be in trouble." The gaolers all had to plead with him. Iron Ox of course remained in the gaol. We shall say no more of this.

When the Blessed Sage told the Magic Messenger all the above, the latter was very upset and begged him to release Iron Ox. The

Blessed Sage retained the Magic Messenger in his quarters for the night and asked him for information about the affairs of the mountain stronghold. The Magic Messenger told of the many good qualities of the two leaders, their loyalty and generosity, their obedience to heaven's will, their vow never to harm honest officials and upright citizens, filial sons and chaste women, and all their various virtues. The Blessed Sage was most impressed. The Magic Messenger stayed five days, daily kowtowing and pleading with the Blessed Sage for Iron Ox's release. The Blessed Sage said: "It's best to expel such people, don't take him back with you."

The Magic Messenger said: "But you see, although Iron Ox is a bit of a fool, and rather undisciplined, he has his good points. For one thing he's absolutely straight and would never pick on anyone. Also he's no toady, he'll stick to his guns even if he has to die for it. And thirdly, he's not a philanderer, nor is he greedy or treacherous, and he is always foremost in a fight. For all these reasons Song Jiang loves him. If I were to go back without him, it would be very difficult for me to face my leader."

The Blessed Sage said: "I know full well that this person is one of the baleful stars come down to earth. Because men have committed too many sins he has been sent as a scourge. How could I go against heaven's will and harm this person? I intend only for him to suffer a while, afterwards I shall return him to you."

The Magic Messenger prostrated himself in gratitude.

The Blessed Sage called out: "Where is my yellow-turbanned bodyguard?" and a sudden gust of wind swept through the Pines and Cranes Pavilion. When it had passed, a mighty yellow-turbanned bodyguard stood before them. Here is what they saw:

Face red as a beetroot and hair like black silk, he seems at least ten feet tall and built with strength enough to lift a ton. His yellow turban is tilted on one side and secured with a gold ring which throws back the sun's bright rays; over his embroidered robe the iron armour spreads a frosty shadow that would swallow the moon. He stands guard over the altar of the law and every evil spirit that draws near to earth is vanquished forthwith.

"What is your command, Master?" said the yellow-turbanned bodyguard.

"That criminal I sent you with to Jizhou has served his term," said the Blessed Sage. "I want you to go back to Jizhou and fetch him. Go quickly and return quickly."

The bodyguard saluted and left. About an hour later Iron Ox tumbled out of the heavenly void.

The Magic Messenger immediately helped him to his feet and asked: "Where have you been for the last two days, brother?"

But Iron Ox had seen the Blessed Sage and was busy kowtowing and saying: "Forgive me, Master!"

The Blessed Sage said: "From now on you had better control yourself. Do all you can to help Song Jiang and do not nurture evil tendencies."

Iron Ox prostrated himself again, saying: "I shall never dare to disregard the Master's words."

"But where exactly have you been all this time?" the Magic Messenger asked again.

"That gust of wind the other day blew me to Jizhou district court," Iron Ox replied. "I bounced off the roof of the courtroom and they seized me. Governor Ma said I was a magician so they tied me up and then the guards from the prison poured dog's blood and shit all over me and beat me till my legs were like pulp. They put a cangue on me and chucked me in the main gaol. When they asked me how I had managed to fall out of the sky, I told them I was the Blessed Sage's favourite disciple and chief bodyguard and that I was being punished like this because of a little fault I committed, and that in a few days time he would come and release me. Although I was beaten, I got quite a lot of wine and food out of them, because they're so scared of the Blessed Sage. They bathed me and gave me clean clothes. While I was in one of the inner rooms enjoying a bit of wine and meat, this yellow-turbanned fellow suddenly dived out of the sky, took off my cangue, told me to shut my eyes, and I was wafted here like in a dream."

Taoist Gongsun said: "The Master has more than a thousand of these yellow-turbanned bodyguards, all at his service."

"My God!" Iron Ox cried. "Why didn't you tell me that before? I would never have misbehaved!" He hurriedly prostrated himself again.

The Magic Messenger said: "We have been here many days now, and the troops in Gaotang are in a desperate situation. I humbly beg the Master to allow Taoist Gongsun to go with us to rescue Song Jiang and destroy Gaotang before returning to the mountain."

The Blessed Sage said: "Originally I didn't want to let him go, but now on account of your great loyalty I shall permit him to absent himself for a while. But I have some words for him which I want him to remember."

Taoist Gongsun stepped forward and knelt to hear the Blessed Sage's instructions. He was indeed filled with ambition to bring peace and salvation to the world and destined to ride the phoenix and tread the clouds.

But if you want to know what it was the Blessed Sage told Taoist Gongsun, you must read the next chapter.

Chapter 54

The Taoist uses magic to defeat Gao Lian; Iron Ox descends the well to rescue Chai Jin!

Now here is what the Blessed Sage said to Taoist Gongsun: "My son, you have studied magic. You can match Gao Lian. I am going to reveal to you the orthodox technique of the Five Thunders. Following this method it is possible to rescue Song Jiang, protect the country and pacify the people, and perform heaven's will. Do not become entangled in human desires and neglect the great task, concentrate on following the essence of Taoist practice which you have learnt. As for your mother, I will send someone morning and evening to see that she is all right, so have no sad thoughts about her. I know that you are one of the stars from the upper regions of heaven, and that is why I give you leave to go and assist Song Jiang. I have this eight character verse which you must have in mind if you are to avoid future mistakes."

Here is the verse the Sage pronounced:

On encountering darkness halt,
Reaching Kaifeng turn back.

When Taoist Gongsun had humbly received the secret doctrine, the three of them bade farewell to the Blessed Sage and the other Taoists and went down the mountain. When they reached Taoist Gongsun's home he got together his priest's cloak, his two swords, his iron circlet, jade sceptre and other religious objects and bade farewell to his mother and then off they went.

When they had gone some ten miles, the Magic Messenger said: "I shall go on ahead to let Song Jiang know, and you Father must continue along the road with Iron Ox. I'll return later to meet you."

"Right you are," said Taoist Gongsun. "We'll press on by ourselves."

"Mind you serve the father faithfully on the journey," the Magic Messenger commanded Iron Ox. "If there's any trouble I shall make sure that you regret it."

Iron Ox said: "He's got the same magic as the Blessed Sage. How could I dare not treat him with respect?"

The Magic Messenger tied on his amulets and raced on ahead, doing his magic walking.

As for Taoist Gongsun and Iron Ox, after leaving the Two Immortals Peak they took the main road and at evening sought accommodation for the night. Iron Ox, fearing Taoist Gongsun's magic, served him most attentively on the journey: he didn't dream of misbehaving! After travelling for three days they came to a place called Battle Knoll. Here they found a populous community and Taoist Gongsun said: "We've been travelling several days and we're tired. We'd better buy ourselves some non-alcoholic wine and some plain noodles before we go on."

"Hear hear," said Iron Ox.

They found a small inn beside the highway, so they went in and sat down. Taoist Gongsun took the place of honour, while Iron Ox removed his belt and sat down next to him. They called the waiter, to ask for wine and some vegetarian food.

"What kind of vegetarian snacks have you got?" Taoist Gongsun asked.

"We only sell wine and meat," the waiter said. "There isn't anything vegetarian. But they sell date cakes in the market."

"I'll go and buy some," Iron Ox said. He got some silver out of his pack and went off to the market, where he bought a bag of the date cakes. He was about to return when he heard the sound of applause somewhere off to one side, and cries of "What strength!" People were crowding round a big fellow who was putting on a performance with an iron hammer the size of a melon, to the admiration of the onlookers.

The man was very tall, with a pock-marked face and big scar on his nose. The hammer must have weighed something like thirty catties. The big fellow swung his hammer and "pow!"

smashed it down into a paving stone, which was reduced to powder. The crowd applauded.

This was too much for Iron Ox. He tucked the date cakes inside his shirt and went to grab the hammer. "Who the fuck are you?" the big man shouted. "How dare you steal my hammer!"

"What's so fucking wonderful about what you're doing?" said Iron Ox. "What is there to get excited about? It offends my eyes! Let me show you how, just watch me for a bit!"

"I'll lend you the hammer," said the other. "But if you fail to lift it, I'll give you a good thrashing!"

Iron Ox took the hammer like someone picking up a marble. He swung it around for a bit and then gently put it down. He was not even flushed. His heartbeat was measured and his breathing unhurried. Seeing this, the other man threw himself down, and said: "Please tell me your name."

"Where do you live?" Iron Ox asked him.

"Just over there," the other answered. He led Iron Ox to a place with a locked door. He unlocked the door and invited Iron Ox in to sit down. The house was full of anvils and hammers, there was a furnace, forge, chisels and other tools of the trade. "This fellow must be a blacksmith," Iron Ox said to himself. "He'd be very useful to us in the stronghold. Why not persuade him to join?"

So Iron Ox said to the stranger: "Would you mind telling me your full name, sir?"

"My name is Tang Long. My father was an officer of the Yan'an garrison. Because he could work iron he happened to be of service to old Marshal Zhong and was employed on his staff. A little while back my father passed away up there and I became addicted to gambling and fell into the way of the rivers and lakes, which is why I come to be here and spend my time working as a smith. I am passionately fond of spear and staff play. Because I am covered in these pock marks people call me Spots. May I ask what your name is?"

"I am Li Kui, the Black Whirlwind, from the Marshes of Mount Liang," said Iron Ox.

Spots prostrated himself all over again, and said: "I have heard so much about you. I never expected to meet you here today!"

"How will you ever make a career for yourself here?" said Iron Ox. "Wouldn't it be better to go with me and join the band on Mount Liang? We'd make you one of the leaders."

Spots said: "If you're really willing to take me with you, I would do anything for you." So saying he prostrated himself to Iron Ox as to an elder brother, while the latter accepted him as younger brother.

"I have no family or other ties," Spots said. "Why don't we go into town and have a few cups of wine together, to celebrate our becoming brothers? We can rest tonight and start early tomorrow."

"I've got this priest at an inn up the road," said Iron Ox. "He's waiting for me to bring him some date cakes to eat before we go on. We can't waste any time. As soon as possible we must continue our journey."

"Why are you in such a hurry?" Spots asked.

"It's like this, our leader Song Jiang right now is attacking Gaotang and he is waiting for us to take this priest back to lend a hand."

"Who is he then, this priest?" Spots asked.

Iron Ox said: "Don't ask so many questions. Pack your bags quickly and let's go!"

Spots hurriedly tied his bundle, got some silver for travelling expenses, donned a hat, buckled on a sword, grabbed a halberd, abandoned his tumbledown old house with its rough furnishings and accompanied Iron Ox to the inn where Taoist Gongsun was waiting.

"Why have you been so long?" Taoist Gongsun grumbled. "If you're going to waste so much time, I shall go back home."

Iron Ox dared not answer back. He presented Spots and explained how they had become brothers. When he heard that Spots was a blacksmith, Taoist Gongsun was mollified. Iron Ox got out the date cakes and told the waiter to serve them. After drinking several cups and eating the date cakes, they called for the bill. Iron Ox and Spots shouldered their packs and with Taoist Gongsun left Battle Knoll and took the road for Gaotang. Early one morning, after three stops and two full days of travel, they saw the Magic Messenger coming to meet them. Taoist Gongsun was very pleased and quickly asked: "How has the battle been going?"

The Magic Messenger said: "That bastard Gao Lian has recovered from the arrow wound. Every day he marches out and issues a challenge. Song Jiang stands firm and doesn't venture forth."

"We shall be all right then," said Taoist Gongsun.

Iron Ox presented Spots to the Magic Messenger and explained all about him. The four then hurried on to Gaotang. When they were just over a mile from the camp, the Little Duke and the Halberdier came out to meet them with a hundred cavalry and some extra horses. The four mounted and rode into the camp where they found Song Jiang and the Professor awaiting them. After the greetings, a celebratory wine was served, questions were asked and answered, and then they were invited into the command tent where there was a banquet for all the leaders. Iron Ox presented Spots to Song Jiang, the Professor and all the rest. After courtesies had been exchanged the whole camp settled down to feasting.

Next day in the command tent Song Jiang, the Professor and Taoist Gongsun discussed how to defeat Gaotang. Taoist Gongsun said: "You must give the order to strike camp and advance. We'll see what the enemy does, but don't worry, I have a plan."

The same day Song Jiang spread word throughout the camp that everyone was to muster their troops and advance on Gaotang. They pitched camp again beneath the walls. After an early breakfast, they armed themselves. The three leaders rode out in front of the army, and with banners waving, drums beating, men cheering and gongs sounding, they bore down on the city.

Inside the city Governor Gao Lian had been recovering from his arrow wound. That night a soldier reported that Song Jiang's army was on the march. At dawn next day the Governor put on his armour, had the city gates opened and the drawbridge lowered, and marched out of the city to encounter the enemy, with his three hundred Celestial guards and all his officers. As the two armies drew close enough for the banners and drums of the other side to be clearly seen, the ranks deployed in battle formation. On either side special drums were beaten and many-coloured banners waved.

Ten riders now detached themselves from Song Jiang's ranks in a V formation. On his left wing were five leaders: Colonel Hua, Thunderclap, Whiskers, Golden Wings and the Little Duke, on the right another five, namely Leopard's Head, Colonel Sun, Redeye, the Flautist and the Halberdier. Three horsemen remained in the centre, the chief of them the commander-in-chief Song Jiang. He was dressed like this:

> *On his head a cloth of alizarin red, his waist girt with an outlandish belt with lion's head clasp. His brocade military robe has a big eagle on the back, his burnished helmet has a brilliant phoenix in flight on the brim. Green boots tread jewelled stirrups, gold armour shines like the rippling scales of a dragon. His gilt saddle flap consorts with the purple silk whip; the embroidered saddle cloth perfectly matches his horse, which is dappled like peach blossom.*

The rider on Song Jiang's left was the chief military adviser of Mount Liang, Professor Wu Yong, and on his right was the deputy military adviser, Taoist Gongsun. Together the three commanders rode out in front of their troops.

On the other side Governor Gao Lian also rode out in front and in stentorian tones roared out: "Now listen here, you bunch of swamp-dwelling ruffians, since you've come here to seek us out, there's got to be victory and defeat, there's got to be a winner and a loser, the one who turns tail is no man!"

Song Jiang's response was to shout: "Who will take that bastard for me and cut his head off?"

Immediately the Archer, Colonel Hua, levelled his lance and urged his horse forward, charging into action. Gao Lian in turn shouted: "Who will capture that bandit for me?"

Someone rode out from a group of staff officers, waving a pair of sabres and mounted on a fiery horse. He charged into action to encounter Colonel Hua. There in front of the armies they fought several bouts, till Colonel Hua suddenly turned his horse and fled back towards his own side. His opponent did not realize it was a trick. Giving his horse its head and brandishing his sabres he galloped in pursuit. Colonel Hua deliberately reined in his horse, took his bow and arrows, and twisting in the saddle loosed a shaft which sent his pursuer tumbling head over heels from his horse. A cry arose from the watching armies on both sides.

Gao Lian was enraged. He hurriedly grasped the special brass shield for calling out wild beasts which hung from the pommel of his saddle, and took a firm grip of his sword. He knocked three times on the shield and from among the ranks of the Celestial guards a cloud of yellow sand arose engulfing everything so that the sky was veiled and the earth grew dark and the sun's brightness was extinguished. A great cry arose as this cloud of yellow sand spewed forth jackals, wolves, tigers, leopards, together with divers unknown beasts and poisonous reptiles. All the troops naturally fled.

Taoist Gongsun, however, grasping his famous sword, with its ancient pattern of pine trees, faced the enemy forces and pointed as he pronounced a muttered spell, climaxing in a shout of: "Chrrr!" Immediately a golden ray shot out and the whole pack of strange beasts and venomous reptiles fell back writhing and squirming into the cloud of yellow sand in front of the armies. The soldiers were now able to observe that they were all white paper cut-outs. The cloud of sand also subsided and vanished. Song Jiang now pointed with his whip stock and the three wings of his army charged forward together. Soldiers died and horses fell, the standards were scattered. Gao Lian hastily withdrew his Celestial guards into the city. Song Jiang's troops pursued them to the city walls, but the drawbridge was quickly drawn up and the gates closed, while blocks of wood and ballista missiles poured down on them like rain. On Song Jiang's orders, a gong sounded the order for his troops to return to camp. Numbers were counted and a great victory was celebrated. Back in the tents praise and thanks were given for the magic powers and virtue of Taoist Gongsun, and the army was rewarded.

Next day the army, in four divisions, mounted a furious attack on the town from every side. Taoist Gongsun said to the other two

公孫勝鬥法破高廉

leaders: "Although we destroyed the greater part of their forces yesterday, the three hundred Celestial guards evidently managed to retreat into the town. If we press them hard today the buggers will undoubtedly try to steal into our camp by night. This evening we must take up a position somewhere. At night we'll pull out our forces after dark, and lay an ambush in four separate groups. We'll build false defences. All the commanders are to wait till they hear a loud report and see fires within the camp and then attack."

Orders were given accordingly. The attack was continued until midday, and then the troops on all four sides returned to camp, where there was music and feasting. As night began to fall, the leaders quietly led their separate forces away and set up the ambush all around.

Song Jiang, the Professor, Taoist Gongsun, Colonel Hua, Thunderclap, the Little Duke and the Halberdier waited on top of a small rise. At nightfall Gao Lian had, as expected, assembled his three hundred Celestial guards each carrying an iron gourd filled with sulphur and brimstone, gunpowder and explosive materials. Each man also carried a hook, an iron broom, and a reed whistle between his teeth. Some time before midnight the city gates were opened, the drawbridge lowered, and with Gao Lian leading them the Celestial guards, followed by another three hundred cavalry, went into action. When they were close to the camp, Gao Lian made a magic signal: a black cloud enveloped the sky and a violent wind arose, flinging sand and stones about and shaking the earth to its very foundations. The Celestial guards took out their tinder-boxes and lit the touch-papers at the mouth of the iron gourds, blew a blast on their whistles and amid the darkness, their bodies masked by the blaze, with swords and axes whirling, swept into the camp.

Taoist Gongsun on top of the hill made magic with his sword and a clap of thunder rang out across the whole flat area of the camp. The three hundred Celestial guards recoiled in dismay. The empty camp was now alive with flickering lights, casting a red glow everywhere. There was no way of escape. The troops lying in ambush on every side closed in. Surrounded as they were by the stockade and darkness, not one of the three hundred Celestial guards got away. All died there in the camp.

Gao Lian with some three hundred cavalry raced back to the city. Some troops were in close pursuit. This was Leopard's Head Lin Chong's force. Seeing the pursuers were so close behind, the drawbridge was raised in a hurry. Only eight or nine horsemen got back into the city with Gao Lian. The rest were taken alive by Leopard's Head and his men. Back in the city Gao Lian ordered the citizens onto the battlements to defend it. His army, including the Celestial guards, had been wiped out by Song Jiang and Leopard's Head.

Next day Song Jiang was quick to deploy his troops around the city again. Gao Lian said to himself: "All those years I spent studying magic, who'd have thought they could defeat me! What am I going to do now? My only hope is to send someone to request help from the neighbouring districts." He hastily composed two letters and sent them to two cities that were not far off, whose governors had both been preferred by his brother. He asked them to come by night with troops to reinforce him. Two aides-de-camp were entrusted with the letters, the west gate was opened and they galloped off on the road westwards.

When the commanders of the besieging force wanted to pursue them, the Professor said: "Let them go. We'll match their plan with one of our own."

"How do you propose to do that?" Song Jiang asked.

"The forces within the city are greatly reduced in numbers. That is why they are sending for help. We can use two detachments of our own troops to play the part of a relieving force, caught up in a fight with us on their way to the city. Gao Lian will naturally open the gates and come to their assistance. This will give us the opportunity to take the city and also to entice Gao Lian onto a narrow path where we can capture him."

This was all greatly to Song Jiang's liking. He told the Magic Messenger to return to Mount Liang and form two detachments of troops, with instructions to approach separately.

Now every day Gao Lian was having sticks piled up in an open space in the city and lit as a signal bonfire. In the city they were continually on the lookout for a relieving force. After a few days the sentries on the city walls saw confused fighting in Song Jiang's lines and immediately reported it. Gao Lian hurriedly armed himself and went up onto the battlements to look. He saw two columns of troops advancing, raising a cloud of dust that cloaked the sun and wildly cheering, whilst the besieging troops fled in all directions. Gao Lian decided it must be that two relief columns had arrived. He quickly ordered the gates to be opened and the defending troops sallied forth, dividing in pursuit of the enemy.

When Gao Lian ran into Song Jiang's army, he saw the latter with Colonel Hua and Thunderclap riding away down a small path. He immediately gave chase. But when he suddenly heard a string of explosions, he began to suspect something. He ordered his troops to turn back. Gongs began to sound on either side. On the left the Little Duke came down, on the right the Halberdier, each with five hundred troops. Gao Lian tried to flee but the greater part of his troops were destroyed.

When Gao Lian fled from the thick of the battle, it was only to find that the banners of Mount Liang were now flying over the city walls. Raising his eyes for a second look, he noted that there was no sign whatsoever of a relieving force. His only resort now was to lead the remnants of his army away into the mountains by a small lonely path. But had barely gone three miles when a troop of men and riders led by Colonel Sun appeared from behind the mountain and barred the way. "We've been waiting a long time for you!" Colonel Sun shouted. "Dismount and allow us to tie you up!"

Gao Lian tried to turn back, but there was another body of troops barring the way behind him. The leader of these was Whiskers. Trapped between these two forces, with every escape route blocked, Gao Lian could only abandon his horse and flee up the mountain. From all sides now his opponents pursued him over the mountainside. Gao Lian desperately gabbled a spell and shouted "Rise!" Immediately he began to ascend slowly into the sky on a black cloud, till he was level with the peak.

At this point Taoist Gongsun appeared on the side of the mountain. When he saw what was happening, he waved his sword towards the sky, muttered a spell and shouted: "Chrrr!" He pointed up with his sword and Gao Lian came crashing down out of his cloud. Immediately Sergeant Lei rushed over and cut him in two with one blow of the halberd.

Thus did this wretched governor learn the illusory nature of power, like the man who awoke from a dream of glory to find he had been lording it over an anthill:

Heaven's scrutiny can't be fooled.
By the powers of Earth be ruled.
The law should be observed;
The spirits must be served.
The cruel are cruelly rent,
The despot's power is spent.
Be on the look-out all your life,
For hardship, danger and strife.

Sergeant Lei picked up the head and they all trooped back down the mountain. First they sent an urgent message to the commander-in-chief. When Song Jiang heard that Gao Lian was dead he marshalled his forces and marched into Gaotang. Orders were first issued not to harm the people. Peace was declared, and a total amnesty. Then they went to the gaol to rescue Mr. Chai. The chief gaoler and all his staff had fled by this time and only some forty or fifty convicts remained. They all had their cangues removed and were set free. But there was no sign of Mr. Chai among them. Song Jiang was extremely anxious. Then in a detention room he came upon all the family of Mr. Chai's cousin, Chai Huangcheng. In another cell he found all the members of Mr. Chai's family who had been brought from his home province and locked up there. Because the fighting had been continuous for several days, they had not yet been questioned or dealt with. But he could find no trace of Mr. Chai.

The Professor had the Gaotang gaolers rounded up and questioned. Among them was one who said: "I am Lin Ren, a warder from the prison. The day before yesterday His Excellency Governor Gao Lian gave orders for Chai Jin to be locked up under tight security, lest he should escape. The order said: 'If anything goes wrong you must put him to death.' Three days ago the Governor wanted to take Chai Jin away for execution. I could see he was a good man and I did not want to do it. So I got out of it by saying: 'The man is seriously ill; the execution cannot be carried out.' Later when they put even more pressure on me, I reported that Chai Jin was dead. Because of the continual fighting the Governor had no time to check up, but I was afraid he would send someone to do so and my crime would be discovered, so yesterday I took Chai Jin to a dried-up well at the back of the prison. I removed his cangue and told him to hide in the well. I don't know whether he is still alive or not."

Song Jiang told this warder to take him there at once. They found the dry well behind the prison and looked down it. It was pitch black and it was impossible to say how deep it was. They shouted down, so anyone there should have heard. They lowered a rope to the bottom: it was over eighty feet deep. "Obviously Mr. Chai is long since dead," Song Jiang said. He shed tears.

"It's no use grieving, commander," said the Professor. "Who dares go down and investigate, to see if he's there or not?"

Before he'd even finished speaking, Iron Ox popped up and shouted: "Just let me go!"

"Good," said Song Jiang. "Since it was you who got him into trouble in the first place, it's fitting for you to make recompense."

Iron Ox merely laughed. "I'm not afraid of going down there," he said. "Only don't cut the rope!"

"What a joker you are," said the Professor.

They got a big bamboo basket and a thick rope, which was tied to a wooden frame, and then thrown into the well. Iron Ox stripped to the skin, took his two axes and sat in the basket while they lowered him. Two bells were attached to the rope.

Slowly Iron Ox descended to the bottom. He clambered out and started to feel about on the floor of the well. Presently he touched a pile of something. It was a skeleton. "Well, blow me!" he exclaimed. "What a fucking horrible place this is!"

As he went on feeling about, he found the bottom of the well to be soaking wet, with no firm ground to stand on. He threw his two axes into the basket and began to feel about with both hands.

井

He stretched his arms out in all directions and eventually touched a human body huddled in a pool of water. "Mr. Chai!" Iron Ox shouted out. There was a slight movement. When he touched the body he seemed to hear a faint whisper. "Thank heavens, it seems as if it's still possible to save him!" he said. He climbed into the basket and shook the bell till they pulled him up.

When Iron Ox told them what he had found below, Song Jiang said: "You'll have to go down again and put Mr. Chai into the basket. We'll pull him up first and then lower the basket again for you."

"Listen," said Iron Ox. "I was made a fool of twice on the way to Jizhou. I hope this isn't going to be a third time someone plays a trick on me."

Song Jiang laughed. "Why should I play tricks on you? You get down there again, quickly." So Iron Ox had to get into the basket and go down the well again.

When he reached the bottom and clambered out, he lifted Mr. Chai bodily and put him in the basket. He gave a tug to the rope and those above hearing the bell began to haul on it. When the basket and its load reached the top, all were overjoyed. Chai Jin's head and face were swollen and cut and his legs coated in mud and he could not open his eyes. He was a sorry sight to behold, and Song Jiang implored the doctor to cure him.

Iron Ox, meanwhile, had been left bellowing at the bottom of the well. Song Jiang hurriedly ordered the basket to be lowered again to bring him up. When he rose to the surface Iron Ox indignantly exclaimed: "You're not very kind, all of you! You didn't want to send the basket down again for me!"

"We were too concerned about Mr. Chai," Song Jiang said. "That's why we forgot you. I'm sorry."

Song Jiang had them lay Mr. Chai in a cart. The two families went first, together with a lot of their possessions that had been recovered. Altogether there were more than twenty carts. He told Iron Ox and Sergeant Lei to guard and escort them to Mount Liang. Then he had Gao Lian's family, young and old, good and bad, thirty or forty people in all, executed in the market-place. The helpful warder Lin Ren was rewarded. The coffers and granaries of Gaotang, together with all stores of private wealth, were emptied and everything in them transported to the mountain. Then all the commanders left Gaotang and returned victorious to the Marshes of Mount Liang. They exacted no penalties whatsoever on the places they passed through. They travelled several days before reaching the stronghold.

Despite his weakness, Chai Jin got up to thank Chao Gai, Song Jiang and all the others. At Chao Gai's instance, another house was built on the summit, where Song Jiang had his residence, for Chai Jin and his family to live in. Everyone was pleased with this. Two new leaders, Chai Jin and Spots, had now been added to the company and a banquet was held to celebrate. Of this no more.

Meanwhile the news of Gao Lian's death and the fall of Gaotang to the rebels had reached the governors of the two neighbouring districts. They wrote to the Emperor. The fleeing Gaotang officials also arrived in the capital and recounted what had happened. Marshal Gao heard how his younger brother had been killed.

Next day before dawn Marshal Gao was up and awaiting the dawn bell in the court of the Waterclock. All the courtiers had assembled there in ceremonial dress to await the dawn audience. In the third drumbeat of the fifth watch the Emperor entered the hall. Three taps of the staff and the officials civil and military lined up in their ranks. When the Emperor was seated, the master of ceremonies called out: "If there are matters to report stand forth and declare them; if not, take leave and depart."

Accordingly, Marshal Gao came forward and said: "Recently in Jizhou the leaders of the Mount Liang bandits, Chao Gai and Song Jiang have been creating mayhem. They have plundered cities and robbed government stores. They have raised an army of ruffians who recently massacred the forces of Jizhou. They caused havoc in Jiangzhou and Wuweijun, and still more recently they wiped out Gaotang and made off with all the government stores. This activity poses a grave threat to internal security. If it is not dealt with soon, the rebel power will grow day by day, till it becomes difficult to control them. I beg Your Majesty to take action."

The Emperor was greatly perturbed by this report and handed down the following order: Marshal Gao was to pick commanders and deploy troops to eradicate the evil. The marshes were to be swept clean and total extermination effected.

Marshal Gao submitted: "To deal with a bunch of outlaws like these there is no need to raise a big army. I can do the job with just one man whom I shall recommend."

The Emperor said: "If it is someone appointed by you, I have no doubt that he will be excellent. Let him set off at once and return quickly with news of victory. He shall have promotion and an ample reward. He can expect to be given the highest responsibility."

Marshal Gao said: "The man I have in mind is from Hedong, and is a direct descendant of General Huyan Zan, who won fame at the founding of the dynasty. His name is Huyan Zhuo. He fights with two steel rods, and his valour is such that a thousand men cannot stand against him. He holds the position of military commander of Runing and has many brave soldiers and valiant officers under his command. This is the man I recommend for the pacification of Mount Liang. If he is given command of a force, with sufficient foot soldiers and cavalry and keen officers, he will in short order clean out that nest of bandits and return in triumph."

The Emperor graciously gave his consent and an imperial order was issued requiring the council to send a messenger immediately to summon Twin Rods, as he was popularly known. After the dawn audience Marshal Gao conferred with the council of ministers and appointed a military officer to bear the imperial order and deliver the summons. The man left the same day, bearing strict orders for Twin Rods to report to the capital without delay and receive his instructions.

Twin Rods was holding a meeting of his military council when the usher announced: "An imperial order is on its way, sir, requiring your presence in the capital to hear about an important assignment."

Twin Rods and his officers received the bearer of the imperial command at the city gate and invited him to the council chamber. When Twin Rods had read the edict he laid on a feast for the messenger. He hurriedly got together his helmet, armour, horse and weapons, and with a personal retinue of thirty or forty followers travelled non-stop to the capital.

Nothing of importance happened on the journey. Arriving in the capital he dismounted before the palace and sought out Marshal Gao. Gao the Ball was in session at the time. The usher called out: "Marshal Huyan Zhuo from Runing is here."

Marshal Gao was well pleased and called him in at once. This Twin Rods was a most striking figure:

> *Descendant of an official who helped found the dynasty, great great grandson of a famous general of the first emperor, he has inherited a truly miraculous technique with the rods; he is bold and experienced in battle. He would beard the tiger in its den with a bare sword, and flights of eagles are not beyond the reach of his arrows. This is the famous warrior who is nicknamed Twin Rods.*

After the interview Marshal Gao rewarded him financially. Next morning at dawn he had an audience with the Emperor. The Emperor recognizing that this was someone quite out of the ordinary, looked upon him with a gracious smile and presented him with a "snowy-footed raven-hued steed," that is to say a horse black as an ink-stick, but with four white socks, as white as mourning sackcloth. That is why it is called a "snowy-footed raven-hued steed." It could do three hundred miles a day and was a personal gift of the Emperor's to Twin Rods.

Twin Rods expressed his thanks and then Marshal Gao took him back to the military council chamber to discuss matters relating to the raising of an army to annihilate Mount Liang.

Twin Rods said: "May I say something? According to my intelligence, the troops of Mount Liang are well led and have a high level of fighting skills. They should not be underestimated. I would like to recommend two officers to lead the attack. With their forces added to our own we can be certain of success."

Marshal Gao was glad to hear this. "Who is it you recommend then, to lead the attack?" he asked.

Now if Twin Rods had not recommended these two officers, things would have been different. As it was, important new leaders joined up in the Place of Many Meanderings, and in the Marshes of Mount Liang the government troops got a hiding. Although the two names may not appear on the imperial roll of honour, they are certainly good enough to grace the Assembly Hall of the Heroes.

Who it was that Twin Rods recommended to Marshal Gao you must read the next chapter to find out.

Chapter 55

Marshal Gao finds himself three commanders; Twin Rods deploys his linked cavalry!

Now when Marshal Gao asked Twin Rods: "Who is it that you recommend for leading the attack?" the latter replied: "The man I refer to is district commander in Chenzhou. His name is Han Tao. He was originally from the Eastern Capital. He has passed the second grade military examinations. His weapon is a spear of jujube wood. They call him Victorious because he wins so often. He is just the man to lead the main attack. Another is the district commander of Yingzhou. He is called Peng Qi and hails from the Eastern Capital too. His family have been soldiers for generations. His weapon is a double-edged blade with three prongs. His martial skill is so outstanding they call him the Supremo. He can be second in the attack."

Marshal Gao was well satisfied with what he heard. "With these two leading the attack, we can forget about those brigands," he said. He immediately signed two orders prepared by the Chancellery and had the Council send messengers to ride post-haste to Victorious and the Supremo and order them to report with all speed to the capital. Within a short space of time the two commanders had arrived. They went straight to the Chancellery where they met Marshal Gao and Twin Rods. Next day Marshal Gao took them all to the imperial parade ground where they practised manoeuvres. After reviewing the troops, they returned to the Chancellery and met with members of the Council to discuss important military matters.

Marshal Gao asked: "How many troops do you have altogether, in your three armies?"

Twin Rods replied: "About five thousand cavalry, and if you include the foot soldiers perhaps as many as ten thousand."

高太尉大興三路兵

Marshal Gao said: "I want all three of you to go back to your districts and choose another three thousand spirited cavalry and five thousand foot soldiers. Then you can start on your mission to destroy the bandits of the Marshes of Mount Liang."

Twin Rods said: "Our three armies of cavalry and foot are all hardened troops, tough soldiers and well-trained horses, you can have absolute confidence in us. But I am afraid we still lack some clothing and armour. I don't want to miss the deadline and fail to carry out our mission on time. Would you consider giving us a few weeks' grace?"

Marshal Gao said: "If that's your problem, you can go to the imperial armoury and choose whatever you like of clothing, armour, helmets and swords, no matter how much. I'll make out a requisition. It is essential that the troops should be fully equipped, in order to cope with the enemy. When you are ready to leave I will personally send someone to inspect you."

So Twin Rods took the order and went with the others to the imperial armoury to get the equipment. He took out three thousand suits of armour, five thousand sets of good leather guards for the horses, three thousand brass helmets, two thousand long spears, a thousand swords, an unspecified number of bows and arrows and more than five hundred iron cannonballs. These were all loaded onto carts. Shortly before they were due to leave, Marshal Gao himself presented them with three thousand war-horses. Each of the three leaders was handsomely rewarded with silver and silk and their armies were fully provisioned. All three handed in written guarantees of victory, bade farewell to Marshal Gao and the other members of the Council, mounted their horses and rode off in the direction of Runing. Nothing worthy of note occurred on the journey.

Arriving back at his base, Twin Rods ordered the other two to return to their districts, muster their troops, and march back with them. In less than a fortnight the three armies were ready. Twin Rods now divided among them the items received from the government: clothing, armour, helmets, swords, banners, spears and saddles, and also some chain-mail that he had had made and some other items of weaponry. Now all that was needed was the order to march. Marshal Gao sent two officers from the Chancellery to inspect them. A bounty was distributed among the troops, and then Twin Rods marched them out of the city. Here's how it was:

> *The riders are wearing iron armour, their mounts are fitted with brass bells. Streaming banners fill the sky with colour, gleaming swords flash white for miles around. The curved bows are painted with magpies, sheaves shaped like flying fish are full of arrows. Eagle feathers decorate the panniers; lion-mouthed pots are tied on securely with leopard's tail thongs. Helmets deep enough to guard the nape and fringed with pearls leave only the eyes visible; the heavy armour of the horses, decked with tassels, exposes nothing but their legs. Those who will pioneer the route carry big axes, behind them come the fighting men with long spears. A thousand armoured cavalry leave the city. The three commanders are advancing on the Marshes.*

They marched out of the city in formation, Victorious with the vanguard, Twin Rods leading the central force and the Supremo bringing up the rear. The three armies of cavalry and foot raced towards the Marshes of Mount Liang.

Advance scouts from Mount Liang returned to the stronghold and reported the event.

Chao Gai and Song Jiang, the military adviser Professor Wu Yong, his deputy the magician Taoist Gongsun and the rest were all in the Assembly Hall, occupied with day-long celebrations of Chai Jin's arrival, when they received the report: "Marshal Twin Rods Huyan Zhuo from Runing is approaching with an army to attack us."

Together they debated how to meet this attack. The Professor said: "I know of this character. He is a relation, a direct descendant in fact, of the famous general Huyan Zan, who made a name for himself at the founding of the dynasty. He's an experienced and valiant fighter. With his preferred weapon, the two rods, no one can get near him. We need a bold and resolute commander. We must first oppose him with force and then capture him by guile."

Before he'd finished speaking, Iron Ox said: "I'll go and capture the bastard for you."

Song Jiang said: "Who asked you to go? I've already got it worked out: we will ask Thunderclap to lead the first party, Leopard's Head Lin Chong the second, Colonel Hua the third, Steelbright the fourth, and Colonel Sun the fifth. These first five forces will attack in rotation, each moving subsequently to the rear. I myself with ten comrades and a large body of troops will follow in support. On my left I will have five commanders: Whiskers, Sergeant Lei, Mu the Unstoppable, the Tamer, and the Little Duke. On my right will be Morbid, Madcap, Golden Wings, the Flautist, and the Halberdier. We will ask the White-Water Dragon, the Pilot, White Eel and the three Ruan brothers to reinforce us by water in boats. Finally, Iron Ox and Panther will conceal themselves with two separate forces in reserve."

When Song Jiang had completed these dispositions, Thunderclap led the first force down the mountain to take up their position on a flat area of wasteland. Although it was winter the weather happened to be pleasantly warm. Nothing happened for a day, but then the government army was seen approaching. The advance guard led by Victorious encamped and built a palisade. They made no attempt to engage the enemy that evening.

At dawn the next day a roll of drums sounded three times from both camps and the troops formed up. Thunderclap now appeared on horseback resting his wolf's-tooth mace, riding out from the opening in the ranks which was marked by a gate of pennants. Victorious, leader of the advance guard with his long lance, reined in his horse and began to insult Thunderclap in ringing tones: "The imperial army is here. If you don't surrender quickly and still dare to resist, you'll really be asking for it! I am going to flatten your place in the bogs, I shall smash your Mount Liang to pieces and take you all alive, you rebel scum! I shall take you back to the capital to be cut into a thousand pieces!"

Now Thunderclap was not a patient man. He said no word in answer to all this but simply slapped his horse, whirled his mace and charged at Victorious. The latter likewise levelled his lance and galloped at Thunderclap. The two fought twenty bouts or more, till Victorious began to flag and tried to break off. By now Twin Rods and the main force had come up from behind and, seeing Victorious was in difficulties with Thunderclap, he galloped forward whirling his two rods. He was riding the horse the Emperor had given him, the snowy-footed raven-hued steed. Ranting and raving he rode out in front of his troops. But just as Thunderclap was about to attack him, the second contingent from Mount Liang arrived, led by Leopard's Head, who cried out to Thunderclap: "Time to take a break, General Qin, while I fight a few hundred bouts. I can manage this one!" Leopard's Head raised his halberd and charged Twin Rods. Thunderclap pulled his troops back from the left flank and withdrew up the slope to look on while Twin Rods fought with Leopard's Head. They were a perfect match. Halberd clashed prettily with rod, and rod elegantly parried halberd. They fought as many as fifty bouts and neither had the advantage.

Now the third detachment from Mount Liang arrived, under Colonel Hua, who shouted out under the gates: "Take a rest, Major Lin, and let me capture the bastard for you."

Leopard's Head withdrew his troops. Having seen the military prowess of Leopard's Head, Twin Rods also returned to his ranks. Leopard's Head wheeled his troops about and withdrew up the mountain, making way for Colonel Hua, who charged forward with levelled lance. By now the government rearguard had come up to relieve Twin Rods.

The Supremo, wielding his double-edged blade with three prongs, which also had four holes and eight rings, and mounted on his hundred-league bay charger rode forward out of the ranks and challenged Colonel Hua: "You miserable renegade! You're not fit for anything! Now you're going to feel the strength of my arm!"

Colonel Hua was too angry to reply. He merely urged his horse forward to encounter the Supremo. They fought more than twenty bouts. Twin Rods saw that the Supremo's strength was beginning to fail, so he gave his horse its head, whirled his rods and charged Colonel Hua. Before they had had three bouts the fourth Mount Liang detachment arrived, led by the woman warrior Steelbright. She shouted: "Time for you to take a rest, Colonel Hua! I'm going to get that bastard!"

Colonel Hua pulled his troops out to the right and withdrew to the mountain slopes. But before the Supremo had time to engage Steelbright, the fifth Mount Liang detachment under Colonel Sun arrived. Colonel Sun reined in his horse and lined up his troops to watch the contest between Steelbright and the Supremo. The two of them had disappeared in a baleful cloud of dust. One fought with a blade on a long pole, the other with two swords. When they had fought more than twenty bouts, Steelbright put up her two swords, turned her horse and rode away. The Supremo, thinking to snatch glory, galloped in pursuit. Steelbright now hung the two swords on her saddlebow and from beneath her robe took out a red cotton lasso with twenty four metal hooks attached to it. She waited until the Supremo had almost caught her up, then turned in the saddle and let fly with the lasso. Her aim was perfect and before the Supremo could even raise his arm he was dragged from his horse. Colonel Sun ordered his troops forward immediately to take the Supremo captive.

Twin Rods was livid. He rode furiously to the rescue. Slapping her horse Steelbright rode to meet him. Twin Rods was prepared to eat her alive. But after twenty bouts he still wasn't able to get the better of her. He said to himself: "This bloody amazon has stood up to me for I don't know how many bouts. She is really something!" Increasingly desperate, he resorted to a trick: he allowed her to come in and then tried to hammer down on her with the two rods. Her two swords were still inactive as the rod in his right hand began to descend towards the crown of her head. But so sharp of eye was she and quick of hand that in a flash she was parrying with the swords. Her right hand went flying upwards, so that the rod came crashing down only to meet the blade of the sword with a great clang, sparks flying in all directions.

Steelbright turned her horse and galloped back to her own side. Twin Rods galloped in pursuit. Colonel Sun levelled his lance, urged on his horse and charged towards him. Behind him Song Jiang and his ten picked leaders had arrived and were deploying their forces. Steelbright retired with her troops to the mountain slope. Song Jiang was delighted when he heard they had captured the Supremo and he came to the front to watch the combat between Colonel Sun and Twin Rods.

Colonel Sun with his lance and with the jointed steel rod hanging from his wrist, galloped to encounter Twin Rods. They both fought with the rods, a form of combat at which both were equally skilled. Colonel Sun wore a cross-barred helmet, a scarlet silk headcloth, and a black robe studded with jade green decorations.

His gilt armour had a blackish sheen to it and the horse he rode was a piebald. Wielding his "tiger's eye" rods, jointed like bamboo, he outshone the heroes of olden days.

Twin Rods had a great spiked helmet, a golden headcloth and a black robe studded with the seven stars. He had a black armoured vest and rode his famous black charger with white socks. He wielded his two octagonal rods of specially hardened steel. The one in his left hand weighed twelve catties and the one in his right hand thirteen. He was the very image of his famous ancestor.

The two of them traded blows there in front of the armies. They fought more than thirty bouts and there was nothing to choose between them. Song Jiang could not stop applauding.

Each on a piebald strong as a dragon,
Twin Rods versus Colonel Sun;
The skill of each is truly a marvel, they'll
Kill each other before they're done!

Among the government forces, Victorious now heard that the Supremo had been defeated. He mustered his troops, who were bringing up the rear, and charged forward. Song Jiang, to prevent his breaking through, pointed with his whip and the ten leaders, with a mixed body of men, quickly deployed in defence. The four detachments behind formed into two halves and mounted a pincer movement. When he saw this, Twin Rods hastily wheeled his forces round so they could face the attack on both sides.

Why could the Mount Liang forces not win this battle outright? Well the force commanded by Twin Rods consisted of what is called "linked cavalry." The horses bore leather armour and the men wore chain-mail. The horses' armour left only their hooves showing, while the men's chain-mail allowed only their eyes to be seen. Although Song Jiang did have some armoured cavalry they were equipped with no more than red-tasseled masks and brass bells and pheasants' feathers and the like. There was no way this could give them protection against arrows. Twin Rods' three thousand cavalry were all equipped with bows and loosed off arrows, so their adversaries dared not close with them. Song Jiang hurriedly gave the signal to withdraw. Twin Rods likewise retreated some six or seven miles and pitched camp.

Song Jiang marshalled his troops and retired to the western slopes of the mountain where they halted and made camp. At his orders, his bodyguards brought in the Supremo, clustering closely around him. Song Jiang immediately stood up and ordered them back. After untying the bonds himself he led the Supremo into his tent and gave him the guest's seat. Then he prostrated himself. The Supremo hastily returned the compliment, saying: "I am a prisoner. I should expect to die. Why, sir, do you treat me like an honoured guest?"

Song Jiang said: "It is only because we have nowhere else to shelter that we have temporarily occupied the marshes. We are forced to take refuge there for a while, the times being so evil. The Emperor has sent you to arrest us. By rights we should surrender to you, but that would be to give away our lives. We are guilty of opposing you and have caused you much offence. I entreat you to forgive us."

The Supremo replied: "I have long known of your loyalty and humanity, how you help those who are in danger and relieve those in distress, but this is generosity beyond all expectation. If you should choose to spare my worthless life, then in recompense I must devote myself entirely to your service."

Song Jiang said: "We all confidently await the Emperor's pardon. We hope for an amnesty which will allow us to offer our services to the country, in defence of which we will not flinch from ten thousand deaths."

As the poem says:

呼延灼擺布
連環馬

Because such greedy officials abound,
These loyal brothers go to ground.
If they weren't all loyal and lovers of right,
Why would the hundred and eight unite?

The same day Song Jiang had the Supremo taken up to the stronghold and presented to Chao Gai. He stayed there in the camp. The three armies and all the leaders were rewarded and the military situation was discussed.

As for Twin Rods, he withdrew to the camp and conferred with Victorious as to how they could overcome the forces of Mount Liang. Victorious said: "Did you see when we pushed forward today how eager those bastards were to attack us? Tomorrow we must attack with massed cavalry and we can be sure of victory."

Twin Rods said: "That's what I was going to do. I just wanted to make sure we are in agreement."

Accordingly he gave the order. "Tell the three thousand cavalry to form up in ranks of thirty, linked together with iron rings. When they encounter the enemy they are to set up long range fire with arrows; when they close they must charge with spears. Divide the three thousand armoured cavalry into a hundred linked units. The five thousand infantry will follow in support. Tomorrow there must be no retreating. You and I will clean up behind. If we are attacked we will take up a three-sided formation and charge."

So the plan was made and the next day they marched out at dawn to do battle.

Song Jiang next day organized his cavalry with five divisions in front, ten commanders bunched together behind them and two concealed divisions, left and right. Thunderclap was first in the field. But when he challenged Twin Rods, the only response from the opposing army was a loud cheer. They did not offer to engage.

The five leading divisions now spread out in a straight line. Thunderclap was in the centre, Leopard's Head and Steelbright on the left and Colonel Hua and then Colonel Sun on the right. Soon Song Jiang arrived with the other ten, in tightly massed ranks of cavalry. Opposing them they could see around a thousand infantry, beating drums and shouting, but not a single cavalryman rode out to do battle. Song Jiang was greatly troubled by what he saw. Quietly he gave the order: "Tell our rearguard to withdraw." Then he rode over to Colonel Hua's position to observe from there. Suddenly a series of reports were heard from the enemy front ranks. The ranks of the infantry immediately parted and out rode the linked cavalry in a three-sided formation. They advanced, volleying arrows from the two sides and with levelled lances in the centre. Desperately Song Jiang ordered his troops to fire back. But they could offer no serious resistance. All the horses in the linked units of thirty had to gallop forward together; there was no chance for anyone to hold back.

The linked cavalry filled the whole field of battle. And still they came charging on. Song Jiang's five leading divisions were thrown into utter confusion and could not stick to their plan. The large group of cavalry behind them could not make a stand and all ran for their lives. Song Jiang galloped off, surrounded by his ten commanders. A unit of linked cavalry was hard on his heels, when the troops hidden in the reedbeds — led by Iron Ox and Panther — charged out to the rescue. Song Jiang's forces retreated as far as the water, where the six water leaders — the White-Water Dragon, the Pilot, White Eel, and the Ruan brothers — were waiting. Six war boats were drawn up ready. Song Jiang hurriedly embarked and ordered each captain to go under his own steam to rescue the other leaders and get them on board. Having continued the pursuit up to the water's edge, the linked cavalry set up a barrage of arrows. But the boats were protected by shields, so these caused no casualties.

The boats were now hurriedly rowed across to Duck's-Bill Landing, where everyone disembarked. In the waterside camp the troops were counted. There had been heavy losses, but fortunately all the leaders were safe. Although some had had their horses killed, they had escaped themselves.

In a little while the Guv, the Flea, Blackface and Auntie Gu all came racing up the mountain and said: "Their infantry are attacking now. They've practically demolished the inn. But for the signal boat we would have been captured."

Song Jiang comforted each of them. When they checked all the leaders it was found that six of them had been wounded by arrows: Leopard's Head, Sergeant Lei, Iron Ox, Madcap, Blackface and the Tamer. Of the men, countless numbers had received arrow wounds. When Chao Gai heard, he came down the mountain with the Professor and Taoist Gongsun to find out more. Song Jiang's brows were knit in an unremitting frown, his expression deeply gloomy. The Professor did his best to reassure him: "No point in grieving, brother. Victory and defeat are part and parcel of the soldier's trade. What's the good of moaning? We've got to think of a new plan to overcome the linked cavalry."

Chao Gai now issued the following order: "The water-borne troops are to strengthen their defences and secure their boats, defend the landing place and keep watch day and night. Song Jiang is to go up the mountain to rest."

But Song Jiang refused to go. He remained in the camp at Duck's-Bill Landing, and instead ordered the wounded leaders to be taken up the mountain to recuperate.

Twin Rods, after his great victory, returned to camp. The linked cavalry were disconnected and came forward in turn to ask for their reward. Countless numbers of the enemy had been killed, more than five hundred taken alive, more than three hundred warhorses seized. Accordingly Twin Rods sent someone to the capital to report the victory, whilst he distributed rewards to the three armies.

Marshal Gao was presiding in his chancellery when it was reported: "General Huyan has had a great victory over the forces of Mount Liang. He has sent someone with the report." Gao was delighted with the news. Next day at dawn he hurried off to tell the Emperor, without even waiting his turn. The Emperor was exceedingly well-pleased. He graciously bestowed on Gao ten bottles of yellow seal imperial wine and a fine embroidered robe. He also ordered an official to carry a hundred thousand strings of cash to the army camp to divide among the troops. Marshal Gao returned to the chancellery with the imperial edict and duly dispatched someone with the reward.

When Twin Rods heard that an envoy from the Emperor was on the way, he and Victorious rode out several miles to meet him.

When they had brought him back to the camp and expressed thanks for the great favours received, they entertained him with wine. Victorious was told to distribute the money among the troops, and the five hundred captives were ordered to be brought, so their heads could be cut off and sent to the capital, as evidence of what had been achieved.

The emissary inquired: "How did you come to lose Colonel Peng?"

Twin Rods said: "He was so eager to capture Song Jiang that he attacked deep behind the enemy lines and got taken himself. But those bandits won't dare show themselves again. I shall press home the attack however. It is essential to clear out the mountain stronghold and sweep the marshes clean. We're going to capture the whole lot of them and wipe out the nest of vipers. The problem is there's water on every side of them and no access by road. You can view their defences from a distance but the only way to get rid of them is to bombard them with cannon and smash that thieves' den to pieces. I have heard that in the capital there is a famous gunner called Ling Zhen, also known as Thunderer, from the sound of his guns. He's an expert with cannon, and can throw a shell fifteen miles or more. Wherever his shells fall they cause huge devastation. If we can get him, we'll pound their stronghold. He's even an expert in martial arts, and can handle a bow or a horse brilliantly. When Your Excellency returns to the capital, please acquaint the Marshal with this matter and ask if this man can be sent to us as a matter of urgency, so we can capture the thieves' den within the time-limit."

The emissary agreed to start next day. Nothing worth telling occurred on the journey. Back in the capital he went to see Marshal Gao and told him about Twin Rods' request for the master gunner Ling Zhen and about the contribution he was to make. Marshal Gao immediately issued an order instructing the master gunner Ling Zhen to report to him.

This Ling Zhen was in fact a native of Yanling. He was the top gunner of the Song Dynasty. People called him Thunderer. In addition he was an expert in martial arts.

City walls crumble when he opens fire;
Ghosts, gods grieve as the smoke mounts higher.
His explosions set the heavens aflame.
Four hundred provinces know his name.

When Thunderer reported to Marshal Gao, he received his commission, with orders to requisition horses and all necessary equipment and get going. So he got together the necessary guns and ammunition, with explosives of every kind. The cannon-balls and guns were loaded onto carts. He equipped himself with suitable clothing and armour, a helmet and a sword. Then with all his luggage and equipment and with thirty or forty troops he left the capital and took the road to Mount Liang. On arrival he went first to see Twin Rods, then he saw Victorious, leader of the vanguard. He found out all he could about the camp in the marshes, distances and routes, and the inaccessible parts of the mountain stronghold. He chose three kinds of missile for the bombardment. The first were wind shells, the second gold wheel shells and the third shrapnel shells. First he had the soldiers secure the guns to their carriages. These were set up on the water's edge and prepared for firing.

Now in the smaller camp at Duck's-Bill Landing, Song Jiang and the Professor had been discussing how to regain the initiative, but they could find no workable plan. Then a scout reported: "They've sent a master gunner from the capital. He's called Ling Zhen or Thunderer. He's been setting up his guns at the edge of the water. They're preparing to bombard us and break down our defences."

"That's not too serious," said the Professor. "We're surrounded by water, there are many channels and the Place of Many Meanderings is set back from the water a long way. So even if they had cannon that would shoot down the sky, they'd hardly be able to hit us. Let us evacuate the little camp at Duck's-Bill Landing, and wait and see what they can manage with their guns. After that we'll make up our minds what to do."

Song Jiang gave the order to evacuate the little camp at once. Everyone moved up the mountain. Chao Gai and Taoist Gongsun received them in the Assembly Hall. "But what's your plan for defeating the enemy?" they asked.

The question was scarcely out before an explosion was heard down below. Three guns had been fired in rapid succession. Two of the shots fell in the water, but one hit the camp at Duck's-Bill Landing, spreading gloom in Song Jiang's heart and causing the others to turn pale.

The Professor said: "If someone could tempt Thunderer down to the water's edge, we could capture him. Then we'd be able to work out how to defeat the enemy."

Chao Gai said: "Then let the White-Water Dragon, the Pilot, White Eel and the Ruan brothers row over and put this plan into action, supported by Whiskers and Sergeant Lei on land."

When the six boat captains had received their orders they formed into two parties. The White-Water Dragon and the Pilot went first, with some fifty troops who were good swimmers in two fast boats. Stealthily the boats glided out from the reeds, and behind them a second group led by White Eel and the Ruan brothers with forty or more small boats. When the White-Water Dragon and the Pilot reached the other shore they charged at the guns with wild shouts and overturned them.

The gunners immediately reported this to Thunderer. Thunderer got two cannon with wind shells, loaded them onto horses and raced to the scene with a thousand troops. The White-Water Dragon and the Pilot then withdrew with their men. Thunderer pursued them as far as the reedbeds on the edge of the water, where he found forty or more small boats drawn up in a straight line, manned by several hundred sailors. White-Water Dragon and the Pilot had already escaped to their boats, but these boats had deliberately not rowed away. When they saw the enemy the crews gave a great cheer and all dived into the water. As Thunderer's troops were about to attack the boats, Whiskers, Sergeant Lei and their troops began shouting and beating drums on the opposite bank. Thunderer seized a lot of the boats and ordered all his men to board them and attack the enemy on the other side. When the boats were right out in the middle of the water, Whiskers and Sergeant Lei on the other bank beat gongs, and fifty sailors rose from the depths and grabbing the boats by the stern pulled out the bungs, so that the water rushed in. They then capsized them, flinging all the troops into the water. Thunderer tried desperately to turn back but his boat's rudder had been torn off and sent to the bottom. The two leaders now surfaced on either side of his boat and tilting it suddenly hurled him out. Ruan the second was waiting for him underwater. He embraced him and dragged him out onto the other bank, where the leaders were ready to receive him. They trussed him up securely and carried him off to the mountain. Two hundred enemy troops were plucked alive from the water, about half the force drowned, and only a few escaped with their lives and returned to base.

Why did they let those crews get away?
Why not use their guns like they ought to?
Of their thunderous barrage we've nothing to say,
More lethal are storms in a few feet of water.

When Twin Rods heard what had happened, he rushed there with his troops. But the boats had all disappeared into Duck's-Bill Landing. It was too far for arrows to carry, and anyway there was no one to be seen. He had to swallow his anger. He stood there fuming for a long time, but in the end had to withdraw.

The leaders took Thunderer up the mountain, sending someone on ahead to report to Song Jiang. Song Jiang and the other leaders went down as far as the second gate to receive them. When he saw Thunderer, Song Jiang hurriedly loosed his bonds with his own hands and blamed everyone, saying: "I told you to invite the commander politely to come and see us, why have you treated him in such an unmannerly fashion?"

Thunderer prostrated himself in gratitude for their sparing his life. Having given him a cup of wine, Song Jiang took him by the hand and invited him up the mountain. When they reached the main stronghold and he saw that the Supremo had become one of the outlaws' leaders, Thunderer was rendered speechless.

The Supremo reassured him: "Chao Gai and Song Jiang are obedient to heaven's will. They welcome good men here and strive for the nation's peace. Since we are here it behoves us to obey them."

Song Jiang also reassured him and he replied: "I would have no objection to staying and serving you. But my mother and wife are still in the capital, if people there get wind of this, I am afraid they will be executed. So what am I to do?"

Song Jiang said: "There's nothing to worry about. In a few days' time we will send you back."

Thunderer thanked him and said: "Such is your kindness, I shall die content."

Chao Gai said: "This calls for a celebration."

Next day a grand assembly of all the leaders was held in the hall. While they ate and drank, Song Jiang and the other leaders discussed how to defeat the linked cavalry. They were getting nowhere, when Spots stood up and said: "I have no qualifications to speak, but I would like to propose a solution. The linked cavalry can only be broken by a weapon which a good friend of mine possesses."

"What is this weapon you say we could use, my friend?" the Professor asked. "And who is this good friend of yours?"

Spots explained, taking his time and with his hands crossed respectfully in front of him. And the answer to these questions was to have important consequences: several leaders will make the journey to the capital, and more than three thousand cavalry will meet an evil genius. Truly there was to be:

A plan to steal the Unicorn from the jade city;
A plot to grab the fabled beast in the golden palace.

But if you want to hear of what weapon Spots spoke to the assembled leaders, and of what person, you must read the next chapter.

Chapter 56

The Professor gets the Flea to steal some armour; Spots lures the Spearsman to the mountain!

Now Spots addressed the assembly of leaders as follows: "I was born into a family of weapons makers. On account of this expertise, my father came to serve under His Excellency the Old Field Marshal and was made garrison commander at Yan'an. This system of linked cavalry was used already by the last dynasty to achieve victory. The only way to break it is to use a special hooked spear. Our family inherited drawings of this and if you wanted me to make one I could set my hand to it. But even though I can make you one, I don't know how to use it. If you want someone who can use it, this cousin of mine is the man you need. He is the only person who holds the secret of using these hooked spears: it's a secret art his family have inherited and they won't teach it to any outsider. On horseback or on foot, there's a special way to do it, it's really amazing!"

When he finished, Leopard's Head asked: "Are you by any chance speaking of Xu Ning, instructor of the imperial armoury, known as the Spearsman?"

"That's exactly who I mean," said Spots.

"I'm glad you mentioned him. I had forgotten," said Leopard's Head. "This 'hooked spear' method of the Spearsman's is quite unique. We saw a lot of each other when I was in the capital, we used to compare fighting techniques. There was a great deal of mutual respect and friendship between us. The only thing is, how can we get him to join us?"

"The Spearsman's forebears left him one very important heirloom," Spots continued. "There's nothing else like it in the world. It provides absolute protection. In the days when my father was garrison commander and went to the capital to visit his aunt I often saw it. It is a suit of armour made of wild goose quills bound with metal strips. When you wear it, it is both light and strong, no sword or arrow can pierce it. People have called it the Lion's Pelt. Many a nobleman has asked to have a look at it, but the Spearsman has never been keen to let people see it. This armour is as dear to him as his life. He stores it in a leather case which he hangs from a beam in his bedroom. If we can first get our hands on this armour of his, he'll have no choice but to come to us here."

The Professor said: "In that case, there shouldn't be any problem, seeing that we have a very light-fingered gentleman among us. We'll send the Flea off to get it."

"My only fear is that the armour might not really exist," said the Flea. "If it does, you can be sure I won't come back without it."

"If you can steal the armour, I undertake to get its owner here," said Spots.

"How are you going to do that?" Song Jiang asked.

Spots went up close and whispered something in Song Jiang's ear. Song Jiang laughed and said: "That's brilliant!"

The Professor said: "We want three more people to go to the capital with them. One must go to buy smoke-bombs, gunpowder and other supplies needed for the guns. The other two are needed to fetch Thunderer's family."

When he heard this, the Supremo stood up and said: "If someone could be sent to Yingzhou to fetch my family, I should be truly grateful."

"Don't worry, commander," said Song Jiang. "Just write out a letter, each of you, and I shall tell someone to do it."

Panther was now told to take some money and the appropriate letter and go with a small company to Yingzhou and fetch the Supremo's family. The Pill Monger was to disguise himself as a mountebank and go to the capital to fetch Thunderer's family. Green-Eyes dressed as a merchant was to go to the capital to buy gunpowder and other supplies. Lungs would accompany Spots and the Pill Monger would travel with them.

The Flea was sent off first. This done, Spots was asked to prepare a model of the hooked spear. Sergeant Lei would oversee its production, since Sergeant Lei's family had been blacksmiths. Spots produced the example of a hooked spear and showed those in the camp responsible for arms production how to make spears according to the pattern, under the supervision of Sergeant Lei. Of this no more.

A big send-off party was held in the main stronghold, and then Panther, the Pill Monger, Green-Eyes, Lungs and Spots bade farewell and left. The following day the Magic Messenger was also sent down the mountain to keep an eye on things.

It now becomes difficult to tell everything at once.

Let us follow then the Flea, who after leaving Mount Liang, collected all the necessary tools and equipment and secretly, carefully disguised, made his way by a roundabout route to the capital, where he found himself an inn for the night. Next day he strolled into the city and started asking for the address of imperial armourer Xu Ning.

Someone gave him directions: "Go into the government quarters and it's the fifth house on the east side, the one with a black door."

Having entered the compound and located the front door of the house, the Flea strolled round to the back. There was a high wall, and above it two small watch-towers. To one side stood an ornamental column. The Flea inspected this for a while. Then he went back to the street and asked someone: "Is Instructor Xu at home?"

"Most likely he's at work and hasn't come back yet," they replied.

"Do you know when he will return?" the Flea asked.

"Not till evening," they replied. "He goes out early in the morning and works in the palace."

The Flea apologized for troubling the man and went back to his inn. He got his tools and concealed them on his person. Then he said to the waiter: "I probably won't be back tonight."

"Don't you worry," said the waiter. "There won't be any problem."

The Flea entered the city again and got something to eat for his dinner. Then he strolled over to the Spearsman's house in the imperial armoury. He looked around but couldn't find anywhere to hide. It was already dark, however, so he slipped inside the compound. It was a cold winter's night and there was no moon. Behind an earthen shrine there was a tall cypress tree. Gripping the trunk with his legs he shinned up it and sat astride a branch at the top. He watched quietly and saw the Spearsman return and enter the house. He also saw two men with lanterns enter and close the gate of the compound, drawing the bolt across, before retiring each to his own house.

Soon the drum sounded the hour in the watch-tower. It was cold and overcast and no stars were visible. The dew gradually turned to frost. When all was quiet in the compound, the Flea slipped down to the ground and stole across to the Spearsman's back door. He climbed over the wall effortlessly and crept inside. He was in a small garden. He paused outside the kitchen and watched. There was a light on in the kitchen and two maids were still clearing up. By scaling the column he was able to reach the eaves. Here he paused to observe for a while. Looking at the upper floor he saw the Spearsman and his wife sitting beside the stove, facing the fire. She was holding a small child, about six or seven years old. He looked at the bedroom. As expected, there was a big leather case tied to a beam. A bow and arrows and a sword were hanging by the door. In the wardrobe hung brightly coloured clothing. At this moment the Spearsman called out: "Peachblossom, come and fold up my clothes!"

A maid came up the stairs and on a small side table proceeded to fold up a robe with purple embroidery and round collar, then another lined with imperial green and with embroidered parted skirts, followed by a brocade kerchief of many colours, a red and green knotted sash, and a handkerchief. She also used a small yellow handkerchief to wrap up a lichee-coloured gold belt with otter tails and put it in the bundle which she placed on the rack near the stove. All this the Flea carefully noted.

Shortly after nine o'clock the Spearsman got ready for bed. His wife asked: "Are you on duty tomorrow?"

"Tomorrow is the day the Emperor visits the Dragon Hall. I have to be there before dawn to wait for him."

The wife said to the maid: "The master has to be up before dawn tomorrow and go out to work. You'd better get up at three to warm the water for him and prepare some dim sum for breakfast."

"Obviously that leather case hanging from the beam is the famous armour," the Flea reasoned to himself. "It'll be good if I can get my hands on it during the night. But if I cause any disturbance I won't be able to get out of the city tomorrow and the whole business is likely to fail.... I'd better wait till early morning, that'll be the time to get to work."

The Spearsman and his wife went to sleep, while the two maids made up their beds outside the room. A night light was left burning on the table inside.

The five people were sleeping. The two skivvies, having spent the whole day serving till evening, were exhausted and fell fast asleep. The Flea came down from his perch and took out a reed which he poked through a hole in the window and with one puff blew out the night light.

In the early hours the Spearsman rose and told the maids to get up and warm his water. When the two girls roused themselves from their dreams they found the light had gone out in the room.

"Oh dear, the light's gone out!" they exclaimed.

The Spearsman said: "Then go and ask for a light next door, what are you waiting for?"

The Flea heard them open the door and grope their way down the stairs. He slid down the column and went to wait in a dark place near the back door. When he heard them open the back door, go out, and open the gate in the wall he slipped into the kitchen and squeezed under the kitchen table. The maids returned with the light someone had given them, closed the door and went to light the fire in the stove. They then went to light the charcoal fire upstairs. When the water started to boil they took it upstairs. After washing and rinsing his mouth, the Spearsman asked them to warm some wine and bring it up. They prepared food and cakes and took them up. The Spearsman ate and then asked them to take food to his orderly who was waiting outside. The Flea heard the Spearsman come downstairs and tell his orderly to eat. Then he picked up his bundle, took his steel spear and went out of the door. When the two maids lit a lantern and went out to see him off, the Flea emerged from his hiding-place under the table and went upstairs. By means of the partition he clambered up into the rafters and crouched there. The two maids shut and bolted the door, blew out the light, and went upstairs and undressed. Then they threw themselves down and slept.

As soon as they were asleep the Flea took out his reed again and blew out the upstairs light. He gently lifted the leather case down from its beam. He was about to go downstairs when the Spearsman's wife woke up and hearing a noise called out to the maids: "What's that noise in the rafters?"

The Flea made a noise like a rat. One of the maids said: "It's a rat, can't you hear madam? That's the noise they make when they're fighting."

The Flea again imitated the sound of rats fighting. Then he lowered himself down, opened the landing door, very slowly raised the leather case and put it on his back, felt his way down the stairs, and opened the back door. By the time he reached the gate of the compound, the patrol were already out and about. They had unlocked the main gate before dawn. Firmly grasping the leather case, the Flea attached himself to a group of people and took advantage of the general hubbub to slip out of the city unnoticed and return to his inn. It was still dark when he knocked on the inn door. He went to the room and got his luggage. He made up a bundle for the carrying-pole. He paid the bill, left the inn and set off on the road east.

When he stopped at an inn about ten miles out of the city to have some breakfast, he ran into someone he knew. This was none other than the Magic Messenger. When he saw that the Flea had the goods, there was a muttered discussion and then the Magic Messenger said: "I'm going to take the armour back to the camp, you follow on slowly with Spots."

The Flea opened the leather case and took out the precious armour. They rolled it up and made a bundle of it. The Magic Messenger tied it on securely. As soon as he left the inn he started his magic walking and returned to Mount Liang.

吳用使時迁盗甲

The Flea now fastened the empty case on his carrying-pole, in such a way that it was clearly visible. He breakfasted, paid, picked up his pole and left. After six or seven miles he encountered Spots. The two of them went to an inn to talk.

Spots said: "Just do as I say and continue along this road. When you come to an inn or eating place or rest house, look to see if there is a white circle painted with flour. If there is, go in and buy wine or food. If it's a rest house, stop there for the night. Put the case where it can be clearly seen. After a day's travel from here wait for me."

The Flea went off to carry out this plan. Spots calmly had another drink and then set off in the direction of the capital.

It was daylight now, back at the Spearsman's house. When the two maids got up they found the door to the upstairs landing open, and the downstairs door and the front door also unlocked. They looked around the house anxiously but everything seemed to be in its place. They ran upstairs and told their mistress: "Somehow the doors are all unlocked, but nothing seems to be missing."

"I heard that noise in the rafters early this morning," said their mistress. "But you said it was only rats fighting. You'd better go and see that nothing has happened to the leather case."

When the maids saw, they raised an outcry: "The leather case has disappeared!"

Panic-stricken, the mistress said: "Quickly, send someone to the palace to tell the master, tell him to come home and look for it as soon as possible!"

The maids rushed away to try and find someone who would go to the palace and tell the Spearsman. They asked three or four but they all returned and said: "The armourers are in attendance in the Emperor's inner garden. The entrance is strictly guarded. No one can enter! You'll just have to wait till he comes back."

The Spearsman's wife and the maids were like ants on a hot plate. They rushed about aimlessly this way and that, and didn't eat a bite. It wasn't until dusk that the Spearsman was able to take off his ceremonial robes and go off duty. He picked up his steel spear and returned home. When he reached the gate of the compound a neighbour told him: "Your wife has been robbed. She's waiting for you. She's frantic for you to get home."

The Spearsman had a terrible shock. He rushed to his house, where the two maids met him at the door. "When you went out this morning, master, a thief slipped into the house. The only thing he took was that leather case you keep hanging from the beam."

A great wail arose from the Spearsman when he heard this, right from the pit of his stomach it came, rolling up to issue from his mouth.

His wife said: "I really can't imagine when the thief got in."

"Everything else is unimportant," he said. "But this special armour has been handed down through four generations, and has never been lost till now. Marshal 'Flash' Wang offered me thirty thousand for it, but I wouldn't sell. I was afraid that one day I would need it in battle and I was so worried something might happen to it, that's why I tied it to the beam. So many people have asked to see it, but I've always pretended I didn't have it any longer. Now it's been stolen. I shall be a laughing-stock! It's gone, and whatever am I going to do?"

He did not sleep a wink that night. He kept turning it over in his mind. "Who could it possibly have been? It must be somebody who knows about that armour of mine."

His wife gave her opinion. "The thief must have crept in last night, when the light went out, don't you think? There must be someone who envies what you've got, he offered you money and you wouldn't sell, so he got this master thief to come and steal it. You'd better go out and tell someone to make thorough inquiries, it's no good just talking about it. And you want to be careful too not to put the culprit on his guard."

But despite this good advice, when day came the Spearsman got up and just sat at home moping.

Around breakfast time, there was a knock on the door, and after going to see who it was the orderly returned and said: "Someone called Tang Long is asking to see you — he says he's the son of Commander Tang who was head of the Yan'an garrison."

The Spearsman told him to show the guest in. Spots kowtowed most respectfully to the Spearsman and said: "I hope you are keeping well?"

The Spearsman replied: "I heard that your father had passed away. But you know I've been so tied up with official duties and it's such a long way too, I just haven't had time to get over there and offer my condolences. And I have had no news of you. Where are you living these days? Where have you come from?"

"It's a long story," said Spots. "Since father died I've been a bit down on my luck. Lately I've been wandering among the rivers and lakes. I was in Shandong. I came to the capital so I thought I'd pay you a visit."

"Won't you sit down?" said the Spearsman, calling for wine to be brought.

Spots felt around in his pack and brought out two twenty tael gold ingots in the shape of garlic bulbs, which he gave to the Spearsman saying: "Before he died my father left this for you as a memento. I didn't have anyone I could trust to bring it, that's why I didn't send it before. I've come here now specially to give it to you."

The Spearsman said: "It was really kind of your father to remember me. I've done nothing to deserve it. How can I ever repay his generosity?"

"Don't say that," said Spots. "When my father was alive he often spoke admiringly of your fighting skills. But unfortunately the world's a big place, so you never happened to meet again. That's why he wanted to leave you this little remembrance."

The Spearsman thanked Spots and took the gifts. Then he called for wine. While they were drinking the Spearsman remained pensive and gloomy and eventually Spots rose and said: "Why do you look so unhappy? Something seems to be weighing on your mind."

The Spearsman heaved a sigh and said: "I ought to explain, but it's a long story. Last night we had a robbery here."

"What exactly was stolen?" Spots asked.

"The thief took just one thing: that special armour bequeathed to me by my ancestors, known as 'the Lion's Pelt.' That's what

I lost yesterday, and that's what presses so heavily upon my spirits."

"I can remember seeing this armour of yours," said Spots. "It really is matchless. My father could never stop admiring it. Where were you keeping it when it was stolen?"

"I kept it inside a leather case which I tied to one of the rafters in my bedroom. I really don't know when the thief got in and took it."

"What is it like, this leather case you kept it in?" Spots asked.

"A red sheepskin case," the Spearsman replied. "And it was wrapped in scented cotton."

Spots pretended to be very surprised. "A red sheepskin case? Don't tell me it had a white cotton cover decorated with a green sceptre of good fortune? And a lion in the middle playing with an embroidered ball?"

"Good heavens, have you seen it somewhere?" the Spearsman exclaimed.

"Last night I stopped at a country inn about fifteen miles from the city to order some wine. I saw a thin dark fellow with prominent eyes. He was carrying it on a pole. When I saw it I said to myself: 'I wonder what he keeps in that leather case?' I asked him as I was going out: 'What do you use that leather case for?' He said, 'It used to be for storing armour in, but now I've just got some old clothes in it.' That must be the man. I happened to notice his legs moved like lightning. He went dashing off. Why don't we follow him?"

The Spearsman said: "It will be a miracle if we can catch him!"

"Stop dithering, then, and let's go!"

The Spearsman hurriedly changed into his hemp sandals, buckled on his sword, picked up a halberd and he and Spots left the city by the eastern gate. They travelled at a good pace. They came to an inn with a white circle on the outer wall, and Spots said: "Let's have a bowl of wine before we go any further, and we can make some inquiries here."

When they were seated inside, Spots asked: "Tell me landlord, has a thin dark chap with staring eyes, been through here, with a red leather case on a carrying-pole?"

The innkeeper replied: "A fellow like that did come by yesterday evening. Carrying a red leather case he were — seemed to be something wrong with his legs too, he were limping a bit."

"Do you hear that, brother?" Spots said to the Spearsman. But the Spearsman was too excited to say anything.

They paid up and left. Further along the road they came to another inn with a white circle on the wall. Spots stopped and said: "Brother, I can't go another step. Let's spend the night at this inn. We can start early tomorrow."

The Spearsman said: "But I'm a government official. If I don't turn up for duty tomorrow I shall be in trouble."

"It's no good worrying about that," said Spots. "Your wife will make some kind of excuse for you."

When they inquired at the inn that night, the waiter said: "Last night a man like the one you describe stayed here. He only slept till the early hours of this morning, then he left. He kept asking the way to Shandong."

"Then we'll be able to catch him," Spots said. "If we start before dawn we're sure to get the bugger tomorrow. Once we've nabbed him, then we'll see."

They spent the night at the inn and left at dawn to continue the pursuit. Whenever Spots saw a white circle on the wall he went in to buy wine and food and to make inquiries, and everywhere they said the same thing. The Spearsman was so desperate to have his armour back he forgot about everything except the chase. When dusk was approaching they came to an old temple, in front of which, under a tree, the Flea had put down his carrying-pole and was sitting on the ground.

When Spots saw this he cried out: "Got him! Under the tree there, look, isn't that the case your armour was in?"

The Spearsman raced ahead and grabbed hold of the Flea, saying: "You villain, what do you mean by stealing my armour?"

"Hold on!" the Flea protested. "Stop shouting. Suppose I did steal your armour, what do you want from me?"

"You ... you shameless animal!" the Spearsman spluttered. "How can you ask me that?"

"Why don't you look and see if there's any armour in that case?" said the Flea.

Spots opened the case and looked inside. It was empty.

"What have you done with my armour, you monster?" the Spearsman yelled.

The Flea said: "Let me explain. My name is Zhang. I'm the eldest in my family and I come from Tai'an. A certain rich man of this district, who wants to get in with the Old Field Marshal, heard that you had this special armour and wouldn't sell it, so he paid me and a mate of mine, third brother Li, to go and steal it from your house. He promised us ten thousand for it. But when I was climbing down the pillar in your house I twisted my ankle, so I couldn't walk properly. I told friend Li to go on ahead with the armour and leave me to carry just the empty case. If you want to do something to me you can take me to the police, but not even to save my life, not even if you beat me to death, will I confess. It's no good thinking I will betray another person. So if you will spare me the official investigation, I am willing to help you try and get the armour back."

The Spearsman hesitated for a long time, unable to make up his mind. Spots said: "Brother, you needn't be afraid he'll get away. Why don't we take him with us to get the armour back? If we haven't got the armour, what's the point of going to the police and making an accusation in this place?"

"You're right," said the Spearsman. So now the pursuit continued with all three of them. They stopped at inns to rest. Whenever they spent the night somewhere the Spearsman and Spots kept a close watch on the Flea. The Flea, of course, had bandaged his leg to make it look as if it was hurt. The Spearsman seeing that he had difficulty walking, was only half on his guard. Next morning they rose early to continue their journey. The Flea paid for all their wine and food, in order to curry favour with them. They travelled all day.

Next day on the journey the Spearsman became quite worried. He had begun to wonder if he would ever get his armour back.

As they were walking along, they saw three or four oxen yoked to an empty cart beside the road. Behind was the driver and next to him a merchant, who prostrated himself when he saw Spots.

"What are you doing here, friend?" Spots asked.

"I've been doing business in Zhengzhou and now I'm returning home to Tai'an," the other replied.

"That's great," Spots said. "We'd like to ride in your cart. We're heading for Tai'an also, on holiday."

"Of course I can take three of you. It wouldn't matter if you were more."

Spots was delighted. He called the Spearsman over to be introduced. The Spearsman asked: "Who is this?"

"Someone I got to know last year when I went to Tai'an to burn incense. He's called Li Rong, and he's a very good man."

"In that case, since our friend Zhang can't walk properly, let's all ride in his cart."

The carter was ordered to drive on, with the four men sitting in the cart.

"Friend Zhang, will you tell me the name of that rich man, please?" the Spearsman asked.

The Flea could not be prevailed upon. The first three or four times he made excuses. Then he said in a vague way: "He's the famous Mr. Guo."

The Spearsman asked Li Rong: "Do you have a famous official called Guo in Tai'an?"

Li Rong replied: "Our Mr. Guo is both aristocratic and rich. He's on very good terms with all the officials. He shelters all kinds of idlers in his house."

Hearing this the Spearsman thought: "If there's someone powerful behind it, we're not likely to be taken seriously."

Li Rong talked as they went about spear and staff play. Sometimes he sang songs. Thus the day slipped past. We needn't bore you with this.

Now they were in fact not more than a couple of stages from Mount Liang when Li Rong told the carter to take a gourd and get a fill of wine and some meat so they could drink a few cups on the wagon. Li Rong got out a dipper and the first measure of wine was ladled out and offered to the Spearsman, who drank it off. When

Li Rong called for more wine, the carter feigning clumsiness spilt the whole gourd-full of wine on the ground. As Li Rong was cursing the carter and telling him to go and get more, the Spearsman collapsed on the floor of the cart with a thud, saliva dribbling from his mouth.

And who exactly was this Li Rong? He was Lungs, of course. The other three jumped down from the cart and drove it on to the Crocodile's inn. They carried the Spearsman down to the boat and rowed him across to Golden Sands Landing. Song Jiang had already been alerted and came down the mountain with the other leaders to receive him. The effects of the drug were already beginning to wear off on the Spearsman but they also gave him the antidote. He had quite a shock when he opened his eyes and saw everybody. "How did you get me here?" he asked Spots.

"I'd better explain," Spots said. "I had always heard that Song Jiang welcomed good men from every corner of the empire and so I and Li Kui, the Black Whirlwind became brothers in Wugang. I returned with him to the mountain stronghold and joined the band. Recently Twin Rods has been using his linked cavalry against them, and they don't know how to counter it. I suggested the hooked spear method. You are the only one who knows how to use it so we devised this plan. We sent the Flea on ahead to steal your armour. My part was to tempt you to take to the road. Later Lungs played the part of Li Rong. As we were coming through the mountains we drugged you. We want you to join us here and become one of our leaders."

The Spearsman said: "So you've really done for me then!"

Song Jiang now stepped forward, cup in hand, and apologized, saying: "I myself for the time being have taken refuge in the marshes, awaiting a future imperial amnesty."

Leopard's Head also came forward cup in hand and apologized. "I sang your praises to everyone here. Please do not refuse."

The Spearsman said: "Spots my friend, you have inveigled me here, but at home my wife will be arrested and what then?"

Song Jiang said: "That's no problem. Set your heart at ease, commander, because you can take my word for it that before long we will fetch your family and you will all be together again."

Chao Gai, the Professor and Taoist Gongsun all came forward with conciliatory speeches and a great reception banquet was organized.

Time was now devoted to selecting the strongest of the troops to learn the method of fighting with hooked spears, while the Magic Messenger and Spots were instructed to travel with all speed to the capital and fetch the Spearsman's family. In a few days' time Panther was back with the Supremo's family and the Pill Monger returned from the capital with Thunderer's family. Green-Eyes returned to the stronghold with five cartloads of explosives and ammunition. A few more days passed, and then the Magic Messenger and Spots brought the Spearsman's family in.

The Spearsman was surprised to see his wife and asked her how she had got there. "When you disappeared and didn't turn up at the office for the roll call," she said, "I told them that you hadn't reported for duty because you were ill in bed. Then cousin Tang suddenly appeared with your armour. He said: 'We got it back, but your husband caught an infection on the journey and he is lying desperately ill at the inn. He wants to see you and the children.' He persuaded me to get into a carriage, but I had no idea where it was taking me till we arrived here."

The Spearsman said: "Fair enough, friends. But it's a pity you left that armour of mine at home."

Spots grinned. "Cheer up," he said. "As soon as I'd got your wife off in the carriage I went back and got the armour again. I also persuaded these two girls to pack all the valuables in your house into bundles so they could be carried here."

"Then I suppose it's no good my thinking about returning," said the Spearsman.

"I have another confession to make, cousin," said Spots. "On the way back here we bumped into a company of merchants. I dressed up in your armour and painted my face. Using your name I stripped those merchants of all their goods. Before long this will be posted up all over the capital and they'll be looking to arrest you."

"Well, you've really done your best to ruin me, haven't you?" said the Spearsman.

Chao Gai and Song Jiang now excused themselves, saying: "If we hadn't done these things, how would we ever have got you to stay?"

Following this, accommodation was allotted to the Spearsman and his family, and the leaders settled down to discuss how to break the power of the linked cavalry.

Sergeant Lei by now had completed the manufacture of hooked spears, so Song Jiang, the Professor and others invited the Spearsman to give a demonstration of their use. "I am ready to divulge all I know and train every troop leader," he said. "We must pick the strongest men for it."

Everyone sat in the Assembly Hall and looked on while the Spearsman selected his recruits and explained the method of the hooked spear. And much was to depend on this, for:

Three thousand armoured cavalry are about to be beaten,
The time has come for a hero's capture.

But if you want to know all about this method of the hooked spear which the Spearsman expounded, you must read the next chapter.

Chapter 57

The Spearsman teaches the hooked spear; Song Jiang destroys the linked cavalry!

Now in the Assembly Hall Chao Gai, Song Jiang, the Professor, Taoist Gongsun and the rest had requested the Spearsman to teach them the moves with the hooked spear. The Spearsman was as might be expected a fine figure of a man, extremely tall, with a pale face and a fine black moustache and whiskers, a solid trunk and broad shoulders.

When the Spearsman had chosen his trainees, he left the Assembly Hall and taking up a hooked spear started to do exercises with it. The onlookers applauded. Then he began to instruct them: "Generally when we use this weapon on horseback we strike from the waist and it goes step by step: seven forward moves — three hooks and four parries, followed by a thrust and a slash, making nine moves in all. If you are using the hooked spear on foot, then it's even better. First eight steps and four thrusts. That opens the gate. On the twelfth step, the first change. On the sixteenth turn about, hooking with the spear. On the twenty-fourth push up, then down. Hook to the east, parry to the west. On the thirty-sixth step keep your guard up and you've got 'em. That's how you fight with the hooked spear."

The Spearsman explained the method move by move, demonstrating each one to the assembled leaders, who were highly appreciative of the performance. From that day on those who had been selected, the nimblest and strongest, practised from dawn to dusk, while the infantry were also taught how to conceal themselves in the woods and trip the enemy horses. In less than a fortnight six or seven hundred had been trained, to the

徐寧教使鈎鐮鎗

great satisfaction of Song Jiang and the other leaders. They were now ready to take on the enemy.

Now since the loss of the Supremo and Thunderer, Twin Rods had been coming daily to the water's edge to challenge his opponents to combat. But the mountain stronghold only gave orders for the boat captains to strengthen all shore defences and to fix concealed stakes in the water. Although Twin Rods had reconnoitred the roads on the north and west of the mountain, he could find no way of reaching the main stronghold.

Mount Liang now gave Thunderer a fixed time-limit for preparing various kinds of missile to be taken down and used against the enemy. Those who were to use the hooked spear technique had already completed their training.

Song Jiang said: "I may well be wrong, but I have a plan and I'd like everyone's opinion."

The Professor said: "We would like to hear your plan."

"For the coming engagement, let us not use cavalry. Let everyone fight on foot. We will use a tactic of Sunzi's, taking advantage of the rough and marshy terrain. The infantry will march down the mountain in ten divisions, with the objective of luring the enemy on. When their attack starts, everyone will take off into the reeds and undergrowth. Troops with hooked spears will already be lying in ambush there, and with every group of ten trained in the use of the hooked spear there will be ten more with snaring hooks. When the cavalry charge they will throw them down with their thrusting and hooking, and the others will use their snaring hooks to snag them. We will also have ambushes like this along the narrow paths in the flat areas. What do you think of it?"

"A great way to preserve our numbers and capture their leaders," said the Professor.

"This is exactly the right way to employ hooked spears and snaring hooks," said the Spearsman.

Song Jiang divided his troops into ten sections. The Red-Haired Devil and Skyscraper led one section; the two Mu brothers led another; one was led by Morbid and the Nine-Tailed Turtle; another by Whiskers and Redeye; one by Snake and Scorpion;

one by the Forester and Rhinoceros, uncle and nephew; one by Steelbright and Short-Arse, the husband and wife team; one by the Pill Monger and the Flautist; one by the Dandy and Whitey; one by Panther and Green-Eyes. These ten sections of foot soldiers went down the mountain first, to draw the enemy on. After them went the White-Water Dragon, the Pilot and White Eel, the three Ruan brothers, the two Tong brothers and Flagpole. These nine boat captains were to support the campaign in boats. Then six leaders on horseback, Colonel Hua, Thunderclap, Skyhawk, Mr. Chai, Colonel Sun and Golden Wings were to challenge the enemy on the slopes of the mountain. Thunderer and Uglymug were to command the artillery. The Spearsman and Spots were in charge of the troops with hooked spears; the troops of the main contingent were led by Song Jiang, the Professor, Taoist Gongsun, the Magic Messenger, the Little Duke and the Halberdier. These dispositions were announced and the remaining leaders were charged with guarding the various camps.

When Song Jiang had completed these arrangements, in the middle of the night, the troops with the hooked spears went down first and were ferried across the water and placed in ambush all about. In the early hours of the morning the ten contingents of infantry set off. Thunderer and Uglymug took wind shells and set up their guns on a high point, erecting racks and placing the shells on them. The Spearsman and Spots crossed the water with their signals. At first light Song Jiang surrounded by his troops beside the water, began drumming, shouting and waving banners.

Twin Rods inside his tent heard the noise. After receiving the reports from his lookouts, he sent Victorious with the advance guard to reconnoitre. The cavalry units were now linked together and Twin Rods himself donned full armour and mounted his famous black charger with the white socks. Brandishing his two rods and urging on the horses and carts he thundered towards the Marshes of Mount Liang.

Song Jiang could be seen beside the water, leading a detachment of his troops. Twin Rods ordered his forces to deploy. Victorious, leader of the vanguard, rode up to consult him: "Over there to the south there's a company of infantry. Do we know how many there are?"

"Don't worry about that," said Twin Rods. "Just get the linked cavalry to charge!"

Victorious took five hundred troops to make a quick reconnaissance and found that another group of enemy infantry had appeared to the south-east. He was about to send some of his men to investigate when he noticed another cluster of banners over to the south-west, where a great deal of flag-waving and shouting was going on. He led his troops back and reported to Twin Rods: "There's three companies to the south all with Mount Liang banners."

Twin Rods said: "The blighters have been lying low for such a long time. They must have some plan."

He had hardly finished speaking when a loud explosion was heard to the north. Twin Rods began cursing. "That must mean Thunderer's gone over to the bandits and taught them gunnery."

Now they all turned from the south and saw the banners of three divisions waving to the north. Twin Rods said to Victorious: "So that's their dastardly plan. We'd better divide our army in half. I'll attack the ones on the north and you attack the lot to the south."

But before they could put this plan into action, four more divisions appeared to the west. Twin Rods began to feel uneasy. A whole string of explosions was now heard from the north and shots began landing on the hillside nearby. The firing came from a big gun that was surrounded by forty-nine smaller ones, known as the "Mother and Sons." The noise when it fired was truly awesome. Twin Rod's troops were thrown into confusion before the fighting had even begun. Running this way and that, they become mixed up with the troops led by Victorious.

The ten divisions of enemy infantry, when attacked, simply melted away on every side. Enraged, Twin Rods concentrated his attack on the north. Song Jiang's men ran in all directions taking cover in the reedbeds. Twin Rods now attempted to sweep them away with his linked cavalry. The armoured horses galloped all together and had no means of stopping. They galloped straight into this tangle of withered reeds, and dead undergrowth. There amid a cacophony of whistled signals the experts with the hooked spears went into action. They attacked the legs of the horses on either end of the row and those in the middle panicked. The troops with the snagging hooks then subdued them and all over the wasteland people busied themselves tying up the prisoners.

Twin Rods realized that he had been caught in a trap with the hooked spearsmen. He pulled up his horse and galloped away south to look for Victorious. From behind him the wind shells began to whistle over his head. On this side and that, on every hill or stretch of wasteland, it was nothing but pursuing infantry. The linked cavalry of Victorious and Twin Rods had galloped pell-mell into the undergrowth where they were tripped and taken. Both leaders now realized that they had been outwitted. They galloped about in all directions trying to locate their cavalry and find a way out. But all these paths were thick with the banners of Mount Liang and there was no route they could take with any confidence. In the end they turned north-west. When they had gone not much over a mile a group of bandits appeared. The two fellows who commanded them blocked the road. One was Mu the Unstoppable and the other was Mu the Irrepressible. Each held a stout halberd. "You're defeated!" they shouted. "It's useless trying to escape."

Twin Rods was furious. Weaving his rods he galloped straight at them. After four or five bouts Mu the Irrepressible galloped off. Fearing a trap Twin Rods did not give chase but took the main route to the north.

At this point another group of bandits appeared on the mountainside and blocked his path. One was Snake and the other was Scorpion. They bore down on him, each armed with a trident. Twin Rods whirled his rods again and attacked. After five or six bouts Snake and Scorpion broke off and fled. But Twin Rods had not gone more than a few hundred metres when twenty-four hooked spear specialists appeared from either side and swept towards him. Twin Rods had no more stomach for the fight. He turned his horse's head north-eastward and fled along the road. Here he came upon the husband and wife pair, Short-Arse and

宋江大破連環馬

Steelbright, standing in the way. His road was blocked and in addition escape on either side was hindered by thorny grass. Twin Rods slapped his horse, whirled his rods, and tried to force a way through. Short-Arse and Steelbright followed, but they couldn't catch him. He got away to the north-east.

Twin Rods had suffered a huge defeat and his forces had been scattered like raindrops.

The foe like a threatening storm appear;
The black horse turns and gallops free.
Linked cavalry fall to the skill of the spear.
The general into the wilds must flee.

Now our story divides. Song Jiang ordered the gong to be sounded, signalling withdrawal to the mountain stronghold, where all claimed their reward. Of the three thousand linked cavalry, a good half had been demolished by the hooked spears. The dead and dying horses were flayed and then used for food. The remaining good horses were taken up the mountain and fed well, to be used for riding. Their armoured riders were captured alive and also taken to the mountain. The five thousand foot soldiers found themselves surrounded on three sides and fled towards the army in the centre, where they were thrown down and captured by men with hooked spears. Those who fled towards the water were cut off by the sailors and picked up in their boats, after which they were rowed across to the landing and taken up the mountain.

All the horses and men previously captured by the government troops were rescued and returned to the stronghold. The camp that Twin Rods had set up was razed to the ground. The small camp at the water's edge was rebuilt, as were the two inns and other buildings that served as the stronghold's eyes, with Blackface and Auntie Gu, the Guv and the Flea reinstated as the landlords. The Red-Haired Devil and Skyscraper having captured Victorious bound him and took him a prisoner to the mountain stronghold. When Song Jiang saw him he personally loosed his bonds and invited him into the hall, where he courteously apologized and entertained him with a banquet. They got the Supremo and Thunderer to encourage him to join the company.

Victorious was in fact one of the seventy-two baleful stars, so it is no surprise that he willingly consented to join them and became one of the leaders on Mount Liang. Song Jiang then prepared a letter and sent someone to get the family of Victorious and bring them to join him on the mountain. Song Jiang was delighted to have broken up the linked cavalry and to have gained new troops, armour, helmets and weapons, and there was feasting every day. The stronghold's defences and lookouts were put back on their old footing. Of this no more.

As for Twin Rods, having lost many troops, he dared not return to the capital. He rode away by himself on the black horse with white socks, his armour tied on the horse's back. He was looking for a refuge, but he had no money for his expenses. He unfastened his silver belt and sold it to provide himself with funds. As he rode along he thought to himself: "Who would have thought that today I would be so down on my luck? Where can I take refuge?"

Suddenly the thought came to him: "Governor Murong of Qingzhou and I have known each other many a year, why don't I go to him? If I can get his sister the imperial concubine on my side I may be able to get hold of another army to avenge all this."

After travelling for two days he found himself hungry and thirsty when evening came. Seeing a country inn beside the road, he dismounted, tethered his horse to a tree outside and entered. He laid his two rods on the table and sat down. He asked the waiter to bring him wine and food.

"We only sell wine here," the waiter said. "But if you want meat, they've just killed a sheep in the village. I can go and buy some mutton if you like."

Twin Rods unslung his provisions bag and took out some money in loose silver which he gave to the waiter, saying: "See if you can get a mutton leg to cook for me, and make sure you feed my horse. Tonight I shall stay here in your place. Tomorrow I go on to Qingzhou."

The waiter said: "Your Honour, you can stay here if you like, but I can't offer you a good bed."

"I'm a soldier," said Twin Rods. "So long as there's somewhere to lie down it'll be good enough."

While the waiter went off with the silver to buy mutton, Twin Rods unloaded his armour from the horse, loosened his belt and sat down in front of the door. It seemed a long time before the waiter reappeared, bearing a leg of mutton. Twin Rods told him to boil the mutton, make some pancakes with three catties of flour and bring three measures of wine. While he was cooking the meat and making the pancakes the waiter also heated water for Twin Rods to wash his feet. Then he put the horse in a little stable at the back of the house. He cut grass and cooked some oats for the horse. Twin Rods told him to warm some wine so he could have a drink first. Soon the meat was done and Twin Rods asked the waiter for more wine to drink with the meat. Then he said: "I am an officer of the imperial guard. Because I have suffered a setback in my plan to destroy Mount Liang I am heading for Governor Murong's in Qingzhou. Make sure you take good care of my horse. He's a very special horse, known as a snowy-footed black steed, a gift from the Emperor himself. You can be sure that I will reward you well."

"I am very grateful to Your Honour," said the waiter. "But there is something Your Honour should know. Not far from here there's this mountain, called Mount Peachblossom. There's a band of robbers up there. The chief is called Li Zhong, the Tiger-Killer, and his henchman is Zhou Tong, the Big Chief. They've got together an army of six or seven hundred and they go around robbing and plundering. They're always stirring up trouble in the region. The authorities keep sending out special troops to catch them but they've never been able to. You'd best be on your guard, Your Honour, and sleep lightly tonight."

Twin Rods said: "Ten thousand men could not stand up against me, let them all come, if they like, the whole bloody lot of them, who cares? You just make sure you look after my horse properly."

When he had eaten and drunk enough, the waiter made up a bed for him.

Now partly because Twin Rods had been having such a wearisome time, and partly because he had drunk a few cups too many, he lay down without even bothering to undress. He slept undisturbed till around midnight, when he awoke suddenly to hear the waiter cursing away to himself at the back of the house. He jumped up at once, grabbed his two rods and ran to the back of the house. "What are you making such a noise for?" he asked.

The waiter replied: "I got up to fetch grass and I saw that the fence was broken and Your Honour's horse had been stolen. I could still see some torches away in the distance. That must be where they're heading."

"Where do you mean?" Twin Rods asked.

"It's the road those robbers from Mount Peachblossom take, no doubt about it," said the waiter.

Twin Rods was devastated. He made the waiter lead him across the rice fields for several miles, but the torches had vanished and they had no means of knowing which way to go.

Twin Rods said: "I've lost the Emperor's horse! Now what am I going to do?"

"Tomorrow Your Honour must go to the authorities and report it," the waiter said. "They'll send troops to catch them and then you'll get your horse back."

But Twin Rods' sorrow knew no bounds. He sat there till day came and then, telling the waiter to carry his armour, set out for Qingzhou. It was getting dark when they reached the city and they spent the night at an inn. Next day at dawn he was outside the courtroom asking to see Governor Murong. The Governor had quite a surprise. "I was told you had been sent to apprehend the bandits of Mount Liang, Commander," he said. "What are you doing here?"

Twin Rods told him all that we have just recounted. Governor Murong said: "Although you've lost a lot of troops, it wasn't deliberate, you were caught out by the bandits' wiles, there was nothing you could do about it. In this district which I govern we have suffered many depredations from bandits. Since you are now here, you can clean up Mount Peachblossom and get the Emperor's horse back. Then you can go on to Twin Dragon Peak and White Tiger Mountain and hunt down the robbers in those two hideouts. When you've dealt with that mess, I will do my utmost to have you reinstated to lead a force against Mount Liang and have your revenge. How about that?"

Twin Rods prostrated himself again and said: "I am deeply grateful to you for your concern in this matter. If you will do this I shall be indebted to you till my dying day."

Governor Murong invited Twin Rods to go to a guest-room and rest. He provided him with clothing, lodging and food. The waiter who had carried the armour was sent home.

After three days, Twin Rods was impatient to recover the Emperor's horse, and kept asking Governor Murong for the troops. The Governor accordingly let him have two thousand infantry and gave him a black horse. Twin Rods thanked him, armed himself and mounted and led his troops forth in search of the missing horse, heading for Mount Peachblossom.

Now on Mount Peachblossom the Tiger-Killer and the Big Chief had spent every day since the capture of the Emperor's horse in carousing. That day one of their hidden scouts returned and reported: "Troops from Qingzhou are heading this way!"

The Big Chief rose to his feet and said: "You look after the camp, brother, while I go and send them packing!" He chose a hundred troops, grasped his spear, mounted and rode off down the mountain to encounter the government forces.

When Twin Rods and his two thousand government troops reached the mountain, they deployed in battle formation. Twin Rods rode out in front and bellowed: "Come out and surrender, you thieves and robbers!"

The Big Chief ordered his troops to spread out in a straight line. Then he rode out in front with his spear at the ready. Twin Rods charged him. The Big Chief urged his horse on to the encounter. The two horses clashed, but after only half a dozen bouts the Big Chief feeling that his strength was failing turned his horse's head and galloped off up the mountain. Twin Rods pursued him some way, but fearing a trap hurriedly turned back and set up camp at the bottom to wait and fight another day.

When the Big Chief returned to the stronghold, he told the Tiger-Killer: "Twin Rods is a great fighter. We can't handle him. All we can do is withdraw up the mountain, and if he follows us up here I don't know what we are going to do!"

The Tiger-Killer said: "I have heard that Lu Zhishen, the Flowery Monk, is at the Temple of the Precious Pearl on Twin Dragon Peak. He's got a lot of followers. And there is also someone called Yang Zhi, the Blue-Faced Beast. And there's a new arrival there, 'Pilgrim' Wu Song, who's got the courage of ten thousand. We'd better write them a letter, asking them to send troops to relieve us. To get ourselves out of this mess we'd better accept their authority over us. At the end of the month we can pay them some tribute."

"I know only too well how courageous they are. I'm just afraid that that monk may remember about what happened before and not want to help us," said the Big Chief.

The Tiger-Killer laughed and said: "Remember how he beat you up and stole a whole lot of our gold and silver cups? But why should he bear us any grudge? He has a generous nature. If he sends troops here to help us, I'm sure he will lead them himself."

"No doubt you're right," said the Big Chief.

They wrote the letter and sent two quick-witted men with it. The messengers stole down the far side of the mountain and headed for Twin Dragon Peak. They reached it in two days. First they made detailed inquiries. They were told that there were three leaders in the great hall of the Temple of the Precious Pearl. Chief of them was Lu Zhishen, the Flowery Monk, second in command was Yang Zhi, the Blue-Faced Beast, third was "Pilgrim" Wu Song.

There were four lesser chiefs on the gate lower down the mountain: one was Shi En, the Young Master (this was the son of the Warden of the Mengzhou prison camp. After Wu Song killed General Zhang and all his family, he fled with all his family and took refuge in the rivers and lakes. Later his parents died and hearing that Wu Song was on Twin Dragon Peak he rushed off to join them). Another was Cao Zheng, the Knife (he was the butcher who had been with Zhishen and the Blue-Faced Beast at the outset, when they seized the Temple of the Precious Pearl, after killing Deng Long). Also there were Zhang Qing, the Gardener and Sister Sun, the Ogress (these two were husband and wife. They had resided at Crossways Rise on the Mengzhou road, selling meat pies made with human flesh. They had joined the band because the Monk and the Pilgrim had written many letters inviting them).

When the Knife heard there was a letter from Mount Peachblossom, he asked for details, and then sent some one up to the great hall to inform the three chiefs. Zhishen, the Flowery Monk, said: "When I first left Mount Wutai, I spent the night in the neighbourhood of Mount Peachblossom, and I gave that Big Chief a bloody good hiding. As for that Tiger-Killer, when he knew it was me he invited me up the mountain for a day's drinking and called me his brother, wanted me to join them as one of their leaders. But they were stingy bastards, so I decamped with some of their silver. Now they're asking for help. Well, let's see what they have to say. Let their men come on up."

The Knife had only been gone a few moments when the messengers appeared in the hall. They saluted and said: "Governor Murong has recently received Commander Huyan known as Twin Rods, after his defeat at the hands of Mount Liang. Governor Murong has now ordered the destruction of the three strongholds, that is to say, our Mount Peachblossom, Twin Dragon Peak and White Tiger Mountain, and is going to let Twin Rods have troops to subdue Mount Liang and have his revenge on them. Our leaders are now asking you to come and help them. Later, when things are quieter we will pay you some tribute."

The Blue-Faced Beast said: "Supposing we just guard our own stronghold and protect the mountain, without offering them any help. I see two problems: firstly it will not improve relations between the heroes of the rivers and lakes, and secondly, if those bastards capture Mount Peachblossom, they will not have much respect for us here. Let us leave the Gardener, Sister Sun, the Young Master and the Knife to look after our stronghold while we three go and lend them a hand."

Accordingly five hundred foot soldiers and more than six hundred cavalry, fully equipped and armed, were detailed to go to Mount Peachblossom.

When the Tiger-Killer heard the news from Twin Dragon Peak he took three hundred troops down the mountain to meet them.

But Twin Rods heard about this and quickly drawing his troops up to block the way, rode out to receive the Tiger-Killer, whirling his rods.

This Tiger-Killer was a native of Dingyuan in Haozhou and his family had always made their living by giving demonstrations with spear and staff. People called him the Tiger-Killer because of his great bodily strength. But when he came down the mountain to join battle with Twin Rods, how would he fare? After ten bouts he saw that things were not looking good for him, so he put up his weapon and fled. This behaviour was contemptible to Twin Rods, who galloped in pursuit. The Big Chief, who was stationed halfway up the mountain, began raining down ballista missiles the size of goose eggs and Twin Rods was obliged hurriedly to turn his horse and gallop down again.

The government troops were now raising a continuous outcry. "What's all the shouting about?" Twin Rods asked. "A column of troops is approaching," they told him.

He rode to the rear to see for himself. He saw a cloud of dust and at the head of the troops a big monk, riding a white horse. Now who was this? Well, listen:

Since the day he was shaved, when he came to the monkhood, far and wide has he wandered, in search of good men. There's huge strength in those shoulders, violence is his birthright. He'll swindle the Buddha and shout at Guanyin! His monk's knife and staff give off a cold glint. Scripture is unknown to him, he's a stranger to fasting. It's the Flowery Monk, of course, it's Lu Zhishen.

Monk Lu Zhishen shouted out: "These fuckers are the rabble defeated by the company from the Marshes of Mount Liang, and they think they can come here and frighten us!"

"You're the first I'll kill, you bald scoundrel!" Twin Rods shouted back. "You've really wound me up!"

The two horses converged, with Zhishen twirling his monk's staff and Twin Rods flourishing his rods. They fought forty or fifty bouts but neither had the advantage. Twin Rods was secretly admiring his opponent: "What skill he has, this monk!"

Gongs were now sounded on either side and the two rejoined their armies to rest awhile. After a brief respite, Twin Rods urged his horse forward again and cried: "Come out and meet me again, you bald scoundrel! Your hour has come, you're going to taste defeat!" The Monk was about to ride forth, but another hero had taken offence and shouted: "Take a rest brother, I'll capture the bugger for you!"

Who was this then, charging at Twin Rods with whirling sword? Listen:

> *Once a commander of the imperial guard in the capital, disaster struck when he was involved in the transport of precious plants and stones: the stars were unpropitious. His sword can subdue the universe, his bow can settle the world. His strength combines the tiger's ferocity, the wolf's flexibility, the monkey's agility; he rides a fiery stallion, seated firmly on an embossed saddle. This hero's fame will enhance Mount Liang. This is the leader whom men call Yang Zhi, the Blue-Faced Beast.*

And so the Blue-Faced Beast rode out to do battle with Twin Rods. They fought more than forty bouts but neither could prevail. When Twin Rods saw how skilful his opponent was, he said to himself: "Where have these two come from? They're real professionals! This is not the kind of thing you'd expect from the greenwood."

When the Blue-Faced Beast saw that Twin Rods fought with such spirit, he feinted and then turned his horse and galloped back to his own ranks. Twin Rods likewise reined in his horse. He did not give chase. Both sides now withdrew their troops.

The Monk discussed matters with the Blue-Faced Beast. "We have got this far, but we must not try to reach the lower camp. Let us withdraw a few miles and tomorrow we will come to fight again." They withdrew their troops to a camp at the foot of a nearby ridge.

Twin Rods sat in his tent, gloomily turning things over in his mind: "I had thought it would all be as simple as splitting bamboo to capture this bunch of rebels. Who would have thought I was going to meet adversaries like these! It's just my luck!" He had got no further when a messenger from Governor Murong suddenly appeared and shouted: "You are to bring your troops back to protect the city, General! Two bandits from White Tiger Mountain, 'Blazing Comet' Kong Ming and 'Red Star' Kong Liang are marching with their troops on Qingzhou in search of provisions. The provincial stores are at risk. I am sent to ask you to return and organize the city's defences."

Twin Rods needed no further prompting. He led his troops back to the city by forced marches.

Next day the Monk, together with the Blue-Faced Beast and the Pilgrim, led the army forth with much cheering and waving of banners. When they reached the foot of the mountain, not a single enemy soldier was to be seen. They were quite amazed. The Tiger-Killer and the Big Chief led their troops down from the mountain and invited the three leaders up to their stronghold. Oxen and horses were slaughtered and a big feast was held in the guests' honour, while scouts were sent down to find out what was going on in the area.

When Twin Rods arrived back in the city with his army, he saw a column of troops approaching. Heading it were the two sons of Squire Kong of White Tiger Mountain, Blazing Comet and Red Star. These two because they had a quarrel with a rich man of the district, had killed his whole household, worthy and base, had gathered six or seven hundred men and set up shop on White Tiger Mountain, robbing and pillaging. Because their uncle, Kong Bin, lived in Qingzhou City he was arrested and imprisoned by Governor Murong. So Blazing Comet and Red Star marshalled their troops in the stronghold and moved to attack Qingzhou, with the aim of rescuing their uncle. Now they came up against the army of Twin Rods. The two sides engaged in a furious skirmish. Twin Rods rode out in front of his troops. Governor Murong, watching from the city gate tower, saw Blazing Comet lead the attack, charging with levelled lance straight at Twin Rods. The two horses clashed and they fought some twenty bouts. Twin Rods was eager to show off his skill in front of Governor Murong. Not rating Blazing Comet's fighting ability particularly highly, he contented himself with blocking and parrying. At the height of the contest, Twin Rods suddenly took Blazing Comet prisoner. Red Star could only lead his men off the field. Governor Murong from his tower signalled to Twin Rods to give chase. The government troops ambushed and captured a hundred or more, while Red Star's troops were routed and fled in disarray. At nightfall they found refuge in an old temple.

Having captured Blazing Comet, Twin Rods brought him into the city and went to see the Governor. The Governor was well pleased. He ordered Blazing Comet to be fitted with a heavy cangue and confined to prison, in the same cell as his uncle. The troops were rewarded and Twin Rods was entertained and questioned about Mount Peachblossom.

Twin Rods said: "I had thought it was just a case of 'To catch a turtle in a jar, put your hand in and there you are.' But a whole gang of bandits came to their rescue, one of whom was a monk, and another a big blue-faced fellow. I fought them both and had no success. Both have skills that are quite out of the ordinary, not at all what you would expect from outlaws. Otherwise I would have beaten them."

"That monk," said Governor Murong, "is the Old Field Marshal's former camp commandant in Yan'an, Major Lu Da. Nowadays he has shaved his head and become a monk under the name of Lu Zhishen, also known as the Flowery Monk. The one with the blue face is a former colonel of the palace guard, Yang Zhi, known as the Blue-Faced Beast. And there's another one, a wandering monk called Pilgrim Wu Song, who used to be Captain Wu Song, the one who killed the tiger on Jingyang Pass. These three have occupied Twin Dragon Peak, and devote themselves to plundering and pillaging. They have repeatedly clashed with the government forces and killed four or five hundred personnel of the anti-brigand brigade. Until now we haven't been able to capture them."

"Well, I can vouch for their military prowess," said Twin Rods. "So it's Colonel Yang and Major Lu, is it? Their reputation is no lie! But put your heart at rest. I know all about their skills now. Sooner or later I will capture all of them, one by one."

This was just what the Governor wanted to hear. He held a banquet in Twin Rods' honour and then invited him to rest in a guest-room.

Meanwhile Red Star was leading the shattered remnants of his army through a wood when he suddenly came upon a body of troops, led by a fine-looking warrior.

When this turned out to be Pilgrim Wu Song, Red Star quickly slid from the saddle and prostrated himself. "I trust you are in good health, sir?" he said.

Pilgrim Wu Song hastened to raise him up, saying: "I have heard about you and your brothers occupying White Tiger Mountain and raising a company. I often wanted to come and see you, but either I couldn't get down the mountain or the way was not clear, and so we were not able to meet. What brings you here today?"

Red Star told all about how they had wanted to rescue his uncle and how he had lost his brother.

Wu Song said: "Don't worry. There are six or seven of us who have a company on Twin Dragon Peak. We have been asked for help by the Tiger-Killer and Big Chief of Mount Peachblossom who were being attacked by the government forces. Our two leaders, Lu Zhishen and Yang Zhi took the men out to fight General Huyan, known as Twin Rods. They fought for a whole day, but then in the evening Twin Rods took himself off. The Mount Peachblossom lot gave us a banquet and made us a gift of the Emperor's horse. Now we are all heading for home. The other two are not far behind. Suppose I get them to go and attack Qingzhou and rescue your uncle and brother?"

Red Star thanked the Pilgrim most humbly. After a long wait, Monk Lu Zhishen and the Blue-Faced Beast came riding up. The Pilgrim introduced Red Star to them and said: "That time when I was with Song Jiang at the Kong's we were in all sorts of trouble. Now I think we should put honour first and combine the troops of all three mountain strongholds in order to attack Qingzhou, kill Governor Murong, capture Twin Rods, and seize enough government stores and money to supply all of us. How about it?"

"I am of the same opinion," said the Monk. "Let us send someone to inform them on Mount Peachblossom and tell the

Tiger-Killer and Big Chief to bring their men here and we'll all of us go and attack Qingzhou."

But the Blue-Faced Beast said: "Qingzhou is strongly defended, it has good troops. And besides, there's Twin Rods, who is a brave fighter. I'm not trying to belittle our strength, but if you want to attack Qingzhou, the only way is to do as I say. If you do, we will succeed in due course."

"What do you suggest, then, brother?" said the Pilgrim.

The Blue-Faced Beast replied briefly, but his words cannot be given in one sentence, and they were to have an important result:

In Qingzhou, a mass of broken tiles and the smoke rising;
In the Marshes, each hero will rub his hands with glee.

But if you want to know what the Blue-Faced Beast told Pilgrim Wu Song they had to do to capture Qingzhou you must read the next chapter.

Chapter 58

Three mountains join forces against Qingzhou; All the tigers agree to repair to the Marshes!

When Wu Song took Red Star to meet Monk Lu Zhishen and the Blue-Faced Beast and he asked them to rescue his brother and uncle, the Monk wanted to attack at once with the combined troops of the three mountain strongholds. But the Blue-Faced Beast said: "You can't take Qingzhou without a very big army. We know the reputation of Song Jiang on Mount Liang. Among the rivers and lakes he's known as the Opportune Rain. Twin Rods, moreover is his special enemy. We can combine our forces with those of the Kong brothers. I shall wait here till the troops from Mount Peachblossom are ready and then go to attack Qingzhou. Red Star, you go as fast as you can to the Marshes of Mount Liang and ask Song Jiang if he will come and help us mount a determined assault on the city. That's my idea. After all, Song Jiang is a good friend of yours, isn't he? What does everyone say?"

The Monk said: "Well, this is how it is. All the time I hear this one say Song Jiang is a good man and that one say Song Jiang is a good man, but unfortunately I've never met the gentleman. His name is on everyone's lips, it's perpetually buzzing in my ears. I'm sure the person in question really is a good man, or he wouldn't have such a reputation. Previously when he was with Colonel Hua on Windy Mountain I had the idea of going to see him. But just as I was about to start I heard that he had moved on, and it turned out once again that I didn't meet him. So there you are! Red Star, if you want to save your brother, go there quickly and ask them for help. The rest of us will stay here and have a go at the buggers first."

So Red Star handed over his forces to the Monk and disguised as a merchant, with just one companion, travelled night and day to Mount Liang.

The Monk, the Blue-Faced Beast and the Pilgrim went back to Twin Dragon Peak and told the Young Master and the Knife to bring several hundred more troops down in support. The Tiger-Killer and Big Chief on Mount Peachblossom heard the news and came with nearly all their troops, leaving only fifty or so to guard the camp. They all assembled before Qingzhou city and mounted a joint attack. But of this we shall say no more for the moment.

We turn now to Red Star and his companion, as they leave Qingzhou and travelling towards Mount Liang arrive at the inn of Li Li the Executioner where they stop for wine and to ask the way. Since their faces were unfamiliar, the Executioner invited them to sit and then asked: "Where have you gentlemen come from?"

"From Qingzhou," Red Star replied.

"Who do you want to see on Mount Liang?" the Executioner asked.

"There is someone I know there. It's him I want to see," said Red Star.

"The main stronghold on Mount Liang is where all the chief leaders live, why should you go there?" the Executioner asked.

"It is Song Jiang I want to speak to," said Red Star.

"If you are looking for Song Jiang, then I've got something special for you," the Executioner said, and he called the waiter to bring some special wine.

Red Star said: "We've never met before, what makes you so hospitable?"

"Well, you see, if you are looking for one of the leaders on the mountain, you must be one of us and an old friend of the company, so how could I be neglectful towards you?" said the Executioner. "I must go and report this."

Red Star said: "I am Kong Liang, and I come from a manor at the foot of White Tiger Mountain."

"I have heard Song Jiang speak highly of you, welcome to Mount Liang!"

二龍山
桃花山
白虎山
三山聚義打青州

When they had drunk the special wine, a window was opened in the water pavilion and a whistling arrow fired off. From the reeds on the other side of the creek a boat was rowed across. The Executioner motioned Red Star into the boat and they rowed across to Golden Sands Landing and then headed up the mountain. Looking at the defensive strength of the three gates, with their forests of spears, swords, halberds and pikes, Red Star said: "I had heard that things were prospering in the Marshes of Mount Liang, but I didn't realize the setup was as big as this!"

A soldier had already reported their arrival, and Song Jiang hastened down to meet them. Red Star immediately prostrated himself.

"Why have you come here, my dear friend?" Song Jiang asked.

As soon as Red Star finished paying his respects, a great sob escaped him. Song Jiang said: "Obviously some painful thought assails you, my friend. Please feel free to tell me about it. No one can escape trouble, one must always do one's best to help others, so please rise, my friend, we want to help you."

Red Star said: "After you left us, Master, and my father passed away, my brother Blazing Comet became embroiled in a petty dispute with a local landowner and killed him and all his family. The authorities came to arrest him so we ran off to White Tiger Mountain and collected a band of six or seven hundred men, and set up as robbers. We have an uncle in Qingzhou called Kong Bin. He was placed under arrest by Governor Murong and thrown into prison with a heavy cangue round his neck. So we went to attack the city, aiming to set our uncle free. Unfortunately outside the city we ran into a chap known as Twin Rods, because he fights with a pair of rods. My brother fought him and got captured and taken into the city. He's in prison there now, I don't know whether alive or dead. They chased me also and destroyed my army. A day or so later I ran into Pilgrim Wu Song who spoke about you and introduced me to his companions. One of them is the Flowery Monk Lu Zhishen, another is the Blue-Faced Beast Yang Zhi. We hit it off immediately and I discussed with them how to rescue my brother. The Pilgrim said: 'I will ask my two friends, along with the Tiger-killer and Big Chief from Mount Peachblossom and the combined forces from the three mountain strongholds, to attack Qingzhou. You ride as fast as you can to the Marshes of Mount Liang to tell Song Jiang about it and ask him to come and help rescue your uncle and brother.' And that's why I'm here."

Song Jiang said: "It's quite a simple matter. Don't worry about it. First come and meet Chao Gai so we can all discuss it together."

Song Jiang took Red Star to meet Chao Gai, the Professor and Taoist Gongsun and the other leaders. He told them all how Twin Rods was in Qingzhou, staying with Governor Murong, how the Governor had captured Blazing Comet and how Red Star had come to ask for help.

Chao Gai said: "Well, seeing that there are good men, honourable and humane, in both those places and they are your friends, how could we not go and help? But my good friend, you have been down the mountain many times in succession, this time you should stay here to guard the camp and let me go instead."

Song Jiang said: "You are our chief. You mustn't go anywhere. Besides, this is entirely my business. Since he has taken the trouble to come all this way, they naturally would not be happy if I didn't respond myself. I'd just like to ask a few of our comrades to go with me."

Before he had finished speaking, everyone in the hall was clamouring to go, saying they'd give an arm or a leg to be part of it.

Song Jiang was well pleased. That day a banquet was held in Red Star's honour. While they were eating, Song Jiang asked Sterling to draw up a list of those who were to accompany him down the mountain. The group was divided into five contingents. The first, commanded by Colonel Hua, Thunderclap, the Dandy and Short-Arse, was to lead the attack. The second was led by the Unstoppable, Morbid, Snake and Scorpion. The main force was under the command of Song Jiang, the Professor, the Little Duke and the Halberdier, the fourth contingent was led by Whiskers, Mr. Chai, the White-Water Dragon and the Pilot, while Colonel Sun, Panther, Golden Wings and Thunderer were entrusted with forming the rearguard. These were the five forces under twenty leaders appointed by Mount Liang, together with two thousand men, horse and foot. The remaining commanders were to remain with Chao Gai and guard the stronghold.

Song Jiang now bade Chao Gai farewell and accompanied Red Star down the mountain. When the forces of Mount Liang set out in their five columns it was like this:

> *As they march out from the Marshes it is like a great dragon uncoiling out of the ocean. As they leave Mount Liang it is like tigers and leopards rampaging through the sky. Led by their twenty heroes, the five columns advance. Each unit comprises thirty officers and men. Brilliantly coloured banners wave in dense clouds. Deadly steel blades glitter like frost and snow. Warhorses gallop forward with jingling bridles, warriors march proudly to the beat of ceremonial drums. Dust is raised in copious clouds, filling the sky with murk and gloom. Multi-coloured banners throng about the clever and resourceful Professor Wu Yong; upright under the green oiled umbrella sits Song Jiang the Just, he who does heaven's will. Passing spirits bestow respectful greetings; bystanders sing songs of celebration.*

Thus Song Jiang marched out from Mount Liang, at the head of twenty leaders and two thousand men, drawn up in five columns. Nothing of importance happened on the way. They passed through the province causing not the slightest harm to any of the people.

When they reached Qingzhou, Red Star first made contact with Monk Lu Zhishen and the leaders of the other force and a reception banquet was organized. When Song Jiang and his army arrived, Pilgrim Wu Song took his six comrades along to introduce them. After Song Jiang had persuaded him to be seated, the Monk said: "I have heard so much about you, yet for some reason we have never met. I am delighted finally to make your acquaintance."

Song Jiang replied: "You are too kind! Men of honour among the rivers and lakes are loud in their praise of your clear virtue. I count myself forever blessed to have seen you for myself."

The Blue-Faced Beast also stood, prostrated himself again, and said: "I once passed by Mount Liang and was honoured with an invitation to stay, but in my folly I declined. Now it is my great good fortune to see you here in our stronghold. This is the greatest favour heaven could show me."

Song Jiang said, smiling: "Your reputation is universal among the rivers and lakes. My only regret is that it has taken so long for us to meet."

The Monk now ordered wine and all the leaders introduced themselves to each other.

Next day Song Jiang asked: "Tell me about Qingzhou, how has the campaign fared?"

The Blue-Faced Beast replied: "Since Red Star left we have fought four or five times but have not defeated them. Their fortunes depend entirely on Twin Rods. If we could only capture him I believe we'd have them in the palms of our hands."

The Professor smiled craftily. "You won't take that one by force," he said. "We must use guile."

"What can we do to capture him?" Song Jiang asked.

"The only way is this," said the Professor and whispered something.

"Brilliant!" said Song Jiang delightedly.

Troops were given their orders that day, and next morning they marched. Arriving before the city all the troops deployed around it. Drums were beating, banners waving, the sound of cheering and challenges filled the air. When report of this reached Governor Murong's ears, he hurriedly demanded the presence of Twin Rods.

"These bandits have now gone and brought Song Jiang of the Marshes of Mount Liang here to help them," he said. "What are we going to do about it?"

"Rest easy, Your Excellency," said Twin Rods. "If the bandits come here they lose their advantage. These scum can only afford to be insolent within their marshes. Now that they have ventured out of their den we shall catch them one by one, they'll have no chance to show off round here. You can stand on the city walls and watch me slaughter them."

Twin Rods armed himself at once and mounted. He ordered the city gates to be opened and the drawbridge lowered and led out a thousand cavalry. He deployed his troops under the city walls.

A certain warrior now rode out from Song Jiang's ranks. He was carrying a wolf's-tooth mace, and he berated the Governor in stentorian tones: "You thieving bureaucrat, you scourge of the people! You murdered all my family! Now I'm going to have my revenge and wipe out your offence!"

Governor Murong recognized Thunderclap and replied in kind: "You, an officer of the imperial guard, the state never broke faith with you yet you had the nerve to turn rebel! When we catch you, you shall die the death of a thousand cuts! Bring me that villain!"

In obedience to the command Twin Rods galloped forward with whirling rods, intending to capture Thunderclap. The latter, brandishing his mace, rode to the encounter. Their horses met.

What a contest it was! Forty or fifty bouts they fought, and neither had the advantage. Finally Governor Murong, fearing that Twin Rods might lose, ordered the gong sounded for his troops to withdraw into the city. Thunderclap made no attempt to pursue them and also retired to his own lines. Song Jiang ordered all the leaders and field commanders to pull their troops back five miles or so and pitch camp.

Back in the city, Twin Rods dismounted and went to see the Governor. "I was on the point of capturing Thunderclap," he said. "Why did Your Excellency order the troops to withdraw?"

"You had fought so many bouts," said the Governor. "I was afraid you were tired. That's why I ordered the army back to take a break. That villain Thunderclap used to be my commander-in-chief. He turned traitor along with Colonel Hua. But you shouldn't underestimate him."

"Don't worry, Your Excellency. I will certainly get the better of that shameless turncoat. When I was fighting him just now, I noticed a flaw in his technique. In a few days' time you'll be able to see me dispatch him!"

"Since you're so brave," said the Governor, "open up a passage next time you're fighting and we'll send out three messengers. One can go to the capital to request reinforcements. The other two can go to neighbouring provinces to ask them to recruit troops to assist us in suppressing the bandits."

"You are a master strategist, Your Excellency," said Twin Rods.

The Governor wrote the letter that same day to request reinforcements and three officers were picked to set off when the opportunity arose.

Twin Rods after returning to his residence, took off his armour and went to bed. Before it was fully light an officer came to report: "There's three horsemen up on that little hill outside the north gate, spying on the city. One of them has a red robe and is riding a white horse. There's two others, one on each side of him. I know the one on his right is Colonel Hua, the Archer. The one on his left is dressed like a scholar."

"The one in red must obviously be Song Jiang," said Twin Rods. "The one dressed like a scholar must be the Professor. Don't do anything to frighten them. Find me a hundred cavalry and we'll ride out and get them."

Twin Rods armed himself and mounted immediately and put himself at the head of a hundred or more cavalry. The north gate was unobtrusively opened and the drawbridge lowered and they trotted up the hill. Song Jiang, the Professor and Colonel Hua seemed quite lost in their contemplation of the city. But when Twin Rods slapped his mount and urged it forward up the slope, the three turned their horses' heads and slowly rode off. As Twin Rods raced towards them they simultaneously reined in their horses beside a clump of ancient trees. Just as Twin Rods drew level with the trees a loud shout was heard and he plunged into a pit. Horse and rider both went in. Fifty hooks reached out on either side and pinned Twin Rods down while they bound him and took him away. The horse was led off after him. Of the cavalry who had also been in the pursuit, the leaders were shot down by Colonel Hua with his bow, while the rest managed to rein in their mounts and flee.

Song Jiang returned to the camp and seated himself, while his guards pushed Twin Rods into the room. Immediately Song Jiang stood up and shouted: "Untie him at once!" And with his own hands he raised Twin Rods up and seated him. Then he prostrated himself.

Twin Rods said: "Why are you doing this?"

"How should I dare to go against the Emperor? It is only because of a corrupt official, who oppresses the people and perpetrates injustices that I have been forced for the time being to take refuge in the marshes, and only until such time as the Emperor declares an amnesty. I have had the misfortune to offend you and provoke your fearsome anger. I am a true admirer of your valour. For this unintentional offence, I humbly beg you to pardon me."

Twin Rods said: "A prisoner must count death a trifle, why do you offer me courtesy and consoling words?"

"How could I dare to do anything prejudicial to your life?" Song Jiang said. "I pray to heaven that my simple thoughts may find favour and my humble request be heard."

Twin Rods said: "Can it be that you want me to go to the capital and plead for your amnesty?"

"But how could you do that?" said Song Jiang. "The infamous Marshal Gao is a mean-spirited man. He forgets any favours he owes, and remembers everyone's faults. You have lost many troops, money and materials, how could he not hold you responsible? But now Victorious, the Supremo and Thunderer have all consented to join our company on the mountain. If you do not regard our stronghold as too unworthy I would like to offer you a place among our leadership — but only until the Emperor sees fit to grant an amnesty. After that we will all be able to dedicate our services to the country."

Twin Rods gave it long and careful consideration. Well, he was, you see one of the baleful stars, so he was naturally favourable to their spirit of righteousness! And then, Song Jiang was so courteous and so persuasive!

Twin Rods sighed and then knelt on the ground and said: "It is not that I wish to be disloyal to my country. But I feel you are exceptionally honourable, it is impossible for me not to trust you. I agree to serve you. In the circumstances, I can have absolutely no argument against it."

There is a poem about this:

Sent by the Emperor to clean out the stable,
Soon he's a henchman, not a new broom.

To explain such disloyalty how is one able?
Evil doings in the palace this puzzle illume.

Song Jiang was delighted. He presented Twin Rods to all the other leaders, and ordered the Tiger-Killer and Big Chief to bring the black horse with white socks, the Emperor's gift, for Twin Rods to ride on.

A meeting was now held to discuss plans for rescuing Blazing Comet. The Professor said: "If Twin Rods can persuade them to open the gates it will be easy as falling off a log. It will have the added advantage of cementing him to our cause."

Song Jiang listened and then reassured Twin Rods with these words: "It is not because I want to gain control of the city. It is simply that the Kongs, uncle and nephew, have been locked up there, and it is impossible to do anything for them if you don't get those gates opened."

Twin Rods said cheerfully: "Since you have enlisted me, I shall certainly do my best."

It was agreed that evening that ten leaders should go with Twin Rods, namely Thunderclap, Colonel Hua, Colonel Sun, the Dandy, the Little Duke, the Halberdier, Snake, Scorpion, Golden Wings and Short-Arse — all dressed in army uniform. When these eleven horsemen reached the city, Twin Rods rode right to the edge of the moat and shouted across: "Ahoy there, guards! Open up! I've escaped!"

When they heard in the city that it was the voice of Twin Rods, they rushed to report it to the Governor. The loss of Twin Rods had plunged the Governor into gloom. When they told him that Twin Rods had escaped and come back, he cheered up at once. He immediately mounted and rode to the battlements. As he could see there were another dozen or so riders and could only hear Twin Rods' voice, not see his face, he asked: "How did you manage to escape, commander?"

Twin Rods replied: "The bastards tripped my horse. They captured me and took me into their camp. There was an officer there who had served with me before, and he managed to steal the horse for me and we escaped together."

Reassured, the Governor ordered the gates opened and the drawbridge lowered. The other ten followed Twin Rods in, and when they drew level with the Governor, Thunderclap knocked him from his horse with one blow of his mace. Snake and Scorpion started a fire. Golden Wings and Short-Arse rushed into the city, killing and scattering the enemy officers. Song Jiang's main force saw the fires in the city and all came pouring in. Song Jiang hurriedly issued orders for the people not to be molested in any way; stores and money were to be taken from the government coffers only. They went to the gaol and released Blazing Comet and his uncle, with all his family. Next they put the fire out. Governor Murong and his family were executed and their property seized and divided among the troops. When it was light a list was made of people whose houses had been burnt in the fire and provisions were distributed in compensation. The contents of the government coffers and grain stores were loaded onto five hundred or so carts. More than two hundred horses were rounded up. A big feast was organized in the government office to celebrate and the chiefs of the three mountains were invited to join the main stronghold. The Tiger-Killer and Big Chief sent someone back to Mount Peachblossom to fetch out all the horses, money and provisions, after burning down the camp. Monk Lu Zhishen sent the Young Master and the Knife back to Twin Dragon Peak to help the Gardener and Sister Sun collect up people, horses, money and stores and burn down the compound of the Temple of the Precious Pearl.

It took a few days to assemble all the troops from the three mountains. Then Song Jiang led this large contingent of troops and comrades back to Mount Liang. Colonel Hua, Thunderclap, Twin Rods and Whiskers were sent on ahead to clear the road. They passed through the province without any disturbance. The villagers, old and young, flocked to see them, offering incense and falling on their knees before them.

In a few days they had reached the Marshes of Mount Liang. All the boat captains came across to meet them. Chao Gai and the other leaders from the main camp were at Golden Sands Landing to receive them. On reaching the stronghold, they all went to sit in

衆虎同心歸水泊

the Assembly Hall of the Heroes and a great feast was organized to celebrate the arrival of new leaders: Twin Rods, Monk Lu Zhishen, the Blue-Faced Beast, Pilgrim Wu Song, the Young Master, the Knife, the Gardener, Sister Sun, the Tiger-Killer, Big Chief, Blazing Comet and Red Star — altogether there were twelve of these new arrivals. During the banquet Leopard's Head told how the Monk had once rescued him. The Monk asked: "After I left you in Cangzhou, Instructor, did you ever have news of your wife?"

"After we had that dust-up with Wang Lun, I naturally sent someone back to fetch my family, but I heard that my wife had been forced by Marshal Gao's son and had hanged herself. Her parents fell ill with grief and also died."

The Blue-Faced Beast then recalled the time when they had gone to the mountain while Wang Lun was in charge, and everyone said: "Something like this must be preordained; it was no accident!"

Chao Gai recounted the story of robbing the birthday convoy on Yellow Mud Ridge, which caused great mirth.

They took turns to organize the banquet on the days that followed. Of this no more.

Song Jiang was naturally well pleased to see so many additions to the company on the mountain. He made Spots overseer of the blacksmiths, with responsibility for supervising the manufacture of arms of every sort, including linked chain-mail armour. The Ape was manager of banners and clothing with orders to produce flags depicting the three powers, the nine planets, the four polar stars, the five directions, the twenty-eight constellations of the zodiac, together with flying dragons and pards, yellow halberds and white long-tailed banners, scarlet tassels and black umbrellas. Beacons were constructed on all four sides of the mountain and two more inns to the west and south were built to receive good men heading for the mountain, as well as to gather military intelligence. The inn on the west was put in the hands of the Gardener and Sister Sun — since this husband and wife team had originally kept an inn. The inn on the south was committed as before to the other husband and wife team — Blackface and

Auntie Gu. The inn on the east was still to be run by the Crocodile and Lungs while the Executioner and the Flea were still at the inn on the north. The three gates leading up the mountain were reinforced and leaders appointed to man them. Everyone complied with these new regulations. Of this no more.

One day Lu Zhishen, the Flowery Monk, suddenly announced to Song Jiang: "I have a friend called Shi Jin, the Tattooed Dragon; the Tiger-Killer is also acquainted with him. He is on Little Mount Hua near Huayin in Huazhou. He is with Zhu Wu, known as the Strategist, and also one Chen Da, the River-Jumping Tiger, and Yang Chun, the White-Spotted Snake. They have formed themselves into a company there. I often think of my friend. He came to my rescue once, in the Temple of the Ceramic Tiles, I shall never forget it. I would like to go and pay him a visit, and persuade all four of them to join us here. What do you say?"

Song Jiang said: "I have heard good things of the Tattooed Dragon. I think it's a great idea for you to go and invite him to join us. However, I don't think you should go alone. I would like to ask Pilgrim Wu Song to accompany you. He is got up as a pilgrim, a kind of monk, you'll make a good pair."

"Certainly I will go with the master," said the Pilgrim.

So that same day they packed their bags. The Monk just went as a contemplative and the Pilgrim took on the role of his attendant priest. They bade farewell to the assembly of leaders on the mountain, and crossed over at Golden Sands Landing. Starting early, resting late, and travelling every day, they soon reached Huayin and headed for Little Mount Hua.

After the two of them had left, Song Jiang found himself uneasy, so he told the Magic Messenger to follow after them and listen out for news.

As they approached Little Mount Hua a guard sprang out and stopped them. "Where have you two monks come from?" he asked.

"Is a Mr. Shi to be found here on the mountain?" Wu Song asked in reply.

"If it's chief Shi you want, you'd better wait here a bit," the man said. "I'll go up and report to the leaders and they'll come down to see you."

"Tell them Monk Lu Zhishen has come to visit," said the Pilgrim.

The soldier had only been gone a little while when Zhu Wu, the Strategist appeared, with the River-Jumper and the White-Spotted Snake. But there was no sign of the Tattooed Dragon.

The Monk asked: "Where is Mr. Shi? Why can't I see him?"

"Excuse me, but are you Major Lu from Yan'an?" the Strategist asked.

"I am indeed," said the Monk. "And my attendant here is Captain Wu Song, killer of the tiger on Jingyang Pass."

The other three hurriedly saluted and said: "Your reputation is well known to us. We heard that you had set up camp on Twin Dragon Peak. What brings you here today?"

The Monk said: "We are not on Twin Dragon Peak any longer. We have joined Song Jiang's company on Mount Liang. We have come here to see Mr. Shi."

The Strategist said: "Since you are here, please come on up to our stronghold and let me explain everything to you properly."

The Monk said: "If you've something to say, then say it! All this messing about, who the fucking hell is going to put up with it?"

The Pilgrim said: "My friend is a little impatient. But if you've something to say, there's nothing to stop you saying it."

The Strategist said: "We had been doing very well in our stronghold here, ever since Mr. Shi came to us. Then he happened to meet a painter called Wang Yi, a native of the northern capital, who had come to fulfil a promise he had made to paint a mural at the Temple of the Golden Lord of Heaven on the western peak of Mount Hua. He had also brought his daughter, whose name was Jade, to keep him company. The district governor, Ho by name and originally a member of Grand Preceptor Cai's staff, a greedy official who unjustly persecuted the people, happened to visit the temple one day to burn incense. He saw the girl and fell for her, just like that. He kept sending people to say that he wanted her as a wife. When her father would not hear of it this governor abducted and raped her and sentenced the father to exile in a distant frontier post. The father passed through here on his way and met Mr. Shi, to whom he recounted the whole affair. Mr. Shi rescued him and gave him refuge on the mountain. He killed the two guards who had been sent with him, and then went to the government office with the intention of killing Governor Ho, but he was detected first and arrested and imprisoned. Now they intend to raise an army to wipe out our camp here, and we simply don't know what to do about it!"

The Monk was outraged: "Those fucking officials are shameless! The harm they do! You and I will go and kill the bastard!"

The Strategist said: "Please come up to the stronghold and discuss it all first."

When this party of five leaders had arrived in the stronghold and seated themselves, the offended father was invited in to explain to them what a greedy drunken despot Governor Ho was and how he made a habit of raping the daughters of respectable families. The Strategist and his comrades had oxen and horses slaughtered to provide a banquet for the other two visitors. As they were feasting, the Monk gave his views: "This bloody Ho is an utter disgrace, I shall go with you to the city and execute him!"

The Pilgrim said: "Don't be so hasty, brother. Let us ride back with all haste to Mount Liang and report the matter. We can ask Song Jiang to bring a big army to attack Huayin and rescue the Tattooed Dragon."

"If he has to wait while we go all the way back to the stronghold and fetch an army, who knows what will happen to the Tattooed Dragon," the Monk objected.

"But even if you kill the governor," said the Pilgrim, "how will you rescue the Tattooed Dragon?" He was totally opposed to letting the Monk go.

The Strategist also advised against it: "Please calm down, Master. Captain Wu is absolutely right."

The Monk grew even more angry: "You're such a cold unfeeling bunch, you'd let our friend Mr. Shi perish. Well, you needn't go back to Mount Liang, you can just stay and watch me!"

No one could dissuade him from it, their pleas that evening fell on deaf ears. In the morning he was up before dawn. He took his monk's staff and sword and hurried off to Huayin.

Pilgrim Wu Song said: "He refuses to listen to anyone. No good will come of this!" He sent off two sharp-witted soldiers to listen out for news.

As for the Monk, he went rushing into Huazhou and started asking for the government office. "Over the city bridge, and then turn east," they directed him. He was just crossing this pontoon bridge, when people started shouting: "Out of the way monk, His Excellency the Governor is about to pass."

"Well," he thought, "I was just looking for him, and here he is coming to find me! It really seems he's fated to die!"

The guard of honour began to pass in pairs, one after another, and then the Governor, in a luxury sedan. On either side the windows were protected by a dozen or so guards tightly packed around it, each carrying a steel-shafted spear.

"It's not a good idea to attack those bastards," the Monk thought, "because if I failed I should be laughed at."

Now the Governor happened to be looking out of the window and he saw the Monk, apparently hesitating about whether to approach. They went on over the bridge, and when he got out at the government office he told two of the guards: "Go and invite that big fat monk on the bridge to come and have a vegetarian meal here at the office." Accordingly the guards went up to Monk Lu Zhishen on the bridge and said: "His Excellency the Governor invites you to a vegetarian meal."

"The bugger has fallen right into my hands," the Monk thought. "I wanted to kill him but I couldn't think of a way to reach him so I let him go. I was wondering how to get to him, and he goes and invites me!" He followed the guards to the government office. The Governor had already made his arrangements. As soon as the Monk was outside the courtroom he was ordered to put down his staff and surrender his sword and then invited to go to have his meal in an inner chamber. The Monk was unwilling to comply at first, but they all told him: "We know you're a monk, but how can you be so ignorant of etiquette? How could you be allowed inside carrying a sword or a staff?"

The Monk thought: "Anyway, my two fists are enough to beat the bugger's brains out!" So he put down his staff and took off his sword in the corridor and followed the guards inside. The Governor was sitting there waiting. He made a gesture with his hand and shouted: "Seize the bald scoundrel!" Forty police officers leapt from the wings and pulling him this way and that secured the Monk.

Well now, you can be Ogre in Chief, but you won't escape Heaven's net! You can be the fiery-headed door-god, but you won't come whole from the dragon's pool and the tiger's den! It was truly a case of:

The moth flies into the flame that burns it up;
The turtle enraged swallows the hook that kills it.

But if you want to know what happened to Monk Lu Zhishen when Governor Ho captured him, if he was to live or die, you must read the next chapter.

Chapter 59

The Professor purloins the Emperor's bell; Song Jiang fights on the Western Peak!

After Governor Ho had enticed Monk Lu Zhishen into an inner room and shouted "Seize him!" the policemen shoved him in front of the bench and the Governor bellowed: "Where have you come from, you bald reprobate?"

The Monk replied: "What crime have I committed?"

"Tell the truth," said the Governor. "Who sent you here to assassinate me?"

"I am a monk," Lu Zhishen protested. "How can you ask me something like that?"

"I saw you, you bald ass," shouted the Governor. "You wanted to attack my sedan chair with your staff, you were thinking about it but you didn't dare. You'd bloody well better confess, you scoundrel!"

"Yes, well I bloody well didn't attack you, did I, so why have you arrested me? It's a fucking false accusation!" said the Monk.

"Who ever heard of a monk who uses language like that?" said the Governor. "This bald villain must be one of those bandits from west of the pass, come here on behalf of that robber Shi Jin. He'll never confess unless he's beaten. Guards, take him away and give him a bloody good thrashing."

The Monk cried out: "Keep your hands off me. I'll tell you myself. I am Lu Zhishen, sometimes called the Flowery Monk, from the Marshes of Mount Liang. I don't care if you kill me. My brother Song Jiang will hear about it and when he comes down from the mountain he'll execute you double-quick, you whole bloody gang of donkey's heads!"

The Governor flew into a towering passion. After the Monk had been beaten for a while, a heavy cangue was ordered for him and he was thrown into the dungeons. A letter to the Emperor was composed, requesting instructions. The staff and sword were placed under seal in the courtroom.

By now the whole district was in an uproar. The two scouts raced back to Little Mount Hua with the news. Pilgrim Wu Song, horrified, said: "We came here to do a job, one of us has now been lost, how can I go back and tell the leaders?"

As he was wondering hopelessly what to do, a soldier from the mountain appeared and said: "There's a leader here sent from Mount Liang. He's called Dai Zong, the Magic Messenger. He's waiting down below."

Pilgrim Wu Song hurried down to invite him up to the stronghold, where they held a meeting with the Strategist and the others, and they explained how the Monk had fallen into the trap after refusing to listen to their admonitions. The Magic Messenger was greatly distressed: "I mustn't stop long," he said. "I must go back to Mount Liang and tell the others, so they can send troops to rescue him."

The Pilgrim said: "I shall wait here. I beg you, go quickly and return soon."

After eating some vegetarian food, the Magic Messenger started his magic walking and raced back to Mount Liang. Within three days he was at the stronghold and recounted to the two leaders how the Monk in trying to kill Governor Ho in order to rescue the Tattooed Dragon had fallen into a trap.

Song Jiang said in great agitation: "If two of our friends are in trouble, of course we must help. I won't hesitate for a moment." He named the troops and divided them into three contingents. The first party consisting of five commanders, Colonel Hua, Thunderclap, Leopard's Head Lin Chong, the Blue-Faced Beast and Twin Rods, with a thousand armoured cavalry and two thousand foot, was to lead off and pioneer the route. The main party had six leaders, Song Jiang, the Professor, Whiskers, the Spearsman, Snake and Scorpion, and two thousand troops. The rearguard, responsible for stores and fodder, consisted of

Skyhawk, Madcap, Morbid, the White-Water Dragon and White Eel with two thousand troops. Seven thousand troops in all left Mount Liang and set off for Huazhou. They marched flat out, making no stops. When they were halfway there, the Magic Messenger was sent on ahead to inform Little Mount Hua. The Strategist and his comrades laid on pigs, sheep, oxen and horses and brewed up some strong wine in readiness.

When Song Jiang's three divisions reached Little Mount Hua, Pilgrim Wu Song took the Strategist, the River-Jumper and White-Spotted Snake down to pay their respects to Song Jiang, the Professor and others, and then they all went up to the camp and held a meeting. Song Jiang asked for information about the city, and the Strategist said: "Governor Ho has got the two leaders in the prison, and is only waiting for the Emperor's instructions to execute them."

Song Jiang and the Professor said: "What's our best plan, then, for rescuing the Tattooed Dragon and the Monk?"

"The city's suburbs are extensive and the moat is broad and deep," said the Strategist. "It's very difficult to attack. We can't get them unless we have someone on the inside."

The Professor said: "Tomorrow we'll go and see what the moat is like. Then we'll talk about it again."

Song Jiang sat drinking till late, and then wanted to go and view the city at once, without waiting till dawn. The Professor advised against it. "They've got two tigers shut up in the gaol there," he said. "Of course they'll be taking precautions. We certainly can't go in full daylight. But tonight there will be a moon. If we leave the mountain in the afternoon we'll get there at dusk and we can have a good look."

So next day they waited till the afternoon and then five of them, Song Jiang, the Professor, Colonel Hua, Thunderclap, and Whiskers rode down the mountain and set off. Some time after seven o'clock they were outside the city walls of Huazhou. They halted at the top of a steep slope to observe the city. It was typical clear March weather and the moon was as beautiful as a picture, without a trace of cloud in the sky. Huazhou had several city gates. The walls were high and the earthen ramparts solid. The moat was broad and deep. They gazed long at it. Far off the peaks of Mount Hua, the great mountain of the west, could be made out. It was a fine sight:

> *This famed peak is often called the Immortal's Hands; here is Guanyin's platform in the clouds. At the top there's the Jade Lady's wash basin; below the waters where the Milky Way can gaze upon itself. This is a whole universe of beauty: the pointed peaks rise heavenward as if the clouds grow from them; reverenced by all is this sacred mountain, whose strange rocks and awesome peaks invade the regions of the Dipper. Here every shade of blue and green is to be found. The most brilliant poet would find it hard to put into words; the brush of the most gifted painter could scarcely encompass it. In profound caves pale light awakes a myriad delicate hues; towering peaks and cliffs reflect the sun in a thousand purple flames. The disciple points into the distance; in the ornamental pond the lily breasts the ripples like a boat. In olden times, 'tis said, flowers fed by the waters of the well grew to an incredible size. Monstrous spirits grew angry, and split the mountain top to release the gods. The famous anchorite, lofty and pure, came to the simple hut to sleep. This is renowned Mount Hua, known for a thousand years, where incense has risen to heaven since time immemorial.*

Having appreciated the sight of Mount Hua, and noted that the city moat was broad, the defences solid, Song Jiang still had no idea how to proceed.

The Professor said: "Let us return to the mountain stronghold and discuss what to do."

Riding all night, they returned to Little Mount Hua. Song Jiang's brows remained knit; his concern showed clearly on his face.

The Professor said: "Let us send out a dozen sharp-witted scouts to listen all around for news."

Two days later one of these men suddenly appeared on the mountain and reported: "Recently the Emperor has sent an officer of his personal staff to take his personal gift of a pair of golden bells to the Western Peak and burn incense there. He is coming by way of the Yellow River and the Wei River."

The Professor said: "No need to worry now, brother, this has given me an idea." He called the White-Water Dragon and White Eel and said: "I want you two to do this … and this…."

The White-Water Dragon said: "The only problem is neither of us knows the way. Wouldn't it be a good idea if we could take a guide along?"

White-Spotted Snake then spoke up: "Can I come with you?"

Song Jiang liked the idea, and the three of them set off down the mountain.

Next day the Professor asked seven of the leaders, Song Jiang, Skyhawk, Whiskers, Twin Rods, Colonel Hua, Thunderclap and the Spearsman to go down the mountain quietly with five hundred troops. When they reached the crossing of the River Wei, the White-Water Dragon, White Eel and White-Spotted Snake had already provided a dozen large boats. The Professor ordered four of his party, Colonel Hua, Thunderclap, the Spearsman and Twin Rods, to set up an ambush on the bank. The others, Song Jiang, the Professor, Whiskers and Skyhawk, got into the boats, which the three water leaders steered to a hiding-place along the bank.

They waited all night. When it grew light in the morning they heard the distant sound of gongs, drums and fifes and then three government boats drew near, all flying yellow banners proclaiming "Marshal Su Yuanjing, officer in charge of the imperial mission to burn incense on Mount Hua."

Song Jiang quietly rejoiced at what he saw: "The Mystic Lady said 'Chance lodgings will bring many joys.' Now I chance to meet this person whose name, Su, is the same as the word for lodging. There must be a meaning to it."

As the Marshal's boats approached the river mouth, Whiskers and Skyhawk grasped their long spears and stood behind Song Jiang and the Professor. When the boats reached the landing place, they were obstructed. Twenty or more guards in purple coats and silver belts appeared on the boats and shouted: "You there, on the boats, how dare you obstruct the channel and get in the way of the Marshal's convoy?"

Song Jiang, lance in hand, saluted. The Professor, standing at the prow, said: "Song Jiang, leader of the company in the Marshes of Mount Liang, respectfully requests an interview." The purser of the other boat appeared and said: "This is an officer of the imperial court, on his way to burn incense on the Western Peak, you are rebels from the Marshes of Mount Liang, how dare you stand in his way?"

The Professor said: "We are loyal subjects, we only ask to see the Marshal's face, we have a request to make of him."

The purser said: "Who do you think you are, to insist on seeing the Marshal?" The guards on either side shouted: "Lower your voice!"

Song Jiang said: "I would like to ask the Marshal to come ashore. There is something I want to discuss with him."

The purser said: "What rubbish! The Marshal is a high official of the court. How could he have anything to discuss with you?"

Song Jiang said: "I am afraid if the Marshal refuses to speak to me, my men may be a little rough with the Marshal."

Whiskers jabbed at the little banner on the boat with his spear, while on the bank Colonel Hua, Thunderclap, the Spearsman and Twin Rods advanced with their cavalry. They fitted arrows to their bows, and when they reached the river spread out along the bank. The steersmen on the boats all went and hid in their cabins in terror. The purser anxiously disappeared inside to report and the Marshal was obliged to come out and take a seat on deck.

Song Jiang saluted and said: "I do not wish to be discourteous."

The Marshal said: "Why do you interfere with our progress like this, my man?"

Song Jiang said: "I would not dream of trying to interfere with your journey, Marshal. I merely wish to invite you to disembark because I have a request to make."

The Marshal said: "I am travelling on imperial business. My mission is to burn incense on the Western Peak. What can you possibly have to discuss with me? How can you expect an important official of the court to disembark just to please you?"

Song Jiang said: "If you do not, I am afraid my companions over there may have something to say about it."

At this Skyhawk waved his signal flag and the White-Water Dragon, White Eel and White-Spotted Snake rowed their boats up. The Marshal appeared quite taken aback. White-Water Dragon and White Eel, swords flashing in their hands, leaped into the boat and with a shove sent the two guards flying into the water. Song Jiang immediately shouted: "Behave yourselves! You are frightening an important man!"

Splash! The two of them had dived into the water and were hauling the two guards out again. They moved as easily over the water as if it were level ground and effortlessly shot back onto the boat, causing the Marshal's heart almost to jump out of his mouth. Song Jiang again shouted: "Withdraw, men, stop frightening the great man. I will help him slowly to disembark."

The Marshal said: "What is your business, then, sir? Please tell me."

Song Jiang said: "This is not the place for it. I invite you to come to our mountain stronghold to hear our request. I intend no harm to you. If I harm a hair of your head, then let the Western Peak fall and crush me!"

By now it was clear that the Marshal could not avoid going ashore. He was obliged to leave the boat and step off onto the bank. A horse was brought and he was helped onto it, and then perforce must go where they led him. Song Jiang ordered Colonel Hua and Thunderclap to take him on up the mountain. Then he mounted himself and ordered the boat crews to unload the incense, religious objects, and the golden bells, and carry them up the mountain. Only the White-Water Dragon and White Eel remained behind with a hundred men to guard the boats.

All the other leaders now went up the mountain. Song Jiang rode into the camp and escorted Marshal Su to the Assembly Hall where he was given the place of honour, with the leaders ranged in their places on either side. Song Jiang prostrated himself four times, and then knelt before the Marshal and said: "I, Song Jiang, was previously an official in the Yuncheng administration, but official persecution forced me to take to the mountains and forests, and for the time being I have found refuge in the marshlands of Mount Liang, until such time as an amnesty allows me to serve my country again. At this moment two of my comrades are subject to groundless persecution by Governor Ho who

吳用賺金鈴弔掛

has thrown them into gaol. I wish to borrow your Excellency's imperial incense, ritual objects and the golden bells to practise a deception on Huazhou. When our business is concluded you shall have them back and your person will suffer no harm whatsoever. That is my proposal."

Marshal Su said: "If you take the incense and the other ritual objects away, it will all come out in the end and I shall be in trouble."

"When you return, Marshal, you can put all the blame on my shoulders," said Song Jiang.

The Marshal saw from their looks that there was no way he could refuse, so he had to give permission. Song Jiang expressed his gratitude with toasts and a banquet. Then the uniforms of the Marshal's retinue were all borrowed from them. A likely-looking soldier was chosen. His head was shaved and he was dressed up in the Marshal's clothes to impersonate the Marshal. Song Jiang and the Professor dressed as pursers. Snake, Scorpion, Morbid and Madcap dressed as guards. The troops wore the red coats and silver belts and carried all the imperial standards, banners and insignia, and the religious objects, the boxes of imperial incense, the sacrificial offerings and the golden bells. Colonel Hua, the Spearsman, Whiskers and Skyhawk dressed as guards. The Strategist, the River-Jumper and White-Spotted Snake kept the Marshal and all his followers entertained, plying them with wine. Finally two bodies of men marched out towards the city, one commanded by Thunderclap and Twin Rods, the other by Leopard's Head Lin Chong and the Blue-Faced Beast. Pilgrim Wu Song was sent on ahead to wait at the gates to the Temple of the Western Peak for the signal to act.

To spare you more details, the main party now left the mountain stronghold and made their way to the river bank where they boarded the boats. They did not announce themselves to the governor of Huazhou but instead went straight to the Temple of the Western Peak. The Magic Messenger went first to give the news to the abbot at the Hall of Clouds and the lay brothers from the monastery came down to the boats to welcome them ashore. With incense, flowers, lamps and candles, with banners and streamers, precious relics and umbrellas, they lined up on the bank. The incense was unloaded and taken to a tabernacle specially prepared for it, which the people from the temple hoisted on poles. Behind it came the golden bells. When the abbot came to pay his respects to the Marshal, the Professor said: "The Marshal caught some infection on the journey and is not in good health. Please bring a sedan chair for him."

Attendants helped the Marshal into the sedan chair and he was carried to the abbot's quarters to rest. The Professor, pretending to be a purser, said to the abbot: "This is an important imperial delegation, bringing you the Emperor's gift of imperial incense and golden bells. Why is the provincial governor so neglectful that he is not here to welcome us?"

The abbot replied: "I have sent word to him. I am sure he will be here soon."

He had hardly finished speaking when the public prosecutor from the provincial administration with fifty or more police officers arrived to greet the Marshal with wine and dried fruit. Now although the soldier who was impersonating the Marshal looked very convincing, he obviously couldn't open his mouth. That is why he had been told he must pretend to be ill and sit on the bed muffled in quilts. When the public prosecutor saw him, together with all the banners, insignia, badges and the like, which were the prerogative of palace staff, why should he suspect anything? The purser bustled in and out, and petitioned twice. Then he took the public prosecutor in and made him prostrate himself far away at the bottom of the steps. The false marshal simply motioned with his hand, and his words were inaudible. As the Professor led the official forward he delivered a reprimand: "The Marshal is an important official of the court, he has taken the trouble to come all this way, bringing the imperial incense to you, he has even had the misfortune to contract an illness on the way which is not yet cured, why are the officials of the provincial government not here to welcome him after his journey?"

The public prosecutor replied with a conciliatory smile: "Although we received advance notification of the journey, we have had no more recent news, that is why we missed meeting you. It is unfortunate that the Marshal came first to the temple, because at present the Governor is much occupied with the robbers from Little Mount Hua, who have allied themselves with the Mount Liang outlaws and are planning an attack on the city. We have to watch out for them every day and for this reason he does not dare absent himself. He sent me here first to do the honours. He will come himself to meet you later."

The Professor said: "I warn you, the Marshal will accept no wine, not a drop. All he wants is for the Governor to come as quickly as possible so they can discuss the presentation."

The public prosecutor therefore had wine served to the purser and his own people. Then the Professor went inside to report and came back with a key and took the public prosecutor to see the golden bells. He opened the case and drew the golden bells, the emperor's gift, from their sheaths of perfumed cotton and hung them on a bamboo pole, so the official could have a good look. They were indeed of incomparable workmanship:

> *The golden bells are cast in solid metal, and supplied with gorgeous multi-coloured trappings, including silk fringes, strings of pearls, and jewelled covers. They are swathed in yellow silk and eight-clawed green dragons twine about them. They are festooned with purple ribbons and pairs of gold phoenixes chase each other round the sides. Each bears a rich inlay of coral and cornelian, with amber and rare pearls. The fine porcelain of a lamp reflects the red gauze shade; a pink lotus is exquisitely framed in jade green leaves. Truly these bells deserve to hang in a palace, their quality would grace the most luxurious of settings.*

These golden bells, in fact, were made by one of the most skilled of the palace craftsmen. They were inlaid with the seven precious stones and with pearls and between them a red lantern was set. Originally they had hung in the centre of the Hall of the Heavenly Lord. Where else could they possibly have been made but in the palace?

After allowing the official one look, the Professor locked the bells away again in their case. Then he handed over to the official various documents from the Chancellery and demanded that the

Governor come to discuss matters and fix the day for the presentation ceremony. The prosecutor and his men, having seen the various objects and documents, took their leave and returned to Huazhou to report to the Governor.

Song Jiang was secretly rejoicing, saying to himself: "This bugger is a slippery customer, but I think we've pulled the wool over his eyes." By this time the Pilgrim was already in position at the gates of the temple. The Professor told Madcap to conceal a sharp sword about him and go to the temple gate to assist the Pilgrim's work there. He also told the Magic Messenger to dress as a guard.

The abbot now served a vegetarian meal in the Hall of Clouds and ordered the temple's administrator and his staff to get the place tidied up in readiness.

Song Jiang meanwhile went for a stroll around the Temple of the Western Peak. It was certainly a fine building: a series of halls quite out of the ordinary, a true heaven on earth! When he came to the main hall he lit some incense and prostrated himself. Having said a silent prayer, he returned to the official hall. At that moment the door-keeper announced: "The Governor is here!"

Song Jiang called Colonel Hua, the Spearsman, Whiskers and Skyhawk and told them to stand with their weapons on either side. Snake, Scorpion, Morbid and the Magic Messenger all with hidden weapons also stood on his left and right.

Governor Ho and over three hundred men now arrived at the temple, dismounted, and began to crowd inside. The two false pursers, the Professor and Song Jiang, saw that these three hundred men were all trying to enter without relinquishing their arms. The Professor shouted: "A marshal of the imperial court is present, no outsiders without business here are permitted to enter!" The crowd halted and the Governor entered alone to pay his respects to the Marshal. The purser announced: "The Marshal invites the Governor for an audience." The Governor entered the ceremonial hall and prostrated himself before the false marshal.

The Professor said: "Governor, do you admit your fault?"

"I should have known that the Marshal had arrived. I beg to be forgiven," said the Governor.

The Professor said: "The Marshal has come here to the Western Peak on an imperial mission to burn incense. Why were you not here to receive him?"

The Governor replied: "We have had no recent news at the government office, that is why I failed to receive him."

"Seize him!" the Professor commanded in a loud voice. Snake and Scorpion had already got their swords out. They tripped him and then cut off his head.

"Go to it, lads!" Song Jiang now shouted.

The three hundred troops who had come with the Governor had remained standing there open-mouthed, too horrified even to run for it. Colonel Hua and his men rushed on them and began knocking them off like beads on an abacus. Some made a dash for the gate, but there the Pilgrim and Madcap began laying into them, their swords whirling; the troops from Mount Liang followed suit. Of the three hundred government contingent not one got away. Those who arrived later at the temple were killed by White Eel and the White-Water Dragon.

Song Jiang hurriedly called for the imperial incense and the hanging bells to be brought and taken back to the boats. In the city two fires were to be seen so they charged in and went straight to the gaol where they freed the Tattooed Dragon and the Monk. They broke into the treasury, removed all the valuables and loaded them onto carts. The caravan then left Huazhou and returned by boat to Little Mount Hua. Here they respectfully greeted the real Marshal and restored to him the imperial incense, the golden bells, the pennants, banners and religious items and so on, politely thanking him. Song Jiang ordered a tray of silver to be brought and presented and all the Marshal's followers, regardless of their position, were rewarded. A farewell banquet was held in the stronghold to thank the Marshal. Finally all the leaders accompanied him down the mountain to see him off. At the river bank all the boats and other possessions, without exception, were returned to their rightful owners.

Having thanked the Marshal and bade him farewell, Song Jiang returned to Little Mount Hua and when he had talked to the four leaders there, they collected all their money and provisions, set

宋江鬧西
岳華山

fire to the defences, and in a big column of troops and provisions set off for Mount Liang.

Now when the Marshal disembarked and entered Huazhou, he learnt that the Mount Liang bandits had slaughtered the garrison and sacked the treasury and stores. More than a hundred officers had died in the city and all the horses had been taken. At the Temple of the Western Peak many more had lost their lives. He made the public prosecutor prepare a report for the Council to present to the Emperor. In it, it was said that "Song Jiang waylaid the imperial incense and bells and used them to entice the Governor to the temple where he killed him." Marshal Su went to the temple and burnt the incense and presented the bells to the abbot. He then hastened back to the capital to report all these matters. Of this no more.

Song Jiang having rescued the Tattooed Dragon and Lu Zhishen, collected the four leaders from Little Mount Hua. As before, the troops were formed into three columns and they set off for Mount Liang. They crossed the province without in any way inconveniencing the populace. The Magic Messenger was sent ahead to report to Chao Gai and the others came down the mountain to meet them. Soon they were all back in the Assembly Hall of the Heroes, where greetings were performed and a big banquet held in celebration.

Following this the Tattooed Dragon and the other three each in turn paid for a banquet to show their gratitude to Chao Gai and the others. Several days passed in this manner, but I will spare you the details.

Then one day, out of the blue, the Crocodile came up the mountain and reported: "There's a new band of robbers on Mount Mangdang over in Xuzhou. They've got together three thousand troops. The chief is a Taoist called Fan Rui. His nickname is the Demon King and his tactical skill is brilliant. He has two lieutenants. One is called Xiang Chong, alias the Eight-Armed Ogre. He carries a collection of twenty-four throwing knives, stuck in a round shield, and wields a steel-hafted spear. The other is called Li Gun, alias Winged Ghost. He has twenty-four javelins, also stuck in a round shield, and he wields a trusty sword. These three are sworn brothers and they have occupied Mount Mangdang and devote themselves to plunder and pillage. They have been talking about coming here to take over the Marshes of Mount Liang. As soon as I heard about this I thought I ought to tell you."

Song Jiang was highly indignant. "The cheek of these bastards!" he exclaimed. "I shall have to go down and see about this!"

At this point the Tattooed Dragon jumped up and said: "The four of us have just joined the stronghold and we have as yet made no contribution whatsoever. Please let us take some of our troops and go to capture this bunch of brigands."

Song Jiang was pleased with the idea. So the Tattooed Dragon detailed some of his troops and when he and the Strategist, the River-Jumper and White-Spotted Snake had armed themselves, they said farewell to Song Jiang and set off down the mountain. They crossed by boat at Golden Sands Landing and took the road to Mount Mangdang.

In three days they were in sight of this mountain, the very place where in days gone by the first emperor of Han scotched the snake and set the ball rolling. The horsemen were spotted and one of the lookouts went up the mountain to report.

The Tattooed Dragon deployed the troops he had brought from Little Mount Hua. Dressed in full armour and mounted on a flame-coloured steed he rode out in front of his forces, wielding his three-pointed double-bladed halberd. Behind him came the other three, the Strategist in the middle with his two swords. On his left was the River-Jumper, with a gleaming steel spear, and on his right, with a blade on a long pole, White-Spotted Snake.

The four horsemen reined in their horses in front of their ranks and after a few moments' wait they saw troops beginning to file down the slopes of Mount Mangdang. In front were two warriors, chief of them being the Eight-Armed Ogre with his twenty-four throwing knives. He could hit a man at a hundred paces, never once missing. In his right hand he brandished a short spear, and on his back was his personal banner with the words "Eight-Armed Ogre" painted on it.

The one behind him was Winged Ghost with his twenty-four javelins. He too could hit a man at a hundred paces. In his left hand he held the shield and in his right a sword, while on his back was his personal banner with "Winged Ghost" written on it.

Marching down the mountain these two came face to face with the Tattooed Dragon and his friends on horseback in front of their army. No word was spoken, but the soldiers started beating gongs and the two warriors from Mount Mangdang whirled their shields and charged into the attack.

The Tattooed Dragon and his forces were powerless to stop them. The troops at the rear went first. Shi Jin in the front rank put up some resistance. In the middle rank the Strategist and the others yelled in panic. It was an occasion when, as they say, there was no holding the horses. They bolted and fetched up over ten miles away. The Tattooed Dragon was almost hit by a throwing knife. The White-Spotted Snake, slow in dodging, had his charger wounded. He abandoned it and fled for his life on foot.

Of the troops which the Tattooed Dragon had brought, half were lost. He discussed what to do with the Strategist and the others who were all for going back to Mount Liang to ask for reinforcements. Whilst they were still anxiously trying to make up their minds, one of their officers rushed up and announced: "There's a big cloud of dust on the highroad to the north. Looks like two thousand troops marching this way." When the Tattooed Dragon and his companions went to meet them, they saw the Mount Liang flag and two commanders riding in front of the column. One was Colonel Hua the Archer, and the other was the Spearsman. The Tattooed Dragon proceeded to tell them about the terrifying weapons and rolling action of the Ogre and Winged Ghost and how the troops could not withstand it.

Colonel Hua said: "After you started Song Jiang was uneasy about you and regretted the decision he had taken so he sent us along as reinforcements."

The Tattooed Dragon and his companions were greatly relieved. They all made camp. Next day at dawn they wanted to muster their troops and attack, but an officer reported: "There are more troops coming along the road to the north."

Colonel Hua, the Spearsman and the Tattooed Dragon all mounted and went to meet them. It turned out to be Song Jiang himself, together with the Professor, Taoist Gongsun, Mr. Chai, Whiskers, Twin Rods, Mu the Unstoppable, Colonel Sun, the Tamer, the Little Duke and the Halberdier, with three thousand troops.

The Tattooed Dragon told them all about the Ogre and Winged Ghost, with their whizzing knives and javelins and whirling shields, and how you couldn't get near them and how he had lost men. Song Jiang was alarmed. But the Professor said: "We should take up a defensive position first and then have further discussions."

Song Jiang was impatient and wanted to go in pursuit, as far as the mountain. By now it was getting dark. Looking up at Mount Mangdang they could see a mass of bright lanterns. Taoist Gongsun said: "Those bright lanterns in their camp must mean that they have magicians amongst them. Let us withdraw for the moment. Later I will propose a strategy for capturing those two."

Song Jiang was well pleased with this. He ordered the troops to retreat eight miles or so and set up camp. Early next morning Taoist Gongsun announced his plan, which was to have important results.

The Demon King consents to join Mount Liang;
The Winged Ghost is ready to go to the Marshes.

But if you want to hear what Taoist Gongsun's plan actually was, you must read the next chapter.

Chapter 60

Taoist Gongsun defeats the ghosts of Mount Mangdang; Chao Gai is struck by an arrow at Zengside!

Now what Taoist Gongsun proposed to Song Jiang and the Professor was this: "My plan is that of the famous general Zhuge Liang during the early years of the Han when he used stones instead of troops. Draw up the army so that it faces in all directions, with eight sections of eight, making sixty-four in all, the commander-in-chief in the middle. This is like a beast with four heads and eight tails. It can wheel to the left or turn to the right, it's a device like the wind and clouds that float over our heads, it has the adaptability of dragon, tiger, bird or snake. Now, wait until the enemy charge down the mountain and attack, then open out on two sides, and calmly invite them in. Then when you see the signal of seven stars, reform into a long snake. I now perform my little magic, and the result is that these three and their army will find themselves unable to go forward or back, left or right. Somewhere we will have prepared a trap, a concealed pit. We drive them towards it. Troops with snagging hooks are lying in ambush on either side, ready to pin them down."

Song Jiang was impressed with the scheme and issued orders at once, with strict instructions to all officers to keep to them precisely. Eight of their strongest, boldest leaders were to command the forces on the periphery. These eight were Twin Rods, Whiskers, Colonel Hua, the Spearsman, Mu the Unstoppable, Colonel Sun, the Tattooed Dragon and the Tamer. The main force in the centre was put under the command of Mr. Chai with the Little Duke and the Halberdier. Song Jiang, the Professor and Taoist Gongsun would control the signals given by the River-Jumper. The Strategist with five officers was to take up a position on a high point to report on the enemy movements.

The morning was well advanced when the army ranks spread out at the foot of the mountain and began to wave their banners, sound the drums and shout challenges. Then from Mount Mangdang the gongs began to reverberate like thunder and the three leaders marched down the mountain. They deployed a force of more than three thousand troops. The Ogre and Winged Ghost commanded the two flanks. In the centre on horseback was the chieftain called Fan Rui, a native of Puzhou, who had once been known as Father Purity and had acquired great skill with arms among the rivers and lakes. On horseback he wielded a flying hammer with devastating effect, and he seemed to have the ability to be everywhere at once, slaughtering generals and capturing ensigns. No one could touch him. He was nicknamed the Demon King. There is a poem which tells what he was like:

> *About his head floats hair like black silk, his embroidered robe is all black and he is totally encased in armour which gleams like the winter sky. He uses the hammer with miraculous skill. He is truly an image of the Great Warrior of the North, and weird sprites are at his beck and call. His personal banner features wandering clouds, rivers and seas; his nickname is Demon King.*

Mounted on a black charger, the Demon King rode out in front of his ranks. On his left was the Eight-Armed Ogre, on his right Winged Ghost. Now although the Demon King had quite a few magic tricks up his sleeve, he was no military strategist. When he saw the formation in which Song Jiang's army was drawn up, facing all directions, he secretly rejoiced. "If you spread your troops out like that, you're playing into my hands," he thought.

"When the wind begins to blow," he commanded the other two, "break through their ranks with five hundred men whirling swords."

They responded by grasping their outlandish shields and readying their javelins and throwing knives and waited for the Demon King to act. The latter now stood up in his stirrups and raising his left hand with the flying hammer and brandishing his trusty blade in the right hand, muttered some magic spells, culminating in a shout of: "Chrrr!" Immediately a violent wind arose on all sides, which set sand and stones flying. The sky grew dark as night, with no gleam of light from sun or moon. The other two cheered and leading five hundred dervish swordsmen charged forward. Before this onslaught Song Jiang's forces parted into two halves. As the two enemy leaders charged into the middle they were subjected to a rain of ballista missiles from either side. Only fifty or so of their troops followed them forward; the rest returned to their own ranks. Watching from his hilltop, Song Jiang saw the two enemy leaders had entered the trap and told the River-Jumper to wave the seven-stars flag. At this signal the troops, dividing and wheeling about, transformed themselves into the snake formation.

Now the two enemy leaders, however they might drive east or west, twist or turn to right or left, could find no way out. On the hilltop the Strategist was using the little flag to point with: when they turned east, he pointed east, and when they turned west he pointed west. Taoist Gongsun was there on the hilltop too, of course, observing. He now drew his famous sword inscribed with pine trees, muttered a spell and cried out: "Chrr!" The wind began to wildly swirl at the feet of the Eight-Armed Ogre and Winged Ghost. They saw the world go dark, no ray of light was visible. Not a single enemy soldier was to be seen either, nothing but darkness wherever they looked. They could not even see their own troops behind them. They became extremely anxious; all they wanted was to turn back, but it was absolutely impossible to find a way out. And now suddenly there was a shattering peal of thunder. Unending curses burst from them as simultaneously they were both tripped and fell head over heels into a huge pit. Hooks reached out on either side and in no time at all they were subdued and bound with rope.

Their captors took them up to the top of the hill to claim their reward.

Song Jiang pointed with the stock of his whip and the three leaders of his main force went into action. The Demon King tried to withdraw to the mountain, but half his force was destroyed before he got away.

公孫勝芒碭山降魔

Song Jiang now called in his troops and the leaders held a meeting outside the commander's tent. The two enemy leaders were paraded under the banner. When Song Jiang saw them he immediately ordered them to be untied, and presenting the cup in his own hands said: "Do not be angry. These are the fortunes of war. I myself have heard so much about you. I wanted to invite you to join our company on the mountain. It is only because there was no opportunity to do so that we have had this misunderstanding. If you do not refuse, and consent to come back with us, we shall count it a great blessing."

The two prostrated themselves humbly and said: "We too know your great reputation. It is just that for some reason we have not had the opportunity to meet you. Obviously you have great loyalty and virtue, but we failed to recognize the fact. We went against the will of heaven and earth. Now we are your prisoners. We thoroughly deserve death, yet you treat us with such courtesy. If you spare us, we pledge to serve you till death, to repay your magnanimity. As for the Demon King, how can he carry on without us? If you would permit one of us to go back and speak to the Demon King, we would tell him to come here and pay his respects, what do you say to that?"

Song Jiang said: "There is no need to keep one of you here as a hostage. Why don't you both go back to your stronghold. I will wait for you to return with good tidings."

They thanked him and said: "What a gentleman you are! If Demon King refuses to submit we will capture him ourselves and make a gift of him to you."

Song Jiang was well satisfied with this, and told one of his men to bring in wine and food. He also ordered two new suits of clothes and two good horses for them, and told some men to fetch their shields and escort them back to their stronghold. As they rode back both of them were full of praise for Song Jiang's generosity. When they reached Mount Mangdang the guards were amazed to see them and admitted them into the camp.

The Demon King asked what they had come for. "We are a pair of unfortunates," they said. "We deserve a thousand deaths."

"Why do you speak like that, brothers?" asked the Demon King.

So they told him all about Song Jiang's noble spirit.

"If Song Jiang is really so noble, so generous, then we had better stop opposing heaven's will and quickly go down to pay our respects to him," said the Demon King.

"That's exactly what we wanted to suggest," they said. They packed up the camp that same evening, and next morning at daybreak they all went down together. When they reached Song Jiang's camp they threw themselves on the ground. Song Jiang raised them up and invited them to sit in his tent. From the outset they felt not a moment's awkwardness with Song Jiang; rather there was an immediate sympathy and trust between them and they exchanged views on everything. They invited all the Mount Liang leaders back to Mount Mangdang, and had oxen and horses slaughtered to feast Song Jiang and his commanders, whilst they also rewarded the men. After the dinner the Demon King begged to become Taoist Gongsun's disciple. At Song Jiang's insistence, Taoist Gongsun explained the technique of the Five Thunders to the Demon King, to the latter's delight. In a few days' time the cattle and horses were rounded up, all the valuables and stores were packed and loaded, the troops were mustered, the compound was fired and everyone left with Song Jiang and the others to return to Mount Liang. Nothing need be said of the journey.

When they were close to Mount Liang and only needed to make the crossing, a tall fellow approached Song Jiang along the road beside the reedbeds and prostrated himself.

Song Jiang hurriedly dismounted and raised him up and asked: "What is your name and where are you from?"

The other replied: "My name is Duan Jingzhu, but people call me Yellow Dog, on account of the colour of my hair and beard. I am from Zhuozhou. I've always been a horse thief, up in the north, in Tartar territory. Last spring north of the Spearbutt range I stole a magnificent animal, with a coat whiter than snow, not a single hair of a different colour. It was three metres from nose to tail and stood fully sixteen hands. A big strong horse, that would easily do three hundred miles a day. It was quite famous up there in the north. They called it the 'moonlight charger.' It had belonged to a Tartar prince, before I stole it up there in the mountains. Now I've heard a lot about the Opportune Rain, from brethren of the rivers and lakes, only I never had the chance to meet him. So what I wanted to do was to bring this horse and make a present of it to him as my pledge for entering the company. Unfortunately as I was passing through the village of Zengside in southwest Lingzhou it was stolen from me by the five sons of the Zeng family. I tried to convince them that it really belonged to Song Jiang of Mount Liang, but they just swore at me most horribly and I didn't dare pursue the matter. When I managed to get away I came straight here to tell you."

The speaker was a gangling, coarse-looking individual of a most strange aspect. What exactly was he like? Well, there's a poem for him:

A head surrounded with wild yellow hair,
Legs that will carry him anywhere.
He's invisible as a man in a fog
When he steals a horse. He's called Yellow Dog.

When Song Jiang saw how unusual this man looked, he secretly rejoiced. "In that case," he said, "why don't you come to the mountain with us and discuss matters?"

He took Yellow Dog into the boats with them and they crossed to Golden Sands Landing. When Chao Gai and the others received them in the Assembly Hall, Song Jiang introduced the Demon King, the Eight-Armed Ogre and Winged Ghost, and Yellow Dog also paid his respects. A drum began to sound clamorously and a great feast was organized. Seeing that a lot more troops had been added to the stronghold and heroes seemed to be flocking in from all directions as if blown by the wind, Green-Eyes and the Nine-Tailed Turtle were ordered to build more houses and extend the stronghold's defences. And since Yellow Dog went on extolling the virtues of that horse, Song Jiang told the Magic Messenger to go to Zengside and find out what had happened to it.

After four or five days the Magic Messenger returned and told them: "There are three thousand or more families in Zengside.

One of them is the Zeng family. Old Zeng is a Tartar. He has five sons, known as the Zeng Five. Starting with the eldest they are called Zeng Tu, Zeng Mi, Zeng Suo, Zeng Kui and Zeng Sheng. There is also an instructor there called Shi Wengong and he has an assistant called Su Ding. They've mustered an army of six or seven thousand troops in the village and built solid defences. They boast more than fifty prison carts. They are on record as saying that there's not room round here for both us and them. They are determined to capture all of us here in the stronghold; they're spoiling for a fight. The horse, Moonlight, is now being ridden by Instructor Shi Wengong. The bastards have done one particularly hateful thing. They've invented some verses which they teach the children of the village to sing:

When our jingling irons are heard,
Gods and ghosts are sore afeared.
We lock our foes in prison carts
With iron spikes to quell their hearts.
We'll sweep Mount Liang and the Marshes clean,.
Seize Chao Gai and turn him in,
Take the Opportune Rain alive,
And the Professor's fall contrive.
The Zengside Brothers Five are we,
We shall forever famous be."

Chao Gai was hugely incensed. "How dare these animals speak so disrespectfully!" he said. "I'd better go myself. If I don't capture that lot, I vow never to return!"

Song Jiang said: "You are our chief. You cannot risk your own safety. I will go instead."

Chao Gai said: "It's not that I grudge you the glory. But you've been down so many times. You must be tired of fighting. This time let me go instead. Next time there's trouble it will be your turn."

When Song Jiang tried to insist, Chao Gai became quite annoyed. He selected five thousand troops and asked twenty of the leaders to go with him. The remainder were to stay with Song Jiang and guard the camp.

The twenty leaders appointed by Chao Gai were Leopard's Head, Twin Rods, the Spearsman, Mu the Unstoppable, the Red-Haired Devil, the Pilot, the three Ruan brothers, Morbid, Madcap, Colonel Sun, the Tamer, Skyscraper, the Door-God in the Clouds, the Dandy, Redeye, Golden Wings, Panther and the Daytime Rat. They led three columns down the mountain to attack Zengside. Song Jiang, the Professor and Taoist Gongsun accompanied them as far as Golden Sands Landing. As they were drinking wine there, a violent wind suddenly got up, splitting in two the new banner which Chao Gai had had made. Everyone turned pale at the sight of this. The Professor warned them: "This is not an auspicious omen. You had better postpone the attack."

Song Jiang also tried to talk him round: "You can go another time. This business of the wind tearing the banner doesn't look good for the army. It would surely be best to wait for a while before going off to deal with those villains."

Chao Gai said: "Sky and earth, clouds and wind, how can they be held to account? If we don't take advantage of this spring dawn to go and get them, we're just allowing them longer to build up their power, and when we do attack it may be too late. Don't stand in my way. Whatever happens I intend to go!"

Song Jiang could say nothing to dissuade him and Chao Gai led his army off across the water.

But Song Jiang felt most uneasy. When he got back to the stronghold he sent the Magic Messenger off after them, to listen out for news of their progress.

Chao Gai with his five thousand troops and twenty leaders reached the vicinity of Zengside and stopped before the stockade. Next day he and the other leaders rode out to take a good look at the place. What they saw was a site most dangerous to attack:

> *All around it a desolate expanse of water; it's surrounded on three sides by a high ridge. Next to the moat is a river harbour like a coiled snake; close to the water a thicket of willows dense as rain. As you look down on it from afar, it is all green shadows with no sign of habitation. If you watch from close to, the perimeter fence is lost in blue shade. But there are youths there in the village fierce*

as door gods, there are children in the fields who spring from the soil like spirits. Evidently the defences are strong; obviously this is a village of tough men and strong horses.

As they were watching, a detachment of some eight hundred troops suddenly appeared from a grove of willows. The leader wore a helmet of beaten copper and was dressed in linked armour. He wielded a spear of tempered steel and rode a fiery stallion. This was Zeng the Fourth. "You rebel scum from Mount Liang," he began to shout. "I was just coming to get you and hand you over to the authorities for the reward, apparently heaven is kind to me! You should have dismounted already so we can tie you up, what are you waiting for?"

As Chao Gai turned towards him with a look of fury, a warrior from his ranks rode forward and charged Zeng the Fourth. It was one of the founder members of Mount Liang, none other than Leopard's Head Lin Chong. The two horses clashed and they fought twenty bouts and neither had the advantage. After the twentieth bout, Zeng the Fourth, reckoning he could not get the better of Leopard's Head, rested his lance and turned his horse and raced back to the woods. Leopard's Head reined in his horse and did not follow. Chao Gai ordered his troops back to camp to discuss plans for defeating Zengside.

"Next time let's go and challenge them right outside the village," Leopard's Head suggested. "It'll give us a chance to see how things really are there, before we make our plans."

When daylight came the five thousand troops were marched to a deserted part of the level land at the entrance to the village and drawn up in battle formation. Drums rolled and the troops cheered. Loud reports came from Zengside and a large body of troops advanced, with seven leaders spread out in front in a straight line. In the centre was Instructor Shi Wengong. On his left was his assistant, Su Ding, and on his right the eldest Zeng. Also on the left Zeng the Second and Zeng the Fourth, while Zeng the Third and Zeng the Fifth were on the right. They were all in full armour. Instructor Shi Wengong had a bow with arrows and was riding Moonlight. He held a square-bladed halberd, finely carved.

Three drumrolls were now heard and from the Zengside ranks a number of prison carts were wheeled out and placed in full view. Zeng the First pointed at the enemy and shouted: "Do you see my prison carts, you rebel scum? We are going to finish you off, or we're not men! We'll take you alive, one by one, and put you in the prison carts to take to the capital. There you'll die the death of a thousand cuts. But if you surrender now, there may be room for discussion."

Chao Gai responded by levelling his lance and furiously charging Zeng the First. Fearing for his safety, the other leaders went with him and the two armies met in confused combat. Gradually the Zengside forces were driven back into the village. Leopard's Head and Twin Rods gave Chao Gai close protection, hacking down the enemy on either side. Eventually Leopard's Head saw that the way forward was too difficult and hurriedly called the troops back to regroup. It was clear that they had suffered quite heavy losses and Chao Gai's heart was heavy when they returned to the camp. The other leaders rallied him, saying: "Be of good cheer, brother. It's no use grieving and it's bad for your health. When Song Jiang fights he generally has losses too. But in the end he always returns victorious. The fighting was fierce today, and both sides lost men and horses, but we weren't beaten. Why must you be so sad?" But Chao Gai's gloom was not dispelled.

Three days now passed in the camp. Each day they challenged the enemy but no one from Zengside put in an appearance.

Then on the fourth day two monks suddenly turned up in Chao Gai's camp, seeking help. Some guards brought them to the command tent, where they knelt and declared: "We are monks from the Fahua temple to the east of Zengside. Those Zeng brothers are always coming to our temple to pester us with demands for money or gifts. We are fed up with it! We haven't been able to find any way of escaping them, so we have come to beg you to go and raid their camp and get rid of them for us. It will be a blessing to the whole district."

Chao Gai was very excited by this. He asked the two monks to sit and regaled them with wine. But Leopard's Head warned him: "Don't be too trusting, brother. This may be a trap."

The monks said: "We are holy men, how could we tell a lie? We have heard so much about the reputation of Mount Liang for loyalty and honour. Wherever you go you never harm the people. That's why we decided to throw ourselves on your mercy. Why should we try to cheat you? Especially as the Zengs are not going to win against you. You've absolutely no reason to suspect us."

Chao Gai said: "Don't be so suspicious, brother. We could miss a great opportunity. I'll go myself to have a look this evening."

"Don't you go," Leopard's Head said. "I will take half the troops to raid the camp, while you stay outside to back us up."

Chao Gai said: "If I'm not going to go, why should anyone else? No, you can stay outside with half the troops and back me up."

Leopard's Head said: "Who do you want to take with you?"

Chao Gai said: "I'll take ten leaders and two thousand five hundred men." These ten leaders were: the Red-Haired Devil, Ruan the Second, Twin Rods, Ruan the Fifth, Golden Wings, Ruan the Seventh, the Dandy, Skyscraper, the Door-God in the Clouds and the Daytime Rat. That evening when they had eaten, with bells removed from the horse's bridles and the troops gagged to prevent sound, they swiftly and silently followed the two monks to the Fahua temple. They found it to be an ancient structure. Chao Gai dismounted and went in. He saw no monks inside. He asked the two monks: "Why is there not a single priest in this temple?"

"The monks were all vexatious creatures, they had to be expelled. There is only the abbot left and a few novices. They live in the court at the back. Halt your men here and wait for a while. When night thickens we will lead you to their camp."

"Where exactly is their camp?" Chao Gai asked.

"They've got four camps," the monk replied. "But I have a friend who is stationed in the northern camp. If you can capture that one, it's all that matters. You can forget about the other three."

"What time can we start?" Chao Gai asked.

The monk said: "Let's see, it's now only the second watch. If we wait till the third watch, they'll be totally unprepared."

For some time they went on hearing clearly the beat of the Zengside drum giving out the time. This continued for upwards of an hour and then there was silence.

"They must be all asleep now," the monk said. "We can start."

The monks led the way. Chao Gai ordered everyone to mount and they left the temple.

When they had gone less than two miles, it was so dark that they lost sight of the two monks and the troops in front feared to advance. There were paths leading in all directions, and not a soul to be seen. An officer came in great trepidation and reported this to Chao Gai. Twin Rods ordered a hurried retreat by the way they had come. But they had not gone much more than a hundred paces when all around them gongs and drums broke the silence together with earth-shattering cries, and there were torches wherever they looked. Desperately Chao Gai and his commanders sought to escape. But after two more turns in the path they ran into the enemy troops. The foremost of them shot a volley of arrows, and unfortunately one of these struck Chao Gai in the face, knocking him from his horse. The horses of Twin Rods and the Dandy bolted. The Red-Haired Devil and the Daytime Rat who were coming up behind them helped Chao Gai back onto his horse and galloped through the village. Leopard's Head and the others were waiting to assist them outside the village and put up a fierce resistance. A confused battle raged till dawn, when both sides returned to their respective camps.

When Leopard's Head got back and called the roll of his troops, it was found that the three Ruan brothers, the Door-God in the Clouds and Skyscraper had swum to safety, but of the two thousand five hundred troops who had gone less than one thousand three hundred remained. Together with Golden Wings they all repaired to the command tent. When they examined Chao Gai, they found that the arrow had hit him in the jaw. When it was pulled out he fainted from loss of blood. The arrow itself bore the name of Shi Wengong. Leopard's Head ordered the wound to be dressed with salve. It was however a poisoned arrow and the poison deprived Chai Gai of the power to speak. Leopard's Head had him placed on a litter and ordered the three Ruans, Skyscraper and the Door-God in the Clouds to go on back to Mount Liang with him. The remaining fifteen held a discussion.

晁天王曾頭市中箭

The general view was this: "Remember the accident this time when our dear leader Chao Gai came down the mountain? The wind tore our banner. All we can do now is collect our troops and return. We'll never be able to capture this place."

Twin Rods said: "We must wait till we get orders from Song Jiang before we withdraw."

That day their gloom knew no bounds. The army had no more stomach for fighting. All they wanted was to return to the mountain.

In the evening around nine o'clock when it had just got dark they were sitting miserably in the camp. Truly it was a case of "A headless snake goes nowhere, a wingless bird cannot fly; they can but sigh and weep, since they can neither advance nor retreat." At this point a sentry suddenly rushed in and reported: "There's four or five columns of troops attacking. We can't even count the torches!"

Leopard's Head immediately ordered everyone to mount their horses. On the mountains which surrounded them on three sides the torches made it bright as day and there was shouting from every direction. Leopard's Head's forces did not stand and fight but struck camp and retreated. With the Zengside forces harrying them in the rear, they were forced to fight a rearguard action. It was not till they had gone twenty miles or so that they shook off the pursuit. When the roll was called they were found to have lost six or seven hundred men. After suffering this serious reverse, they took to the road by which they had come and headed for Mount Liang. Halfway there the Magic Messenger met them with orders to return to the stronghold and not to engage in further action. When they had marched their men back to the marshlands and up into the mountain, everyone attended the wounded leader, Chao Gai.

Neither food nor drink had passed Chao Gai's lips, he could eat nothing. His whole body was swollen. Song Jiang kept watch at his bedside, dressed his wound with his own hands and bathed it in hot water. The others stood watching outside. That evening in the third watch, towards midnight, Chao Gai's condition worsened. Turning his eyes on Song Jiang he ordered: "Dear brother, take care. Whoever catches the one who shot me, let him be lord of Mount Liang!"

Then his eyes clouded over and he was dead. For Song Jiang it was like losing a father and mother and he wept till his head swam. The others raised him up and urged him to take control of affairs. The Professor and Taoist Gongsun exhorted him: "You must spare yourself such grieving, life and death are man's portion, what use is grief? You must look to what has to be done now."

Song Jiang pulled himself together and gave orders for the body to be bathed in scented water and dressed for burial and then placed in the Assembly Hall. All the leaders came to pay their last respects. An inner casket and coffin were made, an auspicious time was chosen, the body was encoffined and placed in the hall, a screen was set up and a memorial tablet was fashioned bearing the words: "Duke Chao, lord of the Marshes of Mount Liang, inspired commander." All the leaders, from Song Jiang on down, wore full mourning. The lesser chiefs and all the men wore mourning headbands. The arrow was preserved as a pledge before the altar. Long banners were strung up around the stronghold and local monks were invited up the mountain to perform a memorial service for the benefit of Chao Gai's soul. Every day Song Jiang led the company in mourning. He had no heart for attending to the business of the mountain stronghold.

After discussion, Leopard's Head, Taoist Gongsun, the Professor and all the leaders now decided that Song Jiang should rule on Mount Liang. Everyone was in favour.

One day at dawn, when incense, lamps and candles had been lit, Leopard's Head led the company in requesting Song Jiang to come and take his seat in the Assembly Hall. The Professor and Leopard's Head opened the proceedings, saying: "Brother please hear us. 'A nation cannot survive a single day without a leader, a household cannot survive without a master.' Our leader Chao Gai has passed on. How can the stronghold remain leaderless? Your name is known everywhere within the four seas. Let us choose an auspicious day and time to inaugurate your rule as our chief, to be obeyed by everyone in all your commands."

Song Jiang replied: "Before he died, Lord Chao proclaimed: 'If anyone manages to take Shi Wengong, you'd better make him master in the Marshes of Mount Liang.' You all know this. Have you forgotten it, even though his mortal remains are not yet cold? His death has not even been avenged yet, or the bitterness wiped out. How then can I occupy this seat?"

The Professor urged him: "Though indeed Lord Chao said this, we have not in fact captured this person. How can we remain leaderless? If you refuse it, who else will dare take up the post? How will the troops of the stronghold be led? We respect all that you say, but please accept the position at least temporarily, until such time as another policy presents itself."

"What you say is reasonable. I will accept the position for the time being, but when the day of our vengeance arrives and the bitterness is wiped out, he who takes Shi Wengong, whoever it may be, must occupy this seat."

Iron Ox who was standing on one side suddenly exclaimed: "You shouldn't just be lord of the Marshes of Mount Liang, brother, you should be emperor, that's what!"

Song Jiang shouted angrily: "That big black fellow is talking rubbish again! Keep your big mouth shut or I'll have your tongue cut out!"

Iron Ox grumbled: "I wasn't asking for you to be just a local chieftain, I wanted you to be emperor. And you want to cut my tongue out!"

The Professor said: "This idiot has no sense of what's proper. Don't waste your time with him. Please give your attention to important matters."

Song Jiang lit incense and was installed as temporary incumbent of the first seat. His first deputy on the left was the Professor, his second, on the right was Taoist Gongsun. Next on the left was Leopard's Head and on the right Twin Rods. All the leaders paid their respects and took their seats on either side.

Song Jiang spoke as follows: "Today I shall temporarily occupy this position, relying entirely on the support and cooperation of all of you to advise me, in order that together we may follow heaven's path. Our numbers now in the stronghold are very great, not as in the past, and I would like you to separate into six main camps where you will reside. The Assembly Hall will in future be known as the Ceremonial Hall. Before it and behind it, on the right and on the left, there will be four land camps. On the other side of the mountain there will be two smaller posts. In front there will be garrisons for the three main gates. At the bottom there will be the waterside camp and a small post at each of the two landings. I would like you now all to accept these dispositions.

"The Ceremonial Hall will for the time being be my seat of residence. My second-in-command there will be the Professor, and after him in order Taoist Gongsun, Colonel Hua, Thunderclap, the Little Duke and the Halberdier. The left-hand camp will be commanded by Leopard's Head, with the Red-Haired Devil, the Tattooed Dragon, Morbid, Madcap, Skyscraper and the Door-God in the Clouds. The right-hand camp will be commanded by Twin Rods, with Whiskers, the Magic Messenger, Mu the Unstoppable, Iron Ox, Golden Wings, and Mu the Irrepressible. The forward camp will be commanded by Skyhawk, with the Spearsman, the Monk, the Pilgrim, the Blue-Faced Beast, the Flautist and the Young Master. The rearward camp will be commanded by Mr. Chai, with Colonel Sun, the Tamer, Victorious, the Supremo, Redeye and the Pill Monger. The waterside camp will be commanded by the White-Water Dragon, with the three Ruan brothers, the Pilot, White Eel, the Cave Dragon and the River Rider. Altogether in these six camps there will be forty-three leaders.

"The first of the gates will be guarded by Sergeant Lei and the Demon King, the second by Snake and Scorpion, the third by the Eight-Armed Ogre and Winged Ghost. The post at Golden Sands Landing will be run by the Dandy, Whitey, Red Star and Blazing Comet, the post at Duck's-Bill Landing by the Tiger-Killer and Big Chief, the Forester and Rhinoceros. Of the two land posts the other side of the mountain, the left hand one will be occupied by Short-Arse, Steelbright and the Knife, the right hand one by the Strategist, River-Jumper and White-Spotted Snake. Within the Ceremonial Hall the left hand chamber will be occupied by the Hand, as Master of the Rolls, by Chief Justice Sterling, by the

Craftsman, our publisher of inscriptions, and by the Calculator, our treasurer. The right hand chamber will belong to Thunderer, chief of artillery, Flagpole, our shipwright, the Ape, our wardrobe chief, and the Nine-Tailed Turtle, superintendent of fortifications. In the chamber to the rear of the hall will reside other administrative staff: Green-Eyes, our housing officer, Spots, the supervisor of arms manufacture, Smiler, superintendent of wine-making, my brother, Iron Fan, supervisor of banquets, and Uglymug and the Daytime Rat as general overseers. The four inns or listening posts down below will be run by the Crocodile, Lungs, the Flea, the Executioner, Blackface, Auntie Gu, the Gardener and Sister Sun the Ogress, the same arrangement as before. Panther, the Guv and Yellow Dog will be responsible for buying horses in the territory to the north. Let everyone now respect these arrangements. Let there be no violations."

Every single one of the chiefs in the waterlands of Mount Liang was pleased that Song Jiang had become chief of the stronghold and all accepted his provisions without demur.

One day at a general assembly Song Jiang said: "I am anxious to avenge Chao Gai. Let us raise an army and attack Zengside."

The Professor said: "Brother, according to custom the period of mourning should be respected. Let us wait till the hundred days are past before raising an army."

Song Jiang followed the Professor's advice. He remained in the mountain stronghold, every day performing religious works to gain blessings for Chao Gai.

One day he invited a certain monk, called Dayuan, who was a member of the congregation at the Glorious Dragon Temple in the northern capital. Because he passed by the Marshes of Mount Liang on his way to Jining, they invited him to perform a service at the stronghold. As they were eating a vegetarian meal, and idly conversing, Song Jiang happened to ask about local customs and personalities in the northern capital and the monk said: "How come you haven't heard the name of the Jade Unicorn of Hebei? For Song Jiang and the Professor it was like a moment of illumination. They said: "We are not old, as you can see, so how can we be so forgetful? In the northern capital there is indeed a gentleman called Mr. Lu Junyi who is known as the Jade Unicorn, one of those famous three from Hebei, but now living in the northern capital and the possessor of wonderful fighting skills. His technique with the staff is quite unparallelled. If we had that man here with us, there'd be no reason to fear capture by the government troops, how could any troops get near us?"

The Professor said pleasantly: "Brother, what are you worried about? If you want him to come here, it's no problem at all."

Song Jiang said: "He is one of the great men in the northern capital. How could he be persuaded to become an outlaw?"

The Professor said: "I thought about it before, but for some reason it went right out of my mind. I've got a plan that will get him here."

Song Jiang said: "It's certainly not for nothing that people call you the Beacon of Learning! May I ask what method you intend to use to attract the person in question here?"

The Professor's reply was unhesitating. Laying two fingers craftily across each other, he expounded his plan. It was to have an important result, for the Jade Unicorn was to exchange the company of courtiers and the luxury of palaces for the dragon's pool and the tiger's den. Truly:

All so that one man should come to the marshlands,
The people suffered the soldiers' axes.

But if you want to know how the Professor planned to lure the Unicorn to the mountain, you must read the next chapter.

Chapter 61

The Professor has a plan to trap the Unicorn; White Eel fights at Golden Sands Landing!

Now when that monk from the Glorious Dragon Temple happened to mention the Jade Unicorn, the Professor boasted: "I can easily go to the Northern Capital and get him to come here, just by using the persuasive powers of this little tongue of mine. It would be easy as falling off a log. All I'd need is a bold companion to go with me."

Before he had finished speaking, Iron Ox shouted out: "Professor, my dear friend, take me along with you!"

Song Jiang said sternly: "Absolutely not, brother, you'll stay here! For killing and arson, for plunder and pillage, for looting and destruction, you're the one we'll employ. But this is delicate business, you've not got the temperament for it. You're not to go."

"You all despise me, because you think I'm ugly," Iron Ox complained. "That's why you won't let me."

"We don't despise you," Song Jiang said. "But just now the capital will be packed with police. If you were to get caught you'd simply have thrown your life away for nothing."

"I don't care!" said Iron Ox. "I still want to go along with him."

The Professor said: "I'll take you with me if you'll obey three conditions. If you're not prepared to do as I say, you'd better stay here in the stronghold."

"Not only three, I'd obey thirty conditions!" cried Iron Ox.

"First condition: when you drink you blaze up like fire, so from today you've got to cut out drinking, no wine till we get back again. Second condition: you'll dress for this trip as a Taoist acolyte, my disciple, and if I call you, you must come immediately. Third condition — this is the hardest: from tomorrow you're not to speak a word, you're to pretend to be dumb. If you accept these three conditions, I'll take you."

"The bit about not drinking and dressing as a Taoist acolyte is all right. But to make me keep my mouth shut and not say anything, that'll kill me!"

"If you open your mouth, you're bound to stir things up," said the Professor.

"All right then," said Iron Ox. "I'll put a copper coin in my mouth, that'll do it!"

"Dear friend," said Song Jiang. "If you're really determined to go, you mustn't blame me if anything goes wrong."

"Of course, of course," said Iron Ox. "I'll be taking these two axes along. If the motherfuckers give me any trouble I'll cut a thousand fucking heads off!"

Everyone laughed. It was quite impossible to dissuade him. A farewell banquet was held that same day in the Ceremonial Hall and everyone went to bed late. Early next morning the Professor packed his bag and told Iron Ox to get dressed up as a Taoist acolyte and carry the luggage down the mountain on a carrying-pole. Song Jiang and the others accompanied them as far as Golden Sands Landing. They warned the Professor many times to be careful, and to keep a tight rein on Iron Ox. Then the two travellers said goodbye and the rest returned to the stronghold.

So the Professor and Iron Ox headed towards the Northern Capital. They travelled four or five days, each day stopping late at an inn to sleep and early in the morning making their breakfast and taking to the road again. Iron Ox gave the Professor many a headache along the way.

Before long they reached the Northern Capital and found an inn just outside. In the evening when Iron Ox went to prepare food in the kitchen he gave the waiter such a beating he was spitting blood. The waiter went to complain to the Professor: "That attendant of yours, the fellow who can't speak, is really horrible. Just because I was a bit slow with lighting the fire, he beat me up. Coughing up blood, I was."

The Professor hastened to apologize and gave him ten strings of silver to get himself fixed up. And, it goes without saying, he told Iron Ox off. When Iron Ox got up and cooked food for them again in the morning, the Professor called him in and said sternly: "You insisted on coming, damn you, and you're a continual nuisance on this journey. But we're going into the city now, and that's no laughing matter. Please don't put my life in jeopardy!"

"Of course not, I wouldn't dream of it," Iron Ox replied.

The Professor said: "We must have a secret signal. If I nod it means I want you to stop whatever you're doing at once."

Iron Ox took note.

They put on their disguises at the inn and made their way into the city. The Professor wore a sweat-band of black crepe over his forehead, a black Taoist robe with white borders, and a multi-coloured girdle of the kind you see on the Immortal Lu Dongbin. He had blunt-toed shoes of black cloth and was also holding a staff with a gilded copper bell on the end. Iron Ox's brown hair, usually unkempt, was coiled on either side of his head and fixed with a bone pin, his swarthy frame was enveloped in a short brown cassock of rough cloth, his thick waist was girt with a coloured sash with a short fringe, and he wore a pair of light climbing boots on his feet. He carried a pole taller than his own height bearing a placard with the words: "One tael of silver to hear your fate and fortune."

When they were dressed, they locked the door of their room and headed for the south gate of the city. It was only a quarter of a mile or so before they saw the gates of the Northern Capital. What a sight!

The walls are high, the ramparts rugged, the moat broad and deep. Deers' antlers are planted all around, sharp tines are set on every side. The drumtowers are imposing, all bedecked with many-hued banners of silk. The battlements are flat and level, piled high with swords, lances, pikes and halberds. The coffers are overflowing, the citizenry flourishing. From courts to east and west music fills the heavens, shops to north and south are bursting with the goods that enrich earthly life. A thousand officials hold sway over the many-tiered city. A million of our people are dwelling in this land.

Now in those days many thieves and robbers roamed the world and every region, every province and district was strongly guarded. Especially here in the Northern Capital, the most important city of Hebei, defended by the garrison troops of Governor-General Liang: here one would naturally expect things to be well organized.

As the Professor and Iron Ox strolled up to the city gate, therefore, they found forty or fifty men guarding it, presided over by a seated officer. The Professor approached and bowed. One of the guards said: "Where have you come from, master?"

"My name is Zhang Yong," the Professor said. "This disciple of mine is called Li. I make my living among the rivers and lakes casting horoscopes. I am coming to the capital to tell fortunes." He took out his false certificate which he showed to the corporal.

Someone said: "That disciple's got a way of looking at you just like a bloody criminal!" Iron Ox was about to take offence at this, but the Professor gave a quick nod and Iron Ox hung his head. The Professor went up to the gatekeeper and said apologetically: "It's a long story. This disciple of mine is deaf and dumb, but he's got prodigious strength. He was brought up by my family and I have no choice but to take him with me. I am afraid he doesn't know the ways of the world. I beg you to forgive him!"

They bade farewell to the guards and went on their way, heading for the centre of town, Iron Ox striding behind with his head held high. The Professor was shaking his bell and intoning: "To some it comes early, to others late; to each is given a different date. You may end poor, you may get rich, come to me if you want to know which." From time to time he would say: "Come along then, hear your fate and fortune, all you want to know about births and deaths, noble and base. Just a tael of silver to know what lies ahead," and then he would give his bell a shake. Fifty or sixty urchins followed behind, making fun of him. They came thus to the gate of Mr. Lu's pawnshop, amid much song and laughter and toing and froing, the children in a great uproar.

Mr. Lu, the Jade Unicorn, happened to be sitting in front of his warehouse, watching his assistants checking in goods, when he heard this commotion in the street and asked the man in charge: "What's all the excitement for out there?"

The man replied: "It's a laugh, sir! There's this travelling fortune-teller in the street. He's asking a whole tael of silver to tell your fortune, but who's going to pay that much? And there's this really uncouth novice with him who walks like nothing on earth. The children are all running after them laughing."

The Unicorn said: "He must be a man of great learning or he wouldn't ask so much. Go and ask him to come in."

The employee dashed out and shouted: "Master, the boss wants to see you."

"Who wants to see me?" said the Professor.

"Mr. Lu asks you to come in," said the man.

The Professor turned back, with the acolyte at his heels. Drawing aside the curtain he went in and stopped before the hall. He ordered Iron Ox to sit on a little goose-necked chair and wait for him. Here is what met his eyes as he went on in:

> *Large, round eyes surmounted by clear eyebrows like a circumflex accent, a tall and upright stature, majestic bearing, god-like demeanour. The staff is his preferred weapon and in defensive technique he is indisputably a master. Of distinguished lineage, he inherits one of the most famous names in the capital. On the battlefield he will take on ten thousand horsemen, drive back a thousand infantry. Noble and generous he is, ever a defender of right. His talents are truly universal. This is Mr. Lu, known as the Unicorn.*

The Professor made his obeisance, and the Unicorn bowed in return and asked: "May I ask where you are from, Master, and what is your name?"

The Professor said: "My name is Zhang Yong and my religious name is Heaven's Spokesman. My people are from Shandong and I know how to cast a horoscope according to the official rules. I can predict births and deaths, riches or poverty. If you will give me a tael of gold or silver, I will tell your fortune."

The Unicorn asked him to come inside and took him to a little pavilion at the back of the house where he gave him the seat of honour. When they had drunk tea he told the servant to bring a tael of silver, and after handing over the fee, asked if he might trouble the holy father to cast an eye on his life.

The Professor said: "Please let me have the day and month of your birth for the calculation."

The Unicorn said: "I would like to know the bad, not the good, Master. There's no need to go into anything about wealth and honours, I'd just like to know about present actions, that's all. My age is thirty-two ..." He went on to give the year, month, day and hour of his birth.

The Professor took out an iron abacus and placed it on the table. He did a few calculations, and then pushed the abacus away, crying in a loud voice: "Oh, my God!"

Somewhat taken aback, the Unicorn asked: "Is it something very good or bad?"

The Professor said: "Please excuse me if I speak bluntly."

The Unicorn said: "I ask for nothing else but to receive your directions. Please speak freely."

The Professor said: "According to your fortune, there is going to be some bloody event within the next hundred days; your wealth and property cannot protect you from violent death."

The Unicorn laughed at this. "You must have got it wrong, Master. I happened to be born in the Northern Capital. I grew up in a rich man's house. My ancestors were faultless citizens. Among my female relatives none was ever unprincipled enough to remarry. Besides all this, I always act circumspectly and never do anything unreasonable or risky. How can some event involving bloodshed be hanging over me?"

The Professor's face had changed; he had turned pale. He quickly picked up the money he had been given and handed it back. Then he stood up to leave. He said with a deep sigh: "Verily heaven flatters men with false hopes. Well, well! My warning is clear and straightforward. But if honest advice is to be construed as an evil intent, I beg to be excused!"

The Unicorn said: "Do not be angry Master. I was only joking. I do wish to hear what you have to tell me."

吳用智賺玉麒麟

The Professor said: "Then please do not be offended if I speak plainly."

"I shall listen carefully. Please conceal nothing."

"With all respect then, you have until now been blessed with good fortune, but this year your stars are contrary and you must expect ill effects. Within the next hundred days there will be dead bodies and strange signs. This is predestined. It cannot be prevented."

The Unicorn said: "Is there not some way I can escape?"

The Professor made some more calculations on the abacus, before replying: "Only if you go to reside in the south-east. If you are beyond a radius of three hundred miles this catastrophe can be avoided. Although there are still some reasons for fear, there will be no serious physical danger."

The Unicorn said: "If I manage to avoid the trouble I shall be truly grateful."

The Professor said: "Four verses are relevant to your fate. I will tell them to you and you must write them on the wall. Later they will be confirmed and you can verify my clairvoyance."

The Unicorn called for a brush and ink in order to write on the whitewashed wall. The Professor recited these four verses: "Through the reeds a small boat steers. All of a sudden a hero appears. The loyal man must seek a way out. There's nothing to do but to turn about."

When the Unicorn had written all this down, the Professor picked up his abacus, bowed and prepared to leave. The Unicorn tried to persuade him to stay. "Won't you sit down for a little, Master," he said. "Leave in the afternoon."

"I am most obliged to you," the Professor said. "But I have other fortunes to tell. I will come and pay my respects another day." He rose to leave. The Unicorn saw him to the door. Iron Ox took up his staff and went out. The Professor bade farewell to the Unicorn and with Iron Ox in tow left the city. They returned to the inn, paid for their room and food, and packed their bags. Iron Ox carried the sign and as they left the inn the Professor said to him: "Good work! Now we must hurry back to the stronghold and complete our strategy, prepare a trap for the Unicorn. Because he will be coming, that's for sure!"

We shall say nothing of the Professor's and Iron Ox's return to the stronghold. Rather we shall turn to the Unicorn, who after having his fortune told felt extremely ill at ease. He simply could not sit still. He was of course another one of the stars, destined to join the company. Anyway, having heard those predictions, he couldn't stand it another day and told his servant to summon all his employees for a meeting to discuss the business. Soon they were all present, including the chief administrator, a fellow called Li Gu. This Li Gu was originally from the Eastern Capital. He had come to the north to stay with a friend whom he had not been able to find. The Unicorn had found him freezing to death outside his gate and had rescued him and looked after him. Seeing that he was conscientious and could write and do sums, he gave him a post in his business. Within five years he had promoted him to chief administrator. He was now responsible for the whole business both in the house and outside. Under him he had forty or fifty storekeepers. Everyone in the household called him Manager Li. On this occasion all the employees, great or small, followed Manager Li into the hall and saluted.

The Unicorn looked them over and said: "How is it a certain person is missing?"

The words were hardly out of his mouth when a man entered. He was a tall young man of about twenty-four or twenty-five, with a neat beard and moustache, very narrow-waisted and broad-shouldered. He wore a handkerchief on his head, formed into the shape of a papaya, and a white silk robe embroidered with silver thread. A red sash spotted like a spider circled his waist. He had brown boots of oiled leather. His hair was gathered at the back of his head by two gold rings shaped like animals and a scented scarf protected the back of his neck. A fan painted by a famous artist was stuck in his belt. At his temple he wore some seasonal flower.

This man was a native of the Northern Capital, whose parents had died when he was small. He had been brought up in the Unicorn's house. Because his skin was exceedingly white, the Unicorn had a tattoo artist tattoo him all over, from head to foot. The effect was like kingfisher blue inlay on a white marble pillar. For beauty of physique no one, no matter who, could compete with him. But he didn't only have physical beauty. He could play all kinds of musical instruments, sing and dance, he was brilliant at word games, there was nothing he couldn't do, nothing he didn't have knowledge of. He knew every dialect and understood the jargon of every profession. For physical dexterity no one surpassed him; he used a Sichuan bow and just three short arrows. When he went hunting in the surrounding countryside he never missed: the arrow always hit its mark and he would return to the city in the evening with hundreds of different kinds of birds. When an archery club held a competition you can be sure the prize would go to him. Moreover he was extremely smart, the kind of person who really knows his way around. His name was actually Yan Qing — just the one character for his given name — but people in the Northern Capital called him the Prodigy. There is a poem which describes his qualities:

> *The lips are as if painted with vermilion, the eyes shining like lacquer, the features might be carved in jade. His courage is exceptional, his spirit vaulting, his intellectual endowment tremendous. His manners are natural and easy, he would be an ornament even to Mount Liang. When he sings the old airs his voice control is superb, he is naturally a great connoisseur of art, and in the groves of carnal pleasure he is always a leading player. On the drums he can produce a thunderous sound, the tone is clear and ringing when he plays the pipes, his conversation is philosophical and profound. His moves with the staff are impossible to read and with his fists and his flying kicks he can put four hundred troops to flight. All are envious of his powers: they call him the Prodigy.*

Naturally this Prodigy was a trusted member of the Unicorn's household. He now entered the hall, gave a loud greeting and took the second place, so that Manager Li was standing on the left, the Prodigy on the right.

The Unicorn opened proceedings as follows: "I have just had my fortune told. I was informed that within the next hundred days some bloody event would occur, unless I leave home and take refuge more than three hundred miles away in the southeast. It has occurred to me that there is somewhere I can go in the southeast. That is where Mount Tai is, the Eastern Peak, the Temple of Divine Benevolence, where they help people who are caught up in catastrophes. In the first place I can go there and burn candles and incense to limit the danger and alleviate the effects. Secondly I can shelter there from this particular disaster. Thirdly I can do some trade and enjoy a change of scene. Manager Li, please find me ten wagons and load them up with Shandong goods. Then get your luggage packed because you're going travelling with me. Prodigy, you will look after the household. From today on you will hold the keys to the stores jointly with Manager Li. I want to start in three days' time."

Manager Li said: "You're making a mistake, Master. Have you forgotten the proverb, 'Fortunes are told to suit the hearer'? Don't listen to all that fortune-teller's nonsense. What danger can there be if you stay home?"

The Unicorn said: "My fate is preordained. Don't argue with me. If disaster should strike, it would be too late to do anything about it afterwards."

The Prodigy said: "My dear master, please hear me. If you take the road to Tai'an in Shandong, you have to pass by the Marshes of Mount Liang. Nowadays Song Jiang is there in the marshes, with a bunch of cutthroats who pillage and plunder; the government forces can't even get near them. If you want to go and burn incense, wait for a time of peace. Don't trust all that rot the fortune-teller told you yesterday. Who knows if he isn't a criminal from Mount Liang dressed up as a Taoist, come here to deceive you? I'm only sorry I wasn't at home yesterday. If I had been, I'd have put a question or two to that priest, and I bet we'd have had a few laughs."

The Unicorn said: "Stop talking nonsense. Who'd dare come here and play a trick like that on me? And as for that bunch of fools in the Marshes of Mount Liang, who gives a fig for them? I consider them a mere bagatelle. I've thought of going to arrest them myself. After all, everyone praises the skill I have acquired in martial arts. I'm known to be a magnificent fighter!"

Before he'd finished speaking, a woman made her appearance from behind a screen. This was the Unicorn's wife. She was twenty-five years of age and her name was Jia. They had been married five years. She now said: "Husband, I've been listening. There's an old saying: 'Even a mile away from home, is not as good as at home.' Don't listen to all that fortune-telling rubbish. Why abandon your vast business interests and go in fear and trepidation to trade in the tiger's den and the dragon's pool? You'd much better stay home and practise meditation to purify the mind and suppress desire, and live in peace and tranquillity, at one with nature."

The Unicorn said: "What would a woman know about it? It's better to believe something is true than ignore it. Disaster has always been man's best teacher. One must bear both good fortune and ill. Anyway, I've made up my mind, so all of you had better shut up!"

The Prodigy again said: "I live always in the shadow of your good fortune, Master. I too have learnt a few things about staff play. I don't want to boast, but I could help you if I went with you. If you happen to meet some bandits on the road, I could deal with forty or fifty of them. Why not leave Manager Li at home and let me serve you on the journey?"

The Unicorn said: "There are things about trading I don't understand, that's why I am taking Manager Li along. I need his knowledge; he is a great help to me. So I'm leaving you to look after the business. Someone else will keep the books, and you will only be in temporary command here."

Manager Li now said: "I'm afraid I've been having a bit of a problem with my feet lately. I definitely won't be able to walk very far."

The Unicorn blew up. "'Feed troops for a thousand days, you'll only get a morning's work out of them!'," he said. "I ask you to go travelling with me and all you can do is offer excuses. If anyone else tries to make difficulties he shall have a taste of my fists!"

Manager Li's face was ashen with fear and no one dared to say anything else. They parted thus.

Concealing his anger and holding his tongue, Manager Li went to prepare the luggage. He procured ten wagons and ten porters, around fifty draft animals, had the luggage loaded on and a number of bales of goods securely tied.

The Unicorn went to get dressed. On the third day he burnt offerings and distributed money in his household, giving to everyone, young and old, male and female. That evening he told Manager Li to get two servants, have everything packed up and leave the city. When Li was leaving, the Unicorn's wife saw the wagons and went away weeping. Next day at dawn the Unicorn rose, bathed himself, put on new clothes and breakfasted. He got offerings and went to the hall at the back to take leave of his ancestors and burn incense. Just before departing he exhorted his wife to take good care of the house and said he would be back in somewhere between forty days and three months.

"Go carefully," she said. "And write home often."

The Prodigy then prostrated himself.

"I leave you in charge here," the Unicorn said. "See that everything goes smoothly. Don't go out whoring and creating trouble."

"If you are going to be away, how could I possibly neglect my duty?" the latter said.

The Unicorn picked up his staff and left the city. When he met up with Manager Li, he said to him: "Take two companions and go on ahead. When you find a nice clean inn, prepare some food there and wait. When the wagons and porters catch up, we'll eat. That way we'll avoid wasting any time."

Manager Li went off staff in hand, with his two companions. The Unicorn and a number of servants followed behind, escorting the wagons. There was beautiful scenery, fine mountains, wide waters, a broad and level highway, and the Unicorn rejoiced at what he saw. "If I had stayed at home, I would have missed such sights!" he thought. After something over ten miles, Manager Li approached with some dim sum for lunch. After they had eaten, he again went on ahead. They did another fifteen miles or more, and then they came to an inn where Manager Li arranged accommodation for the whole caravan. The Unicorn entered the room, leant his staff against the wall, hung up his hat, took off his sword, and changed his shoes. Nothing need be said of that night's food and lodging. They were up very early next morning to make breakfast. When they had finished eating, the teams were harnessed to the wagons and they took to the road again.

So they went on, for several days, travelling till late in the evening, starting early. Then at one inn where they stayed, the waiter came to the Unicorn as they were about to set off in the morning and said: "I think as how I ought to let you know, sir, not ten miles from our inn here you'll pass by a road that leads to the Marshes of Mount Liang. Although Song Jiang, who's the chief of them up there on the mountain, doesn't usually harm travellers, you want to watch your step round there, don't make too much of a stir like."

"So that's the way it is," was all the Unicorn said. He told his servants to get out the trunk with his clothes. He opened it and took out a package, from which he took four silk banners. He asked the waiter to let him have four bamboo poles. To each of them he then attached one of the banners. On each banner was written in characters the size of a bucket:

Here comes the Unicorn,
To martial arts and exploits born.
Though bent on trade in distant lands,
He'll first destroy the robber bands.

When Manager Li and the others saw this, they cursed their fate. The waiter asked: "Is that lot on the mountain friends of yours, then, sir?"

"I am a rich merchant from the capital," the Unicorn replied. "How could a lot of robbers be my friends? I'm going to catch that villain, Song Jiang."

"Please sir, not so loud. Don't involve me in it. It's no joke! Even with a hundred thousand troops, you wouldn't get nowhere near him."

The Unicorn said: "Bollocks! You villains are all in league with them!"

The waiter could only lament, while the drivers were struck dumb. Manager Li knelt down and said: "Master, please take pity on us all and let us go home alive instead of provoking heaven's wrath."

The Unicorn shouted: "What do you know about it? How could that bunch of paltry sparrows expect to compete with a swan? I've been in training all my life, but so far I haven't met anyone prepared to take me on. Now I've got a wonderful opportunity. If I don't seize it, when will I ever have another like it? In a bag on that wagon over there I've got a quantity of good hemp rope. If those bandits really want to die, just let them attack me. I shall knock them over one by one, a halberd blow for each. You lot just tie them up for me and chuck them on the wagons. If necessary we'll throw out all the merchandise to make room for the prisoners and deliver the whole gang to the capital and demand the reward. It will fulfil a lifelong ambition of mine. If any of you don't want to go on, I can kill you here first."

The banners were now strung up on the four leading wagons. The other six followed on behind. Manager Li and the others, despite their bitter complaints, had to do as they were told. The Unicorn took out a blade and mounted it on his staff, securing it with three tight knots. He set off after the wagons on the Mount Liang road. When he saw the mountains ahead, Manager Li dragged his feet, whereas the Unicorn simply couldn't get along fast enough. They had been travelling from first thing in the morning till nearly midday, when they saw far ahead a large wood, consisting of more than a thousand trees of immense girth. When they reached this wood, they heard a loud whistle. There was nowhere for the terrified Li and the two servants to hide. The Unicorn ordered the wagons to draw to one side. The drivers all cowered underneath, cursing their luck.

"If I knock them down, you tie them up for me!" the Unicorn shouted.

He had hardly finished speaking when four or five hundred men marched out of the wood. Then gongs sounded behind and another four or five hundred troops now stood blocking the way back. A gun went off in the wood and a hero leapt out.

Iron Ox, for that's who it was, gripped his two axes and bellowed: "Hello Mr. Lu! Do you recognize the mute Taoist novice?"

This made the Unicorn wild. "I've often thought about coming to get you, you band of desperadoes," he shouted. "And now I'm here, so you can go and tell Song Jiang to come down from the mountain and surrender. If he refuses, I shall see that you all die, every man jack of you!"

Iron Ox roared with laughter. "Mr. Lu," he said, "you've fallen into the Professor's trap. Don't waste any more of our time, there's a seat waiting for you on the mountain."

The Unicorn enraged grasped his halberd firmly and charged Iron Ox, who came to meet him whirling his two axes. Before they had fought thirty bouts Iron Ox slipped from the circle of combat, turned and ran off towards the trees. The Unicorn levelled his halberd and raced after him. On reaching the wood Iron Ox dodged this way and that among the trees. The Unicorn stumbled after him, mad with rage, till Iron Ox plunged into a dense thicket and disappeared. The Unicorn followed, but he could see no one. When he tried to turn back, a group of men came out from the pines, one of whom shouted: "Don't go away, Mr. Lu. Do you recognize me?" It was a strapping great monk, wearing a black cassock and carrying a staff of steel.

"Where the hell are you from?" the Unicorn exclaimed.

The Monk laughed and answered: "I am Lu Zhishen, the Flowery Monk. I am under orders from our military commander to meet you and escort you up the mountain."

The Unicorn really blew up at this. "How dare you speak to me like that, you bald ass!" Gripping his sword he charged the monk, who came to meet him whirling his steel staff. But before they had fought three bouts, the monk struck his opponent's halberd aside and then turned and left. The Unicorn rushed after him. At this point Pilgrim Wu Song appeared from the ranks, brandishing two swords, and attacked. Despairing of catching the monk, the Unicorn now turned his attentions to the Pilgrim. But again, before three bouts were completed, this new opponent took to his heels.

The Unicorn laughed sarcastically. "I shan't chase you. You're not worth bothering with, you pitiful wretches!"

Before he'd finished speaking, someone shouted down the mountain: "Mr. Lu, what's the matter with you? Have you never heard that 'Men fear water, steel fears fire?' My brother made the plan, how can you think you'll escape?"

"And who the hell are you?" the Unicorn shouted.

The other answered with a laugh: "I'm Liu Tang, the Red-Haired Devil."

"Stay where you are, you scum!" the Unicorn shouted. And levelling his halberd he ran at Liu Tang. But when they had fought three bouts another man shouted from the sidelines: "Mu the Unstoppable is here!" Then the two of them, the Unstoppable and the Red-Haired Devil, fought the Unicorn. Another three bouts and the Unicorn heard footsteps behind him. He gave a fearsome shout which stopped the other two in their tracks, and turned to engage the new assailant, who was Skyhawk. The three leaders now fought him in a T-shaped formation. Quite undaunted, the Unicorn fought all the harder. In the midst of this, a gong sounded on top of the mountain and all three of his assailants slipped away.

The Unicorn was drenched in sweat from his efforts and did not pursue them. When he returned to the edge of the wood and started looking for the carts and their drivers, he could see none of them, not even the draft animals. He climbed a small hill to get a better view. All he saw was far off on the mountainside a group of soldiers driving his carts and oxen before them and Manager Li and his followers strung out behind. They were rapidly disappearing into the pine forest, while the gongs and drums continued to sound.

When he saw this the Unicorn began to breathe out smoke and fire. He took a firm grip on his halberd and set off in pursuit. When he had nearly reached the mountain, two warriors shouted: "Where are you going?" One of these was Whiskers and the other was Sergeant Lei. When the Unicorn saw them, he shouted: "You insurgent scum, give me back my wagons and my porters."

Whiskers, fingering his handsome beard and grinning broadly, said: "Mr. Lu, how come you are so slow on the uptake? You've fallen into our military commander's trap, so even if you were to grow wings you wouldn't be able to get away. Why don't you come straight away to the Ceremonial Hall, where a seat awaits you."

This enraged the Unicorn still further. Grasping his halberd firmly he charged them. Whiskers and Sergeant Lei met him with their weapons at the ready. But before they had fought three bouts they turned and left the field. The Unicorn thought to himself: "I've got to knock one of them over, or I'll never get back the wagons." Throwing caution to the winds, he raced up the hill after them. But neither was anywhere to be seen. From the summit however came the sound of drums and fifes and raising his eyes he saw a banner of apricot yellow embroidered with four characters: "To follow heaven's path," and looking again he saw an umbrella of red silk embroidered with gold thread, and sitting under it Song Jiang, with the Professor on his left and Taoist Gongsun on his right. A company of two hundred or more now sang out in unison: "Mr. Lu, we trust you're in good health!"

This only added fuel to the flames of his anger and caused him to hurl insults up the mountain. The Professor spoke soothingly: "Calm yourself, please. Song Jiang has long admired you. That is why he sent a certain friend to your home, to arrange for you to visit the mountain, in order that together we may do heaven's will. Please do not be angry with us!"

"You unprincipled brigands, how dare you set a trap for me!" the Unicorn bawled.

Colonel Hua, the Archer, now stepped out from behind Song Jiang, holding a bow. He took an arrow and looking the Unicorn straight in the eye shouted: "Mr. Lu, I am not trying to show off. I just want you to see my skill with an arrow." He had hardly finished speaking before an arrow whistled through the air and struck the red tassel on top of the Unicorn's hat.

This had its effect on the Unicorn, who turned and fled. Drums now began to thunder on top of the hill and Thunderclap and Leopard's Head charged down the eastern slope at the head of a cavalry troop, with streaming banners and shouting loudly. At the same time Twin Rods and the Spearsman led another troop of cavalry down the slope to the west, also waving banners and shouting. To his horror the Unicorn saw that he was cut off. It was getting late, and he was footsore and hungry. He was beginning to fear there was no way out, when he spotted a narrow path leading towards the loneliest part of the mountain, and took it eagerly. It was around dusk, and mist was rising over distant waters, fog enveloping the mountains. Stars and moon shed only the faintest of light and it was impossible to see anything clearly. All he could do was keep on walking, even if it led to the edge of heaven or the utmost limits of the earth.

He came in fact to Duck's-Bill Landing. Here all that met the eye was lonely reedbeds and a vast expanse of misty water.

When the Unicorn saw this he raised his eyes to heaven and heaved a great sigh: "It's all because I didn't pay due attention to the holy man's words that I am now assailed by such troubles."

In this unhappy state, he saw the reeds part and a fisherman appear, rowing a small boat. Leaning on his oars, the fisherman shouted out: "Well, you're a bold one, and no mistake! This is forbidden territory in the Marshes of Mount Liang. What brings you here, halfway through the night?"

"I lost my way, that's what," said the Unicorn. "I can't find anywhere to stay. Can you help me?"

"In these parts there is one little place, but you'd have to go ten miles round to get there, and besides the way is complicated, it's very hard to find. By water it's only a couple of miles. If you don't mind parting with ten strings of silver, I'll take you there in my boat."

"If you'll ferry me across to an inn in the village I'll even give you something extra," said the Unicorn.

So the fisherman rowed to the bank to pick the Unicorn up, and then punted off with his iron boatpole. They had just gone a mile or so when they heard the creak of oars in the reeds ahead of them: a skiff shot out. There were two people in it. The one in front was stripped naked and equipped with a fishing rod. The one behind was sculling. The front man rested his pole and began to sing:

For reading the classics I've no inclination,
To live on Mount Liang's my only vocation.
I'll trap you a beast or make you a bait'll
Fetch to your line a bloody great turtle.

The Unicorn got a shock. He didn't dare make a sound. From the reeds on the right hand side came another sound and another

張順夜鬧金沙渡

boat appeared with two men in it. The one in the back was sculling and laughing as he did so, the other was resting his pole and singing:

Since the day I was born I've been counted a tough 'un;
A thieving and fighting and murdering ruffian.
I don't want your gold, and your riches I scorn;
My ambition's to capture the Jade Unicorn.

The Unicorn could only curse his luck. Then another small boat came flying towards them with a man standing in the prow, carrying an iron-tipped wooden pole and singing:

Through the reeds a small boat steers.
All of a sudden a hero appears.
The loyal man seeks a way out.
Nothing to do but to turn about.

When the songs finished, a greeting was shouted out from all three boats together. In the middle boat was Ruan the Second, in the left hand boat Ruan the Fifth, and in the right hand boat Ruan the Seventh. The three boats now joined forces and headed straight for them.

What he heard struck fear into the Unicorn's heart. It occurred to him that he had no idea how to swim. He began to urge the fisherman to take him to the bank quickly. The fisherman only laughed and said: "The blue sky is above, green water below. Me, I was born on the River Yangtze, but now I reside in the Marshes of Mount Liang. I'm not the kind who changes his name every other minute; Li Jun, the White-Water Dragon, that's who I am! Now if you don't surrender right off, you'll just be throwing your life away for nothing!"

The Unicorn was really scared now. Shouting "it's either you or me!" he took his halberd and aimed a blow at the boatman's heart. The latter saw the blow coming and taking a firm hold on his scull, turned a backward somersault into the water. Splash! The boat was left drifting in circles on the water and the halberd disappeared under the waves. At this point a man surfaced at the stern of the boat and shouted "White Eel is here!" Treading water, he pressed down on the rudder and then with a sudden twist turned the boat bottom to the sky, toppling its occupant into the water.

This really was a case of:

Employ a scheme to beat the phoenix and trap the dragon,
Forge a snare for the man of whom heaven and earth go in fear.

But if you want to know whether or not the Unicorn escaped with his life, you must read the next chapter.

Chapter 62

The Prodigy saves his master with well-directed arrows;
By leaping from a balcony Madcap robs the gallows!

Now the Unicorn, although a bold fighter, was quite helpless in the water, and White Eel had capsized the boat and knocked him in. What happened next was that White Eel grasped him by the waist under the water and swam to the other shore. Having relieved him of his weapon, he hauled the man out onto the bank. Torches had been lit and the forty or fifty men waiting there to receive the Unicorn surrounded him, took off his sword, stripped him of all his wet clothing, and were about to tie him up.

At this point the Magic Messenger shouted out an order: "Do not harm Mr. Lu in any way!" Someone was immediately sent with a padded cotton coat and silk robe for the Unicorn to put on. Eight soldiers came with a sedan chair, helped him into it and set off. Before long a score or more of red silk lanterns became visible in the distance, illuminating a small group of horsemen who were advancing to meet them to the beating of drums. At the head of them were Song Jiang, the Professor and Taoist Gongsun. Behind were all the other leaders. They all dismounted and the Unicorn hurriedly descended from the sedan chair. Song Jiang knelt first, and then all the other leaders in turn knelt down.

The Unicorn also knelt to return the courtesy. He said: "Since you have captured me, I would ask you to grant me a quick death."

Song Jiang smiled and said: "Please get into the sedan chair again." They all mounted, the music started up again and they rode up through the three gates till they reached the Ceremonial Hall. There they dismounted and the Unicorn was led into the hall, which was brilliantly illumined with lamps and candles.

Song Jiang came forward and spoke, in a very friendly tone. "Your great reputation has long sounded like thunder in my ears," he said. "Today I have the great good fortune to meet you. It is a pleasure I shall never forget. But I fear we have given you cause for annoyance and I beg you humbly to forgive us."

Next the Professor came forward and said: "The other day I told your fortune. I had been entrusted with visiting you to tell your fortune in order to get you here, to join the great enterprise, so together we can follow heaven's path."

Song Jiang now asked the Unicorn to take the first place among the leaders. The Unicorn replied modestly: "I have no talent, no knowledge or ability, I would count a thousand deaths light punishment, why do you jest with me?"

"How could we jest with you?" Song Jiang reassured him. "We value your nobility as those who hunger and thirst value food and water. Our greatest desire is that you will not leave our humble place but stay as our leader, ever to be obeyed by us."

The Unicorn replied: "Better for me to die, when living is so painful."

The Professor said: "Let's talk about it later."

Wine was poured and food prepared for his entertainment. The Unicorn had no alternative but to accept a few cups, and then a soldier took him to an inside room to sleep.

Next day Song Jiang had sheep and horses slaughtered and gave a big feast to which the Unicorn was invited. He had to be asked many times before he would sit down with them. After several rounds of wine Song Jiang stood up, cup in hand, and said ingratiatingly: "Last night I fear we offended you. I sincerely apologize. Although this stronghold of ours is so small and unworthy, hardly fit for your horse, for the sake of 'honour and loyalty,' two concepts we consider pre-eminent, I beg you to accept this position. Please do not refuse."

"You are mistaken in this," the Unicorn replied. "It was through no fault of my own that I became involved. Besides, I have some family dependents. I was born loyal to the dynasty, I must die loyal to the dynasty. I would rather die than agree to your proposal."

Although the Professor and each of the other leaders pleaded with him, the Unicorn refused to become an outlaw. Finally, the Professor said: "If you are not willing, how can we force you? We have implored you to stay, but it is not to your liking. All we can say is that since you are already here, although you do not want to join us, please allow us to entertain you here for a few days before we send you home."

"I have no objection," the Unicorn said. "Only I am afraid that the members of my family will be worried not having news of me."

"That's no problem," said the Professor. "We will send Manager Li back first with the wagons. You can go a few days later, what's wrong with that?"

The Professor asked Manager Li if he had all his wagons and merchandise.

Manager Li replied: "There's nothing at all missing."

Song Jiang ordered two large silver ingots to be brought and gave them to Manager Li. Two smaller ones were shared by the servants. He gave ten pieces of white silver to the wagon drivers. They all thanked him. The Unicorn said to Manager Li: "You know all about my situation. When you get back tell my wife not to worry. I shall be back in three or four days' time."

Manager Li was eager to get away and wasted no time in replying: "That's fine." Then he said goodbye and left the Ceremonial Hall. The Professor immediately after stood up and said: "Now Mr. Lu, just you relax and sit here for a little while. I will see Manager Li off down the mountain."

This was in fact just a pretext. What the Professor did was go first to Golden Sands Landing and wait. In a little while Manager Li with the two servants, the wagons, the oxen and their other companions came down the mountain. The Professor, surrounded by five hundred troops, was sitting under a willow tree. He called Manager Li over and said: "Your master has come to an agreement with us. He has taken the second place in our command. But this was already set out in a four-verse poem before he even came here. It's written on the wall in his house. Let me explain it to you. There are twenty-eight characters written on the wall, and each line contains an important word. '*Through the reeds a small boat steers*' contains the word *reeds*, which is the same as your master's name, Lu. '*All of a sudden a hero appears*' contains the word *hero*, the first part of your master's given name. '*The loyal man seeks a way out*' contains the word *loyal*, the second part of his given name. '*Nothing to do but to turn about*' contains the word *turn*. So in the four lines taken together you can find *reeds — hero — loyal — turn*, or in other words, *Lu Junyi turns*. What do you expect from us here on the mountain? Originally we were going to kill you all, but then we decided that it would reflect badly on our company. So now we are letting you go, to travel back as fast as possible. Do not expect your master to return home."

Manager Li and his companions thanked him profusely. The Professor ordered the boat to take them across the water and the whole caravan set off, hastening back to the Northern Capital. It was really a case of "Once off the hook the turtle stretches out his tail and shakes his head and doesn't look back."

Now our story divides in two. Let us leave Manager Li and the rest to journey home, while we return with the Professor to the Ceremonial Hall. He rejoined the banquet and flattered the Unicorn with a skilful tongue. The feasting continued until the second watch.

Next day when another feast was held in his honour, the Unicorn said: "I am most grateful to you all for inviting me, but I have to tell you that each day is like a year to me until I can leave."

Song Jiang said: "Unworthy as I am I have had the good fortune to make your acquaintance. I would like to offer you a little drinking party so that we can sit down and chat together. I hope you will not refuse me this." So another day passed.

Song Jiang was host on the next day, the Professor the day after, and Taoist Gongsun the day after that. To cut a long story short, more than thirty of the leaders in the hall took it in turn to host a feast and the days ticked by, the sun and moon going to and fro like a weaver's shuttle. Soon well over a month was gone. As he contemplated this, the Unicorn became ever more anxious to leave. Song Jiang said: "We won't try to keep you, when we know how eager you are to return home. But we must have one last little farewell celebration before you start."

Song Jiang's farewell for the Unicorn was held next day. And then all the other leaders came to the Unicorn and said: "We know our leader honours you greatly, but we honour you even more highly! If you'll only accept his hospitality and not ours, it's like valuing a brick more highly than a tile!" And Iron Ox who was among them cried out: "I risked my life to go to the Northern Capital and invite you here. If you won't accept hospitality from my brothers and myself, I shall take it as an insult that nothing will ever wipe out."

This made the Professor laugh. "What a way of inviting someone!" he said. "That's totally uncouth! Please forgive him, Mr. Lu, and accept their good intentions. Stay just a little longer!" And so another four or five days slipped by. When the Unicorn was absolutely determined to go, the Strategist marched into the Ceremonial Hall with a group of others and began to speak: "Although we are all brothers here, we've a bone to pick all the same. Is there poison in the wine or something? If Mr. Lu doesn't see fit to accept what we offer, that's fair enough. Only it's a bit late to say so now that we've gone to all the trouble."

The Professor rose and said: "Don't get upset. I will plead for you with Mr. Lu to stay a little longer, and I don't see why he shouldn't agree. As the proverb says: 'No need to fight when a cup of wine will set things right'." The Unicorn could not refuse them all, so he stayed a few days more. Altogether that made nearly a month and a half. So since the time he left the Northern Capital in August more than two months had slipped by here on Mount Liang. It was now well into autumn, with its soft breezes and refreshing dew, and the Mid-Autumn Festival was fast approaching. The Unicorn was really missing home and he said so. When Song Jiang saw that he was seriously homesick, he said: "That's no problem. Tomorrow we'll take you down to Golden Sands Landing and send you on your way." The Unicorn expressed his gratitude. As the poem says:

Away from your native mountains, the days pass slowly;
Not a day but the heart longs for home.
At these times a man wishes for wings
To waft him on the winds of heaven over the water.

Next day the Unicorn's original clothes, his sword and his staff were restored to him and all the leaders escorted him down the mountain. Song Jiang offered him a tray of gold and silver as a leaving present, but he refused it, saying: "I do not mean to boast, but I have plenty of this sort of thing at home. All I need is just some travelling expenses to get me to the Northern Capital. A gift like this I definitely cannot accept."

Song Jiang and the others then took him to Golden Sands Landing and said goodbye. Of this no more.

We shall not speak of Song Jiang's return to the camp, but of the Unicorn as he sets off and hastens homeward. In ten days he reached the capital. It was already getting dark so he didn't enter the city but stopped outside at an inn. He departed next morning at dawn and raced towards the city. He had not gone half a mile when he met someone with a ragged headcloth and clothes full of holes who after regarding him attentively pressed his knuckles to his forehead and prostrated himself. Looking carefully, the Unicorn recognized the Prodigy. "How do you come to be in such a state, lad?" he asked.

"This is not a good place to talk," the Prodigy said.

The Unicorn led him round the corner of an earthen rampart and then began to question him closely. The Prodigy said: "Not more than two weeks after you left, Manager Li came back and said to the mistress: 'The Master has given his allegiance to Song Jiang of the Marshes of Mount Liang and accepted the position of second-in-command.' He also went to the authorities and denounced you. He and the mistress had already come to an agreement, and they took umbrage when I disapproved, so they threw me out. They only let me take a single suit of clothes and then hounded me out of the city. They even told all the family and friends that anyone who gave me shelter would forfeit half his possessions and be reported to the authorities, so no one dared have anything to do with me. Since I could find nowhere to stay in the city I had to come out here and beg for a living. At the moment I am sleeping in the street. At first I thought of going to Mount Liang to find you, but I didn't want to do anything in a hurry. If you are thinking of returning from the Marshes, please listen to me and go back there at once. Don't even stop to think about it. If you go into the city you'll be caught in a trap."

The Unicorn shouted: "My wife is not like that! Shut your mouth!"

The Prodigy said: "Master, you can't see what's in front of your nose! What do you know about it? All you ever think about is martial arts, you don't know anything about women. Your wife had a relationship with Manager Li long ago. Now they're quite open about it, like husband and wife. If you go back there you'll meet your end!"

The Unicorn was outraged. He yelled at the Prodigy. "My family has been in the Northern Capital for five generations, everyone knows them. What kind of position does Li Gu have, how could he try something like that on? Most probably you've done something terrible yourself, and now you're trying to tell it the other way round. I'm going to go home and find out the truth of all this. You haven't heard the end of it!"

Weeping copiously, the Prodigy flung himself on the ground and tried to grasp the hem of his master's robe. The Unicorn spurned him with his foot and stalked off into the city.

When he entered his house all the employees looked very frightened. Manager Li hurried to meet him and then took him into the hall and prostrated himself. The Unicorn asked: "Where is the Prodigy?"

Manager Li replied: "You'd better not ask, Master. It's a long story and I'm afraid it will make you angry. I'll tell you later when you've rested."

The Unicorn's wife now appeared from behind the screen, weeping. "Don't cry," the Unicorn said to her. "Just tell me what has happened to the Prodigy."

"Don't ask now," she said. "I'll tell you all in good time."

The Unicorn was beginning to have doubts. He persisted in asking about the Prodigy, so Manager Li said: "Change your clothes and have some breakfast first, Master. Then we can talk about it."

He set about ordering food for his master. Just as the Unicorn raised the chopsticks, a tremendous knocking was heard at the front door and the back door and several hundred policemen burst in. The Unicorn was too shocked to do anything so they tied him up and drove him with a blow at every step to the detention cells. Governor Liang was presiding in the court at the time with his officers drawn up in two ranks on either side and some eighty or so ferocious guards. The Unicorn was flung down before the bench, while his wife and Manager Li knelt to one side. The Governor shouted out: "You're supposed to be a respectable citizen of the Northern Capital, you villain. What do you mean by going to hobnob with the brigands on Mount Liang and accepting the second position among their leaders? I hear you're even conspiring with them to attack this city! But we've got you now. What have you got to say for yourself?"

The Unicorn said: "Fool that I am, I was deceived by 'Professor' Wu Yong from Mount Liang, who came to my house disguised as a fortune-teller. He lured me to the mountain and they held me there under house arrest for over two months. Now I've managed to escape and return home. I swear I am innocent. I rely on your justice."

Governor Liang said: "Why keep pretending? If you weren't in league with that Mount Liang lot, why did you stay there so long? Your wife and Manager Li have already lodged an accusation, so someone's not telling the truth."

Manager Li said: "Master, since you're here you had better confess. I have seen the coded poem about rebellion on the wall in your house. It's the strongest possible evidence. You haven't got a leg to stand on!"

His wife said: "We didn't mean to harm you. We were just afraid you would get us involved. As the proverb says: 'For every traitor nine relatives pay the price'."

Kneeling before the bench, the Unicorn began to cry out that he was unjustly accused. Manager Li said: "It's not true that you've been unjustly accused. It's just that the truth can't be hidden, lies get found out. Hurry up and confess, so you won't have to be tortured."

The wife said: "Husband, falsehood won't easily pass into a court of law, the truth is hard to oppose. You go and get yourself into trouble and you ruin me as well. It's a fact of life that flesh is delicate but the cane has no feelings. Why not confess? You'll only get a limited sentence if you do."

Since Manager Li had given out money to everyone, Registrar Zhang declared to the court: "This feckless vagabond will never confess until he's beaten!"

"Hear, hear!" said the Governor. "Beat him!" he thundered. His officers bound the Unicorn and threw him down on the ground. No need to tell what happened. They beat him till the skin split and the blood streamed down. Three times he fainted. No chance here for the Unicorn to show off his martial skills! He could only look to heaven and sigh: "If it is my fate to suffer calamity, I'd better make a false confession and be done with it."

Registrar Zhang took down the confession and the one hundred catty cangue of a man condemned to die was imposed. The Unicorn was taken to the main prison and locked up. Onlookers inside and outside the court-house were deeply shocked. On entering the gaol the Unicorn received thirty more vicious blows of the cane. He was taken under escort to the inmost office and made to kneel before the warden's bench.

The warden pointed a finger at him and said: "Do you know who I am?"

The Unicorn dared not make a sound. It was in fact the warden of the two prisons, who also doubled as public executioner. His name was Cai Fu and he was a native of the Northern Capital. Because of his great strength, people called him Strongarm. Beside him stood his brother whose name was Cai Qing. He was the under-warden. He always liked to carry a flower and the people of Hebei had dubbed him Blossom. He now stood beside Strongarm, leaning on his staff of office.

"Chuck this felon into the dungeon," Strongarm said. "I'm going to take a walk. I won't be long." Blossom led the Unicorn away.

When Strongarm left the prison, he went to see a certain person down by the city wall. The man was carrying a rice pot and his expression was gloomy. Strongarm knew that this was the Prodigy. "Young Yan," he said, "what are you doing?"

The Prodigy knelt down and looking up with tears in his eyes, said: "Warden, my friend, please be merciful to my master, Mr. Lu, who has been unjustly accused and sentenced and cannot even afford to have food sent him. I have managed to beg this half pot of rice outside the city to provide some relief for my master's hunger. But I beg you to tell me what I can do to help." So saying he continued to weep and prostrated himself.

Strongarm said: "I know all about it. You take the rice to him so he can eat."

The Prodigy thanked him and went into the prison with the rice.

Strongarm now proceeded as far as the city bridge. Here he met a teahouse keeper who shouted out a greeting and said: "Warden, I have a customer upstairs who wants a word with you."

When Strongarm went upstairs, who should he see but Manager Li. When they had greeted each other, Strongarm said: "What is it you want to say to me, Manager?"

Manager Li said: "I'll tell you no evil, I'll tell you no lies. My future is entirely in your hands. This evening I've some business that I want to get completely wrapped up. There's nothing special about it, but here is fifty taels of gold in garlic-shaped ingots. This is for you alone. I will take care of the other officers of the court myself."

Strongarm grinned and said: "Haven't you seen the warning in the courtoom which says: 'It's not difficult to oppress the people but Providence is never cheated'? Do you think I don't know all about this dirty business of yours? You've already taken his goods and seduced his wife and now you give me fifty taels of gold to finish him off. If they review the case later on, I'm the one who will be in trouble."

Manager Li said: "I can understand your anxiety. I'll give you another fifty taels."

Strongarm said: "Manager Li, you are trying to make the cat eat the tail you've just cut off! A man so famous in the Northern

Capital as Mr. Lu — is he only worth a hundred taels of gold? If you really want me to destroy him, let me be honest with you, you'll need to give me at least five hundred."

"I've got the gold here, you can have it. I only want to be sure you'll finish the business a little later tonight."

Strongarm took the gold and tucked it away. Then he stood up and said: "You can come for the body tomorrow morning."

Manager Li thanked him and went away with a light heart.

Strongarm went home. As soon as he got in, a stranger pulled aside the front door curtain and entered.

"Good evening, Warden!" said the stranger boldly. He was a remarkably distinguished looking man, and extremely well dressed. He wore a round-collared robe, the hue of a raven's wing and the belt around his waist was fitted out with jade decorations. His feet were shod in slippers embroidered with pearls and on his head was a coronet decorated with pheasant's feathers. He bowed to Strongarm as he entered the courtyard.

Strongarm hurriedly returned the courtesy and said: "May I ask your name, sir? And what can I do for you?"

"Shall we talk inside?" said the other.

Strongarm took him to a little conference room and invited him sit in the place of honour.

"Do not be afraid, Warden," the stranger began. "My name is Chai Jin. My family are descended from the Zhou Emperor and people call me the Little Whirlwind. For reasons of chivalry and philanthropy I have come to know many of the world's brave men. I had the misfortune to infringe the law and took refuge in the Marshes of Mount Liang. I am here with a commission from our leader Song Jiang, to report news of Mr. Lu. Who would have thought that a conspiracy of greedy officials, corrupt officers, a faithless wife and a scheming lover would land him in prison, on death row, where his life hangs by a thread. And he is in your hands. Death is the lot of mortal men, but I am sent to tell you this: if you can preserve Mr. Lu's life the Buddha's eyes will smile on you and your magnanimity will not be forgotten. But if even a hair of his head is harmed an army will be at the city walls and when the defences are breached every head will roll, without distinction of person, wise or foolish, young or old! I have long heard that you are a loyal and honourable man. I have nothing worthy to give you, but I have here a thousand taels of pure gold, as a very small gift. If you think you should arrest me, then go ahead and tie me up, I will not take it amiss."

What he heard made Strongarm so nervous that he broke out in a cold sweat. For a long while he was quite unable to answer. Finally Chai Jin stood up and said: "It is for you now to act. Please do not waste my time. I must have a decision."

Finally Strongarm said: "You can leave, sir. I will make arrangements."

Chai Jin bowed and said: "If I have your word, then I thank you." As he went out of the door he gave orders to a follower who brought in the gold, handed it to Strongarm, saluted and left. This follower waiting outside was the Magic Messenger — another hero who was not to be taken lightly.

Strongarm could not decide what to do. He thought about it for a long long time. Finally he returned to the prison and told everything to his younger brother. The latter said: "Usually you are so decisive. This is an easy matter, what's the problem? As the proverb says: 'If you kill someone there's bound to be blood, if you want to save someone, do it properly!' Since you've got a thousand taels of gold here, let's both go and buy everyone off for him. Governor Liang and Registrar Zhang both love money. If they've got a bribe in their hands they won't let Mr. Lu suffer the death penalty. They'll probably just banish him or something, then whether he's rescued or not depends on his friends from the Marshes of Mount Liang. Anyway, we'll be shot of it."

Strongarm said: "That's exactly what I was thinking. Now you get Mr. Lu to a safe place, make sure he's got plenty of good wine and food, and tell him the news."

Having made up their minds, the two brothers quietly distributed gold to all and sundry to ensure their support.

Next day Manager Li, seeing no sign of activity, went to Strongarm's home to urge him to get a move on.

Strongarm answered: "We were just about to do him in when His Excellency forbade it. Orders were received that he was to be kept alive. But if you go to the top and persuade them to give the authorization, then I've no objection."

Manager Li accordingly sent someone with money for bribes. But when this man tried to hand the money over, Governor Liang said: "This is the Warden's business. Surely you don't expect me to do it myself? Just leave it a few days and then I'll tell him to do it."

Everyone was passing the buck. Registrar Zhang had received the gold already and all he wanted to do was postpone the case. Strongarm was busy handing out bribes and trying to arrange for an early hearing. Registrar Zhang collected up the papers and presented them to Governor Liang who said: "How are we going to resolve this case?"

Zhang said: "In my humble opinion, although there is a serious accusation against Mr. Lu, there is no concrete evidence. Although he spent a certain time on Mount Liang, it was at most involvement with crime, not a serious crime in itself. Give him forty strokes and banishment to a distance of a thousand miles. Would that do, do you think?"

"A very clear appraisal," said Liang. "Exactly what I had in mind." So then he ordered Strongarm to fetch Lu from the gaol. The cangue was removed in the courtroom, the confession and case summary were read, and he was sentenced to forty strokes. A new twenty catty cangue was imposed and the beating was administered in front of the courtroom. Then two guards, Dong Chao and Xue Ba were appointed to escort him to the island of Shamen, his place of exile. These two had served in the Eastern Capital force and had escorted Leopard's Head on the road to Cangzhou. Because they had failed to kill Leopard's Head they got into trouble with Marshal Gao when they returned and were banished to the Northern Capital. Governor Liang had seen how capable they were and had retained them on garrison duties. He now put Mr. Lu in their charge.

So the two guards left the court and placed the Unicorn in the cells while they went home to pack their things, ready for departure.

Meanwhile, when Manager Li got to hear about all this, he was flabbergasted. He sent someone to ask the two guards to come and meet him. When they arrived at the inn, he asked them to take a seat and offered them wine and food. After three cups, he announced: "I will be frank with you. Mr. Lu is my enemy. Now he has been banished to the island of Shamen. It's a long way and he hasn't a penny, so you will have to waste your own money on the journey. It will be at least three or four months before you get back. I can't give you very much, but please accept these two big silver ingots as an initial payment. After a couple of stages at most, or as little as a few miles if you come to a really quiet spot, finish him off, remove the golden seals from his cheeks and bring them back as proof. When you let me know it is done, each of you will receive fifty taels of gold in garlic-shaped ingots. All you need do is lodge a report at the garrison command, and I will take care of everything."

The two looked at each other. They spent a long time considering it. The sight of the two big ingots naturally aroused their greed.

Dong Chao said: "I'm just afraid it may not work out for us."

Xue Ba said: "Listen, Mr. Li is obviously a reliable person. If we do this business he'll be well disposed towards us. If there's any problems we can ask him to sort them out."

Manager Li said: "I'm not one to forget a favour. I shall repay you very thoroughly."

Having taken the money, the guards went home to get their luggage, in order to leave that evening. The Unicorn said: "I received the beating today and it's still exceedingly painful. Can't we start tomorrow?"

"You shut your fucking mouth!" Xue Ba shouted. "Just my luck to be saddled with a useless bugger like you! It's over two thousand miles to Shamen, there and back, we've practically no funds for the journey, you haven't got a cent yourself, how do they expect us to manage?"

The Unicorn said: "You really ought to show me some consideration, as a victim of unjust persecution."

Dong scolded: "You rich men, you're never ever willing to part with a cent! Now heaven has opened your eyes for you, it'll teach you a lesson! Stop feeling sorry for yourself; we'll give you a hand."

The Unicorn just had to grin and bear it. He was obliged to go with them, passing out of the city through the eastern gate. The guards hung their bundles of clothes and their umbrellas on his cangue.

So there was the Unicorn, once a rich man, now a convict. There was nothing he could do about it. Another thing he had to bear was the late autumn weather, everywhere yellow leaves falling and the wild swans overhead, and nothing to be heard in this scene of desolation but the sound of a flute:

Somewhere a flute, expressing autumn's sense,
Stirring up feelings of sadness without reason,
So heartbreakingly sweet one cannot bear to listen:
How can such heartbreak be lodged in a mere sound!

As they escorted him on the road the two guards treated the Unicorn well or badly by turns. When it was nearly evening and they had done about eight miles, they came to a small market town and found themselves an inn to stay. The waiter took them to a room at the back where they deposited their bags. Xue Ba said: "It's a tough enough job being a policeman, I don't see why we should also have to slave for a convict. If you want anything to eat, go and light the stove, double-quick!"

So the Unicorn, still with his cangue on, had to go to the kitchen and ask the waiter to let him have some straw, which he tied into bundles and took to the stove to get the fire going. The waiter washed the rice for him and cleaned some bowls.

Now the Unicorn was a rich man by birth and was quite incapable of this kind of work. The straw and tinder were damp and it wouldn't light. When by dint of much blowing he managed to get it to take, the smoke got in his eyes and he couldn't see. Dong meanwhile was grumbling and cursing away. When the rice was finally cooked the two guards took it and the Unicorn did not dare ask for any. By the time they had finished, all that was left for the Unicorn to eat was the dregs of some soup and some cold rice.

Dong never ceased cursing the Unicorn. After supper he sent him off to heat water for washing. Whilst he was waiting for the water to boil, the Unicorn ventured to go and sit down. When they had washed their feet, the other two got a bowl of boiling water and encouraged the Unicorn to wash his feet in it. The moment he took off his sandals, Xue thrust his feet straight into the boiling water. The pain was excruciating. Xue said: "Here I am, serving you, and you go and make faces!" The two guards went to sleep by the stove. Using some wire they confined the Unicorn behind the door of their room. They had themselves woken some time before dawn and told the waiter to make breakfast. After eating their fill they packed their bags and were ready to start. But the Unicorn found that his feet had come out in blisters and he could hardly bear to put them down.

It rained heavily that day, too, and the path was slippery. The Unicorn staggered at every step. Xue seized him by the waist and belaboured him with his staff of office, Dong gave him false encouragement. All the way he was complaining of injustice and cursing his luck. When they had gone three or four miles they came to a forest and the Unicorn said: "I really cannot go any further. For pity's sake, please let us rest a while."

So they took him into the forest. The sky was just brightening in the east. There was no one about. Xue said: "We got up very early and we're tired. We could take a little nap here in the forest if I wasn't afraid you might run away."

The Unicorn said: "Even if I grew wings I couldn't go anywhere at the moment."

Xue said: "Let's hear no more from you. Just wait while I tie you up."

He removed a piece of rope he had round his waist and attached it to the Unicorn's waist, Then he put a turn round a pine tree. He took another turn round the Unicorn's legs, securing them to the tree. Then he said to Dong: "You go to the edge of the wood and keep a lookout. If you see anyone coming warn me by coughing."

"All right, but try and do it quickly," Dong said.

"Don't worry. You just go and keep watch," Xue said.

Xue picked up his staff. Looking the Unicorn in the eye he said: "Don't blame us. That manager of yours, Li Gu, he's the one what told us to finish you off on the road. But anyway, if you got to

Shamen you'd be as good as dead there, so what's wrong with disposing of you a bit sooner? Only don't make no accusations against us when you get down below. This time next year it'll be your anniversary."

The Unicorn began to weep. He lowered his head, awaiting death. Xue lifted the staff in both hands. He fixed his eyes on the spot on the Unicorn's skull where he was going to bring the staff down. Dong, keeping watch outside, heard the thump of the blow and hurried back to look. The Unicorn was still tied to the tree. Xue was lying flat on his back under the tree; his staff had fallen to one side. "This is extraordinary!" Dong thought. "Is it possible he used so much force that he fell over?" He examined the lying man's face: there was no sign of life. Blood was coming from the mouth. From the breast protruded several inches of the slender shaft of an arrow. Before Dong had time to cry out, he saw a man sitting up in one corner of the tree. At the same moment he heard the twang of a bowstring and an arrow struck him in the head. His legs went from under him and he fell with a crash. The man in the tree leapt down and taking a knife that was tied to his wrist cut the Unicorn's bonds, smashed the cangue, supported the Unicorn and abandoned himself to tears.

When the Unicorn dared to open his eyes he recognized the Prodigy. "Is it really you, lad," he cried, "or is it a spirit impersonating you?"

The Prodigy said: "Ever since you left the garrison I have been following hard on the heels of those two scoundrels. I saw them lock you up in the guardhouse and I saw Manager Li go to talk with them. I suspected that they meant you no good, so I left the city that same night. When you were staying at the inn I waited outside. I got up before dawn and came here first to wait. I guessed it had to be here in this wood that they would set to work. I've finished them both off with arrows, do you see?"

When this Prodigy had the bow in his hand, he could loose three arrows in quick succession and every one would hit its mark.

The Unicorn said: "Although you've saved my life, you've killed these two guards, which makes my fault even graver. Where can we possibly go now?"

The Prodigy said: "It was Song Jiang who got you into trouble in the first place. There is nowhere else we can go now but to the Marshes of Mount Liang."

The Unicorn said: "The trouble is all my wounds from the beating have opened and my feet are all blistered, I simply can't move."

The Prodigy said: "We mustn't waste any time. I will carry you on my back."

The Unicorn went to the dead guards and took some silver from them. He picked up his bow, stuck his sword in its scabbard, took a police staff, hoisted the Unicorn onto his back and set off northwards. After little more than three miles he was exhausted. When they came to a little inn, he went in to ask for a room and buy some wine and food to allay the pangs of hunger. The two of them rested here for a while.

Meanwhile a traveller had come upon the two dead policemen in the forest. He reported it to a local headman who passed it on to the district chief and a report was sent to the capital. In due course an inspector was sent to investigate and he established that the dead men were Dong Chao and Xue Ba from the garrison command. This was reported to the Governor, who issued a warrant and fixed a time-limit for the arrest of the murderer. Various police officers came to look. "The arrows evidently belong to the Prodigy," they announced. "There is no time to lose." Several hundred police were sent out in all directions, to put up notices with descriptions of the two wanted men and to spread the word in villages, districts and inns far and near, and inform the people in towns and markets so as to enlist them in the hunt.

The Unicorn was at this time still at the village inn, recuperating from his beating, and as he still could not walk, there he had to stay. The waiter heard about the murder case and learnt that there was a description of two wanted men at the district office. Having seen it, he hurried to report to the local headman: "There are two pretty suspicious-looking people at our inn. I wonder if it could be them." The headman went to report to the police.

Now the Prodigy, because there was nothing to eat, had taken his bow and gone to look for some game round about. He was on his way back when he heard a lot of shouting in the village. He

放冷箭燕青救主

hid in the trees to observe, and saw several hundred fully armed police standing around, while the Unicorn was dragged away bound in a prison cart. He wanted to rush out and save him, but he had no proper weapon so all he could do was lament. "Unless I go to Mount Liang and tell Song Jiang and persuade him to come and help, I am going to be responsible for my master's death!" he thought.

He set off at once. Halfway through the night he felt terribly hungry. But he hadn't a cent on him. He reached the top of a ridge where there was a thicket of tangled trees and lay down to sleep till daybreak. His heart was heavy and he kept hearing the chattering of the magpies in the branches above him. He thought: "If I shot one I could get some water from the local people and cook it. That would relieve this hunger."

When he walked out of the wood and raised his eyes, a magpie was looking at him. He quietly took out his bow and silently questioned fate and prayed to heaven, as follows: "This is the only arrow I have left. If I am to save my master, may the arrow hit and the magpie fall from the sky; if my master is fated to die, let the magpie fly away before the arrow reaches it."

He fitted the arrow to the bow and cried out: "May good fortune not desert me!" The bow twanged and the arrow hit the magpie in the tail. With the arrow stuck in it, the magpie flew off down the hill. The Prodigy bounded in pursuit. But he couldn't find it. As he was searching, two men appeared in front of him. Here is what they looked like:

> *The foremost wears a scarf folded in the shape of a pig's snout, secured with two gold and silver rings at the back of the head, and a robe of very black silk. About his waist is a girdle of wrought gold, half length soft boots on his feet and he carries a staff of eyebrow height. The second wears a white felt hat to keep off the dust and a brown embroidered robe. His waist is girt with a purple belt and he wears leather walking shoes. He has a pack on his back, carries a short staff and a sword is stuck in his belt.*

The two newcomers were walking side by side with the Prodigy. The Prodigy eyed them and thought to himself: "I've got no money. Suppose I knock them down with my two fists and take their bags? Then I can travel on to Mount Liang."

He turned away to hide his bow. The two men were walking along with lowered heads, their eyes on the road. The Prodigy stole up and hit the second man, the one who was wearing a felt hat, on the back of the head. He crashed to the ground. As he was about to hit the one in front, he was instead caught himself by a blow from the latter's staff which took him in the left leg and knocked him to the ground. The other now struggled to his feet and planting one foot on the Prodigy drew his sword and was about to strike without more ado. But the Prodigy cried: "Wait, sir! I am not afraid to die, but who will notify my master?"

Instead of striking the other stayed his hand while he asked: "What the devil has a villain like you got to notify?"

The Prodigy said: "Why do you ask?"

The man in front now pulled the Prodigy's sleeve and the tattoo was exposed. He asked excitedly: "Aren't you someone from Mr. Lu's household, the Prodigy or something like that?"

The Prodigy thought to himself. "I'll die anyway, I might as well speak and let them turn me in, so my spirit and my master's can be together after death." Accordingly he said: "Yes, I am the Prodigy, from Mr. Lu's household. I was heading for Mount Liang to report and ask Song Jiang to rescue my master, that's what."

At this the two men both laughed and said: "Lucky we didn't kill you! So it's the Prodigy, is it? Don't you know who we are?"

The one in black was none other than Mount Liang's Morbid. The one behind was Madcap. Morbid said: "We have orders from the chief to go to the Northern Capital and find out how Mr. Lu is. The Professor and the Magic Messenger are following us down to wait for our report."

When the Prodigy knew who it was he gave them a full account of the previous events. Morbid said to Madcap: "In that case the Prodigy and I had better go back to the mountain stronghold to report all this to the chief. He will come up with a new plan. You go on to the capital and find out what is happening, then come back and report."

"Right", said Madcap, while the Prodigy picked up his pack and went with Morbid. They reached Mount Liang after travelling all night. When they saw Song Jiang the Prodigy recounted all that had happened in detail. Song Jiang was extremely worried and summoned all the leaders to discuss the situation and work out a suitable plan.

Meanwhile Madcap, with nothing but the clothes he was wearing, reached the capital as it was beginning to get dark. He couldn't enter the city so he had to spend the night outside. Next morning after breakfast when he went into the city he found everyone muttering anxiously about something. He began to fear the worst. When he reached the centre he found everyone had locked and barred their doors. He questioned some householders there, but the only answer he got was from an old man: "Haven't you heard then, sir, that a certain Mr. Lu of this city, a very rich man, was lured to Mount Liang by the bandits there and when he managed to escape and return he was persecuted by the authorities and banished to Shamen. Then somehow on the way there he killed his two guards. Yesterday they caught him, and today he's going to be brought here to be executed at half-past twelve. You'll be able to watch."

Madcap went to the market-place at once to see for himself. He found a tavern at the crossroads and went in. He found himself a cubicle overlooking the street and sat down. The waiter came bustling up and asked: "Are you waiting for someone sir, or are you on your own?"

Madcap glared at him and said: "Just bring a big bowl of wine and a big piece of meat, and cut out the bloody questions."

Much chastened, the waiter poured a double measure of wine and sliced a big piece of beef and brought it. Madcap ate and drank for a while. Before long there was a tremendous commotion in the street below. He stepped outside onto the veranda to look. Everyone had locked their doors and every shop was shut. The waiter rushed upstairs and said: "Are you drunk sir or what? They've got the criminal down there. You'd better hurry up and pay your bill and take yourself off!"

"What the hell should I be afraid of?" said Madcap. "Get out of here, unless you want me to hit you!"

That shut the waiter up and he went downstairs again. In a little while the clamour of gongs and drums became deafening. Madcap watched from the veranda of the inn, as the execution ground at the crossroads was marked off by a dozen executioner's men bearing swords and staves and the Unicorn with his hands tied was dragged and buffeted to a spot in front of the tavern where he was made to kneel. Strongarm took up the executioner's sword. His assistant, Blossom, supported the cangue and said: "Mr. Lu, you know everything. It isn't that we didn't want to help you, my brother and I, but it all went wrong. I have already arranged your place below in the Halls of the Blessed. When your spirit arrives there, it'll be received."

A voice rang out: "Twelve thirty! The hour has come!" The cangue was removed, the assistant executioner steadied the head, the executioner raised the sword, the registrar read out the crime sheet in a loud voice, the crowd were completely hushed. Then suddenly, from the upper floor of the tavern Madcap, sword in hand, shattered that silence with a great shout: "The forces of Mount Liang are here!"

Strongarm and Blossom let go of the Unicorn, cut the rope and ran for it. Madcap leapt down from the veranda and raising his sword began slashing at people like someone splitting watermelons or picking vegetables. He killed a dozen without drawing breath. Then he grabbed hold of the Unicorn and made off, heading south.

However Madcap did not of course know the streets of the capital. He was further hindered by the fact that the Unicorn was terrified out of his wits and could hardly move a limb.

When Governor Liang heard what was happening, he was horrified. He told his guards to form separate detachments and go to each of the four city gates and close them. All the police were ordered to report for duty.

Well, however much of a hero you may be, how can you scale the high walls and ramparts of a city? Our heroes were indeed in the situation of someone having to burrow through the ground

劫法場石秀跳樓

without the benefit of teeth or claws, or trying to fly up to heaven without feathered wings.

But if you want to hear how the Unicorn and Madcap escaped from their predicament, you must read the next chapter.

Also in This Series

The Broken Seals: Part One of The Marshes of Mount Liang
1994 ISBN 962–201–602–2 448 pages

The Tiger Killers: Part Two of The Marshes of Mount Liang
1997 ISBN 962–201–751–7 456 pages

Iron Ox: Part Four of The Marshes of Mount Liang
forthcoming

Things Fall Apart: Part Five of The Marshes of Mount Liang
forthcoming

Related Titles Published by The Chinese University Press

Classical Chinese Literature: An Anthology of Translations
Volume I: From Antiquity to the Tang Dynasty
Edited by John Minford and Joseph S. M. Lau
2000 ISBN 962–201–625–1 1,240 pages
(Published for North America and Europe
by Columbia University Press)

Leaves of Prayer: The Life and Poetry of He Shuangqing,
a Farmwife in Eighteenth-century China
By Elsie Choy
2000 second edition ISBN 962–201–883–1 320 pages

The Discourse on Foxes and Ghosts: Ji Yun and Eighteenth-Century Literati Storytelling
By Leo Tak-hung Chan
1998 ISBN 962–201–749–5 372 pages
(Published in North America by University of Hawai'i Press)

Tales of Magistrate Bao and His Valiant Lieutenants
Translated by Susan Blader
1997 ISBN 962–201–775–4 416 pages

Fox Volant of the Snowy Mountain
By Jin Yong Translated by Olivia Mok
1996 second edition ISBN 962–201–733–9 416 pages